"I didn't think you would come."

Tristan's voice was as she remembered it.

"I wasn't going to," she said, barely above a whisper.

"Why?"

The electricity between them was so strong that Antonia thought the world must surely erupt into thunder. But this was a storm of their own brewing, a quietly potent one full of energy and intensity and fire.

She felt his hand on her chin, and then she was being forced, ever so gently, to look up at him.

"Why?" he repeated.

"Because there can be nothing between us," came the harsh reply.

"There already *is* something between us."

Dear Reader,

This is it, what we've all been waiting for. The month when history becomes twice as exciting and twice as romantic. Thanks to popular demand, Harlequin Historicals are increasing from two to four titles per month, starting now!

Our four books this month span the globe from the deserts of the American Southwest to the Scottish highlands as we bring you stories by some of your favorite authors.

With *The Silver Link,* Patricia Potter brings to life the early days of New Mexico in a poignant story of love and deception between a Spanish beauty and an American army scout. Heather Graham Pozzessere, in her eagerly awaited *Forbidden Fire,* takes you to turn-of-the-century England and to San Francisco on the eve of the Great Earthquake of 1906.

Contraband Desire by Lucy Elliot is a triumphant love story of devotion and hope set in Tennessee during the dark years of the Civil War. And finally, be sure not to miss Ruth Langan's *Highland Heather,* the next book in her series of adventuresome tales of the Scottish MacAlpin clan.

We hope you enjoy all of our historical romances. And whatever you do, don't forget to look for four Harlequin Historicals each month from now on, and join in the excitement!

Yours,
Tracy Farrell
Senior Editor

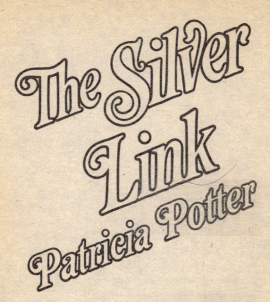

The Silver Link

Patricia Potter

Harlequin Books

TORONTO • NEW YORK • LONDON
AMSTERDAM • PARIS • SYDNEY • HAMBURG
STOCKHOLM • ATHENS • TOKYO • MILAN

Harlequin Historicals first edition February 1991

ISBN 0-373-28663-5

THE SILVER LINK

Books by Patricia Potter

Harlequin Historicals

Swampfire #6
Between the Thunder #15
Samara #20
Seize the Fire #26
Chase the Thunder #35
Dragon Fire #48
The Silver Link #63

Harlequin Books

Historical Christmas Stories 1990
"Miracle of the Heart"

PATRICIA POTTER

is a former journalist with a passion for history and books. While working at the *Atlanta Journal* she met and reported on three presidents and covered southern news stories as varied as the space launches and the civil-rights movement.

A resident of Atlanta, Georgia, Patricia has her own public-relations and advertising agency. Her interests in animals and travel are not especially compatible, but she does manage to fit them both into her schedule, along with her reading, which runs the gamut from biographies to espionage. She is a past president of the Georgia Romance Writers and is now busy winning awards for her historical romances.

The silver link, the silken tie,
Which heart to heart, and mind to mind,
In body and in soul can bind.

—Sir Walter Scott
The Lay of the Last Minstrel

Prologue

Virginia, 1846

The two men sat their horses with equal ease as they looked out over the Shenandoah Valley at the wide river that was the boundary of the Hampton farm. The scene was beautiful this morning, with the mist blending the blue sky, the rich green land and the shining water into a muted tapestry of quiet serenity.

For thirty years the farm had been the source of deep happiness for the older man. He loved the roots he had planted here and the family he and his wife, Samara, had nourished so carefully. He had always hoped this rich piece of earth would be enough for his children, that they would draw their strength and love from the land as he had.

But as he looked at his eldest son, he saw the same devils that had spurred him as a young man. Tristan was so much like he had once been himself... before he found Samara and discovered something other than the exhilarating feel of danger and adventure.

He understood his son's restiveness, but he hated the understanding, for to do so was to give him up. And although he loved all six of his children, Tris had always been special. His birth after two years of war and agony, had been an acknowledgment of Samara's love.

It was not that Tris ever complained. He had accepted the responsibility of being the oldest son, had performed every task given him with stunning competence. But his smile, so open and brilliant as a child, came slower now, and laughter no longer danced in his eyes. It seemed that Tris did most things by rote and little by joy.

"It will soon be time for spring planting," Reese Hampton told his son. After all these years, he was still surprised by the satisfaction he took in such an observation, at his perverse delight in watching things grow.

Tris turned to him, his glittering blue-green eyes glinting in the sun. They were so filled with restlessness, with an unknown wanting, that Reese ached for him.

Reese knew Tris felt too much responsibility to his family. His own twin brother, Avery, had been confined by responsibility, and Reese had vowed that his children would never be saddled that way. It was time to test that vow.

"Conn's coming for a visit," Reese said slowly. The letter from his brother-in-law had come this morning and it had been the reason he had ridden out to meet Tris. It was time, past time, to talk to his son.

Tris always left at dawn to ride alone before tending to his daily duties. Reese had seen him silhouetted against the sky several times, a lonely figure who, no matter how hard he tried, wasn't quite comfortable with the world his father designed.

Reese watched Tris's eyes light and he felt the heart twist become a deep pain. Conn, for God's sake. Of all of Samara's brothers, Conn was Reese's least favorite and a thorn in his side. Conn had done his damnedest to keep Reese and Samara apart. In subsequent years, Reese and Conn had come to some kind of civility, but not much more than that.

Tris had always been intrigued by the West and, therefore, his Uncle Conn, who had become an explorer and adventurer. After the War of 1812, Conn had continued westward, seeking one new danger after another. He had been with Sam Houston during the Texas fight for independence, a trader along the Santa Fe Trail, and led expeditions to California and Oregon.

"I wonder where he's going this time?" Tris said in his soft, clipped voice.

"According to the letter, he's been in Washington, trying to convince the politicians to invite Texas into the Union as a state. Then he's bound west again . . . to fight, I suppose. He's convinced there will be a war with Mexico over the annexation of Texas."

Tris didn't say anything, but Reese could see the sharp interest in his eyes, interest his son quickly hid, as he often did his feelings these days. It cut Reese to the quick.

"Have you ever thought you might go with him?" Reese's question was unexpected, like a knife thrust, and Tris was startled into a candid reaction.

All the time. It was the answer in his heart, but he had responsibilities here. Responsibilities to a mother and father, to sisters and brothers he loved.

But he couldn't lie. Not completely. "I've thought about it," he admitted, "but this is my home."

"Is it?" Reese asked sadly.

Tris's throat caught as he considered the pointed question. No one had ever had a finer, more loving family than he, but there was something in him that was missing. Now, as he thought about his uncle, the embers deep within him, embers that had burned for years, flared anew.

"Francis is thinking about leaving and buying his own land since he believes you will have Hampton Hills."

"Francis!" Tris couldn't stop the exclamation. "By God, why didn't he say anything to me?"

"He didn't want you to think he was trying to intrude on your rights, I suppose. Just as you didn't want him to know that you're not happy here."

Tris's clear eyes searched his father's as his grin grew wider. "Are you chasing me off?"

Reese stared out into the distance. *Was that what he was doing?* He was hardly aware of the slight wetness forming at the corners of his eyes. Nothing he had ever done was harder than this. Nothing. But Tris deserved his chance.

"It's up to you, son," he said quietly. "My brother was chained to a title...he had no choices. I want you to have them."

A shock of bronze hair fell over Tris's forehead and he pushed it back in place. The mist below was clearing, and the fresh green of the valley floor was bright with glistening drops of dew. A movement in the distance drew his attention and he watched a speck appear and move slowly toward the large, comfortable brick home that overlooked the river. He studied the rider and horse as they grew larger until he could make out the tall buckskin-clad form.

A sudden excitement gripped him. He had always felt it when he was around Conn. His uncle's rare letters and fewer visits had only fueled a consuming curiosity about the West...about a land still teeming with vitality and danger and a certain wild beauty described vividly by Conn.

He looked from the house up to the sky. It was so damned big, and there was so much under it. And he wanted to explore it, as his uncle had. He wanted to see the red mountains and the vast plains and the shining deserts. He wanted to be part of the growth of his continent—as his parents and grandparents had been—not just a caretaker of what had already been claimed.

"I'm needed here," he said, trying to swallow his dream.

Reese laughed despite the lump growing in his throat. "I think, Tris, that I'm still quite able to take care of this family. Francis is ready to take on more, and in a few years, Rafe and Seth will be old enough to help him.

Tris's blue eyes bored into his father's. At sixty-seven, Reese radiated the same energy Tris had always loved, even envied. Reese Hampton had always been bigger than life. At times, the image had been daunting.

"I'm sure you can," Tris said slowly, his eyes crinkling with laughter.

"I'll miss you, Tris. We'll all miss you...particularly your mother...but we both know you have to follow your own course. Not ours."

A smile tugged at Tris's mouth as he searched his father's face and finally nodded.

Reese saw the touch of sadness in his son's expression, along with a quiet joy that had been missing for too damned long.

Chapter One

New Mexico, 1846

Antonia Theresa Margarita Ramirez stared at the sleek black mare with admiration and a certain amount of resentment.

She knew the horse was a bribe. But it was a magnificent animal and she wanted it. Badly.

Her father had not put any conditions on the gift. He knew better than that by now. Yet the fact that her father had asked Don Ramon Silvero to bring her birthday gift from Mexico City was another undeniable nudge toward the ambitious neighboring rancher and a marriage that was abhorrent to her.

Antonia did not want to marry Ramon. She didn't, in fact, want to marry anyone. But she was especially opposed to Ramon. There was something cold and ruthless beneath his handsome and charming exterior that made her uneasy. And Antonia was not easily frightened.

Ramon stood in front of her now, his tight lips twisted into a smile, his black eyes boring intently into hers.

Antonia felt her father's arm go around her shoulders, using her partly for balance. He had been badly injured five years ago and had to use either crutches or a chair on wheels to move. Now his crutches were tucked under one arm as he admired the horse. "Magnificent, isn't she?"

Despite her resentment and growing apprehension, Antonia had to agree. The mare tossed her head with spirit and pride, and her configuration was perfect. The inky blackness of her coat matched Antonia's own midnight-dark hair. A thrust of unwanted feminine vanity told the girl that she and the horse would be striking together with only a saddle trimmed in silver between them.

"She truly is, Father," Antonia answered, finally deciding to accept the present. It was her father's birthday gift to her, and a good investment as a brood mare, although her father probably had not considered that aspect. He seldom did, which was one reason they were so indebted to Don Ramon. *"Gracias,"* she said quietly.

"And thank Ramon," Miguel Ramirez replied smugly. "He was kind enough to bring the horse all the way from Mexico City."

Antonia's large dark brown eyes went to Ramon. He was waiting expectantly for her gratitude, just as he had waited these past three years for her hand in marriage. Antonia knew he had little doubt he would eventually have it. What Ramon wanted, he usually got, one way or another.

"Gracias, Ramon," she finally said in a deceptively soft voice as her eyes went over every inch of the horse, looking for whip marks. She had never understood how her father was so blind to the cruelty in their neighbor.

But her father didn't want to see. Ramon was darkly handsome, his hair jet-black and curling, and his sensuous lips framed by a rakish mustache. He could be undeniably charming, and he was always so with her father. Charming and generous and ever so helpful. So helpful, in fact, that Antonia feared he had enticed her father deeper and deeper into his debt. It was more than that, however. Ramon was a Creole. His blood, like hers, was pure Spanish, although their families had lived in New Mexico for more than two hundred years. And he was Catholic. Those two factors were, to her father, the most important qualifications for marriage. Nothing was as important to her father as keeping their blood "pure."

There were other reasons. A marriage between Ramon and Antonia would join their abutting lands and create one of the largest ranches in northern New Mexico. And Ramon represented protection against the hated Yanquis, who had killed Antonia's mother.

Antonia's father chafed at her reluctance to marry Ramon, unwilling and unable to understand her reasoning. She was nineteen today, three years past the usual marrying age in this heavily Spanish, devoutly Catholic society, and her father badly wanted grandchildren, particularly a grandson. It was her misfortune that she was an only child, that she was a girl when Miguel Ramirez so craved a son to carry on the heritage that had started centuries ago with an ancestor who had ridden north with Coronado and stayed to help build an empire. Now all her father's hopes were centered on her willingness and ability to produce a male heir.

But she would not have Ramon, not when his black eyes burned through her and she felt a strange uneasiness when he was around. There had to be someone else . . . and if there were not, she would simply not marry at all. She loved her father dearly, but not enough to submit to the hell she suspected awaited her if she married Ramon. And her father knew he couldn't force his strong-willed daughter, although he would exert every other possible influence to bring the match about.

Ramon, unfortunately, was one of the few eligible young men in this part of New Mexico. Not only was he young and wealthy, he had also served as the alcalde, the appointed governing authority, and he wielded great influence with the governor and with Mexico. He often visited Mexico, ingratiating himself further, Antonia thought contemptuously. Now that there was talk of war with the Yanquis, his visits had become more frequent.

"Ramon," Don Miguel said as he placed his crutches back under his arms. "Come in and tell us the news from Mexico City."

Ramon swung easily from the saddle. He was a good horseman, having, like most New Mexicans, practically lived on a horse since the age of four. Everything in New Mexico was far away from everything else: neighbors, water, the village of Taos where they purchased the goods they didn't raise. But it was obvious that Ramon had no affection for horses, and even possessed a subtle cruelty toward them.

Ramon allowed Antonia to see his darker side infrequently, and then only by accident, but she could never entirely forget those episodes. It sometimes seemed as if there were two Ramons, one charming, attentive and witty, and the other cold and spiteful. While she was attracted to one, she was repelled and suspicious of the other.

She felt Ramon's close presence as his hand took hers, bringing it to his cool lips.

"You look beautiful as usual, *Chiquita,*" he said, but there was little warmth in his voice.

She lowered her eyes. "*Gracias,* Ramon," she said again, feeling his critical gaze at her mode of dress. It *was* unconventional here, although well accepted in California, where she had stayed years ago…before her father's crippling, when the three of them—her mother and father and herself—had been so very happy. It had been a special trip for them all, a visit to Antonia's uncle, who owned a large, sprawling horse ranch near Los Angeles.

Antonia had been only fourteen then, and captivated by the freedom of the young women, who rode astride and wore a form of trousers. When, by necessity, she took over much of the operation of her father's ranch, she had adapted the clothes for herself: a broad-brimmed, low-crowned hat, secured by a thong; a brightly colored embroidered jacket; and buckskin armitas with legs so flared they looked like skirts when she was not sitting a horse. Ramon disapproved, although even her father saw the wisdom of such clothes in this rough land; it was infinitely safer than the usual heavy skirts and sidesaddles. His only request was that she wear more traditional garments when going to Taos or Santa Fe.

But then Ramon disapproved of much about her. So much, in fact, she sometimes wondered why he wanted to marry her. Yet he did, and with Don Miguel's full approval.

Antonia knew her father felt he would eventually sway her to his way of thinking. For had he not opposed his own arranged marriage to Antonia's mother, only to find supreme happiness in it. The same would happen with Antonia, he told her frequently enough. She and Ramon had too much in common for it to be otherwise.

Antonia recalled the love that had flowed between her parents. Her mother had been one of the gentlest people she had ever known. Even now the thought of her brought a rush of emotion and a blur to Antonia's eyes. Her death had been so senseless, so cruel.

But there was little of her mother's gentleness in Ramon. Antonia knew it, if her father did not. He only saw Ramon's strength, his ability to protect her from another invasion by Yanquis or Comanches or Apache. And her safety had become an obsession with him as his health grew worse and his memories closer. There were rumors of another war with the United States, and threats of an invasion. He swore often that he would never allow the past to repeat itself. The Yanquis had killed his wife; they would not claim his daughter.

For her father's peace of mind, Antonia tolerated Ramon and tried to be pleasant to him, although she continually pushed aside or ignored suggestions of marriage. She was not ready, she told her father. She did not tell him she would never be ready.

Once inside the cool adobe hacienda, Luz, who looked after the hacienda, hurried to bring drinks—wine for the men and a fruit drink for Antonia.

"The news?" Don Miguel urged his guest.

"The Americans have sent their general, Zachary Taylor, to the Mexican border. Already they have violated our territory. Mexico has no honorable choice but to declare war," Ramon said.

"War!" Antonia couldn't stop her exclamation. She knew a momentary shiver. She remembered the last encroachment . . . by an expedition of Texans. It had resulted in the death of her mother and the crippling of her father.

Ramon looked at her condescendingly. "Mexico has never recognized Texas as independent; it never will. Texas is still part of Mexico, and the Yanquis are intent on having it, along with New Mexico and California."

Antonia had an uncharitable desire to prick him, even if she did feel a new ball of fear forming in the pit of her stomach. "I don't understand why that would be so bad. The taxes under the Mexican government keep going up...and we get nothing for them."

Her father's face flushed red. "You forget Yanquis killed your mother, Antonia."

"Deserters, Father. They were deserters from Texas volunteers. You cannot blame all Yanquis for that, any more than they can blame all of us for Santa Ana's slaughter at Goliad." It was an argument she made often, for she could not bear to see hate wearing such bitter inroads on her father. Once a very gentle man, he had, with Ramon's help, twisted his grief into a biting hatred of all things Texan and American.

Ramon's face flushed with anger. "You know little, Antonia," he said with condescension. "They were traitors at Goliad...and, yes, at the Alamo. They deserved to die. All of them. And any new invaders will feel the same justice of Santa Ana's sword."

"I didn't think Santa Ana was still in power," she said, her own anger building, her voice silkily challenging. It was one of her worse traits, this teasing, and she disliked herself for it, but she didn't like the way Ramon continually inflamed her father.

"He will be," Ramon said darkly. "The Mexican government will discover they need him. And he will chase the Yanquis back to Washington."

Antonia sincerely doubted it, but the distress on her father's face stopped any further retort.

Instead, she excused herself, saying she had duties. The air was heavy with malevolence and she could no longer bear it.

Her father nodded with relief, and Ramon rose quickly as she did, taking her hand. "I am having a gathering at my home. Your father has graciously said you both will attend. Until then, Antonia."

Her throat caught. It meant she would have to dance with him, feel his arms move possessively around her and probably hear another offer of marriage. She winced inside, but managed a slight smile. "Until then, Ramon," she agreed, before hurrying from the room.

She went to the kitchen where Luz was busy preparing the main meal of the day...a spicy stew with beans, peas and greens, tamales and enchiladas.

Antonia smiled ruefully under Luz's scrutiny. A mestizo— part Mexican, part Indian—Luz had been with the Ramirez family thirty years. Besides cooking and supervising the house servants, she also served as doctor and knew healing herbs as few others.

"He is arrogant, that one," the other woman observed.

Antonia sighed. "He never gives up. Never."

"Did you hold your tongue?"

Antonia's smile brightened her face. "Almost," she admitted. "If it weren't for father..."

"I know," Luz said sympathetically. "He believes Ramon will keep you safe."

"I know," Antonia said with resignation. "But I don't understand why father trusts him so much. There is something so cold about him."

Luz knew **Don Ramon** was unable to keep his vaqueros for very long, unlike those on the Ramirez ranch, and she had heard Jose curse about the treatment of Silvero's horses. Despite Don Miguel's friendship with the neighboring rancher, Luz had never approved of the match Don Miguel coveted so much. But it was not her business, although she felt toward Señorita Antonia much as she would toward her own child.

"He is of the devil," Luz said slowly. "It is in his eyes. But he hides it from your father."

Antonia stared at Luz. It was the strongest criticism she had ever heard the woman voice about anyone. "I don't think he's the devil," she said softly, "but neither do I want him for a husband."

Luz lost her worried look and smiled. "It's time you did marry...though not Don Ramon," she said, "and stop riding all over the countryside." It was a thought voiced often enough, but it seldom did any good. Since Don Miguel's accident, Antonia had taken his place overseeing the vaqueros while Don

Miguel kept the accounts. It was a pattern that had evolved over several years. By the time Don Miguel finally discovered his daughter had grown and should be thinking of womanly things, she was supervising the fencing, making the major decisions about sale of livestock and overseeing the sheep shearing.

Whenever he broached the subject of marriage, Antonia would quickly assure him that she was content as she was and all they needed were each other. It was an argument that usually won him over, until lately, when his health had begun to falter. Now he worried about her. He wanted to see her safely and comfortably married. And he wanted a grandson.

Sometimes, at night, Antonia felt a pang of loneliness, an emptiness she really didn't understand. After all, she had her father, she had the ranch, she had her mountains. But still . . .

Ramon had already made it clear that his *wife* would stay at home, *his* wife would not wear heathenish clothes, and *his* wife would be *obedient*. Antonia grinned. He would find she didn't know what the word meant. Her father had certainly discovered that. She had been independent far too long, ever since that terrible day when she was fourteen. . . .

Now she spent a few more moments with Luz, waiting for Ramon to leave, so she could go riding on her new mount. She did not want to make excuses to avoid riding with him. It was best, she had found, to just try and avoid him.

It was more than an hour later when she finally heard him leave. She wondered, briefly, what he and her father had discussed for so long. She would find out tonight.

Antonia left the cool adobe house through the patio, which was shaded by cottonwood trees. She hurried past the small chapel, the storerooms, the servants' quarters and finally past the big hall designed for dances and other parties, although her father seldom entertained now. The stables were near the blacksmith shop, and a number of saddled horses were, as always, tethered to a hitching post.

Antonia dismissed her lingering disquiet over Ramon and grinned when she saw Jose, Luz's husband and their most valuable horseman, holding the bridle of the saddled black mare. He knew her only too well, knew she would be out to try the horse the moment Don Ramon left.

She swung up on the tooled leather saddle. It was not as grand as the one she used for special occasions, but it was much more practical for ranch riding.

She felt the horse's unease as it danced nervously before sensing her almost immediate control. She was a superb horse-woman, having learned, as Ramon did, at a very young age. Her father had taken her everywhere as a child, and she had no fear of horses or the countryside. Her saddle always carried a rifle, and she knew how to use it. The country was full of mountain lions, cougars, snakes and the occasional bandit or renegade Apache, although most of the Indians in this area were now peaceful farmers.

Antonia kept the horse at a slow pace at first, adjusting her body to its fine natural gait and establishing both trust and command of the horse. When she felt she had finally asserted her authority, she let the horse run, as it so obviously wanted to, and felt an exhilaration that came only with chasing the wind with a magnificent mount under her. She rode to her fa-vorite hill, where she could look up toward the Sangre de Cris-tos Mountains she loved, and dismounted, allowing the horse to rest as she fondled its head.

"What should I call you, girl? You're as black as midnight and as fast as the wind. Night Wind. You will be my Night Wind from now on."

Antonia whispered to the horse, all the time rubbing its fine neck with steady strokes, building trust. The horse neighed its pleasure at the attention, and Antonia laughed with delight. They would get along well together.

She tied the reins to an aspen tree, low enough to allow Night Wind to graze, and went to the edge of the hill where she could look out over the valley below the mountains. It was a shining land of extraordinarily bright colors of silver and gold and red.

Just watching the shades change and meld as the sun moved ever so slowly, filled her with a contentment dimmed only by that sense of loneliness that had increased over the past months. It was a nagging feeling, one she often suppressed by counting her joys: a sunrise, a sunset, a fast ride, a book, a new colt or filly. So many things.

But she missed having friends, a companion with whom she could really talk. All her childhood friends were now married with children of their own, and conversation no longer centered around dreams but household realities. There was Father, of course, but he had, in many ways, slipped away from her. Antonia loved him with a fierce protectiveness, but since the death of her mother, she had watched miserably as both his mental and physical strength deteriorated. She often found him staring at walls or clutching a small portrait of her mother in his hands for hours. He no longer cared so vitally about the ranch, and he depended too much on Ramon for business counsel. The vaqueros came to Antonia when a decision was needed. Antonia would then talk to her father, making him feel the decision was his when it was actually hers. But all too often, in other matters, he succumbed, usually, to the strongest voice, which, Antonia knew, was not always the right one. She particularly feared Ramon's influence over him.

It hadn't always been thus. She remembered her father's strength and gentleness, his love for her. And then the Texans had come.

Her mother and father had gone to Santa Fe, her father on business, her mother accompanying him. They didn't know then that an expedition of Texas volunteers had moved across the border with the intention of trying to annex the northern part of New Mexico.

Nor had they known that the expedition had failed, that there were insufficient supplies and that a large number of the volunteers had been captured by New Mexican troops and several brutally killed. A few Texans had escaped and, filled with bitter anger, desperately tried to make their way to safe territory. Three of them ran into Don Miguel, his wife and a vaquero riding with them as protection.

Antonia had heard the story from Don Miguel. The Texans demanded their horses, and Don Miguel had refused. The vaquero was shot and the horses bolted at the gunshot, galloping madly along the rough trail. The carriage overturned, killing

Antonia's mother and crippling Don Miguel. The Texans took the horses and left Don Miguel there, pinned under the carriage next to his dead wife. It was only providence that a trader passed, helped free Don Miguel and brought back the broken body of his wife.

From that day, everything in Antonia's life had changed. Her father partially recovered but could no longer ride without great pain, and she gradually resumed many of his responsibilities. Because he was numbed by pain and grief, he allowed it. Her role was already well established when he realized she was nearing marriage age, and that he had been derelict in preparing her for it. And with the added threat of another Yanqui invasion, his concern for her had become obsession.

As for Antonia, she had gone through her own period of grief and anger. She, too, had hated the Yanquis. But the padre of the school she attended was a gentle man who taught her to judge men individually, not on the actions of one or two. There were many Yanquis in Taos, good men who could not be blamed for the brutality of a few men. It was a lesson she had accepted but her father had not. The hours of pain beneath the buggy, lying with his hand on his dead wife, had mortally wounded his soul.

Antonia wanted to see him happy. More than anything else, she wanted to see the old twinkling light return to his eyes, the kind smile to his lips.

But she would not marry to do it. She would take care of both of them. And without Ramon.

Antonia sighed. She sometimes wished she would fall in love, that she could fill the emptiness that was often strong within her. If only there were someone strong and wise and gentle. It wouldn't matter whether he was handsome or not. Ramon was handsome on the outside and tarnished on the inside.

But this hard country, beautiful as it was, seemed to drain compassion and love from its inhabitants and breed an arrogance born of defeating such a difficult land. Antonia would not let it drain her. Nor would she allow any person to.

But dear Mother in Heaven, sometimes she was lonely.

* * *

Christ, but Tris learned quickly.

Conn's eyes followed the stealthy steps of his nephew as he stalked the mountain cat that had raided the farm where they had stayed last night. A young calf had been carried off for the second time in as many weeks, and Conn and Tris, grateful for the family's hospitality, had volunteered to go after the cat. They had been tracking the animal since noon, and Tris had not stopped for a rest and had, in fact, found a track Conn had missed.

It was, Conn pondered, disconcerting at the very least.

He had been hesitant when Tris had approached him in Virginia and asked to accompany him west. It took a very special type of man to survive on the frontier, particularly when war was brewing.

And frankly, his nephew had never impressed him as possessing the type of ruthlessness the life required. Oh, he was bright enough, but Conn had never seen that spark of independence and adventure that so marked the men who went west.

Not until after several days on the trail.

He didn't know what he had expected. Perhaps that Tris would quickly tire of the long rides and incessant instruction. Perhaps that he would become bored with the whole idea.

Instead, the young man seemed to thrive on discomfort and deprivation, on sleeping on snow-covered mountains and standing watch after eighteen hours in the saddle. He absorbed Indian lore and language like a sponge and constantly demanded more, his mind never stopping, his intelligence quick and eager.

Until this journey, Conn had seen little of Reese Hampton in his serious son. But now, the devil shone in Tris's eyes just as it had the first time Conn had met the infernal Englishman who had fathered this man. And in a matter of weeks, Tris carried the same cool confidence and aura of danger his father had.

It had been, Conn decided, that damned farm that had stifled Tris Hampton. What surprised him was that Reese and

Samara had not recognized it until now. Perhaps they had not wanted to.

He was continually astonished that he appreciated, in Tris, the same qualities that had so irritated him in his brother-in-law. They made Tris a boon companion. He was easy to be with, a courageous and talented man in a fight, and Conn often found a smile lurking in the back of Tris's eyes, giving the lie to the seriousness, even stuffiness, that Conn had always found there before.

And, Lord, Tris and his father looked alike. Tris's bronze hair had, in the past weeks, bleached to the color of pure gold, while his face darkened, changing his handsome features into striking ones. His eyes, so green-blue they fairly glittered, were always watchful, always alert, and they invariably drew the attention of others. There wasn't a woman along the way, married or unmarried, who hadn't gazed at him with something akin to pure lust.

Now Conn watched as Tris moved easily through the forest, his rifle held as if it were an extension of him. One of the new Colt revolvers was strapped around his waist and he wore buckskins as naturally as he once wore frilled shirts and satin cravats. It was only three months since they'd left Virginia and the dandy was now a deadly predator.

Of course, Tris had already had many of the skills. He had been a good shot and excellent rider, and he had done some tracking for game. But Conn had honed those skills, had taught the younger man caution and expanded his abilities, and now he was proud of his pupil. Damned proud, in fact. He would put Tris up against anyone.

There was a noise ahead that only the most trained of ears would detect, but Tris's rifle moved and Conn knew he had heard. Then came a growl and something hurtling through the underbrush.

Tris knelt swiftly as the cat lunged. Conn lifted his own rifle, but he didn't need to shoot. A loud, sharp crack came from Tris's rifle and the mountain lion fell inches from his nephew's kneeling form.

Conn's lips twisted wryly. "Not bad for a tenderfoot," he said, but there was no sting in his words, only a grudging respect, and Tris grinned in reply.

"The Reynoldses will be pleased. I think we'll eat well tonight," Conn observed. "Cut off those claws," he added with a wicked insinuation in his voice. "You can give them to Susannah as a souvenir."

Tris groaned. They had been staying at Dan Reynolds's farm for three days. Reynolds was an old friend of Conn's and when they arrived to find Dan laid up with a broken leg, Conn had volunteered their assistance for a few days. It was a welcomed rest after days of sunup-to-sundown hours in the saddle. Except for Susannah, who couldn't seem to stop staring at Tris.

"Don't you think we'd better be getting on," Tris said slowly. One more brush of Susannah's leg against his at the dinner table, and he might succumb to her blatant invitations despite his better judgment. She was certainly pretty enough, but Reynolds was a friend of Conn's, and Tris knew rules of hospitality precluded bedding the daughter of the house. Even if she were doing the seducing.

Conn chuckled deep in his throat, although it sounded more of a growl. "I suppose we should," he retorted, "before you're the guest of honor at a shotgun wedding."

Tris glared at Conn for a moment and then his lips started twitching. "Exchange one farm for another? My father would never forgive you."

"Your father has never forgiven me anything," his companion replied with a laugh.

"I thought it was mutual."

"Oh, I like Reese well enough. I just don't want to give him the satisfaction of knowing it."

Once again Tris's lips quivered with amusement. "Don't ever tell him, but I think he feels the same way."

"Damn," Conn said dryly. "It's hell when two old enemies can't stay that way. Takes all the fun from life."

Tris's easy smile touched his eyes. He could well imagine the fireworks when Conn and his father had met the first time. Both were stubborn and passionate men. Conn hid those feelings carefully, but every once in a while they surfaced at the least expected time, and Tris knew he would never have a better friend. The past months with Conn, demanding as they were, had been among the best in his life.

Not wanting his feelings known, he looked back at the cat with no little satisfaction and pride. Dusk had fallen and the first stars lit the evening sky, while a slight breeze cooled his hot tense body.

God, but it felt good. He remembered the surge of blood as the cat leapt, the excitement that ran through his veins as he realized the danger, the thrill of the victory as the cat dropped. He had never felt quite this way before . . . so damned alive.

They left Dan Reynolds's place the next morning, despite protests and Susannah's tears. As they moved across Missouri toward Leavenworth, Kansas, the news of war with Mexico increased. After President Polk—who supported Texas's annexation—had taken office, Mexico had broken off relations with the United States and now, they heard, Mexico was preparing for war on a grand scale. Polk had ordered General Zachary Taylor to Corpus Christi.

Conn was planning to join Stephen Kearny, who was in Kansas and whose orders, if war broke out, were to move to Santa Fe, New Mexico, and then on to California. Conn had served with Kearny during the War of 1812 and later had been a guide and scout for him in the West. He planned to do the same again. He wanted to fight, but he didn't want to be in the army with a required term of enlistment. He liked his independence too much for that.

The relationship between Tris and Conn had changed with the killing of the cat. It was no longer one of teacher and pupil, but of partners and friends. Despite his soft speech and occasional English inflection, Tris found himself more and more comfortable with the taciturn Westerners they encountered, and his own vocabulary widened, but not particularly in the drawing room sense.

As his speech gradually changed, so did his body. Always lean and athletic, he was now whipcord thin from a diet of lean meat and constant exercise. He could ride all day with comfort when the first weeks had been unending misery. He woke easily at the slightest sound and, like Conn, had started to sense danger.

When they stopped at the Missouri River, it was Tris who did the hunting, bringing back a haunch of deer for dinner. After they contentedly chewed the larger portions of the roasted meat, Tris leaned on his elbow, looking up at the darkening sky.

"How long before we reach Kansas?"

"Another four days or so to Fort Leavenworth," Conn replied.

"Do you really think there will be a war?"

Conn snorted. "You can just bet your boots. Mexico's never given up on Texas, damn butchers." Conn would never forgive Santa Ana, the Mexican dictator, for the Alamo ten years earlier. A number of his friends had been killed there. Conn had been elsewhere during the battle of the Alamo, but had helped revenge Houston when the Americans decimated the Mexicans at the Battle of San Jacinto. Santa Ana was currently in exile, but already there was talk that certain elements in Mexico would welcome him back.

"You think Colonel Kearny will take me on?" Tris asked.

"You may be new to this, Tris, but you have the instincts of a damned good scout, and the colonel needs every one he can get."

"Tell me about him."

"Well, he's about as tough as a bear guarding a honey tree."

Tris couldn't quite keep the amusement from his eyes. In the past thirty years, Conn had lost most of the soft South Carolina accent his sister and brothers shared, and any trace of his extensive formal education. He sounded just like all the Westerners Tris was now encountering: bluntly picturesque.

"And how tough is that exactly?" Tris ventured, his lips twitching slightly.

Conn looked at him reprovingly. "Did Samara ever tell you you're impertinent?"

"Occasionally."

"It didn't do any good," Conn observed.

"Not much," Tris agreed.

Conn's eyes narrowed, although there was a gleam of approval in them. He liked Tris's independence. His nephew also had the attractive trait of being able to laugh at himself. "I heard Kearny dress down one of his new officers who had addressed his men as 'gentlemen.' He said that 'there are colonels, captains, lieutenants and soldiers in this command, but no such persons as "gentlemen."'" Remember that, Tris. The only thing Kearny worries about is results. Don't ever let your well-trained gentlemanly instincts get in the way, or he'll have your head for dinner."

Tris grinned, and Conn was reminded once more how much he resembled his father. In the past weeks, he'd also discovered Tris had the same damned dogged perseverance.

They reached Independence in early June, one of the last large trading areas on the frontier. The town was overcrowded with wagons and settlers heading west toward Oregon or California. It was there they learned, by a dispatch rider headed for Kearny's headquarters, that the United States had declared war on Mexico.

They left an hour later, fast on the heels of the dispatch rider, to join Kearny. A day and a half later, they rode into Fort Leavenworth and found Stephen Kearny making preparations to move his camp. More and more Missouri volunteers were arriving daily. They would march to New Mexico and then on to California.

Kearny took some persuading to sign Tris on as a scout. Tris's impeccable good manners and slight English accent drew a raised eyebrow from the Westerner, who had just been promoted to Brigadier General and was everything Conn had said he was.

"I need scouts I can depend on," Kearny said skeptically.

"He's fast," Conn replied. "A faster learner than any man I've ever had. I'll vouch for him."

"Damn you, O'Neill. You'd better be right. I don't need you spending all your time nursemaiding. One mistake and he goes back. Understand."

Angered at being talked about as if he weren't there, Tris broke in. "I'll be the first to resign in that event, General Kearny."

"We don't fight by gentlemen's rules here, Hampton. We don't wait for the enemy to shoot first."

"I understand, General," Tris replied with frosty eyes. "I don't aim to let him."

"Half pay. He's on half pay until he proves his worth," Kearny said to Conn, who nodded.

"Get the hell out of here then. We'll be leaving in three weeks."

"For where, sir?" Tris ventured.

"New Mexico. Santa Fe. Where the hell did you think? And I'm told that the Mexicans will fight for it."

If Tris thought Conn was a hard taskmaster, he knew he had seen nothing until he met Stephen Kearny. They left Fort Leavenworth with cavalry and infantry, and in twenty-nine days covered nearly five hundred fifty miles, the foot soldiers at times outpacing the cavalry and earning the name of the "long-legged infantry."

Tris and Conn spent their time far ahead of the main force, seeking out water and campsites. They encountered no hostile Indians, although occasionally running into friendly ones eager to trade skins for tobacco or whiskey.

Never had Tris felt better or been more content. He seemed born for this, for the adventure, for sleeping under rich blue skies framed by mountains. Each day he grew more confident in his abilities. He was no longer under the shadow of his charming, charismatic father, but his own man. He felt a special pride when he was sent out alone, without Conn's watchful tutelage, and knew then he had been accepted completely.

He didn't know exactly where this was leading him. He only understood that he had a growing affinity with this hard, rough land and its stark brilliant beauty. As they approached New Mexico through Raton Pass, Tris Hampton had the strange feeling of coming home.

Chapter Two

"He should be hung."

Ramon's loud voice greeted Antonia as she approached the door of her father's hacienda.

"*Caramba!*" Antonia wanted to utter something stronger than the mild oath, but she could not think of anything bad enough. She hesitated, listening to the loud voices inside.

It had been a month since the dance, when she had last seen Ramon, and she had prayed nightly it would be forever before she saw him again. Obviously her plea had gone unheeded.

Now all the familiar venom was in his voice. "Governor? Fool and coward. He ran from a smaller force of Yanquis when our soldiers could have trapped them at Apache Pass. The Yanquis took Santa Fe without a shot being fired." A long string of Spanish curses followed.

"They'll be here next . . . a spy told me they plan to appoint a gringo, Charles Bent, as governor," Ramon continued. "You, Don Miguel, should know better than any of us what that means."

There was a silence, and Antonia wanted to cut out Ramon's heart. Ramon's last comment was obviously designed to stir her father, and he was ill enough without such provocation.

"We must drive them from New Mexico," Ramon was continuing. "Are you with us?"

Her father's voice was unexpectedly strong. "*Si*, I am with you."

Antonia said another prayer. She knew how well Ramon could manipulate her father in this matter. She would not give him a chance this time. Throwing open the door, she said in a cool low voice, "Father?"

There was, she noted, a note of relief in his voice as he looked up from the chair he was occupying. "Antonia. Come join us."

Antonia observed with some satisfaction the noticeable frown on Ramon's face as she entered the room.

"Ramon," she said politely, acknowledging his presence.

He bowed. "Antonia." He looked at her riding clothes with displeasure. "Surely, you are not still riding alone. The Yanqui invaders are said to be coming this way. There are reports of rape and worse."

Antonia wanted to say she had been taking care of herself for years now and would continue to do so, but she controlled her tongue. She, for one, rejoiced in the removal of Governor Manuel Armijo. He had been greedy, as had Ramon as his representative in Taos, and she was sure that both men kept as much in taxes as they sent to Mexico. She had often heard her father complain, but now he was silent.

In fact, she thought bitterly, it was probably Ramon's greed, not his patriotism, that lay at the bottom of his hatred.

"I ride with a rifle and I can shoot quite well, Ramon," she said, the pointed warning aimed at him as much as at a stranger. There had been an ugly scene at his gathering when she had refused him once more. He had tried forcibly to kiss her and had stopped only when she had slapped him.

"All the same," he said stiffly to her father, "you should forbid her from riding alone. When she is . . ."

When she is my wife . . .

The words were unsaid but they hung in the air like a dense suffocating fog. Antonia's lips pressed together as her eyes swept him coldly, noting his confidence. She wished she knew why it was there.

Miguel Ramirez sighed. To Antonia's distress, he turned to her. "He is right, Antonia. You should not ride alone now."

Antonia turned her anger on her father. "I will be fine, Papa. You know I can shoot better than most of the vaqueros."

Seeing Ramon's face flush with her ready defiance of his warning, she added. "I have heard from Señor Magoffin that the Yanquis have issued a proclamation assuring us that all our rights and religion will be respected. And I heard Ramon say Señor Bent will be appointed governor. Surely, it is well that someone from Taos, like Señor Bent, is named. He is a fair man."

"Lies," Ramon exploded. "They come to rob and desecrate our churches, to take our land. They are greedy." He eyed Antonia with the possessiveness she hated. "But they will not have New Mexico—or you."

Antonia wanted to retort that it was Governor Armijo who was greedy, who had been endangering their ranch through taxes, but her father's pleading eyes stopped her. Instead, she said icily, "No one will have me that I do not want."

Ramon met her look with unwavering black eyes. Then he turned to Antonia's father. "It is time that Antonia and I married. Her arrogance and independence should be curbed."

Antonia could not longer hold back her fury. "Arrogance? Don Ramon, you are the very essence of arrogance, thinking you can have something you can never have. I will not marry you. Can you understand that?"

"Antonia!" Her father's voice was outraged, angrier than she could ever remember. "You will apologize."

She trembled, both at her own loss of control and her father's unusual anger. She bit her lip, then shook her head slowly. "I cannot, Father. I am not sorry, and I will not lie and say so," she finally said slowly, watching the furious flush grow deeper on Ramon's face as the full meaning of the words penetrated.

Ramon swallowed his fury. She looked so accursedly beautiful, standing there proud and defiant. He had wanted her all his life, since they were children together and he had led their games. She had looked up to him then, but something had happened, and her eyes, once adoring, now regarded him coldly. Her reserve, however, had not reduced his desire for her, but had, instead, spurred it. He always got what he wanted, and a challenge made the reward that much more desirable.

He had rarely been refused by a woman, and Antonia's stubbornness made her an even greater prize. He knew that if he could get her alone and use the sensuous magic of his mouth and hands, she would lose that haughtiness and become like the others, begging for more.

Ramon knew he had Don Miguel's approval for a marriage with Antonia. It was time for him to marry, to breed heirs. And Antonia was the only woman he had ever wanted; she would produce splendid sons. He sometimes wondered if what he felt was love, but he quickly dismissed the idea. There was no such thing as love, only power and desire and winning. He had learned that as a boy when his father's iron hand was his taskmaster. Soft emotions, such as love and sentimentality, had been whipped out of him. Only strong men survive.

He had survived and prospered. He was much wealthier than his father had ever been, which gave him much pleasure. He had proven he was the better man, but even after his father's death the cycle of acquisition never stopped. He wanted more and more, and denial only made the need stronger.

But he had never wanted anything more than Antonia. God, how he wanted her. And he would have her, one way or another. The way he eventually won everything he wanted. Ramon wanted her willingly, but if he could not get her that way, he had few compunctions about finding another. Her father already owed him almost more than he could ever repay. One more loan to pay the exorbitant taxes he and the governor kept raising, and Miguel could lose the ranch... if the damned Yanquis didn't interfere. He was so close, so very close, to getting the Ramirez ranch along with Antonia.

She was beautiful. There was no doubt about that. Even in those heretic clothes she wore. But he could take care of that... along with her haughty disdain. And enjoy every minute of it. He looked at her angry face and felt the hunger eat at him.

He forced a thin smile. "I think it's time to leave. I have a meeting." He bowed slightly to Antonia, then to her father. "We will talk again, Don Miguel, about our little plan."

After the door closed, Antonia and her father stared hostilely at each other.

"What plan, Father?"

"How could you have been so disrespectful?"

"I was only being honest. Why can't he leave me alone?"

"He would make a good match for you. And you will come to love him, just as I did your mother. He is a strong man…and has been a good and loyal friend. It is time you married, Antonia, particularly now. Ramon can protect you."

Antonia was silent. How could she explain her fears about Ramon when she didn't quite understand them herself.

"He is very fond of you," her father continued haltingly. "I don't see—"

"Papa, have you ever wondered about the taxes? On horses and cattle and even wool?"

Don Miguel sighed. "It's the government, Antonia. Not Ramon. He has tried to help."

"Let me help you with the accounts," Antonia suggested unexpectedly. The accounts were the one part of the ranch that her father controlled and he seldom talked of them, no matter how many times she asked.

Her father looked at her sadly. "You do enough, Antonia, more than enough. I fear I've been wrong these years to let you ride with the vaqueros, to take so much responsibility." He suddenly looked very old. "Antonia, *por favor,* consider Ramon's offer."

She wanted to concede, if only for him. She owed him her very existence. A lump formed in her throat as she realized how difficult these last years had been for him. He had been such an active man, such a vibrant one, and now he was only an ill shadow of that person. But something in her heart would not let her bend. "I can't, Papa," she whispered. "I don't love him."

"You can grow to love him. He is a handsome man, a wealthy man. He can always take care of you."

"I only need you, Papa," she said, kneeling beside him.

His mouth gentled. She was his heart, his soul. He wanted only her happiness and security, and he was convinced it lay with Ramon. They were so alike in their blood and heritage. If only she would give Ramon a chance. But responsibility, which had descended on her because of his own injuries, had made her so independent, so stubborn.

"I love you, Chiquita," he whispered. "And I want you to be happy, to have *niños* of your own. Think about it carefully. I won't always be here."

"You will," she said firmly.

He only smiled sadly, and Antonia felt pain crawl into little corners of her heart. He did not look well, and the news about the Yanquis had not helped.

She nodded, hoping to erase some of the lines in his face. She was, after all, agreeing only to give it more thought.

Don Miguel, however, saw the determination in her eyes and knew the consideration would be slight. He had never understood her aversion to Ramon, especially when they had been so close as children. He studied the rest of her, his eyes running over the dark shining hair that was so much like his wife's, his sweet Theresa. His had been an arranged marriage, one made when they were both children, but he had come to love his wife dearly, and she him. When she died, more than his body had been damaged. His heart had been crushed during the long afternoon he had held her still hand beneath the carriage—willing her to breathe again, to whisper words of love—to heal.

He swallowed down the bitter memories. "I won't force you, Antonia," he said, his voice full of sad defeat. "But I think you are wrong about Ramon. He will make you a fine and loyal husband."

Loyal to himself, Antonia thought. She suddenly remembered Ramon's parting words. What was he involving her father in now?

"What was the plan Ramon mentioned, Father?" she asked suddenly.

Miguel looked away.

"What plan, Father?" she insisted.

"It's nothing," her father said. "It's only a discussion as to how to meet the Yanquis when they arrive. We will be civil."

"And . . . ?"

"And nothing," he said, evading her eyes. "There's nothing we can do now. The government in Santa Fe has surrendered. It is over."

"Not for Ramon. . . ."

"It is over," her father said again. He turned away, and she knew he was hiding something. "I must work on the accounts," he said in dismissal.

She doubted she would get any more information from him, but she would keep an eye on him.

For now, she needed to get away. She would take Night Wind and go to her hill. She needed to rid herself of the aftermath of Ramon's presence. She needed to race the wind and feel its freshness.

Jose saddled the horse and Antonia secured the thong of the black hat she wore over her long black braid. She was wearing black *armitas* and a black silk shirt under a fitted jacket. Black suited her mood today. She checked her rifle and secured it on the saddle before swinging easily onto Night Wind's back. The horse pawed restlessly, eager for exercise. She would have it today, and more. Antonia needed to exorcise a few devils of her own, she thought bitterly.

She pushed Night Wind into a gallop, relishing the feel of the strong muscles and superb gait that made riding the mare such a joy. She leaned over the horse's neck, urging her faster. She was so intent on the rush of freedom she felt, she didn't see the horseman emerge from a stand of aspens and follow her at a distance.

Tris halted his golden stallion and dismounted. The Taos Valley lay tranquil below him. He had followed the Rio Grande Gorge from Santa Fe, and had seldom seen such spectacular country. He was tired, but knew a kind of exhilaration. The temperatures had dropped as he climbed steadily up the gorge, and now a light breeze ruffled his hair and cooled his skin.

He had never seen anything quite as beautiful as the scene below him...not even after all the spectacular sights of the past months. Nothing could compare to the absolute perfection of this valley glimmering under a red-gold sun that looked near enough to touch.

It was the end of August, nearly six months since he had left Virginia. He had been elated when General Kearny chose him to go to Taos to find Charles Bent, whom the general wanted to appoint as governor. Bent was a trader, well-known and respected among both the Indians and ranchers in New Mexico. Charles and his brother, William, had established a fort in Colorado before Charles headed south and made his headquarters in the Taos area. Bent's Fort had been one of the stopping places for the Kearny expedition, and Tris had met and liked the crusty William Bent. He looked forward to meeting his brother.

Tris heard a stream nearby and dismounted, walking his tired horse to the source of the sound. The water ran through a forest of aspen and evergreens. He lay down on the bank and drank from the stream, then splashed some water on his face. Despite the late summer, it was cool, flowing, he supposed, from the high mountains. Tris let his horse drink slowly, then he tied the reins to a bush, giving the animal enough slack to graze. Finding a likely looking tree, he slid down next to it, resting his tired back against the white bark.

He didn't know how long he stayed there, lulled by the lazy afternoon and the sprinkling of sundrops against the rich earth. He was tired, but it was a satisfying kind of weariness. This land, this wilderness, had tested every fiber of him, and he knew no man would ever quite conquer it. The sun was like warm honey against his skin, and the sky was so blue it defied description.

Tris knew it was time to leave, but he promised himself a few more moments. He had ridden hard for ten hours and another wouldn't make that much difference. He had just bent his head back once more, his eyes drawn to the mountains across from him, when he heard the sound of another rider.

And then he saw the approaching horse and he stood, stunned in the shadow of a tree.

The rider was slender and dressed all in black except for the striking blue pattern on the short jacket. It was obviously a woman although her hat was pulled down over her forehead, shading her eyes form his vision. A long braid fell down her back, and she was riding astride with a grace he had seldom seen. Mesmerized, he watched as she dismounted and took off her hat, shaking her head. She was, quite simply, the most beautiful woman he had ever seen.

Her hat and riding quirt held in one hand, she stood on the edge of the hill, where he had been minutes earlier, looking out over the valley. Tris watched as her shoulders straightened and set and her slender figure seemed to gather strength from the view. He could see the proud chin, the elegant lines of her cheeks, and he wondered about the color of her eyes. They would be dark with that hair, that coloring . . . and mysterious. Somehow he knew they would.

As Tris watched her stare so intently at the mountains across from them, he thought about approaching her, but he didn't want to break the spell she had invoked in him. Still hidden by the trees, he watched as she turned and buried her head in the silky black mane of her horse.

Once more, he considered approaching her and took a few steps forward, but stopped abruptly. There was something about the woman that held him back. He sensed her need to be alone and he felt like a Peeping Tom, but he couldn't take his eyes from her. He had never believed in love at first sight, but now he felt his heart thumping against the cage that was his body, and he had a difficult time swallowing. He had to ball his fists at his side, for they wanted to reach out and see if her skin was really as soft as it looked.

He tried to suppress the feelings. One of Kearny's most stringent orders had been to do nothing to antagonize the local residents, and he could tell by the woman's bearing, color and dress that she was probably of one of the old Spanish families he had been warned about. The rules of their society were narrow and most definitely not open to an American adventurer. Still, what was she doing alone? Unchaperoned? He had understood that unmarried Creole girls were protected like coffers of gold. Could she be married, then? He felt a gnawing pain in the pit of his stomach at the possibility.

His thoughts were interrupted by the sound of another approaching horse, and the pain grew greater. Was she meeting a lover? If so, should he reveal himself? There was no other way off the hill, and he certainly had no desire to be a voyeur. He felt a surge of disappointment, wondering at the intensity of it, as a man rode up abreast the woman. Tris immediately disliked him, though he didn't know if it was his own envy or the arrogance of the man, which was obvious even from a distance.

The woman turned toward the oncoming rider, watching him. Tris couldn't see her expression, but as the man dismounted, she moved away from him. Something inside Tris lightened as the woman's face turned in his direction and he saw anger and even a touch of fear on her proud face. It was lovelier than he had imagined from the side view, delicate, yet with a certain strength. And her eyes were, as he expected, dark and compelling.

He knew he was still hidden by the thick stand of trees, and he debated revealing himself when her words, hostile and angry, drifted over to him. "You followed me. You had no right."

The man spoke in Spanish, and Tris had to concentrate to understand. "I needed to talk to you alone, Chiquita." His hand went up to her face, stroking it before she jerked away.

"Please...Ramon..."

The man caught her arm as she tried to turn away. "Antonia, there is no more time for games. You are mine. You have always been mine."

"No." The sound of her voice was explosive.

"I think you deny too much." The man leaned down and his lips touched hers forcibly. His arms went around her as she struggled. "And I *will* have you...now."

The woman's hand moved with lightning speed, and Tris heard the whistling sound of the quirt and then the blow. There was a string of Spanish curses as the man's hand went to his cheek.

It had happened so quickly that Tris had not moved, but now he saw the man's hand go from his cheek upward as if to strike the woman, and he hurtled out from behind the tree toward the two figures.

Tris's fist swept out, knocking the Creole's hand down, and then the two men were facing each other. The Creole's fists were balled, his face suffused with rage. "Yanqui," he spit out, and one of his fists went for Tris's stomach.

Tris spun around and deflected the blow, which glanced his side. His own fist connected with his opponent's face, and a spurt of blood poured from the man's nose.

The blow would have stunned any other man, but the Creole appeared unfazed. Tris dropped his guard just long enough for the man to see his advantage and strike Tris's chest. Tris fell, the wind knocked from him, but he managed to get to his knees in time to see the man coming at him, his booted foot aimed for Tris's ribs. Tris stiffened, feeling his muscles flex as he reached out and grabbed the boot, tumbling his attacker. The man went down with a curse and started back up.

God, but the New Mexican was quick. And Tris knew he was tiring. Desperately, he threw himself down on the man, locking him to the ground. The Creole struggled to throw him off, and Tris hit him once and then again.

"Damn you," he said, ignoring his orders about antagonizing the local populace. He hoped that didn't apply to someone who was attacking another member of that same populace.

"Bastard," the man under him spit. "Yanqui bastard."

"Yanqui, yes. Bastard, now that's another matter," Tris said, his voice and eyes icy cold. "But I think the term might well apply to you. Attacking a woman!"

"She's is my *novio*," the man said, his eyes black as onyx and hard as that same stone.

Tris started. *Novio*, he knew, meant fiancée. "You lie," he said.

But Tris's surprise was enough to give Ramon an edge. His leg crashed into Tris's side, upsetting his balance, and both rolled over, their fists once more pummeling each other.

"Stop, Ramon, or I'll shoot."

The woman's voice was cold and deliberate, and the two men, locked together, froze. The woman was holding a rifle, and Tris saw that it was aimed at his opponent.

"Shoot *him!*" the man cried, as if he hadn't heard her first order.

"I will shoot *you,* Ramon, if you don't get up and ride away from here."

Surprised at the iron in her voice, Tris took his hands away from the man and rolled away, watching the tableau unfolding in front of him.

Ramon...that was what she had called him...continued to stare at her in shock, then in arrogant defiance. "You won't shoot me, *chula,*" he said. "You won't take this... invader...this heretic's side." He rose and walked toward her, his hand outstretched.

Tris stiffened. In his mind's eyes, he could see the rifle pointed at him if she handed it to the Creole. His hand reached for the pistol strapped inside his belt holster and drew it out and noisily cocked the weapon, aware that the other man was too intent on the woman to pay him any mind. "Perhaps she won't," he said in a deadly tone, "but I sure as hell will."

The man whirled around. Tris could almost taste the venom he saw in the man's eyes, but his face, now dirty and bloody, had been molded into a cold mask. "You interfere, Yanqui, in matters that don't concern you."

"This territory is under U.S. law now," Tris said tightly, "and we are pledged to the protection of its residents...even one against another."

"This is a personal matter."

"The lady doesn't seem to think so. She has indicated she would prefer you to go." He turned to the woman, who was still very competently holding the gun. "Is that correct, *señorita?*"

Antonia looked at the men. Both were bloodied and tense, as if prepared for another battle. All she wanted, at the moment, was for Ramon to go. She would decide later what to tell her father. She nodded, her dark brown eyes flashing. "Yes."

"You heard the lady," Tris said in a soft, dangerous drawl. "Unless you want to test this pistol and my resolve, I would suggest you mount your horse and leave the lady alone."

"She's mine," the man said again, "and you will pay for this interference, I swear to you."

"And I swear to you I'm fast losing my patience, and I've never had a lot to brag about." The soft drawl was gone, and now there was a strange clipped note to his words. "I will give you the count of five to be on that horse over there...."

The man stood there for a second, as if deliberating the odds, weighing his hate against his caution. He finally turned and walked slowly, painfully, over to his horse and mounted gracefully. He looked down at Tris, whose pistol had carefully followed his every move. "We will meet again, Yanqui." The tone of his voice said it would not be a pleasant reunion.

"I'll look forward to it," Tris replied calmly, but his eyes, like Ramon's voice, promised otherwise. "By the way, Ramon...is it...you can leave your rifle here. You can return later for it. Much later."

Ramon looked at him hard for a moment, then slowly did as he was told. "Yanqui dog," he said before cruelly spurring his horse into a gallop.

When Ramon was finally out of sight, Tris turned to the woman. The rifle was still in her hands, but now they were shaking slightly. He watched as she slowly lowered it and took off her gloves.

"Gracias," she said simply.

"He said he was your *novio?*"

"Him!" Antonia was too angry to hold her tongue. "I have refused him. Time and again, I have refused him. He will not accept it."

Tristan felt a current of relief flow through him. "Then I'm glad I could be of assistance."

"I'm afraid I might have caused trouble for you. Ramon can be dangerous...and vicious."

"I can be dangerous, too, *señorita,*" Tris said with a crooked smile. "But what about you? He might try again."

"I know now," she said. "I will not be caught unaware again. I can take care of myself." She smiled for the first time, and her dark eyes seemed to catch a golden light from the sun. "Usually," she added with a touch of chagrin.

Tris found himself lost in those eyes. They were incredibly expressive. He had thought her beautiful at a distance but now she was pure bewitching magic.

"*Señor....?*"

The soft voice with its musical Spanish accent penetrated a mind suddenly gone besotted. He felt a fool and knew he must look like one. He raised an eyebrow.

"You are...American? You do not sound entirely like one."

Tris bowed slightly. "I am sorry, *señorita*. I have forgotten what manners I once had. Tristan Hampton, a scout for General Kearny. My friends call me Tris."

"But your speech..."

"I have spent some time in England and with English cousins, and some of it stuck to me, I'm afraid. I am teased about it frequently."

"But no. It's very...pleasant." Antonia was baffled at her behavior. She had never spoken at length with a strange man, particularly one who was now an enemy of her country. Despite her brave words to her father, spoken partially to annoy Ramon, she did have a fear of Yanquis. How could she not?

Yet this man seemed so kind, so easy to talk with and so... He looked like a sun god, with his fiery gold hair and rich bronze face. He was dressed in buckskins and they showed every hard lean angle and muscle of his body.

But most striking of all were his eyes. They were a clear blue-green, yet seemed to change color as his emotions changed from anger to concern to humor. There was a devil in them, but a laughing, happy devil, not like the malevolent one in Ramon's. *Madre de Dios,* but he was a beautiful man.

She watched now as the brief humor changed to concern again. "You shouldn't be riding alone, *señorita*."

"Now you sound like Don Ramon," she teased, but there was still a note of fear in her voice. "I have been riding alone since I was sixteen."

"And, of course, that's been for many years," he teased again, his eyes sparkling like the sun glinting off a lake's surface.

She drew herself up to her full height. "Three," she answered indignantly.

"And you have no—duenna?"

"There are no older female members of my family, only Father and myself . . . and he trusts me."

"And he is . . . ?"

Chagrined, Antonia realized she had not introduced herself. But then she was not quite used to meeting men this way. "He is Miguel Ramirez," she said softly. "I am Antonia Theresa Margarita Ramirez."

Tris bowed, a formal one he had used when once introduced at the English court, and his eyes twinkled. "A name as beautiful as its possessor," he said, taking her hand and bringing it to his lips.

He had not expected the flames that suddenly raced between them as his mouth touched her fingers. It was as if electricity had reached down from the sky, embracing them with a sizzling ring of fire. He could only stand there, his heart pounding and his senses soaring, as he watched her brown eyes widen in her own awareness of something special, something extraordinary, happening between them.

In confusion, Antonia pulled away, her face flushing with embarrassment. She did not want to lose his touch, but she must. "I—I must go," she said shakily, trying to keep her eyes away from his.

Tris understood. He knew if he continued to stand this close to her, he would have to do more than kiss her hand. And it was too soon. He did not want to frighten her, not after the earlier incident. But when he tried to move, his legs would not obey.

It was Antonia who stepped back, wondering how she managed those few steps when she wanted nothing as much as to move forward, to look into his eyes, to study even closer the clean, strong features of his face. She whirled around and moved toward her horse, but he moved with her, and when they reached Night Wind, she felt his strong arm as he assisted her onto the mount.

"I will ride with you," he said. It was an announcement, not a request, and she surprised herself by nodding. She did not want him to leave. She suddenly couldn't bear to think of never seeing him again.

"For your safety," he said, as if reassuring her when she needed no reassurance. When she said nothing, he added, "My horse is over in the trees. You will wait?"

"I will wait," she said in that soft voice he knew would lure birds to her fingers.

Tris disappeared among the trees, reappearing in seconds leading a great golden stallion that caused her to gasp in awe. It was the finest horse she had ever seen, and she and her father raised excellent horses themselves. As he swung up, Antonia thought once more of a sun god. She shivered despite the heat of the day, and her mind was a jumble of confused emotions, one of which reigned supreme. She closed her hands tightly around her reins, drawing a protest from Night Wind as she identified that wayward emotion. *Want*. Pure uncomplicated want. She had never before known the intensity of that word. Not until an hour ago.

But now, dear Mother in Heaven, she did. And nothing, she feared, would ever quite be the same again.

Chapter Three

As she rode beside the Yanqui stranger, Antonia felt reason replacing her euphoria at the man's presence. She knew she should not be with him. She particularly should not be with him alone.

Her father had stopped protesting her rides alone because he felt her safe enough among his own vaqueros and the people of the valley. In its role as a trading center, Taos was considered neutral ground for both the Apache and Comanches, and the area's own Pueblo Indians had been peaceful since a bloody revolt two hundred years earlier.

But Antonia knew he would never approve of her being alone with a Yanqui and she felt a quickening in her blood as she herself understood how unwise it was.

She couldn't, however, help stealing glances at him. He was so different from anyone she had ever met. It wasn't only his coloring, though that was rare in this country dominated by dark hair and dark eyes. It was something in his bearing, in his eyes.

His face was strong, as if each feature had been carefully chiseled by a master sculptor, and he was clean shaven, unlike most of the Creoles, who wore mustaches or trimmed beards. His mouth was wide, and she already knew it smiled easily, as did those startling eyes that kept pulling her gaze to his.

There was pride in his carriage and in the tilt of his chin, but it didn't hold the arrogance she associated with Ramon. Instead there was a self-confidence, although she also detected a restlessness in his eyes, a sense of adventure.

His hat hung by a thong from his saddle horn. His uncovered gold hair, laced with sun-painted silver strands, ruffled in the breeze, contrasting with the darkness of his skin. And his clothes, *Muy Dios*. The deerskin molded itself to muscled thighs and powerful shoulders. He was a superb horseman for a Yanqui, who usually had heavy hands and seats.

But most fascinating of all was the great vitality emanating from him. She had the sense he was a man who scooped every minute from life, wasting none of them.

She scolded herself. She was the daughter of Don Miguel Ramirez, who was descended from royalty and was strongly Catholic. She should not be thinking the thoughts that were running insistently through her head. How, for instance, would it feel to touch those hard planes of his face or the golden hair that showed through the rawhide ties at the neck of his shirt?

Tris couldn't miss Antonia's sidelong glances, and each time he felt a surge of something strong and hot and fluid moving through him. He still didn't quite understand what she was doing alone, an unmarried girl of obvious breeding, but he was not about to question his luck. He wanted to feast his eyes upon her, to reassure himself she was not a mirage. Still, in the past months, he had learned caution, and the angry Creole he had defeated could well try an ambush of some kind. He kept his eyes moving, searching every hill, every tree, every jutting rock. There had been something in the Creole's face and manner, that made him wary.

After a long silence, Tris settled his eyes on the woman riding beside him.

"Who is he?" Tris finally asked, and Antonia knew he was referring to his recent opponent.

"Ramon Silvero. A neighbor," Antonia said. "And the alcalde."

Tris stiffened. The alcalde was the local magistrate or authority. And then he grinned. Leave it to him to violate orders in a grand way. 'Don't ruffle the local feathers,' he had been told, and now he had pummeled the magistrate. Not a very auspicious beginning.

Antonia hesitated. After all, this man was an enemy. At least according to Ramon and her father. But everything she had heard had been from their view.

"What is happening in Santa Fe?"

"Governor Armijo fled to Albuquerque. There was no resistance. In fact, most of Santa Fe seemed glad to see us. It seems your governor was not very popular."

Antonia was silent for a moment. "There was no fighting?"

"None, and you are now a U.S. citizen."

"I don't think that will make my father happy."

"Why?" He caught something in her voice.

"He does not care for Americanos. And then there's Don Ramon. He has filled my father's head with tales. He says the Americans will steal from our churches, try to take our religion from us and force us from the land." She looked over at the American, seeking the truth.

"Do you always believe Ramon?"

Antonia's eyes filled with laughter, and her lips curved up in a mischievous smile. Tris had heard from his uncle how shy these Creole women were, how protected, but Antonia Ramirez was like a brightly glowing star.

"I think," she said slowly, "I would doubt any of Ramon's words." The smile faded. "I only wish my father would."

"Perhaps I could talk to him, reassure him. From everything I have heard in Santa Fe, the New Mexicans will fare better as U.S. citizens than as stepchildren of the Mexican government. You will have many more rights."

"And our religion . . . ?"

Tris heard the apprehension in her voice and stopped his horse, expecting her to do the same. "My God," he said, "what in the devil have you heard?"

"That . . . that our churches will be torn down, the holy relics stolen."

"Señorita...Ramirez, probably no other country respects the right of its citizens to choose their own religion more than the United States. General Kearny has given orders that both your property and religion are to be protected. You have nothing to fear from us." An ironic note crept into his voice. "It seems you have much more to fear from your own neighbors."

"I think you are right," Antonia said slowly. "Ramon does not want to lose what power he has."

"He won't . . . at least if he causes no trouble. The general's leaving the present authorities in place for the moment . . . except, of course, for the governor."

"I heard Señor Bent is to be appointed."

He smiled again, the sides of his mouth curving up in an irresistible smile. "News travels fast. I was to inform Charles Bent and accompany him back to Santa Fe to talk with General Kearny. How did you hear?"

"Ramon," she said, feeling no sense of betrayal. If everything the American was saying was true, they would, indeed, be better off than under capricious Mexican rule and taxes.

Tris didn't allow his expression to change, but he absorbed the information with interest. So there were spies in Santa Fe. Charles Bent's appointment was supposed to have been a secret until he accepted.

The sun was spreading a fiery halo in the western sky, and Antonia knew she had to hurry or her father would send some vaqueros after her. She didn't want to be seen with the American or there would be a tremendous explosion. There was enough tension between her and her father now because of Ramon. The doctor had told her Don Miguel's heart was bad and that he needed peace. Knowing she had spent time with a Yanqui would not give it to him. This she knew.

"I must go on alone," she said, her words reluctant.

"I would like to talk to your father, to reassure him about our intentions."

"No," she said, averting her eyes from his steady gaze. "He does not like Anglos."

"Why?"

Yanqui frankness, Antonia thought with a small smile. Her Creole friends would never ask such a question.

Antonia hesitated. She didn't know this man well enough to explain about her mother, how the incident had affected her father. "He has good reasons. Something happened . . . a long time ago."

"If it was a long time ago . . . ?"

"You don't understand, Señor Hampton. It is not just dislike. He is passionate in his hatred."

"And you don't share it?"

"I don't know many Anglos," she said with a small, rather shy smile, a touch of impishness in her eyes.

"I intend to remedy that," he said with an appealing smile of his own.

"I don't know if that is possible, Señor Hampton." The smile disappeared. She wanted it to be possible. She wanted it very much.

"Tris," he said. "My name is Tris."

Antonia regarded him solemnly, at the smile in his eyes, at the easy way his lips turned upward. "Señor Hampton," she insisted, trying to keep a distance despite the increased rhythm of her heart.

"Tristan then. Just try it."

The intensity of his expression commanded it, and she had no more resistance in her. "Tristan," she said softly, her tongue savoring the unusual sound.

There was something about the way she said it, the almost reverence in her tone, that caused Tris's insides to throb.

"Why?" he said again, forcing his mind on the last unanswered question. "Why doesn't your father like Americans? Especially when someone like Silvero is around?"

"He doesn't know what . . . Ramon is really like."

Tris stopped his horse. "Are you going to tell him . . . about this afternoon."

"No," she said softly.

"Why not?"

Antonia's eyes, so deep that Tris felt he could drown in them, were sad. "It is better unsaid. I don't think Ramon will try again."

"I don't understand . . . surely he will protect you."

"My father is crippled . . . and ill. He is no match for Ramon."

"But he should know."

"He believes Ramon is his friend. He wants me to marry him."

"That bastard!" Tris's voice was explosive.

"Ramon and I have much in common," Antonia said defensively.

"You're not going to...?"

"No," she replied so passionately that Tris's frown relaxed.

"I would like to talk to your father," Tris insisted. He had always been able to charm everyone. It was a gift he had inherited from his father and which he often used carelessly. But he knew that when he turned on its full potency, there were few who were immune to it.

"No," Antonia said. "You don't understand... and I really must go on alone. Please."

The distress on her face was so deep, Tris quieted his protests but he couldn't stop worrying. "I still don't think you should be riding alone. What about Silvero?"

"We are on my father's land now. I will be quite safe. Ramon would try nothing here. But thank you."

"I would like to call on you."

I would like that too. Something inside Antonia hurt desperately as she realized exactly how much she would like that. But if her father knew, he would forbid any further contact, and she did not want to be put into a position of openly defying him. Looking at this man now, she knew she would.

"He will not receive you," she said finally.

"I have to see you again."

Antonia tipped her head to the side, studying the determination on this man's face. "How long will you be here?"

"I don't know. It depends on Mr. Bent."

Antonia's words came without plan. "I go riding to the hilltop quite often in the afternoons." Her lips moved into an enchanting smile that was part shyness, part invitation, and once more Tris felt his heart slow, then speed with erratic rhythm.

"What about...?"

She didn't want to hear Ramon's name again, didn't want the memory to spoil the sudden swelling of her heart as she looked at the golden American. "I don't think Ramon will attempt that again. I will be watchful."

Tris wished he felt as confident. "I didn't think Creole girls rode alone," he said carefully, his emotions warring in him. He wanted desperately to see her again, but he also feared for her.

"They don't," she said with a sudden mischievous glint that couldn't help bring a smile to Tris's lips. "But I kept sneaking out until my father finally gave up hiring duennas." She smiled. "I'm like a mole . . . I keep burrowing until the opposition collapses."

"I'll remember that," Tris said with a grin.

"And, *señor*," Antonia added seriously, "there is seldom trouble here. Not in the valley."

"Until now," Tris said tightly. He kept remembering Ramon's possessive hands on her.

"Until now," she agreed. "But I am aware now. And Ramon's pride will not let him try it again."

"He doesn't look like a man who gives up easily."

"No," she said thoughtfully. "He will try, instead, to use my father."

"I still think you, or I, should tell him what happened."

She shook her head. "I can say nothing at the moment. Please."

"All right," Tris reluctantly agreed, then his expression lightened. "The hilltop?"

"The hilltop," she said.

"I'll be there," Tris said. He moved his horse closer to hers and held out his hand. Taking her much smaller gloved one in his, he touched it lightly to his lips. Even through the cloth Antonia felt a burning sensation. *"Vaya con Dios,"* he whispered, grateful for Conn's lessons in Spanish, especially when he saw the smile on her face.

"Vaya con Dios," she replied in a low musical voice that Tris knew would remain with him.

He relinquished her hand reluctantly and watched as her knees tightened against the mare. The horse spurted away at a fast trot. Tris turned slowly, knowing he had already delayed too long in his mission, and rode in the opposite direction. But he couldn't stop looking back at the graceful rider and feeling a terrible longing.

Antonia had not gone far when she saw a group of riders. She hoped against hope that they had not seen the rider just disappearing from view.

When Antonia reined her horse to meet her father and Nicolas, she stared at Don Miguel in amazement. It had been weeks since he had been on a horse; it was much too painful and often dangerous, since he had to be strapped to the saddle.

"We have been worried about you," her father said. "Who was that with you?"

Antonia's heart stopped. "Just someone asking about Taos."

"He was looking for someone?"

"*Sí.*"

"For whom."

"Señor Bent," she said reluctantly.

"A Yanqui?"

"Yes, Papa."

"Just one?"

She nodded as she saw his mouth tighten in the way it did whenever Yanquis were mentioned.

"That is all he wanted?"

"Yes," she said. "He was very polite and pleasant."

"I will not have you around the cursed Yanquis," her father said.

Why couldn't her father see where the real danger lay? It was their neighbor they should fear, not the stranger.

She took the offensive. "What are you doing out here, Papa? You know how much it weakens you."

He sighed. "After talking to Ramon, I worried about you riding alone."

"Papa, you know I can take care of myself...even against Yanquis."

"You should not ride alone any more. If you must go out, Jose or one of the other vaqueros will accompany you."

Antonia had never seen his face so set before. She would remain silent, then continue to do as she had always done. There

was always a reason to go for a ride on a ranch: a fence to
check, work to oversee.

He took her silence as agreement and his expression softened. "It is best, Antonia. You cannot trust Anglos. They are
animals."

"Not all of them. Even Father Luis said many are fine
men—"

She saw the stark pain in her father's face, and wished she
hadn't said anything. But she had to see the American again.
She had to.

"They have no pity, no compassion," Don Miguel said.
"They are seducers, jackals. You must be wary of them." His
hand reached out and touched her face with tender affection.
"I worry about you, Antonia. I should never have been so easy
with you. You should be married and safe, with *niños* of your
own."

He sounded so sad that Antonia wished momentarily she
could be as he wanted, that she could love Ramon. Her heart
swelled with love for this man who had given her life, had given
her love and asked only one thing in return...the one she could
not give him. She would do anything else for him. Protect him,
care for him always, but she would not marry Ramon. If she
had ever had any doubts about that, they had been destroyed
this afternoon.

Tris settled back in a comfortable chair in Charles Bent's
home and watched as Bent went over the packet of papers sent
by General Kearny.

"Governor?" Bent's query was made with a raised eyebrow.

Tris grinned. "That's right. Kearny has a great deal of faith
in your powers of persuasion. Besides, the hostilities seem to be
over now, and he wants someone as governor who has good
relations with both the Indians and the New Mexicans."

Bent looked at his pretty Mexican wife, Maria, who was sitting with her sister, Josefa Carson, Kit Carson's wife. "Would
you like to be a governor's wife instead of a poor trader's?"

The pretty dark-haired woman smiled serenely. "As long as I'm *your* wife."

Tris was surprised at the stab of loneliness that struck him as the man and woman looked at each other, affectionate understanding passing quietly between them. All afternoon and evening he had been unable to rid himself of the image of shining eyes and hair as black as a moonless night.

He shook his head, trying to remind himself of the business at hand.

"You accept, then?"

"I reckon I do," Charles Bent said.

"When can you leave?"

"I have business here I must see to. Five days perhaps."

"I was asked to accompany you back."

"Ah, a nursemaid already. You'll stay with us, then, until we leave." It was a statement rather than a question.

Tris looked at Mrs. Bent and she nodded, smiling.

"I would like that," he said. "It would be a pleasant change."

"And we'll have a party," Bent said. "To celebrate becoming a part of the United States. It will give you a chance to meet some New Mexicans."

"I've already met two," Tris said, deciding it was time to dig for some information.

Bent tipped his head in question.

"A Señorita Ramirez and a Ramon Silvero."

Bent's brow furrowed. "Silvero. I imagine he wasn't very friendly."

Tris's mouth twisted in a wry smile. "You could say that."

"He's one of the former governor's closest allies."

"And a thief," Mrs. Bent spit out.

"That, too," Bent said with a chuckle, then his face creased in seriousness. "Watch out for that one."

"Why?"

"You remember hearing about those Texans who tried to invade New Mexico in 1841?"

Tris nodded. "I heard how badly they were treated."

Bent's laugh was bitter. "They were dragged across the desert at the end of ropes. Those lucky enough to make it to Mexico were imprisoned under terrible conditions. Only a few ever came back. Silvero was a part of that. Sadistic bastard. He and Santa Ana are friends, and he will never concede New Mexico to the United States."

"What about Don Ramirez?"

"Ramirez? He's another who will fight you all the way. He hates all Anglos."

Tris's throat went dry. "Why?" It was the same question he had asked Antonia and now he realized he hadn't received an answer.

Bent looked closely at Tris's frowning face. "How long were you with Antonia Ramirez?"

"Long enough," Tris said with a wry smile.

"Don't even think about it," Bent said. "She's full-blooded Spanish. Her father won't allow her to marry anyone who's not the same."

"Does she do everything her father says?"

Bent laughed. "Hardly ever. But Señor Ramirez was badly crippled years ago and Antonia has practically run the ranch since. She has proved a good manager . . . a fine horsewoman, and she's an independent little thing. But there's an unbreakable bond between those two. She would never hurt Don Miguel and, believe me, an alliance with an Anglo would hurt him."

"Dammit, why?" Tris said, forgetting momentarily the presence of the ladies. Antonia had certainly bewitched him in some way. He had not been able to dislodge her from his mind since the first second he saw her. And Tris, to whom everything had come easily, was unaccustomed to defeat.

Bent hesitated.

"I have to know," Tris insisted.

The American trader sighed. "Miguel Ramirez was married to a Creole, Theresa, who was, like him, a descendent of pure Spanish blood. She was a beautiful woman, a very gentle lady, and she and Miguel had a very happy marriage. . . ."

"And . . . ?"

"It was 1841, the time of the Lamar expedition I just mentioned. Several Texans escaped from the Mexicans and came this way. They happened on Miguel and his wife in a buggy and tried to take their horses. There was gunfire, the horses bolted, overturning the buggy and killing Theresa. Miguel was crippled and the Texans left him there to die. He has reason to hate, Tris."

Tris silently absorbed the words while a tight ball of apprehension knotted inside him. He was surprised that Antonia had even talked to him. "What about Ramon Silvero?" Tris said finally. "He acted . . . possessive?"

"Don Miguel would like nothing better than a match between the two, mainly because of the common heritage and religion, I think. So far, Antonia has resisted." Bent shrugged. "But she loves her father and there's a limit to how much she'll oppose him."

"Can you invite them to your party?" Tris had always been persuasive and persistent when something important was at stake. He didn't know the meaning of the word *surrender,* even now that he knew the full scope of his problem.

"They won't come," Bent said. "Not to the home of Yanquis, especially not to celebrate the liberation of New Mexico from Mexico."

"Ramirez has to eventually realize he's better off with the United States. I understand the government has been corrupt, the protection nonexistent."

"Ah, Tristan." Bent's voice was patient. "You don't understand. These families have been here for two centuries. Their ancestors came with Coronado and stayed, sending for their wives in Spain. Through the years, they intermarried, keeping their Catholic faith and traditions strong. They were not happy when this territory was ceded to Mexico by Spain, but at least there was the common bonds of language and religion. That heritage means more to them than taxes or our concept of freedom or anything else. Their pride is enormous. It is the keystone of their life."

"But in Santa Fe . . . ?"

"Oh, you will find many Creoles eager to throw off the yoke of Mexico, including some in Taos. But Silvero and Ramirez are not among them and will never be. They both carry a burning hatred of Americans for different reasons. Ramirez because of his wife, Silvero because you will destroy his power. Don't underestimate either of them."

Tris was silent, wanting to question more, to protest, but Bent was moving on to another subject. Although his mind was on the dark-haired girl, Tris responded the best he could, explaining that Kearny planned to push on to California with a small force, leaving Colonel Doniphan and his Missouri riflemen to hold New Mexico. General Zachary Taylor would protect the Texas border.

Bent smiled slowly. "At last," he said. "Do you know what this will mean to the United States? The addition of Texas and California will unite the continent."

"There's still Oregon," Tris said, reminding Bent of the dispute between America and England over the northern territory.

"Yes, but once we have Texas and California, Britain won't be able to withstand our claim. They won't go to war again over Oregon."

Tris, who had spent considerable time in England, agreed. The people in Britain wanted peace. They would not countenance the expenditure of money or men for so distant a territory. He felt a thrill of pride running through him as he thought of witnessing the expansion of this rugged, independent country that had already overcome so many odds.

"What about the Indians here?"

"The Pueblos? They're peaceful enough. They have little love for the Mexicans or the Spanish. They've been damned exploited by both over the centuries. They revolted a couple of centuries ago and massacred a number of Spanish, chasing out the remainder until the Spaniards returned years later. But they've been peaceful since then, especially around Taos. There's sort of an unspoken truce around here . . . the trading is too damned important to everyone, the Indians included.

We're the main trading center between Missouri and California."

Tris gave Bent his disarming grin. "Conn told me this is one of his favorite places because of that . . . it's wide open."

"That it is. Americans, Mexicans, Indians, outlaws, you name it. They all come, and no one much bothers them as long as they behave themselves here. Conn stops frequently. He and Kit Carson are good friends."

"I would like to meet Carson."

"He's in California now . . . if you go on with Kearny, you'll probably run into him. There aren't that many trails west."

"I don't know yet where I'll be assigned . . ." Tris said slowly. "I know Conn's going with Kearny to California, but I might be assigned to Doniphan."

"And which would you rather do?" Bent asked curiously.

"Until today, I would have said continue on to California," Tris replied thoughtfully.

"Today?" Bent felt a heavy weight settle in his stomach as he recalled the light in Tris's face when he had talked of Antonia Ramirez. He was struck with a dark premonition of trouble as he watched the determination in Tris's slow, easy smile.

"I like Taos," Tris said simply. "It's one of the most beautiful places I've ever seen."

But that was not the only thing Tris Hampton liked, and Bent knew it. He went over to a table. "Drink?"

Tris nodded. It had been a long day. As he took the glass of whiskey, a gleam entered his turquoise-colored eyes.

Bent's frown deepened. "Thinking of Antonia Ramirez again?"

"I'm afraid so," Tris admitted with a small smile. "I don't think I've ever met anyone quite as beautiful."

Bent took a gulp of whiskey. "That may be, Tristan, but she's not for you, not for any Yanqui."

Tris did not answer. Something in him told him Antonia was his future. He didn't know why or how, but he did know he wouldn't give up.

He held the drink in his hands, his eyes seeing something outside the room, and Charles Bent once more felt a cold shiver as he gulped the burning whiskey, seeking a warmth that didn't come.

Chapter Four

Antonia couldn't sleep. After tossing for hours, she finally rose and went to the doors that opened onto the patio. The moon was hovering, full and bright, over the blue mountains to the west. The stars appeared more brilliant than ever before, clouds of them sprinkling the midnight-blue sky like crystals spread over velvet.

It was all so vast, so complete and harmonious. There was a special magic tonight, or was it just something inside her that had changed, that had come alive?

She fixed her gaze on the north star, which shone brighter than any of its companions, and she wished, all the time knowing it was a hopeless wish. She wished *he* were here, sharing the night's enchantment, and she wondered, hoped, that wherever he was, he, too, could not sleep and had slipped out. Perhaps Señor Hampton was, at this very moment, staring at the same star as she.

Fool. He had probably found a woman. There were many, Mexican and Indian, in Taos, who served the traders and vaqueros. She knew she shouldn't know such things, but she had spent enough time with vaqueros to have overheard conversations.

The thought cut through her like a sword and she knew a heart yearning that cried as mournfully as a wounded animal. She knew she could not have the Yanqui. She might as well try to weave a rope of sand or extract sunbeams from wheat as think of him. It was all as wistful, as impossible.

Holy Mary, but why had she mentioned that she went riding to the hill each afternoon? She had been bewitched by those eyes, by the golden hair, by the soft drawl. But they were from completely different worlds. He was an adventurer, a Yanqui, who probably had dozens of women. She had been taught that the Yanqui traders had no respect for women, for purity, for tradition.

And then Antonia recalled the warmth in the Yanqui's eyes, the open smile that was all admiration, the courteous manner, his rage at Ramon's actions.

But her father would never, ever, accept him, and she could never leave her father. She owed him too much. To love a Yanqui would be to break her father's heart.

"Tristan." She whispered the word in the still night and felt its echo in her heart. She wondered hopelessly how someone could so capture her soul in such a very short time. She would not go to the hill again. Not until she knew he had left Taos. She would not.

Bent's party was long and noisy. Incredibly frustrated, Tris left the hot, crowded room and went outside into the cooler garden. To think. Hell, no. To mope. The thought didn't brighten the gloom that had settled on him in the past two days.

As Bent had predicted, the Ramirez family hadn't attended, although Bent had sent them a personal invitation.

Tris's stomach had stayed in a tight knot for the past three days. He hadn't been able to sleep, to eat, to concentrate. Bent, with admirable restraint, would often jerk him back to attention with some pointed comment.

Tris had ridden to the hill the past two afternoons and waited for hours, waited until the slipping sun told him it was useless. He had spent the time remembering every aspect of Señorita Ramirez. He could almost smell her light fragrance, see the proud tilt of her head, the depth of the brown eyes. He willed her to appear, but the effort went unrewarded.

He worried incessantly that something had happened to her, that perhaps Ramon had cornered her again, but Charles assured him that he would have heard if anything was wrong at the Ramirez ranch. News traveled fast in the valley.

"Señor Hampton."

Tris turned and looked at the smiling face of Carlota, a friend of Mrs. Carson's.

"You look so sad. This is a celebration for your country, no?"

Tris looked at the earnest face smiling up at him. "It is a celebration, yes," he said, crooking his mouth in a half grin.

Carlota was a pretty thing, petite and lively, with friendly dark eyes and a wide, smiling mouth. Four days ago, he would have taken her out for a walk and stolen a kiss. But now he felt no interest, only an increased longing for a person who was not here and who obviously didn't return his damned obsession.

"There is going to be dancing . . . the fandango. Señor Bent thought you might enjoy it, *señor.*"

He nodded and followed her back inside. The soft strum of guitars quickened, and Tris could feel the growing excitement of the rhythm. Two couples took the floor, the women dressed in blouses with large sleeves and ruffled skirts, the men in black velvet with brightly colored serapes.

Tris's eyes studied the guests, the men now scattered around the walls, the women sitting in chairs. It was an incredibly mixed group. Some of the old Spanish families had come, along with others of Mexican descent and the mestizos—those of mixed Spanish and Indian parentage.

"*Señor,* would you try it with me?"

Carlota's face was so expectant Tris could not refuse.

"I think you will find me very clumsy, *señorita,*" he warned her.

"I think not, *señor,*" she replied with a sparkle in her eye. "You just take this step, then this . . . you see."

Tris's concentration was caught in the dance. For all of several minutes, he didn't think of Antonia Theresa Margarita Ramirez more than six times.

"Oh, that Anglo. He is charming. You should meet him."

Antonia tried to blank out the words of her friend, but

Francesca chattered on. She noted that Francesca used *Anglo* rather than the derogatory *Yanqui* her father and Ramon always called Texans or Americans…if they weren't calling them something worse.

"It was a wonderful party. Augustin said we must stay on the good side of the Americans. I don't think he likes them much, but he thinks they might be better for New Mexico than Santa Ana."

"I wish father felt that way," Antonia said, anxious to get away from the topic of the blond Yanqui.

"If they are all like Señor Hampton," Francesca said with a sigh, "I know I will. He was so…courteous…and so handsome."

Antonia busied her hands with some sewing, willing her friend to change the subject. "Who else was there?"

"Many except, of course, you and Don Ramirez and Ramon. Carlota Mendez was there. She was teaching Señor Hampton how to fandango. At first, he was very funny, but he was also very quick to learn."

"Carlota?" Antonia's voice was choked. Carlota was Mexican and had had few of the social restrictions Antonia had. They had attended the same Mass and had been friends for a time, but Antonia's father had disapproved of Carlota's family and they had grown apart. But Antonia had always envied Carlota's carefree ways and good nature. Carlota! Antonia had known the Yanqui would find someone. He probably hadn't even gone to the hill.

"Oh, she had eyes for him, but then we all did." Francesca rolled her eyes dramatically. "But, of course, I have Augustin and the *niños*."

"When does Señor Bent plan to leave for Santa Fe?"

"Tomorrow. And I hear the Yanqui scout goes with him. Carlota will be desolate."

Antonia nodded, trying not to reveal the crushing disappointment that enveloped her. Disgust with herself. Disappointment in Señor Hampton. Her father had been right.

She forced herself to murmur polite answers during the rest of the visit. Francesca had come to call unexpectedly, and Antonia had been initially grateful. She had needed something to keep her mind from the hill and the blond American. She didn't want to count the number of times she had started for the stable and then forced herself to stop. Her father had left early today in the buggy, without word of where he was going, and she suspected he was with Ramon. The temptation to go to the hill had been great. Her initial gratitude at Francesca's visit ended abruptly, however, when her friend discussed the party.

Antonia had not known about it, although Francesca had said everyone in the valley had been invited. A surge of anger filled her when she realized her father had not even mentioned it. But then, he would never have allowed her to attend anyway. Any more than he would have attended.

When she asked eagerly about it, Francesca mentioned the American. He had dressed quite elegantly, she said, and seemed quite at ease. Even when he did the fandango.

Antonia, who had never known jealousy before, was amazed at the anger and resentment that boiled up inside her at the very thought of the American and Carlota together. She knew it didn't make any sense. She had no hold on him. But the image of the two of them—Carlota and Señor Hampton—hurt her in places she didn't know could hurt.

She suddenly wanted Francesca to leave. Just as she realized that some part of her had expected the American to show up at the ranch. It was completely illogical, of course, after she had asked him not to, after she indicated she would meet him, and did not do so.

Still, she felt betrayed.

"Even Augustin liked him," Francesca was saying, and Antonia understood that the conversation was back once more to the American scout. Augustin liked very few people, particularly Americans, whom he considered only a small improvement above the Indians.

Finally, Francesca said she had to leave. Antonia saw her to the door and then to her carriage, where a vaquero waited. Antonia promised to visit soon, and felt a great relief when the vehicle disappeared from sight.

Tristan. Tristan Hampton. And Carlota.

The feeling of being trapped, of infinite, terrible emptiness swamped her.

Night Wind. She would run Night Wind. The horse badly needed exercise, and she needed an escape. But she wouldn't go to the hill. She wouldn't.

An hour later, Antonia hesitated at the bottom of the hill. She could see nothing above. Her gloved hands tightened on the reins, clenching and unclenching as she tried to fight the compulsion that had brought her here.

She told herself he wouldn't be here. He probably had not even come once. He had just been polite when he asked to see her again. And then he had met Carlota, who was much more gay and attractive than she was.

Without urging, Night Wind started the climb up. Antonia merely went along for the ride, dreading the moment they reached the top, knowing he wouldn't be there, hoping he wouldn't be there, hoping he would be there.

Madre de Dios! What had happened to her?

They reached the top and Antonia's eyes anxiously scanned the clearing. She knew he was there even before she saw him.

He was sitting on the grass, resting on a bended knee, his eyes riveted on her. For the first time, she couldn't read his expression. It was guarded.

Tristan did not stand and come to her, but instead watched her warily, as if uncertain whether any move on his part might send her away.

Antonia dismounted and tied the horse to a low-hanging branch. Instead of going to Tristan, she went to the edge of the hill and looked down on the valley, trying to summon what little dignity she had at the moment. She wanted to rush into his arms, to feel, once more, that compelling electric current that had held them prisoner together that first day.

She didn't hear him approach, but in the same instinctive way she had known he was on the hill, she could feel his presence.

"I didn't think you would come." The voice was as she remembered.

"I wasn't going to," she said barely above a whisper.

"Why?"

The electricity was so strong between them now that Antonia thought the world must surely erupt into thunder. But this was a storm of their own brewing, a quietly potent one full of energy and intensity and fire.

She turned around and looked up at him, her eyes full of amber fire. She slowly took off her gloves, each move deliberate, as if by concentrating on the motions she could distance herself from a body that was no longer under control.

She felt his hand on her chin, and she was being forced, ever so gently, to look up at him. "Why?" he repeated.

"Because there can be nothing between us."

"There already *is* something between us."

"No."

"Antonia . . . Tonia . . . God, I've been in misery for the last three days. I've been here every afternoon. If you hadn't come today, I would have gone to your ranch."

"Please. You must not. He might try to kill you."

Tris studied her face. It was even more beautiful than he remembered. "I will not let you go."

"What of Carlota?" The words escaped her mouth before she could pull them back.

"Carlota?"

"Carlota Mendez."

He grinned slowly, his eyes twinkling in a most devilish way. "If that is what gets you here, I must attend her more often." The grin faded as he saw the unhappiness in her face.

"I met Señorita Mendez at the party. She asked me to try the fandango with her. There was no way, without being rude, of refusing to do so. But I could only think, all evening, of how much I wanted to be with you."

His mouth was tender, his eyes concerned and his words sincere. Antonia felt a glow replacing the huge emptiness she had felt so recently.

His hand went from her chin to her cheeks, his thumb stroking them lightly. Antonia felt the warmth, which started with his barest touch, move quickly inward, reaching to the deepest part of her. She closed her eyes, relishing the feeling.

Tris bent down and his lips touched her forehead before moving—very, very slowly—to her eyes and then her cheek, every movement carefully tender and yet urgently possessive. She knew she was trembling, but could not stop herself; she seemed to be drowning. She had never wanted anything as badly as to taste everything he had to offer, to be as close to him as possible, to feel his heart beat and know its rhythm matched her own wildly pulsating one.

"Ah, Tonia." He sighed as his mouth found hers and the words were quieted. There was a sudden urgent hunger in his kiss, raw and naked, as her lips parted under his and he tasted a sweetness he had never known before.

His tongue moved slowly, seeking a response he sensed was new to her and rejoicing when her tongue, tentatively at first, then as fiercely as his own, joined in an exquisitely painful exploration—each touch, each movement giving birth to new sensations. He could feel her body hug his, setting every part of him ablaze. He could feel the awakening passion in her, feel the way her mouth opened wider as she sought instinctively for more.

He ached. He hurt. God, but the pain in his loins was growing beyond bearing. He thought he would explode if he didn't have her, if he couldn't bury himself in the sweetness he knew was there.

But her very willingness, her trembling as she pressed against him, stopped him. All her responses told him she was inexperienced, a virgin, and he wanted much more than a few abandoned moments. He had known from the first time he saw her that he wanted her for a lifetime.

He would not compromise. He would not hurt her. It was the hardest thing he had ever done in his life, but he stepped back and released her lips, feeling her reluctance to let go. Her great dark eyes were glowing with fire, and her lips were a deep rose from the fierce kiss.

"I did not know it could be like that," she finally said, the words touched with wonder.

He took her hand, holding it tightly before bringing it to his mouth. "Neither did I," he observed wryly.

Her eyes grew larger. "But you, *señor,* you must have kissed many times."

His eyes crinkled at the corner, and they fairly seemed to dance. "But never quite like that."

"Is that good, Señor Hampton?"

"Tris," he insisted. "Especially after that kiss. And yes, Tonia, that is good."

"Tris," she said. "It is a strange name."

"Very strange," he agreed, relieved to change the topic.

"I have read the legend," she said. "It is very sad."

He looked at her inquisitively. His own family worshiped books and learning, but for some reason he had not expected to find the same curiosity here in New Mexico, which he considered a wilderness, although a compelling one.

Antonia watched his expression. "We are not barbarians," she said teasingly. "One of my teachers was an Irish priest. He loved to tell old Irish legends."

Tris raised an eyebrow. "An Irish priest? Here."

Antonia laughed. "He was just in Taos for a short while, but I liked him very much."

"And he told you about Tristan and Iseult?"

"I was very young and thought it was very romantic, that they died for love and from their graves two trees grew and intertwined, bringing them together for eternity."

"I think they would have preferred a more happy mortal existence," Tris replied dryly, but his hand tightened on hers. "And it was all due to a love potion."

Antonia looked up at him, at his green-blue eyes sparkling with such life and warmth. "I don't think they would have needed a love potion."

Tris's other hand went to the braid, which had twisted over her shoulder, and fondled it. "Perhaps not," he replied in a low voice. Good Lord, but he had not needed such a thing. He once more recalled the legend he had heard as a boy, how Iseult was to marry King Mark, and her mother made a love potion to be drunk by her daughter and her intended. Instead, Iseult and Tristan, Iseult's escort and nephew of Mark, drank it accidentally and were bound by an imperishable love. Neither, however, could deny their loyalty to Mark, and they separated, Iseult marrying Mark and Tristan marrying a duke's daughter. Years later, Tristan was wounded by a poisoned weapon and sent for Iseult, who was skilled in the arts of healing and the only one who could save him. If she agreed to come to his aid, the returning ship was to carry a white sail; if she refused, a black one.

Tristan's jealous wife, however, seeing the white sail of Iseult's approaching ship, rushed to tell Tristan that it was black. He turned his face to the wall and died, and Iseult, arriving too late to save him, yielded up her own life in a final embrace. Out of their graves two trees grew and intertwined.

As a boy, Tris had always questioned the legend and scoffed at the idea of dying for love. Now, looking down at the huge brown eyes that regarded him so seriously, he understood for the first time how strong an invisible link between two people could be.

Tris led Antonia to a tree and helped her sit, his own body folding easily as he reclined against the aspen and put an arm around her as he thought how natural it seemed. Her body leaned against him trustingly, as if they had been lifelong friends.

"Are your parents Irish, then," Antonia said, thinking once more of the tragic legend.

Tris chuckled. "No. My mother is from South Carolina, my father from England. They now live in Virginia."

Antonia leaned back and looked up at him. "How did they meet?"

"My father was an English privateer, and my mother a fervent American during the War of 1812. He captured her when she stole away on her brother's blockade runner. And later, she captured him when he was a spy. It was an interesting courtship, I hear."

"They were enemies?"

"Yes."

"Like us?"

"I don't consider us enemies. The war is over here."

"My father does."

"Your father will learn he has nothing to fear and everything to gain from the American government."

There was a long doubtful silence. "Are they happy?" Antonia ventured.

"My mother and father?"

"Yes."

"Supremely. They fight sometimes, but I think it's mainly for the joy of making up."

"You are very lucky you still have them both," she said in a small voice. "My mother died five years ago."

His hand tightened on her shoulder. He could almost feel the pain in her.

"She must have been beautiful."

"She was. My father has a painting..."

He couldn't bear the unhappiness in her voice. His lips reached down and touched her forehead. He remembered Bent's words about Antonia's mother.

"Tell me about your father," he commanded softly. The more he knew, the better he felt he could deal with the situation. Everything had always come easily to him. He couldn't imagine, at this moment, being defeated by so small an obstacle as a man's disapproval. He had always made friends easily, had no enemies he knew about and had been able to charm the most antagonistic of fellows.

Antonia hesitated. "I love him very much," she said finally.

He pushed back a curl that had worked its way loose from the braid. "And...?"

"He's a very proud man... proud of his heritage, proud of his land."

"And proud of you, I would think," Tris said gently.

"We are all either of us have," she replied softly.

His arms tightened once more around her. "Not anymore," he insisted.

Antonia closed her eyes, wishing it were so. She had never felt so safe, so happy before. It was as if she had been waiting for this man all her life. And he was a Yanqui, the one thing her father could never, would never, accept. "It cannot be," she said in a whisper.

"But it can, Tonia."

"I can never leave him," she replied with infinite sadness.

"Surely he expects you to marry—"

"Ramon. Ramon, who lives on the neighboring ranch. Ramon, who has the same blood, the same religion, the same background."

"And who is a rapist," Tris added grimly.

Tonia tensed at the word, remembering the scene that took place just feet away. But she said nothing.

"Your father should know . . . I will tell him."

"He would not believe you. He wouldn't believe anything a Yanqui said."

"Then you tell him. He would believe you."

"Ramon is his friend, his only friend. He would only believe that Ramon meant no real harm, that his . . . his love for me led him do something he would never do again."

"Do you believe that?" Tris said gently.

"I don't know," she said, turning her face from his. "But I *can* take care of myself."

"I don't want you to have to," Tris said, his arm tightening around her.

She turned her head and her eyes met his. "I have taken care of myself since my father was hurt. I am not afraid of Ramon. I'm not afraid of anyone." He remembered the way she had held the rifle on the Creole and believed her.

She was silent, and Tris could see tragedy in the dark eyes that now glistened. He looked down. Her hands were clenched together in a tight knot, so tight they were almost bloodless.

Tris remembered Bent's words, and he hated those Texans who had caused so much pain, had put so much responsibility on such young, tender shoulders. He wondered how he would have felt if someone had done to his parents what had been done to hers. Dear God, it was a miracle she even spoke to him.

Tris closed his eyes as her own agony echoed through him. "How badly . . . is your father hurt?"

He knew. Antonia understood that instantly. Someone had already told him about her father and mother. There was aching sympathy in his eyes, a yearning to comfort, a plea not to blame. "His—his legs were badly damaged," she said in a stronger voice. "He can barely walk with crutches."

And you feel protective. He finally understood why she would say nothing about Silvero. It must have taken all her strength to refuse her father what he appeared to want most, and now she wouldn't destroy a friendship the man valued.

If he had thought her beautiful before, Tris believed her magnificent now.

But at the same time, a deep dread filled him. From what he had learned from Charles Bent, and now Antonia, he would have a far more difficult courtship than he had ever thought possible. But for now, he just lay his head against her hair, holding her carefully while some of the tension seeped from her body, sharing with her a silent sympathy and understanding that flowed easily between them. Her hands slowly unclenched, and one of them settled on his large callused one....

So strong, she thought. And so gentle. How could such a large man be so tender? But there was nothing soft about him; she had seen that when he went after Ramon.

Antonia could sense the restrained strength in him, and she felt safe in a way she hadn't in many years, safe and understood and wanted for herself. She closed her eyes, feeling the dried tears flaking them, and wondered at the comfort of just being close to him.

Suddenly she wanted to know more about him, everything about him. She turned her head so she could watch his face. "Why did you come all the way from Virginia?"

To find you, he wanted to say. But he knew that was not an acceptable answer at the moment. "I wanted to see more of this land," he said simply.

"And is it like Virginia?"

He laughed, and she loved the sound of it. It was rich and easy. "No, it's nothing like Virginia. Or England or any other place I've been. Virginia is so very green like an emerald. And New Mexico...it's more like gold. Bright and intense."

"Do you miss your family?" Her voice was wistful.

"Yes," he said softly.

"Did they try to stop you?"

"No. They knew it was something I had to do."

"Will you go back?"

"To visit. I doubt if I will ever live there again. It never . . . quite felt like *my* home, where I belonged."

Antonia didn't want him to stop. She wanted to know the origin of that faraway look that sometimes shone in his eyes. He was so unlike most of the adventurers she had seen: rough untutored men with beards and wild hair and blasphemous speech. Yet he had that same air of confidence, of strength. Without realizing it, her hand tightened on his. She never wanted him to leave. Never.

"Do you feel you belong here?"

His eyes met hers and she wondered at the glittering brightness of them. She had never seen such eyes.

"I belong with you," he announced simply, as if it were incontrovertible fact. And once more his head came down and his lips touched hers with such gentleness and yearning that her blood turned to warm, running honey. Her arms went around his neck and she closed her eyes.

She felt she was drowning in whirlpools of sensation. There was sweetness and hunger, the softness of dawn and the impatience of nightfall, the grace of a spring rain and the thunder of a summer storm. Then there was nothing but Tris Hampton. Nothing else in the world.

Tris knew he had to stop. Every working part of his mind was telling him so. Everything in his body was countermanding those instructions. He felt on fire. Inside and outside. Her fingers, so tentative, so gentle, were like brands on his skin, burning their touch on him forever. Tension, like that of a too-tightly strung wire, hummed inside him, ready to snap at any moment. His hands moved over Antonia, wanting desperately to make their way through layers of cloth and caress the soft skin he knew lay below.

"Tonia." he rasped, his mouth turning more violently searching. "God, but I want you."

But still his hands hesitated. Not this way, he told himself. Not this way. He would have to leave soon with Kearny, and he would not make her his until he could settle their future. But God help him, he wanted her.

Tris almost thrust her away in his frustration, and she looked at him with confusion, not understanding the new harsh lines around his mouth, the way the warmth had fled so abruptly. Her wide hurt eyes wounded him to the core.

He spun upward, rising to his feet in one quick, graceful movement, his mouth tightening into a straight, determined line. Turning, he walked away from her, hoping the distance would soothe the violent ache that was torturing him.

"Tristan."

Her soft voice lured him back, like the distant, lovely sound of a siren.

He turned back and looked at her. Amber lights played in her eyes, and the sun glinted against the intense blackness of her hair.

"Did I do something wrong?" Her voice was low and trembling, once more he felt a fierce pain arch through him.

His hand went down and took hers. As he pulled her up he marveled at how light and graceful she was.

"No," he said. "You did nothing wrong." He touched her face reassuringly. "It's just the things you do to me."

Such as I feel? It was a question Antonia wanted to ask. But she had kept her feelings bottled for years, and she could not say such personal things, not even to this man.

Antonia looked so enchantingly vulnerable. "I want you for my wife," Tris said abruptly, knowing it was too soon, too sudden, but unable to hold back the words.

She jerked away, suddenly aware of what had happened, what had almost happened. Dear Mother in Heaven, she had almost committed a mortal sin.

It was as if he read her mind. His hand touched her face. "We did nothing wrong, Tonia."

But Antonia was stricken as she absorbed his words. *I want you for my wife.*

"We barely know each other," she whispered.

"I feel I've known you all my life."

Antonia felt the same way, and she was stunned at the strength of the feeling. She felt caught up in some tidal wave over which she had no control and was swirling around in totally unfamiliar emotions that would not let her go. She had always been a determined person, a strong one, and now she felt she had no will at all.

"We...can't," she whispered. "I'm Catholic...my father...our land."

"My grandfather was Catholic. If it is so important to you, I will become one."

Antonia looked at him hopelessly. "You don't understand...it's different with us. The Church is so much a part of us. And my father, he will never consent, and I could never leave him. He has no one else."

"It's usually the father who takes care of the child," Tris said stiffly, recognizing the resistance in her voice.

"It—it would kill him if I married a Yanqui," she said, her eyes begging him to understand.

Tris recalled her strength and determination when Antonia had faced Ramon a few days earlier, and he swore to himself.

"I have to leave for Santa Fe with Charles Bent tomorrow at dawn," he said. "I'll talk to your father tonight."

Antonia's chin came up. "No."

He placed a gentle hand on her cheek. "I won't say anything about you...or marriage. I'll just say I'm visiting the landowners to assure them we mean no disruption." He was confident he could make peace with her father. Anything could be accomplished if it were important enough.

"He won't see you."

"If I bring a note from Charles Bent, he will. He must, since Charles is the new governor."

Antonia turned around, unable to look at him. She thought of her father and she knew that if he found out about Tris, he would try to kill him, and one of them might die. Dear God, she could never live with that. Her heart broke as she turned to face Tris. "It would be best if you didn't, if we didn't meet again." Her words were so low he had to lean over to hear them.

"I've waited all my life for you," Tris said slowly. "I won't give you up."

"You have no choice," Antonia retorted, suddenly angry. She knew she shouldn't have come here today, but since she had met him, she appeared to have no more control of her own life. "I must go."

"I will ride over tonight."

"No. It must stop here. I cannot see you again."

He leaned over, his lips touching hers ever so softly, his hands preventing her from moving.

"Tonight," he promised again as she gazed up at him. She felt helpless against his stubbornness, his confidence, and her own lack of will to defy him.

Antonia shook her head and twisted out of his grasp. "If you care for me at all, you will not come."

She ran to her horse before he could reply and swung into the saddle, kicking Night Wind into a gallop. She wanted to look back, to see the tall figure once more. But she gave the mare her head and they raced recklessly down the hill. And she kept her eyes straight ahead as they blurred with tears.

Chapter Five

Ramon sat astride his horse and watched Antonia descend the hill as if something, or someone, was chasing her.

He sat there patiently, hidden by some trees until he saw another rider. There was no mistaking the American who had interfered the other day.

Ramon had ridden here the past three days, the first time to try to see Antonia again and apologize. He had never apologized to anyone in his life and the thought was excruciating. Still, he had done his cause no good the other day.

Ramon had truly thought his touch would convince, that his hands and mouth could seduce her, that her resistance, until now, had been more childish rebellion than womanly conviction. And perhaps he would have succeeded if it had not been for the American.

The subsequent humiliation and rejection brought back memories of his childhood, of the father he had wanted to love, but hated instead. He had ended up besting his father, and he would do the same to the American.

Ramon knew that Antonia frequently came to the hill and, repressing his fury, had set out to apologize, to make amends, before all his plans were ruined forever. And instead he had found the Yanqui.

He had returned the next two days, and each time the Yanqui had come, and Ramon had realized with rage that the man was waiting for Antonia. He thought about challenging the

American bastard or even ambushing him, but he was obsessed with knowing whether Antonia would meet him.

He had been relieved, even gladdened, when she had not.

Until today.

Fury and a new kind of pain knotted inside him like a fist, knowing the two of them—the Yanqui and Antonia—had been together.

He had tried so hard to win her. He had, in fact, been trying since he was a boy. Until the other day on the hill, he had managed to keep his volatile temper in check, had been a gentleman to her, a friend to her father. All for nothing.

Ramon was not used to defiance. He was used to getting exactly what he wanted. Everything except Antonia.

She had always been his weak spot, his vulnerability. He cared little for anyone else. Possessions and power had always been his gods, made so by a fanatically religious father who demanded perfection from an imperfect son. At least he had always been told he was imperfect. His older brother was perfect, though, and had joined the Church, quickly rising to the position of bishop in Spain. He had been his father's favorite, while Ramon could never do anything right.

But he tried and, in trying, he had hardened. Objects took the place of love. Success became the substitute for affection. Winning became everything…regardless of the cost or who was hurt. Through his position as alcalde and his connections in Mexico, he had doubled and tripled his father's wealth. He was not above stealing from fellow ranchers or trading with the Apache or even killing someone in his way. And although he gave allegiance to the Church, he rejected its gentler precepts as weakness and embraced its harsher ones of intolerance. He had thoroughly enjoyed punishing the Texans who had the audacity several years earlier to invade New Mexico.

Ramon had eventually taken everything he wanted, except Antonia. And the more she resisted, the more he wanted her. It was, he knew, like a disease. He remembered her as a girl, laughing and teasing until that one day when his cousin had stolen her attention….

She had never again looked at him in the same way. Wariness had replaced her open admiration.

He wondered if she looked at the Yanqui in that way. It was a singularly painful thought. Except for Antonia, he had always had every woman he wanted. He was proud of his dark good looks, his muscular body, his lovemaking. He was sometimes rough, but he had never had any complaints.

He would have to put more pressure on Miguel Ramirez. And he would have to get rid of the American. Along with Bent and all the others. The land belonged to those who settled here hundreds of years ago, not to upstart heretic Yanquis.

Ramon had already sown the first seeds of rebellion in the Pueblo Indians. It wasn't difficult to do. They had a simmering hatred of the white man. Although Catholic and outwardly peaceful, they never forgot that the land was once entirely theirs and that now they were little more than slaves. They had risen once in bloody rebellion; enough persuasion and they would do it again.

He knew them well, knew they hated the present inhabitants, including himself. He just needed to incite them to hate the newcomers more. He had met with Pablo Montoya and Tomas Romero, two of the Pueblo leaders, this morning, and told them how the Americans always broke treaties, how they moved Indians, like the Cherokees and Creeks, from their homes to places where they would die.

As he watched Antonia disappear, he turned his complete attention to the Yanqui. He had his spies and knew that Hampton would be leaving in the morning with the newly appointed governor. They would have to go through the Rio Grande Gorge. Perhaps he would plan a small surprise and rid himself of two problems.

It would mean a long ride. And probably more bargaining. But it would be worth it. Ramon smiled as he thought of the blond scalp on an Apache belt. He had friends among those who traded with the Apache. He would use them to get the scout and the new governor. None of it would be traced back to him. Ever.

* * *

"You're mad," Charles Bent said. "Absolutely mad. He'll shoot you before he hears you out."

"Not if I take a note from you."

"And just what do you want me to say?" Bent asked sarcastically.

Tris grinned. "Governorlike things."

Charles stared at him, then threw back his head and laughed. "You never give up, do you?"

"Not when it's important."

"It's hopeless, you know."

"Nothing's hopeless unless you allow it to be."

"And what does the lady say?"

"About the same as you. She can't leave her father."

"You sure as hell make up your mind fast."

Tris sipped a glass of whiskey. "How long did it take you to ask your wife to marry you?"

"Not very damned long," Bent admitted.

"I don't have time, Charles. I signed on with Kearny to go all the way to California. I can't leave her here alone with that damn Silvero."

Bent searched the younger man's face. He didn't know when he had taken to anyone quite as quickly as he had taken to Hampton. There was an easy power about Tris, something lying untapped but dangerous. It was rare for anyone to best Silvero, but Hampton had apparently done it.

"Be careful of Silvero," Bent warned suddenly. "He doesn't lack in courage, but he's also been known to stack the odds in his favor. He has few scruples when it comes to something he wants."

"So I've discovered," Tris said wryly. "And he apparently wants Tonia."

"Tonia?"

Tris's eyes glittered. "Somehow it suits her more than Antonia."

"Does it, now?" Charles said, searching back in his mind for images of the girl who had so entranced his new friend. "How?"

"The sparkle in those brown eyes when she's not as serious as she thinks she should be."

"What else?" Charles teased.

"The way she defies convention with those clothes. The way she rides as lightly as a butterfly perched on a leaf. The way—"

"Enough. Enough. I'll write a letter to Don Miguel under some pretext or another and send you to deliver it. But I warn you now, you'll never charm him like you apparently did Antonia."

Tris grinned. "I'll be at my most mannerly and believe me, after the English court, that can be very, very proper."

Charles raised an eyebrow. "English court?"

"My uncle's an earl."

"I hate to disillusion you, Hampton, but I wouldn't mention that to Don Miguel. He doesn't care for the English, either."

Tris gave him a wry grimace. "Any other advice?"

"Yes, but you won't take it, so I'll write your note and you can see for yourself. And we'll leave at dawn for Santa Fe."

Tris rode past fields of wheat and maize, and continued on the hard-packed road to a gate where he saw corrals occupied by fine-blooded horses. A golden adobe structure lay in picturesque splendor before him.

He leaned over and unfastened the gate, ignoring the curious stares from several vaqueros, who stood around in dusty clothes. His eyes darted from a wealth of flowers in the garden to the well-kept barn as he looked for a slim figure with black hair, but Tonia was nowhere to be seen. He saw a figure hurry to the hacienda and enter, and knew his approach was being reported. When he reached the porch to dismount, the door opened and a richly dressed man on crutches struggled awkwardly through.

The Creole had Tonia's dark coloring. His eyes, though dark, had none of Tonia's vitality, although they shone with hatred. His trimmed beard contrasted with the pale face that looked older than Tris had imagined. Heavy pain lines creased the man's face around the eyes and mouth, and Tris felt a surge of sympathy for Antonia's father.

"Señor Ramirez?" Tris said the words politely as he started to dismount, halting only at the rude words of the man he had come to see.

"There is no need to dismount, *señor,*" the man said abruptly. "You can tell me your business from where you sit."

Tris swallowed his anger over the Creole's rudeness and obvious contempt.

"I have a letter from Charles Bent...he is soon to be governor."

"Your governor," the New Mexican said sharply. "Not mine."

"Nonetheless, he will represent the authority, and he wanted you to know that nothing will change...you will be left in peace."

Don Miguel's lips tightened. "Nothing will change, *sí,* Yanqui? Every place you gringos go, you bring change and destruction. And greed. You don't think we know how many families were forced from Texas after your rebellion? How many innocents you have killed? You take us for fools." His lips trembled with anger. "Take your letter and get off my land."

Tris's hands tightened on the saddle horn as he suddenly realized what Tonia and Charles had been trying to tell him. He had seen rage before, and he recognized it now. There was no way of making himself palatable to this man, not now. He would only make things worse if he stayed.

But still something in him tried. He looked over at the corral of horses. "You have beautiful stock, Señor Ramirez." Talk of horses, he had discovered years ago, could usually bridge the widest chasm.

For several seconds he thought his ploy might work as the New Mexican's eyes scanned his own gold stallion with appreciation before they grew, once more, as hard as agates. "If there's nothing else, *señor?*" Ramirez said in an icy voice. Without waiting for an answer, he turned around and went inside, shutting the door behind him, leaving Tris swearing quietly to himself.

But he would have sworn he saw a momentary interest in the man's eyes when he spoke of horses. Perhaps that was the weak link. It was something he would remember.

Once more, his eyes studied the ranch, but there was no sight of Tonia. He felt a ball of frustration swell in his stomach. It would be days, possibly weeks, before he could see her again.

But see her he would. And have her he would. He had never failed at anything he tried to do in his life, and he wouldn't fail now. With that encouraging thought, he turned his horse through the gate and headed back for the town of Taos, unaware that Tonia's eyes were following him as he rode away.

Antonia winced as her father's anger grew with each bite. "Arrogant gringo." *Gringo* was the worst possible insult he could offer, although *Yanqui* did not come far behind.

"Did he . . . offer an insult?"

"Just coming here was an insult," Don Miguel replied. "As if he thought I would recognize Señor Bent's authority."

"What did the letter say?"

"I did not take it. Do you think I would accept the words of these invaders."

"But perhaps—"

"Enough, Antonia. I don't want to hear any more about it. Besides, they will not be here long, I think." There was a certain note of satisfaction in her father's voice that frightened Tonia.

"What do you mean?"

"The Pueblos aren't any happier than we to have the gringos here."

"But they are peaceful."

A gleam shone in her father's eyes. "It would not be the first time they've rebelled."

Antonia paled. She would never forget the stories of the rebellion two hundred hears ago, when the Indians rose and slaughtered every Spaniard they could find, driving them from New Mexico for twelve years.

"What are you involved in, Papa?"

Miguel's eyes lowered. Ramon had warned him against saying anything to Antonia. She would not understand the reason of their plans. "Nothing, Chiquita. It's just that the Indios are no more pleased to see the gringos than we are."

"Ramon," Antonia said bitterly. "You've been plotting with Ramon."

"Ramon is our friend," Miguel said. "And I think it's time you married him." His voice turned pleading. "He would make you a fine husband, a proud father to your *niños*."

"We have discussed this before," Antonia said. "I do not love him, and...there is something that...frightens me about him." She had never expressed that thought to her father before, but she realized it was true.

"Nonsense. Nothing frightens you. And he has been very patient."

No, he hasn't, she wanted to retort. But she merely clenched her hands together. Her most successful defense had always been to change the subject. She tried now.

"The...rider who came here. His horse is very beautiful."

"Was that the Yanqui you met the day you were riding?"

She nodded, hoping her eyes didn't say as much as she was afraid they would.

His eyes searched hers. "He is very handsome."

She nodded, knowing denial of the obvious would only increase his interest.

His eyes suddenly softened. "Be very careful, Antonia. The Americanos...they come, they go. They are ruthless. And cruel. Remember that." There was an intensity in his words she hadn't heard in a very long time, a sadness that bit her to the quick.

"Papa."

His hand touched her hair. "You look so like your mother did," he said slowly. "Before the Yanquis took her life."

Antonia was silent, feeling the weight of his sorrow.

"I could do nothing, Antonia, nothing." The guilt and failure in his voice did more to hurt than anger could. She saw tears in his eyes as he remembered.

"She lay there so still," he continued, reliving the day. "I begged her not to leave me, I begged them to help. And they laughed. They laughed and they left us there.

"But I can do something now," he continued in low bitter voice that drove through her like a spike. "I will never let them take anything from me again. Not you. Not my ranch."

"They won't, Papa, they won't," she said with a tear of her own making a path down her cheek.

"Ramon can keep you safe, Chiquita. I don't know if I can."

Antonia could tell how much the admission hurt him. She looked at his lined face, at the muscles in his cheek that trembled slightly, and she thought of all the pain he had endured.

"I will think about it," she said comfortingly. "But I can promise nothing."

Miguel was satisfied with the answer. It was the closest she had come to even considering Ramon's proposal.

And the tall Yanqui would probably be leaving with Charles Bent. Miguel had sensed another purpose in the Yanqui's visit today, one different from the stated one. He knew instinctively it had to do with his daughter, and nothing could enrage or frighten him more. He could only hope the man was gone for good and Antonia would realize her future lay with her own kind.

He patted her face as he had when she was little. Everything would work out. The Pueblos would dislodge the Americans, Antonia would marry Ramon and the ranch would be safe. His daughter would be protected and there would at last be grandchildren. A grandson of pure Spanish blood. Just as he always dreamed.

Tris and Charles Bent left at dawn for the seventy-mile ride to Santa Fe. Because of the mountainous terrain, they would be fortunate to arrive late that evening.

Mrs. Bent had packed food for them, and they planned to stop only to rest and water the horses.

There was mist over the mountains as the first golden light colored their peaks in soft pastels. It was peaceful and cool, and Tris's stallion was impatient to stretch his muscles. It was all

Tris could do to keep the horse under control, but he needed, and wanted, the challenge. It took his mind from the confrontation yesterday with Miguel Ramirez.

He had briefly told Charles Bent of the meeting and was appreciative that the new governor listened without saying "I told you so."

But Bent had his own concerns. He disliked leaving his wife and children in Taos and shared some of Tris's melancholy.

They had been riding for several hours in silence when a cold chill ran up Tris's back. He knew his instincts were good. They always had been, and his uncle had tuned them to perfection. He didn't need to look to know they were being followed; someone was there, and the fact that they were hiding boded little good.

He moved his horse closer to Bent's and his lips barely moved as he told the new governor that they were not alone.

Bent's eyes flickered, and then he straightened up and nodded almost imperceptibly.

There was a canyon ahead, and Tris felt the chill grow more pronounced. It was an ideal place for an ambush. He saw Bent's eyes on him and knew the man was thinking the same thing. It was, all of a sudden, very quiet. Even the birds had stilled their chatter, except for one plaintive cry above them.

"Apache," Bent said quietly, and Tris nodded, his hands still at ease on the saddlehorn.

"Once we reach the entrance, we'll both swing to the left," Tris said. "There's an outcrop of rocks where there's some protection. You stay there. I'll keep going above and see what I can find."

"The hell you will," Bent said. "We'll stay together."

"And get trapped together? I want to know how many there are." Tris grinned suddenly. "It's the price of being governor, Charles, this being protected."

They slowed the horses just a little as they neared the mouth of the canyon, and then both of them spurred their mounts toward the outcrop. Bent slid in behind some rocks, his rifle in his hands almost instantaneously. Tris went several feet farther and slid from his horse in his own quick movement, quickly blending into the trees and slapping his horse out of sight.

On his hands and knees, he crawled up the rock-layered edge of the canyon, grateful his buckskins blended in with the terrain. His hand tumbled a rock and it went clattering down the hill. He froze, hearing, rather than seeing, a breath of air sweep by him and the ping of an arrow as it hit a rock just feet away.

He heard the sound of a shot and knew it came from Bent below. The Apache had become a target, and Tris saw his body pitch down from the cliff above. He continued to move carefully upward, his rifle in one hand, the other one clawing, getting handholds to pull himself up. It was a slow, laborious process.

Tris finally hoisted himself up behind a rock and looked around. Three figures crouched along the canyon wall. A fourth was on the canyon floor, moving toward Bent's position.

Tris took his rifle and aimed carefully, knowing that the moment he shot, the other three would find his location. He would have to move quickly. Almost as soon as his finger hit the trigger, he rolled backward, behind a rock as arrows came toward him. Two hit the rock in front. The third hit the dirt just inches from his foot.

Tris quickly looked back down. One Apache was lying still, and Bent was shooting at the others on the cliff. Tris grinned. They made a damn good team.

Then another arrow sped toward him and he felt a sudden pain in his leg. He threw away the rifle; he didn't have time to reload. Grabbing his pistol he aimed carefully, oblivious to the flood of blood reddening the earth beneath his leg.

Both he and Bent fired at the same time, and an Indian toppled from the cliff. There were two left—at least two they could see.

Tris looked at his wound. The arrow had ripped along his left calf, tearing a long deep gash, but not embedding itself. Tris took his knife and sliced a long strip from the buckskin trousers, tying it around the heavily bleeding leg. He then signaled Bent below that he was going higher and to cover him.

Dragging the leg and feeling the first stabs of intense pain, Tris negotiated the sharp incline until he found several boulders. From that protection, he looked around. He saw Bent's rifle protruding from behind some rocks, and he was satisfied for a moment that the new governor was fine. His most urgent concern was discovering whether the two Apache were alone.

The pain in his leg intensified, shooting up into his body, but he blocked it out, concentrating all his energy on finding the figures in the rocks. They, like he, had taken cover. It was a waiting game now.

The sun reached its zenith in the sky, and he felt its rays pounding down on him. He would have sold his soul for a drink of water, but his canteen was still on his saddle. Finally, he saw a movement and he sighted his rifle toward it. There was another stirring, and he saw enough of a body to shoot. Grateful for his uncle's patient instruction, he slowly squeezed the trigger and saw the figure crumble.

The shot echoed in the Canyon and Tris heard a bloodcurdling scream as the body pitched forward and landed with a thud.

"Hampton." Tris heard Bent's warning shout from below along with the loud report of a shot from Bent's rifle. Tris twisted around, his pistol ready.

A figure was hurtling itself at him, and he shot, watching a spurt of blood appear on the oncoming body. But the attack didn't stop, and Tris fired again as the Indian, a silver knife in his hand, fell toward him.

Tris tried to twist away, but he was too late, and the Indian's weight hit his wounded leg and knocked the breath from him. An instant of terror hit him as he saw the desperate glitter of the Apache's eyes, but instinct drove his hand to deflect the knife going for his throat. With a sudden movement, Tris rolled the other man over, his own body now taking control. Something in his mind registered all the blood. They were both covered in it, and the Apache was quickly weakening, as was Tris. With his last remaining strength, he struggled to grab the Indian's neck, pull it up and them slam the man's head against a rock. Tris heard a whistling noise and felt the body beneath him relax.

He rolled off and lay for a moment, drinking in air.
"Hampton?"

Tris heard Bent's worried shout from below, but he had no energy left to reply. He had never been so drained, so weak.

He heard the clatter of rocks as someone approached. He hoped to hell it was Bent. His fingers found the pistol where it had slipped from his hand when the Apache attacked, and using all his reserve, he pointed it in the direction of the noise.

"Great God almighty," he heard Bent's voice, and the gun fell from his fingers as he slipped into unconsciousness.

Chapter Six

Tris regained consciousness slowly. He felt water trickling down his face, and his mouth moved in greed for the liquid. As his eyes struggled to open, he saw Bent lean down with a canteen and he parted his lips.

He wanted to take great gulps of the water Bent was so carefully giving him, although he knew he shouldn't. He held the water in his mouth, savoring it before carefully swallowing. Gradually he felt some strength seep back into his body and he tried to rise.

"Careful, Tris," Bent warned. "You've lost a lot of blood."

Tris looked down at his buckskins. They were covered with blood, as were his hands. He saw the dead Indian not far away and he nodded toward the still form. "Some of it's his."

Bent shook his head. "For a moment, I thought you both were dead."

"There weren't any more than the five?"

"Not that I could find. If you hadn't noticed something, it would have been all they needed."

Tris tried to sit again, this time making it as he looked around. Bent had evidently escaped any injury. "That's the first time I've ever killed anyone," Tris said quietly.

"Well, you did one hell of a job on the first, second and third. Might even had been a fourth. We shot at the same time."

"I'll let you claim him," the younger man conceded wryly.

Bent looked at him closely. "Killing's never easy, Tris. Not if you're any kind of a man. Now let's look at that leg."

Tris sat as Bent washed the wound, then poured some whiskey on it. "Go ahead and yell," he said. "No one out here to hear you, and I sure would."

The pain of the alcohol on the raw wound washed over Tris in great waves, and he clenched his jaw in stubborn defiance. Think of something else. Think of Tonia. Of great dark eyes and gentle laughter. Oh, God, it hurt. Tonia.

And then it was over. There was still pain, but it was beginning to dull, and his body started to relax again.

"We'll stay below tonight," Bent said. "I don't think you should ride yet. And I'll wash those clothes for you."

Tris winced as he looked back down at the clothes. They smelled of blood and sweat and were already stiffening with a mixture of both. He nodded.

"Do you think you can make it down with some help?"

Tris nodded and accepted Bent's outstretched hand. Half falling, half stumbling, they climbed down the incline, Bent's arm around Tris, keeping him from tumbling down the hill.

It was dusk when they reached the Rio Grande, a quick-running stream coming down from the mountain. Tris's horse was standing nearby the outcrop, but Bent's was nowhere to be seen.

"If you don't object," Bent said after scouring the area for his own pinto, "I'll take your horse and look for mine or one of the Indian ponies."

Tris nodded. The weakness was back and he felt his legs giving way under him. He found a tree and slid down carefully until he was seated on the ground, his back against the tree. He was so damned tired.

He thought once more of the way the Apache had felt under him as he slammed the man's head against the rock. The other deaths seemed distant, but that one was personal. He had seen the desperation in the man's eyes, and finally the knowledge of death. Tris had always heard about the exhilaration of danger, but he had felt none. He had done what he had to do, but he knew he would never enjoy it or seek it out. Not like Conn.

It wasn't fear. At least he had discovered that. He had reacted purely on his instincts, and they had served him well. But damned if he liked killing. If he would ever like killing.

He pulled off his shirt and painfully unlaced his tattered trousers. He was going to be a fine figure when they rode into Santa Fe tomorrow, he thought wryly as he heard Bent's approach and saw the man riding his own horse, and leading his.

"I found he doesn't appreciate a new rider," Bent observed. "I had the devil of a time with him."

"No one else has ever ridden him."

"He's a fine horse, never seen one quite like him."

"My family raises them, has for better than sixty years."

A flash of pain crossed Tris's face, and Bent dismounted, taking the reins of both horses and leading the animals to the water.

When he returned, he noted a thoughtful look on Hampton's face.

"I thought you said Apache didn't come near Taos," Tris said slowly.

"Not to raid. Going back more than a hundred years, Taos has been a rendezvous for trading—everything from Indian slaves to furs—and it's been so important, everyone has declared a truce around Taos." He laughed dryly. "I suppose this really couldn't be called Taos, and God knows the Apache are active enough around Santa Fe."

"But it's rather strange. It seemed as if they knew we were coming."

"I kinda wondered about that, too," Bent said. "I guess we'll never know, since they're all dead." He paused, looking at Tris's drawn face. "Get some rest, Tris," he ordered. "I'll start a fire...."

When Tris woke the next morning every bone in his body hurt, but he felt stronger and after eating a fresh trout Bent had caught and cooked, he felt up to the trip.

His clothes were damp and still had traces of blood, but they were an improvement over the past day. He swung painfully up into the saddle, knowing it was going to be one hell of a long ride.

* * *

"I want Hampton," Bent declared angrily, pacing from end of the room to the other.

Kearny warily eyed the man he had chosen as governor. "He signed on to go to California."

"I don't give a damn," Bent said. "I need a liaison, and he's the man I want."

"That's an officer's duty, not a civilian scout's," Kearny said. "I need every scout I can get, and he's turned into a damned good one."

Bent couldn't deny it. He was alive because of Tris Hampton. So he changed tactics. "He won't be able to ride for several days."

"I think he can catch up," Kearny said dryly.

Bent shrugged. "There's still some New Mexicans who aren't happy with the American government. I'm already hearing rumors of plots. I need someone I can trust."

The general had heard the rumors, too. He had planned to divide his command and take three hundred dragoons to meet Commodore Stockton, who had already been sent to California with a naval force. The Missourians under Doniphan would stay in New Mexico to hold the territory. Perhaps it *would* be wise to leave Hampton as liaison between the governor and Doniphan. Everyone liked the scout, and God knew that was a rare quality. And he had certainly proved himself in the past week.

"Is that what he wants?" Kearny said finally.

Bent grinned. "I don't think it will be difficult to persuade him. He seems to like New Mexico."

Kearny raised an eyebrow. To him, New Mexico was infernally hot, dry and dirty, and he liked damned little about it. He shrugged and nodded. "He's yours . . . if he agrees."

Bent nodded, pleased. He'd just paid back at least a fraction of the debt he owed Tris Hampton.

Conn entered the military infirmary and searched out his nephew. He found him impatiently limping up and down the small room he occupied.

There were bruises and cuts on his face, and Tris moved slowly but determinedly. He looked up when he heard the door open and gave Conn a quick smile.

But Tris's face had changed. It was not quite as open.

"I heard you had sort of an interesting trip here."

"That's one way of putting it."

"Charles says you saved his life."

"He saved mine, too."

Conn wanted to say something else, but he didn't know how. Praise didn't come easily to him, and he didn't think it important anyway. He could tell from Tris's easy confidence that the past few days had showed his nephew exactly what he was capable of. Conn felt a surge of pride as he watched the man across from him. "The general says you aren't going on with us."

"Governor Bent has asked me to stay with him, and I plan to do it. I like New Mexico."

"No more longing to see beyond the next hill?"

"There's still lots of hills I haven't seen here," Tris retorted.

"So there are," Conn said. Along with the pride, he felt a sudden loss. He would miss Tris, more than he ever thought possible. He had become like a son to him, goddammit. Reese Hampton's son.

Tris saw the half smile and looked questioningly.

"I was just thinking of your father."

It was Tris's turn to smile. He was only too aware of the antipathy between the two men. He had never known how much of it was real and how much habit.

"I don't think you ever really reminded me of him until now," Conn said slowly. "You look alike, but you never quite had that supreme self-assurance of his that I always took as arrogance."

"And I do now?" Tris asked, partly puzzled, partly amused.

"God be thanked, not quite," Conn said, his smile widening. "But I never did relish the thought of being on opposite sides of him in a fight. I'm beginning to think that about you, too."

"That's a compliment, I assume."

"Nope," Conn said, "an observation." He put his hand out. "I'll miss you, Tris."

Tris's grip was strong and it said more than words could. Conn turned abruptly and disappeared out the door.

Antonia hadn't imagined that light could go so quickly from the day, nor brightness from the sun. Everything seemed dulled as one day moved slowly into another and there was no word of Tris Hampton other than that he had been wounded in an Indian attack.

She had first heard the news at Mass. Francesca had learned from her husband that the new governor and the American scout had been ambushed by Apache. Antonia had not been able to find out how badly the scout was injured. No one, except her, seemed to care.

There had been excitement, though, and some measure of concern. The Apache had not attacked in this area for a long time. It seemed amazing that when an attack did come, it was against the new governor. As a precaution, the ranchers and farmers redoubled their guards. Even Antonia hesitated to ride alone if the Apache were raiding in the area. And then there was Ramon.

There was always Ramon. In the days since Tristan left, Ramon visited daily, and he was suspiciously humble and agreeable. Once, while they were waiting for her father, Ramon apologized for those moments on the hill and begged her forgiveness.

"I would like to say it was your beauty," he said carefully, "and it was. But that is no excuse for my behavior. I assure you, Antonia, it will never happen again."

His dark eyes were full of regret, his face pleading. "Please say you will forgive me?"

What amazed Antonia was that he said nothing about Tristan. His newfound humility startled her.

But at least he didn't press her about marriage, and for that she was grateful. They passed pleasant words for the first time in months.

"Augustin and Francesca are having a dance next week," he said as he was leaving. "May I escort you and your father?"

"You will have to ask my father . . . I don't know if he is well enough."

His eyes bore into hers. "I wanted to ask you first . . . I do not want to force you, Antonia."

Antonia thought of another party, one her father hadn't allowed her to attend, and of the blond American who had so captured everyone's hearts. If only she knew. If only she knew something, that he was alive. She could not think of the blazing blue-green eyes dulled or the wickedly playful smile gone. Perhaps at the party she could learn something more. . . .

She nodded, and Ramon's eyes brightened. "You will dance the fandango with me?"

At first he was very funny. And then he was very quick. Why did she have to remember every word Francesca had said? How would it feel to dance with Tris Hampton? Just the thought of his touch sent shivers up and down her spine.

"Antonia?"

Startled from her daydream, she looked up at Ramon, questioningly.

"The fandango? You will dance with me?"

"Yes, Ramon."

"And I am forgiven?"

She nodded slowly, but her eyes were wary. "If it doesn't happen again."

"I swear to the Holy Mother, Antonia. It's just that I've waited, wanted you so long. . . ."

Antonia was spared a reply by her father's return. She cast a suspicious glance his way, wondering whether his absence had been on purpose.

The conversation drifted back to politics and the war. It was uncanny, Antonia thought, how much information Ramon was able to obtain. If only she could ask him about Señor Hampton. It would, she suspected with an inward smile, test Ramon's unusual patience.

After a period of exile, Santa Ana had returned to Mexico and was regaining support. Nothing could have pleased Ramon more, for the Mexican dictator had a hatred of Yanquis equal to Ramon's own. Santa Ana would stop the Americans. If the Americans didn't destroy themselves, he added with some satisfaction. Nearly the entire American army under Zachary Taylor was sitting on the San Juan River. With a malicious smile, Ramon reported that many of the American troops were dying of disease and others were deserting. They had chosen the worst possible spot for a camp with only the muddy San Juan River for water.

Kearny had left Santa Fe for California, leaving the Missourians to hold New Mexico against the Mexican army, Apache, Comanches and a host of other enemies.

Ramon glanced at Antonia and noticed that she had paled. "The Yanqui scout that was here will be with them...unless he died. I heard he was wounded by the Apache."

Miguel Ramirez straightened up at the comment. "We've doubled our guards, but there haven't been any more attacks...."

Ramon shrugged. "Probably just a few renegades out hunting."

"I hope you are right," Miguel said. "We haven't had trouble for a long time."

"I am sure I am," Ramon said smoothly. His contacts with the Apache were not something he shared with Miguel. It was acceptable, in Miguel's mind, to incite the Pueblos against the Americans. That was war. But Miguel hated the Apache as did many others. There had been too many raids in the past, too many stolen women, too many ugly deaths. The old man would not understand Ramon's business relationship with the Apache.

It was all he could do to keep a pleasant expression on his face as he thought of the Apache failure. He had promised them rifles if they succeeded in killing the scout and Bent, and they had assured him they could do it. He had never expected the scout to be good enough to take five Apache braves. Worse luck that the man's wound wasn't fatal. But the last he had heard was that the upstart gringo should be going with Kearny to California.

He was sure Antonia had seen the last of the man. With the confidence of one accustomed to getting what he wanted, Ramon deemed it only a matter of time now before Antonia would be his.

He merely smiled pleasantly when Antonia excused herself, sorry to see her go but relieved to be alone with Miguel. They had important matters to discuss.

Antonia walked outside to the stables. She paused to look up, seeking out the north star as she had days ago and fixing her gaze on it. Tris had to be alive. There was too much life and vitality in him not to be.

Perhaps he was even on his way to California. She had given him no encouragement when they had parted. She had asked him to stay away. Perhaps he had come to believe she was right.

Or perhaps he was as her father had said, an adventurer who would play with her heart. She knew little about Yanquis, but she really didn't think they would be much different from the people she knew. Although she did hope—no, knew—Tris was different from Ramon.

She went into the barn and over to Night Wind, who whinnied in recognition. The horse pawed her straw impatiently, and Antonia knew she needed a long ride. But she was reluctant to ride far afield if the Apache were raiding. Women had been taken from ranches and farms farther south, and she had heard terrible whispers about their fate. She would take a short ride tomorrow and ask some vaqueros to accompany her. It wouldn't be the same as riding alone, but both she and Night Wind needed the exercise. Antonia buried her head in the horse's mane. *Where is he? How is he? Dear Mother, help me bear the loneliness.*

Tris Hampton stood with Charles Bent and watched Kearny's dragoons march out of Santa Fe. His uncle, Conn O'Neill, had left yesterday to scout ahead.

Kearny's troops were a magnificent sight. Their horses were fresh and eager and their riders were proud. They were to take California for the United States, a fine, bold venture that would make history.

"Wish you were going along?" Bent asked Tris.

"Part of me, I suppose," Tris answered honestly. "But another part tells me this is where I belong. There's much to do here, too."

"And there's a pretty young *señorita,*" Bent teased.

"That, too," Tris replied with a grin.

"How's your leg?"

"Good as new."

Bent gave him a suspicious look. "You're still favoring it."

"Habit."

"Are you up to a trip to Taos?"

Tris looked askance.

"For the time being, Kearny wants to keep the present alcaldes, even Ramon Silvero, although I know he's nothing but trouble. I can't do anything until he makes a move."

Tris nodded.

"I have some papers that must be delivered, both there and, when you return, to Albuquerque. I'm explaining in them that you speak for me."

Tris raised an eyebrow. "That's a lot of trust."

Bent smiled. "I have a lot of trust in you."

"Silvero won't appreciate my being the messenger."

Bent's smile disappeared. "Perhaps it will force him into making a move."

"Ah, and I'm to be the tethered goat?"

"I don't know if I would put it quite like that," Bent said with a small twist of his mouth. "You're to take ten troopers with you. I don't want a repeat of the trip to Santa Fe."

"Have you heard of any more Apache attacks in the area?"

"No," Bent replied thoughtfully, "and the more I think about that ambush, the more certain I am it was planned. For us."

"I've been thinking that, too," Tris said. "It was very convenient. But it's hard to imagine. White men conspiring with the Apache."

Bent shook his head. "It's happened before. And they're getting rifles from somewhere."

"Silvero?"

"I can't accuse him without evidence, but I think he's capable of it. That's why I want you to be careful. Very careful."

Tris nodded as a thought started nagging at him. Silvero was close to Antonia's father, and Antonia knew exactly when they were planning to leave. Could she have told her father? Was he involved? God help them all if he was.

Bent watched Tris's face and guessed his thoughts. "Ramirez wouldn't get involved with the Apache," he said. "He hates them as much as he hates Americans."

"When do you want me to leave?"

"As soon as that leg feels well enough."

"Tomorrow," Tris replied with a slight smile. "At dawn."

"I'll ask Doniphan for ten men."

Tris nodded and gave the governor a crooked smile. "Thanks."

"Don't thank me yet. Remember what happens to tethered goats."

"But this one has teeth, Governor."

"So he does," said Bent. "So he does."

Antonia woke to a fresh new morning. She couldn't quite get over the feeling that something fine was going to happen today.

She gave Luz a bright smile and went into the kitchen where her father was already sitting at the table. He looked older than he had last night, a grim expression replacing his usual pleasant greeting.

She had hardly told Luz what she wanted for breakfast when her father fixed her with an intent look. "Have you thought any more about marrying Ramon?"

She shook her head.

"Antonia, please consider it. I would like to announce a betrothal soon."

Antonia jerked her head up. "I am not ready to get married," she said.

"You are nineteen—"

"I don't love him," she cried out, desperately wanting her father's understanding.

"You will learn to. If only you would try...." The harshness had gone from his voice, and once more she thought how old he looked. And sick. His complexion was gray and unhealthy.

"Are you feeling worse?" she asked suddenly.

He tried to smile. "I'm tired, Antonia. And I worry about you. I want to know there is someone to take care of you."

"We take care of each other," she said affectionately, trying to tempt him out of this mood.

"Antonia..." He hesitated before continuing slowly, "The ranch is heavily in debt. If anything happens to me... you will have nothing. You will be alone. It is my wish, my dearest wish, to see you married."

Antonia stared at him. "How much in debt, Father?" She knew he had borrowed money but he had never told her how much.

He sighed. "It's not your worry... or your concern. I just want to see you married with children of your own."

"How much?"

His stubborn proud face said he wouldn't tell her.

"From Ramon?"

"Yes," he admitted.

"And now he's blackmailing you?"

Don Miguel's face relaxed. "Nothing like that. He is a friend. He would never try to take the ranch... but he doesn't think...a woman can run it alone. If anything happens to me, he will be forced to foreclose."

Antonia swallowed. How could her father be so blind? Ramon had neatly boxed her in. To her father, he was the deliverance, not the villain who had sucked him deeper and deeper into debt.

Something fine! How could she have thought something fine was going to happen today? "But nothing is going to happen to you," she assured him.

"Antonia, I have not been feeling well for months. My legs are worse, and the doctor says my heart is weak. I have not wanted to tell you, but now it is important that you know, that you are settled."

Antonia closed her eyes. If she argued with her father, she might cause his illness to worsen. If she did not do as he wished, worry might hasten his death. And she would be responsible.

Don Miguel sat and waited. To push his daughter would be to push her away. She had to make up her own mind, and she would do the right thing. He was sure of it. He only wished he understood her reluctance to marry Don Ramon.

Antonia thought of the trembling excitement she felt at Tris Hampton's touch and the chill of distaste at Ramon's. Tris was gone, and she was a fool to think he would come back. Perhaps she had never really given Ramon a chance.

"He intends to ask for your hand tonight at the dance," Don Miguel said. "I have, of course, already given my approval for him to do so."

So Ramon intended to push.

"I'm going for a ride," she said, not answering the indirect question.

"You will take some vaqueros with you?"

She nodded. The Apache would be worse than Ramon. Maybe.

The party was at the home of Francesca and Augustin Cardona. Lanterns were strung everywhere, and laughter floated from the courtyard.

Antonia had to admit that Ramon made a handsome picture. Dressed entirely in black clothes that hugged his lean, muscular body, he was the epitome of grace and courtesy. His black hair was lustrous in the moonlight and curled attractively around his neck. His neatly trimmed mustache gave him an air of rakishness, and his dark eyes fairly glittered with anticipation.

She took his proffered arm as she descended from the carriage and felt his gloved hand tighten on hers, as her father was helped down and into the chair with wheels. Her throat constricted at his concession. He usually wouldn't use the chair in public, and the fact that he did demonstrated only too clearly how much his health had deteriorated.

Inside she greeted Francesca and Augustin. Francesca leaned over and whispered, "I have a surprise."

But before Antonia could learn what it was, another guest took Francesca's attention and Ramon was hurrying her and her father on to the *sala,* where the dancing would take place.

The room was already crowded with guests. In one corner were the musicians with their guitars, fiddles and flutes. In another was a table loaded with delicacies of all sorts. The room was awash with color and laughter and gaiety, and Antonia surrendered her shawl to Ramon as she looked to see who was present.

Maria Bent was there, as was her sister, Josepha Carson. Antonia's eyes continued around the room until they stopped at Carlota, and they locked in on Carlota's companion. He was by far the tallest man there, and his hair was the color of a vein of gold showered by rays of the sun.

Antonia thought she would be sick, wanted to be sick, as the man she had dreamed of, had sorrowed over, bent toward Carlota and said something that brought forth a peal of laughter. She watched as Carlota's hand reached for his arm and touched it with something resembling intimacy.

In that moment, her heart dropped down to her feet and she looked over to Ramon, who had tensed. Just as Carlota's hand had reached for Tristan's, her hand now went to Ramon, and he looked down at her, surprised. It was the first time she had ever willingly touched him. He stifled his anger at the sight of the American and gave her his most charming smile.

"A dance, *chula?*"

She nodded, still too sick to say anything, although she fastened a smile on her face.

"I will ask for a fandango," he said as he guided them toward the musicians. In a moment, the music had speeded and Ramon's hand guided her to the middle of the floor.

He was incredibly graceful, and Antonia gave herself up to the rhythm of the dance. They were so striking together that no one else joined them and all eyes turned on the swirling figures.

Tris had been keeping his eyes on the door, having been informed on his arrival in late afternoon of the dance and of Tonia's expected presence. Josepha Carson had quickly arranged his invitation. He had looked away only once and that was when Carlota cornered him and asked if he liked her dress. When he looked back, he saw Ramon with Tonia.

His hands knotted in fists, he watched them move as if they had been dancing together forever. Her eyes were shining with what could be excitement, and Ramon's were darkly sensual and possessive.

Tris, already tired from the daylong ride and tense with anticipation at seeing Tonia, felt bitter disappointment flooding him. He tore his gaze from the dancing couple and brought it to Carlota. "Some air, *señorita?*"

Carlota readily agreed, delighted to have the attention of the handsome American. They went through the doors to the lighted courtyard.

As Antonia spun around, she saw them leave and struggled to hold back the tears that glittered like stars in her eyes.

Chapter Seven

Despair enveloped Antonia like a shroud as she watched the tall American leave the room. Other than an almost imperceptible limp, he displayed no signs of wounds or sickness. His face was as sun browned as she remembered, his eyes as clear, his stance as bold as ever.

What was he doing back in Taos when General Kearny was said to be marching west?

Automatically she finished the dance with Ramon, then begged off of another. She saw Ramon look at her with an angry expression, and she summoned a gay smile that meant nothing. She was confused, bewildered and very hurt. She had dismissed Tris abruptly at the hill. He had every right to flirt with Carlota.

Yet, somehow, he had become her life. She hadn't known how much until she saw him with someone else.

She was pitiably grateful when Francesca approached.

"Come," she said, "I'll introduce you to Señor Hampton."

Antonia flinched, realizing she had said nothing to Francesca about meeting the American scout.

"I saw him," she said stiffly. "He seems preoccupied with Carlota."

"Oh, Carlota. She just forced herself on him."

Antonia sought desperately for another reason. "Father would not approve."

A twinkle appeared in Francesca's eyes. "When has that ever bothered, you, Antonia?"

"Nor would Ramon."

"Especially when has *that* ever bothered you?" Francesca retorted quickly, a sparkle in her eye.

Antonia felt her arm being pulled. She had no more will and she let herself be led to the courtyard, where the tall American and Carlota stood talking. Without pause, Francesca pushed Antonia over to him, completely disregarding Carlota's offended expression.

"Señor Hampton," Francesca said with mischief, "you must meet Antonia Ramirez, my very best friend."

Tris's eyes were cool as he bowed politely and took Antonia's hand and touched it lightly to his lips. "I am delighted to meet your very best friend," he said to Francesca, almost ignoring Antonia.

Antonia felt as if she had just been sucked into a tornado as she finally caught the blue fire in his eyes. Although his mouth was smiling, it didn't quite reach his eyes, and she knew it was because she had been dancing with Ramon.

"Are you planning to stay long?" she finally managed to say.

"A few days, *señorita*. I plan to meet with the alcalde and a few ranchers on Governor Bent's behalf."

Ramon! He was meeting with Ramon. Dear Mother in Heaven, didn't he know how dangerous that would be? She thought of the Indian attack, and fear jerked through her. Could Ramon have had anything to do with it? But no. Even Ramon wouldn't traffic with the Apache.

"I heard you were wounded, *señor*," she said softly.

"It was nothing," he said. "Only a slight inconvenience." He tried to make his voice sound indifferent, but even he recognized the jagged edge behind it. Good Lord, but it took all his strength not to take her in his arms. She was beautiful in the moonlight, the soft glow touching the rich ivory of her cheeks, the gloss of her hair. *Why was she dancing with Silvero when she had declared her distaste of him so openly only weeks ago?*

"You did not go with General Kearny?"

"Governor Bent asked me to stay on with him. I've been appointed his aide."

Despite Carlota's glowering presence, Antonia couldn't stem a flood of joy. And apprehension.

Before she could say anything else, however, she felt an arm around her waist and heard Ramon's barely controlled voice.

"So we meet again, *señor?* What brings you back to Taos?"

Tris's voice was smoothly amused as he answered. "A meeting with you, Señor Silvero. Some messages from Governor Bent."

"Orders, you mean."

"Interpret them as you will," Tris said, his voice growing harder as he saw Silvero's hand move tighter around Antonia and saw her try to inch away.

Ramon's face suffused with anger, and Tris didn't know if it was aimed at him or at Antonia. Or both of them.

"You will excuse us, *señor?*" he said in a quiet voice. "But the *señorita* has promised me this dance."

"I don't believe you," Ramon said. "Antonia is my guest this evening.

"Señorita?" Tris said.

Antonia felt rooted to the ground. She looked from Ramon's furious gaze to Tris's expectant eyes to Carlota's jealous ones. Francesca was surveying everything with fascination.

Tonia closed her eyes. She had dreamed of being back in Tristan's arms for endless, miserable nights. She had not missed the flaring anger and contempt in his eyes when Ramon had touched her. No matter what happened this night, she could not bear him thinking ill of her. She could not bear not knowing his touch again.

"I'm sorry, Ramon, but I had accepted." She offered her arm to Tristan.

For the first time since she had seen Tristan tonight, he smiled, a lovely conspiratorial smile. He nodded politely to Ramon, then to Carlota and his hostess as he firmly took Antonia's arm.

He paused when they reached the dance floor. The other dancers were performing something entirely foreign to him.

"The *cuna,*" Antonia said with a quick smile. "The cradle, it is called. I will show you." She stopped suddenly. "Your leg?"

He smiled warmly at her concern. "It needs the exercise . . . it will be fine."

The dance was something like a waltz, Tris learned as he quickly followed her lead. He and Antonia stood face-to-face, their arms encircling each other's waist, and they whirled to the music. As they swung around, they leaned back. It was curiously intimate, this forming of a cradle, and Tris relished the feel of his hands on her trim waist.

It was a decided improvement over the fandango, he thought.

A shyly pleased smile curved her lips. "If Carlota can teach a dance, so can I," she said.

He wished it would go on forever, particularly when he saw that Ramon Silvero had been joined by a glowering Don Miguel Ramirez. He wanted to talk to her, and he suspected from Ramon's fury and Señor Ramirez's grim visage that this might be his only chance.

"Why are you with him?" he asked quietly.

"Both my father and I are with him," she corrected.

"He acts like he owns you."

"He does not, *señor.* No one owns me."

"You will meet me tomorrow? In the late afternoon?"

"What about Carlota?"

They were moving faster now despite a certain stiffness in his leg. Antonia saw the quick grin on his face.

"I think Carlota can entertain herself."

The music ended, and Antonia saw Ramon heading for her. "I must go. I will try to come to the hill tomorrow."

He nodded, feeling a flurry of mixed feelings: relief at her consent; anger at Ramon's obvious possessiveness.

Tris watched for several moments as Ramon and Antonia moved around the room, and then he made his apologies. It had been a long day. It would be a longer night, he thought, as he took one last look at Antonia.

Antonia knew both her father and Ramon were furious, although the latter was struggling to keep it under control.

As she talked to Francesca later, she heard Ramon's angry words as he talked to Augustin.

"How could you invite that gringo?"

"They control New Mexico now," Francesca's husband replied calmly.

"Not for long."

"You are dreaming, Ramon. You cannot keep the sun from rising or the tide from running."

"You are weak, Augustin, and you are wrong. We will force them out."

"Who? Santa Ana? With all the army he had, he could not defeat the Texans. Do you think he can now defeat the might of the American army?"

"Why should the gringos want to die for New Mexico? Enough deaths and they will run for home."

"You're the fool, Ramon. They have never given up on what they want. They have held off Britain twice. You think they will run from Mexico?" Augustin's voice was now full of contempt.

"You will see," Ramon said, menace underlining each of his words. "And you will be branded a traitor."

"If you mean because I invited Señor Hampton to my home," Augustin said with fury of his own, "you can go to hell. I'll invite whom I wish. Señor Hampton is a gentleman and a friend of my friends."

The music grew louder, and Antonia could hear no more of the conversation, but it seemed that a piece of lead had lodged in her stomach. Ramon would not stop, and he would draw her father into whatever mischief he was planning. She had been a fool to think he might have changed even a little.

She endured the rest of the evening with a fixed smile and polite words, certain that the ride home would be miserable. She would hear more about her dance with Tristan, more vindictiveness about the Yanquis.

But surprisingly, it did not come from Ramon. He was quiet and seemingly thoughtful. The angry words came later from her father when they were alone.

"You shamed Ramon, and you shamed me," he said in rare rage.

Antonia stood straight. "By dancing with a guest of Francesca's?"

"You are Ramon's *novia*."

"No," she cried.

Miguel stared at her. He had been so sure she had finally decided to marry Ramon. Ramon had also thought so and had planned to ask her tonight. Until the gringo appeared and seemed to disrupt everything. He remembered the look in his daughter's eyes as she danced with the tall Americano. There had been the flash of something he had never seen in them before.

"Is it the Yanqui? Is that why?" he said with sudden suspicion.

Antonia looked at him directly. "I don't trust Ramon. You know that. I have tried for your sake. I have tried very hard, but there is something cruel about him. I don't know why you can't see it."

"Because it's in your imagination, Antonia. I have known him all his life. He is my friend."

"Only because he wants something from you," she accused.

"And what do you want?" her father asked softly, taking another tack. He realized she had not replied to his question about the American.

"I don't know," she said. But she knew she lied. She wanted the American, but he was out of reach, a part of a different world.

Miguel's fury faded as he saw the sudden desolation on Antonia's face. He did not want to drive her away. He did not want to fight with her. But he could not forget how she looked at the gringo. How could she feel anything for a man like those who had killed her mother? The gringo would take her away from him . . . or break her heart. He could not stand the thought of either possibility.

The old man was at a loss as to what to do. Antonia had had her way since she was a young girl. She supervised much of the work on the ranch, and the vaqueros trusted and respected her. It would be difficult, if not impossible, to order them to keep watch over her. She had their complete loyalty.

He could only try to keep her with him until the Yanqui left. The man would meet with Ramon and be gone, hopefully forever. If not, Don Miguel knew he would have to try some other way, even if it meant killing the Yanqui. He winced inwardly at the thought. He had never before cold-bloodedly planned anyone's death, although he had prayed for that of his wife's murderers many times. But he would to it to protect Antonia. *Sí,* he would do that and more.

"It is late. We will talk about it no more tonight," he said softly.

Antonia smiled. She did not want to lie to him about Tristan and was relieved he did not probe any further. She kissed his cheek. "I love you," she said. "I do not want to make you unhappy."

"I love you, Chiquita. I want only the best for you."

"I know," she replied, and left the room. She wanted to go to bed, to think of Tristan. She knew he would be there in her dreams tonight. And tomorrow. She couldn't stop the tremors that rocked her body as she thought of him, standing so tall and commanding on the hill, his green-blue eyes flashing with their own loving fire.

Tris stood on the hill, watching as the bright sun dipped below the mountains. He readily understood why Tonia came here so often. It was incomparably peaceful. The soft colors of twilight washed the golden earth, red rock and blue mountains with a magic brush of subtly changing hues until the entire landscape glowed a bright crimson that seemed to set the sky ablaze.

He no longer expected Antonia. His meeting with Ramon had taken much longer than he anticipated, and it had been laced with barely restrained hostility, although the Creole had obviously tried to hide his hatred. The attempted pleasantries were more ominous to Tris than outright defiance.

"You will continue most of your duties," he told the al-calde, "until further notice. And you will be responsible for the peace of this area."

Ramon shrugged. "I have no troops as you do," he said. "If the Apache return..."

"For some reason, I doubt if they will," Tris said dryly. "If they do, you can send for help from Santa Fe."

"Our own Indians, the Pueblos—"

"Are peaceful, I'm told," Tris finished for him.

Ramon's lips curled with disdain. "They don't care for gringos—" he gave Tris an insincere but apologetic smile "—I mean Americanos."

Tris fought to control his temper. "If you don't think you can do it..."

"I will manage, Señor Hampton," Ramon said, keeping his anger inside. He needed his authority now, despite the effort it took to be civil to the gringo bastard.

They had talked for another hour, discussing the requirements of the military occupation. As Tris started to leave, he turned to Ramon. "Governor Bent expects you to reassure the ranchers and the Indians that the Americans will respect their property and traditions." He noted the threat in Ramon's eyes and couldn't help but believe Kearny and Bent were making a disastrous mistake in maintaining the present authority. He understood their reasoning, but Ramon Silvero was dangerous.

"And their women?" Ramon said smoothly, with only a touch of acid in his voice.

Tris paused. "More, I imagine, than some of your... caballeros, if what I have seen is any indication." His voice was icy and his eyes contemptuous as he stared Ramon down.

Ramon balled his fists, wanting to strike out at the arrogant gringo. Instead, he said softly, "She is mine, Señor Hampton."

"I think Antonia should be the one to decide that."

"She already has," Ramon said.

"I don't believe you."

"The match is made. Don't interfere."

"Or what? An ambush?" Tris's voice was silky.

Ramon shrugged. "This is dangerous country."

"I know." Tris said. "Full of snakes."

"And you never know when they will strike." Ramon replied with a curl of his lips.

"I appreciate your warning...and your concern, Señor Silvero. I will be particularly cautious."

Tired of playing the malicious game, Tris took his leave, noting with dismay that it was very late afternoon. If Antonia had come, she surely would be gone now. He cursed Silvero and then himself for letting himself be goaded and delayed.

Now he watched the sunset and thought of last night and the acrimonious conversation this afternoon. Again he questioned Bent's judgment. But Bent thought it would be easier to keep an eye on Silvero if he remained as alcalde, and he believed stability would also calm the fears of the ranchers.

He's underestimating Silvero, Tris thought. *He's underestimating him badly.*

Tris slowly went to his horse and mounted. She would not be coming now. He could stay one day longer, no more. If she did not come here tomorrow, he would go to her ranch. He remembered her father's hostile greeting of him weeks ago and the man's snub last night. A cold wind swept through him as he recalled Ramon's words. *She is mine.... The match is made.*

Antonia had risen that day with a sense of euphoria. He had come back. He had not gone west with the American general. Surely that meant something.

She tried not to think of Carlota. Tristan had dismissed her old friend with a few offhand words, and she had not missed the jealousy in his voice when he asked her about Ramon.

She dressed in her riding clothes and slipped down to the kitchen, eating quickly. Luz said her father had already eaten and had gone out to the corral.

The buggy was ready, her father already seated in it as he talked to the head vaquero. When she approached him quizzically, he smiled affectionately.

"It's been a long time since you and I rode over the rancho together, Chiquita. I thought we might do it today."

Antonia's face was anxious as she looked at him carefully. His face looked tired this morning, far more than it should. "Are you well enough," she worried aloud.

"To go for a ride with my daughter? Certainly," he said reassuringly.

It was a lovely October day, bright and crisp and invigorating. Antonia felt an almost uncontrollable pride in this land they owned. The cattle were fat; the sheep contented; the horses lovely in the morning sun. The wheat had been harvested, but the fields lay well tended in neat rectangles. The morning was like the old days when she and her father had shared the joy of the land, of their heritage, except now they rode in a buggy rather than side by side. Antonia was painfully aware of why. Her hand reached over and covered his fists that held the reins. They were pale now, not the dark bronze she remembered as a child. Her gesture was full of love, and Don Miguel's smile returned it in full measure.

Miguel felt a new sense of hope. He could see in his daughter's face the same fascination he had for the land. She would never give it up, not for a Yanqui.

Antonia was grateful he said nothing about the disagreement last night or of Ramon. She tried not to think of Tristan, but it was impossible. He would be waiting for her this afternoon.

Antonia looked at her father and saw the hope in him, and sensed why it was there. Suddenly, she felt like a betrayer. But she knew she could no more keep away from Tristan Hampton than she could stop breathing. Perhaps her father's silence on the subject today meant he would not object so bitterly. Perhaps there was some way to bring the two men together, after all. She knew her father wanted her happiness. If he knew how much she liked...cared for...Tristan, perhaps he could see that Tristan was an honorable man.

But what if he didn't? What if she had to make a choice? She looked at her father, worn and crippled, and knew she could never leave him. The ache deepened in her heart, and some of the brightness of the day was tarnished. She felt terribly empty and alone.

Perhaps just seeing Tristan would change that. This afternoon. She would meet him this afternoon. She bottled her impatience. As soon as they reached home, she would invent some errand.

But the opportunity never came. When they arrived back at the hacienda, her father's face was pale and strained, and he asked her to read to him. Afraid for him, she complied, part of her mind with him, part with Tristan. When he seemed to drift off to sleep, she started to leave, but he stirred and asked her to stay. He looked so ill, she worriedly complied.

Hours went by. She asked one of the vaqueros to go for the doctor, and the physician did not arrive until dusk. After staying in her father's room for a long time, the doctor came out, his face grave.

"He is resting, Antonia. He told me you know his heart is weak. Try to see he is not upset by anything."

Antonia knew her face had paled. "Is he so ill, then?"

"Not if he takes care of himself. And I know you will see that he does." His smile was kindly and confident, and Antonia felt split in two. In the past weeks, she had thought of little but the tall American, barely noticing that her father was apparently more ill than she had expected.

And Tristan. Was he still waiting on the hill? Thinking what? He had seen her dancing with Ramon last night. She had thought the worst when she saw him with Carlota. Did he think the same?

He had dwarfed everyone in the room last night, and his eyes had promised so much. And he was the only man she had ever known to best Ramon. She had to tell him to be careful. She had to. And she had to tell him why she didn't meet him today.

Antonia went to her father's desk and wrote a brief note, sealing it. She wrapped it in a second note addressed to Josepha Carson. She then went to find a vaquero she could trust and asked him to deliver it.

* * *

Tris crumpled the note in his fist. Josepha had handed it to him with the slightest of discreet smiles. She knew what it was to be in love.

Señor Hampton,
My father became ill today and I could not leave him.
I sometimes enjoy a ride at night . . . when the moon is at its highest.

                                        Antonia

It was dark now. He had arrived an hour earlier at the Bent home where he was staying, and had been pacing his room restlessly. *When the moon is at its highest.*

He looked out the window. The blue-black sky was lit by a full moon and sprinkled with stars. He quickly pulled his boots back on and donned his deerskin jacket. It was getting cold these nights. He slipped down the hall to the living area, which was now darkened, and out the doors, stepping quickly to the small stable outside. His horse, catching his master's scent, neighed loudly, and Tris soothed him with gentle hands before saddling the animal with efficient movements.

Tris led Nugget from the stable and swung easily into the saddle, pleased that the moon was giving so much light this night. At a fast gallop, he would make the hill around midnight.

He didn't see her at first. She was dressed in the black riding clothes he had first seen her wear, and her horse blended into the dark landscape. It was the white flash of her cheeks that drew his attention.

He thought how splendid she looked standing so silently. Tris watched as she turned toward him and regarded him so solemnly, her eyes shining in the moonlight, her lips trembling. He held out his arms and she walked into them, pressing her body to his as his arms enclosed her. Without words, they held each other tight as if they belonged that way.

All of his uncertainty melted away.

All of her hesitancy disappeared.

He could feel her trembling.

She could feel the tension in his body.

His lips lowered.

Hers lifted.

And nothing else existed except the other and the inexorable pull they had, one to the other. Their lips met and the world exploded for both of them. But it was a gentle explosion. Tender and fierce. Giving and demanding.

The demand grew.

Tris felt his body react with painful need, with as much raw aching want as his soul felt.

"God," he groaned as he tore his lips away in an agony of confession. "I've missed you."

"Missed me or God?" Antonia couldn't resist teasing him.

He stepped back and stared at her, a chuckle starting deep in his throat. Vixen. Magnificent, wonderful, laughing little vixen.

"You, my love, but I'm very grateful to God for leading me to you."

She snuggled farther into his hard curves. They seemed familiar. Perhaps because she had dreamed so much of being here.

Every emotion she had felt in the past weeks—the deadening fear after she heard he had been wounded, the loneliness, the terrible wicked jealousy when she saw him with Carlota, the joy when he looked at her with such possessiveness—all of them collided in chaos inside her head.

All she could do was press against him so tightly that she would bind him to her forever in her mind. There was so much need, so much aching to have his arms around her.

"Tonia," he whispered, and she felt the same need in him and wondered at it, wondered that this tall handsome man could feel the same debilitating weakness as she.

"You didn't go," she said. "You didn't go with the rest."

"How could I leave? We've settled nothing."

The words brought Antonia to sudden impossible reality. Tris felt her stiffen slightly.

"You feel the same," he said confidently. "I know you do."

"I don't know how I feel," Antonia lied.

"Then I'll show you." His lips once more joined hers, and his tongue flickered in playful mischief, tempting her mouth open. Then the mischief was gone and his tongue swept the most sensitive parts of her mouth, bringing forth spasms of warm heat through her.

Antonia's body was no longer her own. As Tris's hands roved restlessly over her, claiming her with each fiercely tender touch, an ache started deep within her and grew until she thought she would die. Nothing else mattered at the moment but relieving the torment.

Her hands went around his neck and then moved downward as his had. She felt the straining muscles at his shoulders, and his back seemed to shiver under her touch.

She felt something hard against her body, and her own body responded, pressing even closer to him until they were locked together so tightly, Antonia didn't know any longer where one ended and the other began.

With a muttered oath, Tris jerked away. He had pledged to himself this would not happen again. If things went one step further, he would not be able to stop. He could barely do so now.

He knew Antonia Theresa Margarita Ramirez was not a woman who could live easily with physical love before marriage. He knew that as well as he knew anything in his life. If something were to happen to him, she would be destroyed. And he couldn't forget the ambush several weeks ago, or the malicious promise in Ramon's eyes.

For the first time in his life, he loved a woman. Loved her with his heart and his soul and his passion. And he knew the first two took precedence. No matter how painful, he would never knowingly do her injury.

He swallowed as he saw her eyes glittering like amber stars in the moonlight. It would take only a touch, and she would be his. He could almost feel her under him now, joining her to him in the most intimate and beautiful of ways.

Instead, he turned, taking his hands from her as quickly as if he were touching a blazing pyre. He felt her hand on his arm, and both of them were trembling.

"Don't leave me, Tristan," she whispered.

He turned and looked at her upturned face and thought once more how very lovely she was.

"I'll never leave you," he said. "Not in my heart."

"I think I love you," she said.

"I *know* I love you," he said with a twisted smile.

"But it is so impossible."

"Nothing is impossible."

"But . . ." Her voice wavered.

"Tonia. This comes but once in a lifetime. I will not risk losing it."

"My father . . ."

"Your father will have to accept it. I'll make him understand if I have to grovel on my knees in front of him."

The image of Tristan groveling brought a small smile to Tonia's face. "I don't think even that will work." Her face tensed. "And he's ill. I didn't know until yesterday, but the doctor said a shock or worry could kill him."

"I'll be patient, then," Tris said with a soft drawl that held so much caring that Antonia wanted to take it and bottle it and preserve it forever. "But promise me you will be my wife. We will work it out some way . . . without hurting your father."

Can that be possible? But at the moment, Antonia thought he could do anything. He could make the sun rise early, hold back the moon, capture a star.

Her throat constricted with emotion and she couldn't speak. She nodded her head, her eyes saying everything he wanted to hear.

He kissed her again, this time restraining the hunger and bestowing all the gentleness and love within him with a touch so painfully sweet that the earth seemed to hum beneath them and the air seemed to embrace them with a soft, approving caress. An owl hooted its ovation in the distance, and the lonely howl of a coyote provided counterpoint to two hearts swelling with love.

Chapter Eight

They remained together for an hour, just holding each other and talking of a future they hoped they would have.

Tris told Antonia about his meeting with Ramon and how the alcalde had insisted that Antonia was his and that she had agreed to it.

"He lies," she said. "But I think my father has given him reason to think that. My father badly wants a marriage between us."

"Why?" Tris said. "He's treacherous."

"My father does not see that. He just sees the Spanish blood and the Catholic religion and . . ."

"And . . . ?" Tris prompted.

"He truly believes Ramon is his friend, a loyal friend to him and to Mexico. And Ramon has, I think, loaned him much money, although my father has not discussed it with me and will not."

"How much?" Tris asked.

"I do not know, but much, I think."

Tris was silent. He had a great deal of money of his own, money that he had put back into the family business. He had never needed much.

"I have money," he said quietly.

"My father would never accept any from a—a Yanqui."

"I can find another way, then," he said. "Perhaps Charles will know a family who can make your father a loan."

"Charles?"

"Governor Bent."

"He is your friend now?"

"Yes."

"Ramon and my father despise him."

"Because he's American?"

"Yes, and because he is governor."

"I'll find a way, Tonia. I don't like your family indebted to Silvero."

Antonia was silent. She didn't like it, either. But there was little she could do about it. It was like a sword over their heads. All ranchers were land rich and cash poor and lived on credit. It was part of their life, yet she hated knowing it was Ramon who held the notes. She shivered. "He can be so charming, yet there is something dark about him, something I don't understand."

Tris could have told her. He had seen men like Silvero before, men without conscience or scruples. She only sensed what he saw clearly. "It will be all right," Tris said. "I won't let him hurt you or your father."

Her heart pounded faster with love for Tristan. Her father had been disrespectful, even contemptuous toward him, and yet his voice held concern for her father. If only her father could shed his hate long enough to see what a good man Tristan really was.

Tris held her tightly. "I must leave again tomorrow," he said. "I'm going to Santa Fe, then to Albuquerque. I should be back within a month.

A whole month. How could she bear it? Perhaps it would give her time to talk to her father.

He took a ring off his finger. It was gold and bore a complex crest inlaid with glittering stones. He put it in her hand and pressed her fingers against it.

"It was my father's," he said. "Keep it until I return and give you my own ring."

Antonia's fingers closed tightly around the heirloom as her eyes misted. He was giving her a part of him to keep. To add to the pieces already in her memory. He would be with her through the ring. Always and forever.

"I love you," she breathed softly.

"And I love you, Tonia. God alone knows how much."

Tris insisted on accompanying her until they sighted the gates of her ranch. Even then, he waited until he felt sure she was safe before spurring his horse in the direction of town.

He didn't know the hour, but he knew it was late. He slowed his horse, wanting to feel the cool breeze and remember every word that had been said between them tonight. There was a bubbling happiness in him that belied the exhaustion of his body. Nothing mattered except that Antonia loved him, and they would, somehow, work everything out.

Tris was so lost in thoughts of a future with Antonia that he didn't use his usual caution. He never noticed the shadowy figure that followed him from the hill.

Manuel Garcia thought happily about the money he would receive for this night's work. It had been so much easier than he'd expected. He had been warned that the gringo was dangerous, but all he saw was a lovesick calf.

Manuel had been summoned by Don Ramon Silvero early yesterday and told to take an unbranded horse and follow the gringo wherever he went. If he had a chance to kill him, he should take it. The gringo's death would mean a dozen gold pieces. It was a fortune.

He had followed the gringo to Don Silvero's home, to the hill and back to Señor Bent's home, but he had had no opportunity to attack him. He had almost given up for the evening when the gringo had left the Bent home. Manuel had followed cautiously. His eyes had opened wide when he saw Señorita Ramirez waiting. No wonder Don Ramon wanted the gringo dead. Everyone knew he had been courting the Ramirez girl for years. Manuel wondered briefly whether his knowledge would mean more money from Don Ramon or a death sentence. Not certain, he decided to keep it to himself. It was not wise to cross Don Ramon, but perhaps someday the information would be useful.

He had followed the gringo as he escorted Antonia to the Ramirez ranch, and continued on toward Taos. Remembering a perfect place for an ambush along the trail, he had pushed his horse into a trot, circling wide around his quarry. Reaching the spot several minutes before the gringo he slid off his horse, taking his rifle.

Lying on a rock that looked down on the trail below, he quickly sighted the rifle and waited for the rider to appear.

Tris moved his horse into a canter. The night was incredibly still. He was still unused to the deadly quiet of the high desert mountains. Even the faraway coyote that had serenaded him and Tonia earlier was now silent. He heard the rustle of the breeze and shivered, without knowing exactly why.

The loud blast of a rifle split the night's peace and he felt a sting in his arm. There was another report and his choices ran swiftly through his mind. He could run for it, presenting a target for the next several seconds, or he could play dead and try to identify his attacker.

A tethered goat. Very apt. And what good is a tethered goat if it doesn't attract and snare the prey.

He fell from the horse and rolled, drawing his pistol and laying it next to him as he came to a halt in the shadow of a tree. He hoped to Christ the man would come close enough to check his body before firing again.

Tris played dead for what seemed a lifetime. He suspected the man was taking his time before checking. He finally heard the crunch of boots on rocks and the flurry of dirt dislodged by heavy footsteps.

He heard the grunt of satisfaction as the man reached him, and a foot kicked his ribs. Tris stifled a gasp of pain and willed himself to stay absolutely still. Then he sensed the man leaning down toward him. Hoping that his attacker had lowered the gun, Tris moved with lightning speed, rolling and bringing his gun up simultaneously.

The man above him had already lowered his rifle and now he frantically tried to aim it with his left hand. Tris aimed for his shoulder, but the man moved and when the gun fired, the bullet went straight into his attacker's heart.

The man grunted and fell, and Tris cursed his luck. He had wanted a prisoner, not a dead man.

He rose painfully, his ribs still hurting from the kick and his arm bleeding slightly from a flesh wound. He quickly surveyed the body in the moonlight.

His attacker looked like a Mexican peasant, except for the fact that he had two pistols strapped around his waist. There was nothing in his pockets. Tris moved to the stand of trees from where the Mexican had come. A thin roan was greedily eating grass nearby. A quick survey showed it carried no brand. Tris swore fluently. The attack had been no random foray. Though he was no closer to proving the identity of the provoker, he knew with every instinct he had that Ramon Silvero had struck again.

He thought about dumping the body at Silvero's ranch, but that might raise questions about where he had been and why. He wondered if the dead man had followed him from the hill, and he cursed once more.

No, he would leave the assassin here. Let Silvero guess. And wonder. And worry about what happened. And whether the dead man had said anything before he died.

With a small deadly grin, Tris mounted his horse and returned to Taos.

There was trouble in Santa Fe. And Tris found himself involved in one peacemaking mission after another on behalf of Governor Bent.

The New Mexicans, many of whom had initially welcomed the Americans, were becoming weary of the bad manners shown by the restless troops. Governor Bent soon discovered there was something about the combination of Tris's air of authority, quiet courtesy and easy smile that settled disputes no one else seemed able to handle without military force. He was a born diplomat, and Bent used him unmercifully.

In addition to Doniphan's Missourians, General Sterling Price had arrived with seventeen hundred troops, including the

Mormon battalion. For a town of three thousand residents, the numbers were overwhelming and a recipe for disaster.

All of Tris's plans, including the proposed trip to Albuquerque, were repeatedly delayed and his return to Taos was continually pushed back.

Unexpectedly, Conn returned. He had accompanied Kearny as far as Valverde Mesa on the Rio Grande, where they met Kit Carson, who was bound to Washington with messages from Colonel John Fremont in California.

The American flag, he reported, was already flying from every important position in California. The territory was free from Mexican control, and "peace and harmony established among the people."

Kearny, hearing the news, decided he no longer needed such a large force and had sent half of them back to Santa Fe. At his own request, Conn returned with them, there to join Colonel Doniphan, who was to head south to engage the Mexican forces. Kit Carson, who had been returning to Taos and his wife, had been recruited, instead, to lead Kearny into California.

The Americans celebrated the news of California's liberation. Manifest Destiny, the spread westward of the United States to the Pacific, was becoming a reality.

The news of California's conquest spread to the citizens of Santa Fe, and many were not happy. Bent and others started hearing more and more rumors of a rebellion brewing in the four northern counties of New Mexico. Once more, Tris's trips were delayed as Bent asked him to find out what he could. Both were certain that Silvero was involved in Taos, but it was more important to discover the overall leader.

Tris was delighted when Conn returned. His uncle would be in Santa Fe only a few days before Doniphan's troops headed south, and the two met for dinner in one of the small Mexican cantinas,

"Trouble seems to have a way of following you, Tris," Conn said after hearing of his latest Taos adventure. "Every time you go there, you pick up a new scar."

Tris shrugged. "It was hardly a scratch."

Conn shook his head. "Are you going back?"

"As soon as I can."

Conn knew a little about Tris's interest in a New Mexican girl. He hesitated, then waded in. "Ever think the lady might have something to do with these attacks? She's an aristocrat. Could be her family's involved with the plotting."

Tris's eyes narrowed and anger colored his face. He knew Conn didn't have much use for women, but that sure as hell didn't excuse him.

"I'll try to pretend I didn't hear that, Conn."

Conn leaned back and eyed his nephew speculatively. No longer the eager student, Tris now exuded confidence and danger, and Conn had heard from Bent how valuable he had become. Whatever else he was, Tris was no longer a tenderfoot, and he had never been a fool.

Conn nodded. "I've never met the lady, though I've heard of her beauty."

"She had nothing to do with the attacks, and her father is ill. I'm convinced it's all been Silvero, but damn if I can find any proof, and I sure as hell can't as long as I stay here in Santa Fe."

Conn raised an eyebrow in question. "I'm not sure it's wise for you to go back."

"Since when did you ever do the wise thing, Uncle?"

Conn chuckled. "Not often, Tris. But be damned careful. I don't want to have to explain anything to Reese and Samara."

"Why don't you stay? There's trouble brewing here, too."

"I like to keep moving, Tris. You know that. And the Mexican army is south."

Tris leaned back in his chair. "Don't you ever want to settle down, Conn?"

"Nope. Never did. Don't think I ever will. I thought for a while you were like that. But you're not, are you?"

"No," Tris said thoughtfully. "I guess I was just looking for something."

"And you think you've found it?"

"I know I've found it."

Conn exhaled a long breath. "Perhaps you have, Tris, but love can be treacherous."

"Advice from an old bachelor?"

"A smart one," Conn corrected. "And now for some hard drinking."

Conn left in the morning. Doniphan, who had planned to march south to Chihuahua, received new orders from Kearny. The Apache had raided a New Mexican town called Pulvidera, killing the men and taking the women and the horses. As the United States had assumed responsibility for the area, Doniphan was now ordered to march on the Apache. Only after they had been subdued could Doniphan continue on to fight the Mexicans.

Conn greeted the news philosophically. Mexicans or Apache, it didn't matter. At last there would be a chance to fight. He bade Tris farewell, keeping his measurable concerns to himself.

Antonia included in her nightly prayers a plea for Tristan's return. She wasn't sure whether it was an altogether proper thing to do, for it was selfish in the extreme. And she had been taught not to pray for selfish things but, rather, the souls and well-being of others.

Nonetheless, she felt it wouldn't hurt.

She had heard nothing from him since he left her that night, and it had been nearly a month. He was respecting her wishes in not openly contacting her until her father was better. She was grateful, but she longed to hear from him.

At least she had his ring. She had placed it on a ribbon and wore it under her nightclothes and whenever she wore a high-necked dress or blouse. She fingered it frequently and wistfully, almost feeling the heat from his body in its small, sparkling stones.

Antonia filled her days with the ranch. She rode each morning with the vaqueros and spent her afternoons with her father, making decisions about which horses to breed, how many of the cattle to sell, what winter supplies to purchase. She also wondered, when she had time, about hell. And whether she might be going there. She had not confessed her meetings with Tristan to Father Martinez in Confession because she knew he despised the Yanquis almost as much as her father did. And she could not do penance for something she felt in her heart was right and good. It was the secrecy that was a sin, and it weighed heavily on her...that and the physical passion she felt for the American. She comforted herself by knowing she had not done anything really wrong with Tristan, except in her thoughts.

But even those disturbing thoughts were often relegated to the back of her mind. Her father's pallor continued, and she feared he was not improving, although he said little.

It had been a good year for the ranch. The sheep had provided the finest wool, the mares had fine colts and fillies, and the cattle were sleek and fat. Perhaps they would be able to pay back some of the debt they owed Ramon.

Their neighbor came frequently, often closeting himself in Don Miguel's office for hours. Once, Ramon and Don Miguel went riding, Don Miguel strapped in the special saddle. He was gray and tired when they returned, and he would not tell Antonia where they had been.

Much to her surprise, Ramon did not press his suit. He was always courteous and affectionate, but he said no more about marriage. He seemed, instead, preoccupied with other matters. Whatever they were, she couldn't help but be grateful for them.

She started riding alone again. It had been months since the Apache attack on the governor and his companion, and there had been no more. When the work at the ranch was finished, she often went to Francesca's. She was terribly restless, and unable to sit for long.

She was waiting. Always waiting.

Occasionally Antonia went back to *their* hill. Hers and Tristan's. She felt close to him there. She would hold the ring and remember his words the day he gave it to her. She no longer had any doubts about his sincerity. He was not like the other Yanquis.

She counted the days until a month went by. And then another week and another until it was mid-December. She looked for him everywhere, eavesdropped on every conversation, trying to hear news of him.

Antonia finally decided to go into Taos, something she seldom did without her father or an escort. Taos was a wild and boisterous town. It was a neutral territory for all kinds of lawless elements and not the place for a lady. But perhaps she would hear some news.

Knowing her father would try to prevent such a trip, she didn't tell him she was going, but merely had Jose saddle Night Wind and asked him to accompany her into Taos. "I must get a Christmas gift for my father," she explained, ignoring his protests, "and he is to know nothing about it."

Jose finally agreed reluctantly, and they rode the fifteen miles to Taos. The town was rough and ugly. The adobe buildings had been built attached to each other for protection from Comanche raids and though the raids had ended years ago, the tradition continued.

There were more saloons than stores, and men staggered drunkenly in the street. Antonia had carefully dressed, wearing high-necked clothes and a broad-brimmed hat that partially hid her face, but still she attracted rude remarks.

Asking Jose to wait outside with the horses, she hurried into the gunsmith shop, turning away from several Yanqui hunters who were studying a selection of knives.

The owner, Luis Condova, hurried over to her.

"Señorita Ramirez," he said with surprise, looking around for her father.

She leaned over to him conspiratorially. "I'm looking for a handsome rifle for my father."

A twinkle appeared in the gunsmith's eye. "I think I have just the right thing." He reached under the counter and pulled out a rifle with a beautifully carved stock.

"Oh, that is lovely," she said, fingering the carving.

"It handles well, too," he explained. "It is one of the finest guns on the market."

Antonia felt her purse. Money was always short, but her father had given her small sums for dresses and ribbons and other special items. She had hoarded most of it, never knowing when it might come of use.

"How much is it?" she asked, and bartered the price down considerably. Once she had the rifle, she then picked out a staurolite crystal from a small collection Luis kept in stock. The black prismatic crystal formed a perfect cross and was treasured by the Spanish as a good-luck symbol.

Antonia carefully paid Luis, ignoring the admiring looks of the Yanqui hunters, and took her purchases out to the horses.

"I would like to visit Señora Bent," she told the scowling Jose.

"It would be better to return to the hacienda," Jose muttered, knowing that Don Miguel would not be pleased about any part of this venture, gift or not.

"Just a short visit," she said, and her tone did not give Jose a choice.

She was greeted warmly by Maria Bent, who ushered Antonia inside and offered refreshments.

"I cannot stay," Antonia said hesitantly. "I just…wondered if you had…"

Maria took pity on her. "If Señor Hampton was all right?"

Antonia nodded.

"I received a letter from my husband several days ago and there was a note in there for you. I was going to give it to Francesca to give to you, but now I can do it in person." She disappeared into another room and came out carrying a sealed note.

Antonia clutched it, wanting to tear it open, but also wanting privacy.

Maria, who had once felt the same trembling uncertainty, smiled. "There are some things I must do in the kitchen." she said softly.

When she was alone, Antonia opened the note, her fingers touching where she knew he had touched.

Tonia,
Because of certain difficulties in Santa Fe, I am unable to return to Taos as planned. I will come as soon as possible. In the meantime, you have my heart.

Tris

Antonia's mouth curved into a soft smile. Tonia. No one but Tristan had ever called her that. And she loved the sound of it on his lips.

Folding the note carefully, she tucked it into her blouse before she went looking for Maria.

"He is all right?" Maria asked anxiously. She liked the tall American, and she remembered binding his wound the morning he left for Santa Fe. It had been minor, but even minor wounds could become infected.

"Yes," Antonia said. Then something in Maria's voice startled her. "Why would he not be all right?"

"He did not mention the wound?"

"What wound?"

Maria wished she had been silent. Señor Hampton had asked her to say nothing about the bullet wound, and she had not. But she assumed he would have told Antonia. She had not missed the look in Señor Hampton's eyes when she mentioned Antonia, nor was there any mistaking the feeling in Antonia's face.

"What wound?" Antonia whispered again.

"It was nothing," Maria said. "Just a small crease."

"When?"

Maria stared helplessly at her guest.

"When?" Antonia insisted.

"The night before he left."

The night he was with her. Antonia felt her face drain of color. *"Maria Santisima,"* she murmured.

"What is it?" Maria Bent asked.

"Nothing," Antonia said, but her mind was rushing ahead. "You know nothing more?"

"No, I noticed blood on his sleeve in the morning and asked him about it. I don't think he planned to say anything. But he let me dress it. It was a flesh wound, nothing more, but . . ."

"But what?"

"He didn't say. But a man, a *bandito* was discovered dead on the road the next day."

Antonia closed her eyes, thinking. The ambush on the way back to Santa Fe. Now this. Could it be Ramon? But how would he have known about their midnight meeting? It had to be a coincidence. It had to.

If Ramon had learned she had met the Yanqui at night, he would have said something. To her father, anyway. She shivered at the thought. Something terrible would have happened.

"Thank you," she said to Maria.

"It is nothing."

"If you hear from him again, you will send word?"

"Through Francesca," Maria replied with understanding eyes. But she knew Don Miguel's hatred for the Anglos and like her husband, she wondered whether tragedy was brewing.

Spontaneously, Antonia leaned over and kissed her cheek, surprising Maria. Antonia had always been quiet and reserved, although she had a delightful smile when she used it. Now her expression was soft and smiling, and Maria thought how very pretty she was.

"I will get word to you," she said again, thinking what a handsome couple the tall golden American would make with the slender dark-haired Antonia. She had never liked Ramon, though she had never truly understood why.

Antonia said little on the way back. She was too lost in her thoughts of Tristan and the danger he seemed to attract. Twice he had evaded death.

She saw him as he had been on the hill that night in the moonlight. Tall and powerful, graceful and tender. She ached at the memory of the feelings he aroused, and they came flooding back in torrents: the warm rush of heat, the stirring of something deep inside her, the craving for something she didn't understand. Her hand trembled as she sought to bring her body back to normal. *Nombre de Dios,* what had he done to her?

She clutched the small crystal in its package and wished with all her heart she could finger his ring to bring him closer. But that would have to wait until later. Even Jose must not know of it.

But someday...?

How could she bear the waiting?

Chapter Nine

Relaxing on his rangy bay, Conn O'Neill studied the Rio Grande and the mass of tents beyond it.

He shivered despite the sheepskin coat he wore, and his sympathy went out to the foot soldiers with little but summer clothing and a few blankets to keep them warm.

Conn had left Santa Fe on October 26 with Colonel Doniphan and three hundred of his mounted troops to put a stop to the Navaho menace in the area below Albuquerque. It had been a seven-week campaign over wild and snow-covered mountains, and Conn, as chief scout, had seldom stopped moving in all that time.

It had been a bitter and ruthless campaign, ending with a treaty signed by the chiefs with *X*s, promising "permanent peace, mutual trust and friendship." Conn had viewed such sentiments with deep cynicism. As soon as the soldiers were gone, the raiding would start again.

But at least he would be on his way to fight the Mexicans, something he had been waiting for since he joined Kearny. So far, he had been bitterly disappointed, but that, he knew, would soon change. They were to meet with General John Wool and take Chihuahua City, where the Mexican army was said to be massing.

When Doniphan left Santa Fe with his horse soldiers to pursue the renegade Indians, he had sent his foot soldiers south along the Rio Grande toward Chihuahua and now he was heading south to meet the infantry. Conn's job was to find them.

Conn caught sight of them near Valvarde. They looked more like disorganized rabble than any kind of army. The camp was strewed with the bones and offal of the cattle slaughtered for supplies, and the men were unwashed and dressed in an assortment of clothes, few of them bearing any resemblance to uniforms.

It was a sight Conn was accustomed to, although he knew it would horrify most military minds. It had been the same with the Texan army ten years earlier, and Andrew Jackson before that. The mountain men, hunters and other western volunteers had little use for formality or discipline. But God, they could fight!

He would rather have a hundred of the unwashed, bearded fellows sprawled lazily in this camp than a thousand professional military men any day. With a grin, he rode in, greeting old friends as he moved along, regaling them with tales of the Indian hunt. He would share a meal with them, then return to meet with Doniphan.

Doniphan's appearance gave new life to the straggling troops, and they started south once more, marching across a high desert area called Dead Man's March. On Christmas afternoon, they arrived at a spot thirty miles north of El Paso, where the Brazito River flowed into the Rio Grande. Conn, scouting ahead, discovered a Mexican battalion of some twelve hundred men to Doniphan's eight hundred.

As the two sides lined up for battle hours later, Conn thought fancifully that it was a very strange Christmas. Not that he cared much about such things since he left home so many years ago. Christmas had become just another day. But still, there was something sad about the impending violence on this of all days. Damning himself for a fool, he slid from his horse and went to Doniphan's side as a rider approached from the Mexican side.

The Mexican courier demanded Doniphan's surrender and, when it was refused, announced there would be no quarter, words Conn had heard before from the Mexicans. He took his rifle from his horse and sent the animal back with the other mounts near the river.

His grim expression changed to a grin, however, when Colonel Doniphan passed an order down his ranks: "Prepare to squat." He, like the others, knew exactly what it meant.

As the Mexican troops approached, the Americans held steady, holding their fire. The Mexicans fired, once, twice, three, four times and still the Americans didn't fire, although they dropped to their knees, letting the bullets fly over them.

Off balance and convinced the Americans meant to surrender, the Mexicans approached closer, and the American long rifles were cocked and aimed. As one file fired, the other knelt and reloaded. Both the Mexican cavalry and infantry reeled from the carnage, those still alive fleeing from the deadly fire, many disappearing into the mountains where Apache waited with their own form of retribution.

"One hundred Mexicans dead," Colonel Doniphan announced later that night as his troops celebrated with captured Mexican wine and supplies. "And not one American."

"We'll keep going south?" Conn asked.

"El Paso," Doniphan said, taking a celebratory cup of wine himself. The first real battle in New Mexico had been an unqualified victory.

Tris spent a lonely Christmas in Santa Fe. Every time he tried to leave for Taos, another problem seemed to develop. In mid-December, Charles Bent had learned of a plot to assassinate both himself and General Stirling Price. Some of the conspirators were arrested, but the ringleaders escaped.

The capital remained tense, although Charles, confident of his own personal popularity, discounted any additional threats.

But Tris couldn't help worrying. There was something in the air, something ominous that he couldn't dismiss. Dammit, he could smell conspiracy.

It made for a dreary and tense Christmas.

Christmas in Virginia had always been a gay and happy time, full of surprises. With six children in the family, there were always parties and shouts of laughter and teasing and games.

He had selected a lovely silver-and-turquoise ring for Tonia, hoping that he might be able to present it prior to Christmas, but it still remained wrapped in his few belongings at the hotel where he stayed. He wondered how she was celebrating the day, although he had noted that Christmas to New Mexicans seemed a more solemn occasion than a joyous one.

Tonia.

He received word of her through notes Maria Bent sent to her husband. Tonia had received his note. She had asked about him. She was well.

He wished he could send word directly to her but for the time being at least, he would observe her wishes about her father. He sensed she would never forgive him or worse, herself, if anything happened to Don Miguel because of their actions. Tris knew he would just have to find a way to crack her father's antipathy and he was prepared to do anything necessary to accomplish that.

Tris attended Mass at the Cathedral of St. Francis early Christmas morning, and was startled at the peace he found in the beautiful church. It had been months since he had been in a church and, perhaps because of Tonia's strong beliefs, it meant more to him today. He felt close to her here.

He had never been in a Catholic church before, although his maternal grandfather, Connor O'Neill, had been Catholic. Tris's grandmother Samantha was Protestant. Connor and Samantha had married, hurriedly, in the Protestant faith and had remained there.

Tris had no strong convictions one way or the other. He supposed he believed in God, but he had never really tested that belief. Church had been part tradition, part obligation, part social, but had never played a deep role in his life. He knew it did in Tonia's, and he wanted to understand.

And this Christmas morning, he did. There was a richness of spirit in this church that glowed in the faces around him. He heard and understood the Latin words and their meaning struck him with their simple beauty.

When the Mass ended, some of the intense loneliness had left and he felt a certain harmony, if not contentment. He missed Antonia but he had, somehow, captured some of her spirit this morning.

He took dinner with an equally lonely Charles Bent and some bachelor officers. The group discussed the future of New Mexico. They had heard that Doniphan had, temporarily at least, subdued the Indians and was marching south. The rumored rebellion was all but over, Charles believed. New Mexicans were accepting the new government, and California had been taken. There was much to celebrate.

Charles looked at Tris's bleak face. "I'm going to take a short vacation in Taos next week. I assume you would like to go with me."

"Do you think it's safe?" Tris questioned.

"Taos? Of course, it's safe," Charles replied. "It's been my home for years. There's no safer place in New Mexico."

Tris raised an eyebrow.

"Except for an occasional Indian attack," Charles amended.

"Silvero?"

"The conspirators we've captured have been questioned over and over. There's no indication Silvero was involved." Bent looked at Tris with a sly grin. "Nor Ramirez."

Tris sighed with no little relief. The thought had been haunting him. "The ambush?"

"I'm beginning to think it was just a random attack," Bent conceded. "I think what small rebellion there was has been smashed. Most New Mexicans are pleased, particularly since we rid them of the Navaho menace. They've never had any real protection from the Indians before."

Tris hoped he was right. But he couldn't forget Silvero and the hatred that had been so evident in the Creole's eyes.

"And what of the attack on me?"

"A bandit. You said yourself you could find nothing on him."

"That's what made me wonder," Tris said. "I hope you're planning to take troops with you to Taos."

"No. I'm tired of troops and fawning aides."

Tris's lips crooked in a small smile.

"That's why," Bent continued, "I like you. You don't fawn. You aren't even respectful," he added with a twinkle in his eye.

Tris's smile widened. "I can always try."

"You would never succeed. There's too much natural-born arrogance in you, my boy. I don't suppose you even kowtowed to that English king you visited."

Tris didn't reply. He *had* attended court with his cousins, and been bitterly disillusioned. At first, it had seemed grand and glittering and he had been impressed by Queen Victoria's earnestness. But so many of the titled nobles looked as if they had never worked a day and spent their lives in the gambling halls. Tris had worked hard on the farm until he went to Cambridge, and his oak-colored skin and well-developed muscles were oddities among the languid and often cynical aristocrats.

The women, although pretty, had bored him. American women, with their independence and industry, were far more appealing than their English counterparts, who seemed to care for little other than gossip and dalliances. There were exceptions, of course, especially his cousins, whom he liked immensely, and who were raised with the same love of education as his own family.

But he had been eager to return to America and leave the superficiality he felt typified English society. So now he only smiled at Bent, the same self-deprecating smile that had so attracted the older man to him.

In the past weeks, they had become good friends. Bent regaled Tris with his adventures as a trader and the hardships of establishing a trading post with his brother in Indian Territory. Both Charles and Tris were from Virginia—another bond—although Charles was older than Tris by fourteen years and had been engaged in the fur trade for nearly thirty years. Bent knew the Indian tribes as well as Conn and was loquacious in sharing his knowledge. He recognized in Tris a similar sense of adventure and love of New Mexico, and he identified completely with Tris's obsession with Antonia Ramirez. He himself had fallen in love with a New Mexican girl.

The two men were at ease with each other and since the ambush along the Rio Grande Gorge, they trusted each other thoroughly.

Bent offered a Christmas toast. "To our ladies," he said with a wink. "It won't be long now."

It was a toast with which Tris heartily concurred.

Christmas was usually a serene time for Antonia. She loved the solemn processions, the midnight vigil, the Christmas Mass. She had always felt closer to God at Christmas.

Until this year.

Instead, fear had disrupted the peace of the season. Fear and the anticipation of seeing Tristan.

Her father's face, already pinched and gray, had grown even tighter. He seldom smiled now, and worry was heavily etched on his face.

Just before Christmas, Don Miguel had disappeared for two days, saying only that he was going away on business. She couldn't remember when he had taken a journey before without telling her the details. Days later, she had heard about the conspiracy unearthed in Santa Fe and learned that some of the participants had been jailed.

Ramon was a frequent guest, even more so than before, and his black onyx eyes never left Antonia when she was in the room. She couldn't help but think of the attacks on Tristan and wonder whether Ramon had been responsible. Her skin fairly seemed to crawl when she was in the same room with him, and she was torn between wanting to leave and being afraid to leave . . . afraid Ramon would draw her father into some dangerous scheme. Once, she left the room and hovered around the door, which had been closed. It had been opened abruptly by Ramon. "Would you like to join us again," he said smoothly.

"I was just returning to see if you need some brandy?"

"That's very solicitous," he said in the silky voice of his. "But I think we have sufficient."

This time Antonia didn't linger.

Christmas Day was tense. She could even feel it in the Church of San Francisco de Asis. Her father was withdrawn, even when she gave him the rifle. The fact that he did not ask how she had obtained it was more bothersome than questions would have been. She had never seen him so preoccupied.

Ramon came over to share the Christmas dinner, bringing as presents a lace shawl for Antonia and a handsome embroidered rug for Don Miguel. They were entirely appropriate gifts, and Antonia could find no excuse to refuse the lovely shawl, although she knew she would never wear it.

Ramon was at his most charming. If he had been involved in the rebellion, he certainly showed little if any concern. He talked instead of horses and cattle and crops, his eyes frequently moving to Antonia's.

Antonia herself brought up the topic. "Have you heard any more of the rebellion in Santa Fe?" she asked, watching her father's face tense.

"Only that the Americans are looking for Diego Archuleta and Tomas Ortez," he said.

"They've captured some New Mexicans?"

"A few. No one of any importance." Ramon shrugged.

"Do you think that will be the end of it, then?"

"The end? While gringos occupy our country? No, Antonia. It is not the end until they are swept out of New Mexico." Ramon's voice was low but intense.

"But—"

Don Miguel broke in. "Enough talk of war on Christ's day," he said, telling Ramon of Antonia's fine gift. The conversation then went back to the price of horses and cattle.

When Ramon took his leave, he asked Antonia to walk with him to his horse. Once outside, he took her hand and brought it to his mouth. "I would have liked to have brought you a much more personal gift," he said softly. "A betrothal ring."

Antonia met his eyes directly. "I don't love you, Ramon."

"No, but we have known each other for years, and love will come," he said. "We are alike, we have everything in common. I can protect you. And your father."

"I will never marry without love," she said.

"Then I will try hard to make you love me, Antonia," he said. "I am sorry about that afternoon...I just care for you so much."

Antonia could find no words. He *had* been going out of his way to be pleasant lately. But, Holy Mary, she could not rid herself of the feeling he was pulling her father into something dangerous, nor of her suspicion that he had something to do with the attacks on Tristan.

"I'm sorry, Ramon," she said finally.

"I will keep trying," he said mildly. Again, he brought her hand to his lips and kissed it lightly, then quickly mounted his horse and trotted down the packed dirt road.

He was in a strange mood, Antonia thought. He seemed very sure of himself, as if he knew something no one else did. It was freezing now in the Taos Valley, but it was not the cold that sent shivers up and down her back.

Those damned fools in Santa Fe.

Ramon had already cursed each and every one of them for the past week, ever since the rebellion had been uncovered. And all because of a woman. Someone had told the former governor's mistress, who then had gone directly to the American general, Sterling Price.

Her new patrons were the Americans.

He cursed all women in general, including the stubborn Antonia. The more she refused him, the more he wanted her. And the more determined he was to have her.

In the meantime, the rebellion would continue to be fermented. There were many conspirators who had not been identified, and plans were continuing, if delayed.

His part, his and Miguel's, was to incite the Pueblo Indians to revolt.

It was not a difficult task. The Tao Indians were no more enthralled with the Americans than they were with the Spanish or Mexicans. They would like to rid themselves of all whites. Ramon knew that the Indians thought if they could slaughter the Americans by cooperating with the New Mexicans, they might then be able to oust the Mexicans and Creoles. But Ramon had plans of his own.

He and Miguel had been supplying the Pueblos with guns as well as a steady influx of hatred. They would be forced from their ancient homes, he told them. Resentment had been building, and only a spark was needed to ignite the flames. It was a spark Ramon intended to fan when Charles Bent returned to Taos.

Ramon hoped with all his being that Tris Hampton would accompany the governor. It would be an added bounty. He knew how cruel the Indians could be, how they enjoyed torture.

He smiled as he rode home.

Chapter Ten

The cold pierced Tris like a thousand silver needles. Snow and ice lay over the Rio Grande Gorge like an ermine cloak, richly white, and the wind blew strong and hard.

But nothing could quiet the exhilaration in him as he rode side by side with Charles to Taos.

It seemed years rather than weeks since he had seen Antonia, and he kept thinking about the silver-and-turquoise ring in his saddlebag. Would she like it?

Everything seemed more spectacular today. The air was more vibrant, and the red-tailed hawk, perched high in a dead cottonwood, more colorful. Ice hung like crystals from the piñon trees, shimmering like diamonds in the sun. Chipmunks chattered, chickadees played in the trees, and a golden eagle spread its great wings and glided gracefully to a ledge high in the mountains.

Tris had never felt more alive, more hopeful, more expectant.

Charles had continued to refuse a military escort, but he had acceded to Tris's wish that they tell no one of their plans until they were actually ready to leave Santa Fe. And Tris was finally infused with the governor's own enthusiastic confidence. After all, Charles Bent had lived in Taos for a number of years. He knew the people. If he felt safe, who was Tris to gainsay him?

But he would still exercise an extra measure of caution.

His spirits soared when he saw the Taos Valley. Taos Mountain rose like a protective arm around the valley, its huge mauve bulk crowned by clouds that lay in streaks across the vivid blue sky.

"It's becoming home to you, too, isn't it?" Charles asked.

Tris looked with surprise at his traveling companion, who was smiling in understanding.

"I suppose it has. I've never seen anything quite as . . ." Tris hunted for the word.

"Magnificent," Bent finished. "That's the way I felt when I first saw it. And I could never leave again, not without knowing I was going to return. There's a magic here and believe me, it gets stronger the longer you stay."

Tris had already felt its pull and he knew Bent was right. Even if Antonia had not been here, he would feel the same way. This land of mountains and deserts, of sage and rich high grass, of lakes and streams, tumbling cold and pure from the mountains, weaved a spell of incredible strength.

Almost embarrassed by his sentimentality, Charles grinned and spurred his horse into a gallop. "I want to see Maria and the children," he yelled into the wind. "I'll race you to Taos."

Riding against a wind that bit and tore at his skin, Tris quickly moved beside Charles and, their laughter ringing, they raced like two lads across the rich meadow.

Tris had dinner with the Bents. Although he enjoyed the couple's open affection for each other and their three children, he ate restlessly, wanting desperately to ride out to the Ramirez ranch. But he had, in effect, promised Tonia he would do nothing to upset her father, and he would keep his word.

Charles had sent one of his Mexican friends to the Ramirez ranch with a note from Tris and instructions to give it only to Antonia. If her father was present, he was merely to ask for work. Tris hoped fervently that Don Miguel would not be home.

After dinner, he paced restlessly as Charles played with his children. He stopped when he heard a horseman ride up and a few quiet words as Maria slipped outside. In a moment Maria was handing him a note with a conspiratorial smile.

"Sunrise tomorrow," it said in neat, strong strokes, and Tris's heart pumped faster. He could scarcely stand the joy, the anticipation, that swirled around inside him. But there was also a twinge of apprehension. He knew the matter would have to be settled soon. He couldn't wait much longer and he hated this subterfuge and hiding. It went against everything he believed in, everything he was brought up to cherish. Love meant honesty and commitment.

Jealously, he watched Charles and Maria retire, hand in hand, to their bedroom, while he went outside, hoping the cold would cool the heat arising in his body. It didn't, and he knew it would be a long night.

He left the Bent home an hour before sunrise. He was going to make damned sure neither he nor Tonia were followed. He saddled his horse quickly and led the stallion outside, leaping easily into the saddle before sending the animal galloping down the empty streets.

Tris knew Nugget could outrun nearly any other horse in the territory. He had been bred for speed, and Tris called upon it now. He raced the horse to a small ravine, where he dismounted and waited.

He was not disappointed. Within a few minutes, he spied another rider, carefully following the tracks he had left in the first gray light of dawn. The tracks led out of the ravine, but the follower never had a chance to see that they also came back. Tris hurled his body down on the man and knocked him to the ground. He had the advantage of surprise and as he twisted so the man fell under his full weight he heard the quick expulsion of breath.

In another quick movement, Tris tore the bandanna from his stalker's neck and securely tied the man's hands, jerking him up.

"Why are you following me?"

The man looked at him blankly, and Tris repeated his words in broken Spanish.

The man merely shook his head. He didn't know whether the tall American would kill him or not. But he knew Señor Silvero would if he said anything.

Tris jerked him again, wanting to strike, but he wouldn't hit a bound man. From the terrified look in his captive's eyes, he wouldn't get the answers he wanted now, anyway. Perhaps a few hours of cold and fear would make the man more willing to talk.

Tris pulled the smaller man up and pushed him to where Nugget was waiting. Taking a length of rope from the saddle, he led his prisoner to an aspen tree, forcing him down and firmly tying him to it. He tore a piece of cloth from the man's own shirt to gag him.

"I'll be back for you," he announced, his words half promise and half threat.

He was late. The sun had already come over the horizon, sprinkling colors across the patchwork snow. He rode quickly now, but still carefully, his eyes restless and searching. He studied the area around the hill before urging Nugget up. There was no one else around.

She was standing at the edge of the woods, her hat off and her long black braid following the swell of her breasts under the heavy jacket she was wearing. Her cheeks were flushed from the cold, and wisps of escaping hair blew in the wind.

Her face was a mixture of apprehension and disappointment until she saw him, and then it blazed with joy.

He dismounted in a second and she rushed into his arms, burying her head against his heart for a moment before lifting it to gaze into his eyes.

His heart thudded with her nearness. He had never known this kind of wanting before. A kind of glorious splendor.

He touched her ever so lightly, as if afraid she might disappear.

Antonia's hand went to his, touching it with the same delicacy, the same wonder.

For a brief golden moment, the touching was enough.

And then their lips touched with the same terrible, yet tender, need for contact.

Tris was washed with a compelling feeling of belonging, as if a silver chain had been wrapped around them, binding all that was giving, all that was good. He knew that nothing had ever been quite so right as this moment.

The kiss deepened and grew rougher with passion. Sweet passion. Hungry passion. Their tongues played lazy, sensuous games that excited something more vital in each of them, reaching down to the core and stirring the embers that had been burning since they'd first met.

Warm delicious rushes of heat pulsed through Antonia's body, and she wished they were not parted by their heavy clothing.

But perhaps it was just as well, a cautioning voice said. She didn't think she could stand being any closer to him. She was already trembling with something she couldn't identify.

Tris tore his lips away with a small groan and took her arm, leading her into the woods. He saw a broken log and helped Antonia to sit, then settled next to her.

He put his arm around her and drew her near. There was such delight in the simple act that once more his heart raced and the ache in him grew.

"God, I've missed you," he said finally.

Antonia felt as though light had just returned to her life, even while she pondered how strange it was. They had not spent many more hours together than the number of fingers on her hands. Yet it seemed as if they had known each other forever.

"My life stopped when you left," she said shyly. "And started again this morning."

He smiled, not the quick flashing devilish grin she had seen before, but one full of sweetness and caring, and she melted under its impact.

He reached in his pocket and pulled out a small package of green velvet and placed it in her hand. "I'm sorry it's late. I wanted to give it to you at Christmas."

With trembling fingers, she unwrapped the gift carefully, her breath catching as she saw the turquoise in the intricately carved silver setting. She caressed it lovingly. This ring had been chosen by him ... for her. She was so full of joy that she thought she might explode.

The turquoise, small but perfect, looked like his eyes at their brightest, full of depth and hues that changed according to the light.

Tris took her left hand, placing the ring on her finger, and smiled with satisfaction as it fit perfectly.

"I have something for you, too," Tonia said when she could gather the words in her mind and put voice to them. Even then her voice quavered.

She took out the crystal cross and handed it to him, her eyes hopeful that he would understand its significance. The gift seemed almost trivial compared to the ring, but there was delight in his smile, and she felt her own pleasure deepen.

"It is good luck," she said.

His eyes crinkled. "I'll treasure it, love." He smiled. He thought it best not to add that he probably needed luck...much more than she knew. "I think," he added slowly, "it's time to approach your father."

Antonia tensed. In the last month, her father had changed drastically and for the worse; day by day growing paler and more distracted.

She shook her head and tried to turn away from him, but Tris would not let her off that easily. He cupped her chin in his hand and forced her to look at him. "It does not sit well with me to go behind a man's back." His words were slow but determined.

Antonia clenched her fist, her mouth tightening. "Nor is it mine."

"Dammit, Tonia. We can't keep meeting on this hill forever." He didn't say that they had come close to being discovered ... if they hadn't already.

"When father is better—"

She had to turn away from the sudden fierce light in his eyes and the coldness that chilled her more than the icy wind blowing on the hill.

"Don't make me choose between you," she finally whispered. "I don't know if I can do that. He needs me."

"I need you," Tris countered.

"It's only been a few—"

"Do you think time has anything to do with what's happened between us. Those weeks away from you, dammit, seemed like years. But I won't sneak around like a schoolboy."

Antonia, who had always been strong and determined and independent, now felt the earth falling away. Whichever way she leapt, there was a chasm waiting.

She wanted to reach out to Tristan, to take his hand and be led by him . . . anywhere.

Instead, she withdrew from him, taking her hand from his. "I can't," she whispered.

She heard his muttered oath as he whirled to his feet.

"Tris . . ."

He looked at her, and for a moment she thought him a stranger.

"I mean it, Tonia. I love you. God knows I love you. I haven't known a moment's peace since I set eyes on you. But I can't play games like this."

Something in Tonia shattered. She looked at the ring on her finger and felt the large one that lay against her skin inside her blouse. He had brought her life, and now he was taking it away.

"A—a few weeks more," she said hesitantly. "Perhaps he will be better."

"I will be here with Governor Bent for two weeks," Tris said. "Then I return to Santa Fe."

He saw the misery in her eyes, and he touched her cheek but withdrew his hand quickly. He didn't know how long he could stay with her, how long he could touch her without losing control. He knew he couldn't keep meeting her here without doing something that could possibly destroy her, destroy them both. She had to make a decision. He couldn't believe that her father would be so unreasonable when he realized how much in love they were, and that Tris had the means to take care of her and the ranch.

If only she would tell her father or release me from my promise not to, Tris thought.

The sun now hovered in a great gilded ball just over the mountains, but its heat didn't reach Antonia as she thought about a life without Tris.

But she was so sure it would kill her father if she married him.

Her father needed her. Tris didn't. It was just that simple and that painful.

Antonia rose with a dignity that took all her courage to feign.

Slowly, carefully, she reached inside her coat to the chain around her neck, unlatching and removing it. Then she let the heavy ring fall from the chain into her hand. Silently, she held it out to him.

"Tonia . . ."

"You are right," she said, glad her voice wasn't shaking as were her legs. "It isn't fair. Not to you. Not to me. Not to my father."

He made no effort to take the ring.

"Please," she said, and there was so much agony in her eyes, he couldn't refuse.

He slowly put his hand out and felt the ring, still warm from her body, drop into his fingers. Then he saw her tugging on the ring he had just given her. He took her hand and balled it up. "No," he said. "That one is yours."

She started to protest, but his words stopped her. "You don't want your cross back, do you?" He held his breath. He didn't want to give it back.

Antonia met his direct gaze. At least something of hers would be with him. "No," she agreed in a low voice.

Tris felt his heart crack as her head bowed. "I love you, Tonia. If you need anything . . . or change your mind . . . send word to me."

Tears were now snaking their way down her face, and she nodded, afraid to speak.

Tris leaned down and kissed her. The kiss, meant as a farewell, did not stop there. Tris wondered if it could ever stop there.

Her lips were hungry and salty and as he tasted them, his arms wrapped around her once more.

He had not planned to force her to make a choice. Not to-day. But seeing her and realizing the depth of his need for her, he had recklessly plowed ahead. He had not entirely under-stood until this morning when he knew someone was follow-ing him, how deeply he detested these secretive meetings. The fact that someone was following seemed to make them even more reprehensible.

Dear God Almighty. He groaned with pain and denial and several other emotions he couldn't identify. But he couldn't let her go from his arms, even as he knew he should. Instead, they tightened around her as he felt her own desperation.

Tris tore his lips away and stared down at her. He had never seen anything quite as lovely. Her dark eyes were luminous with hovering tears and her cheeks were flushed from the cold. Her lips were full and red from his kisses, and her strong, stubborn chin trembled just enough to let him know the anguish she was feeling.

He wondered what he would do if someone made him choose between love and loyalty to his family. If his mother were ill, and he was the only one left to protect her, could he take the chance of increasing her pain? He was consumed by waves of regret and guilt and tenderness. "I'm sorry," he whispered in a raw, ragged voice. "But God help me, I don't know how long I can bear this."

It was her turn now to comfort. Her hands went up and played with his thick gold hair, possessively, selfishly. The fear of losing him was so great, so overwhelming, that she wanted to hold on to him forever.

Tris sensed the hopelessness in her movements, and he hated himself for making her so unhappy. How long could they con-tinue this way?

But he could no more ignore her upturned lips than he could stop breathing, and once again, their mouths melded in per-fect union, their tongues, tender and wanton, saying things they could no longer say out loud.

When they finally parted moments later, they both knew they would meet again. No matter what promises they made, Tris

PLAY

HARLEQUIN'S

LUCKY HEARTS

GAME

AND YOU COULD GET

★ **FREE BOOKS**
★ **A FREE GOLD-PLATED CHAIN**
★ **A FREE SURPRISE GIFT**
★ **AND MUCH MORE**

**TURN THE PAGE AND
DEAL YOURSELF IN**

PLAY "LUCKY HEARTS" AND YOU COULD GET...

★ Exciting Harlequin Historical™ novels—FREE
★ A gold-plated chain—FREE
★ A surprise mystery gift that will delight you—FREE

THEN CONTINUE YOUR LUCKY STREAK WITH A SWEETHEART OF A DEAL

When you return the postcard on the opposite page, we'll send you the books and gifts you qualify for, absolutely free! Then you'll get 4 new Harlequin Historical™ novels every month, delivered right to your door. If you decide to keep them, you'll pay only $2.89* per book—that's a saving of 36¢ off the cover price. And there's no extra charge for postage and handling! You can cancel at any time by marking "cancel" on your statement or returning a shipment to us at our cost.

★ Free Newsletter!
You'll get a free newsletter—an insider's look at our most popular authors and their upcoming novels.

★ Special Extras—Free!
When you subscribe to the Harlequin Reader Service,® you'll also get additional free gifts from time to time as a token of our appreciation for being a home subscriber.

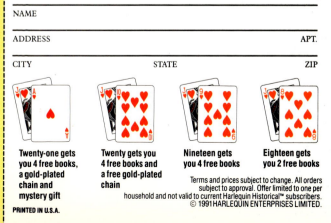

BUSINESS REPLY MAIL

FIRST CLASS MAIL   PERMIT NO. 717   BUFFALO, NY

POSTAGE WILL BE PAID BY ADDRESSEE

HARLEQUIN READER SERVICE
3010 WALDEN AVE
PO BOX 1867
BUFFALO NY 14240-9952

NO POSTAGE
NECESSARY
IF MAILED
IN THE
UNITED STATES

DETACH AND MAIL CARD TODAY

knew he could not stay away from her. Nor she from him. They were like the sun to each other; sun and water and life.

Antonia felt an infinite sadness. She wanted to shout to the world that she loved the tall American. She wanted to stand proud at his side. She wanted desperately to be his wife and know the intimacy of marriage.

She would do something. She had to. Perhaps Tristan was right. She knew her father loved her. Perhaps if he knew how much they loved each other, he would understand.

Antonia didn't have an opportunity to speak to her father until late that night. He had once more taken the buggy and was gone from the ranch when she returned. She was worried that no one knew where he was. He had never taken so many trips alone, especially since his legs had worsened. And each time he returned, he was tense and tired and in pain.

After one such trip, she asked if Jose or she couldn't help. He had looked at her with a sad thoughtful expression. "I must do something, Antonia, to remain a man."

"But you do much."

"I look after the books. There is not much challenge in that."

"And this other thing . . . ? It is a challenge?"

"It is duty, Antonia. And something I must do."

"Duty to what?"

"You wouldn't understand, Antonia. And I am very tired. Come help me to bed."

He would say no more, but now every time he disappeared, she worried. She knew Ramon was somehow a part of it. She couldn't help but believe he was leading her father into something wrong. She had vowed, then, to follow Don Miguel the next time, but it was almost as if he sensed that. He had taken no more trips, until today . . . when she had been gone.

Now she waited for him impatiently. There were so many things that needed to be discussed, including Tristan. There were also a number of decisions to be made. They needed money for supplies and grain to see them through the rest of the winter, and she knew there were stacks of bills on her father's desk. They would have to sell some of their horses. It was always an agonizing choice, for she hated to see any of them go and worried about the care they would receive from new owners. The sale of horses was usually a joint decision between her and her father, but lately he had dismissed such questions with a wave of his hand. He had let that go, as he seemed to be letting many other things go.

Why?

He had never been a good manager, and she knew it. He had loved the outdoors and activity, and when his injuries prevented that, he had taken over the books, wanting to be important to the ranch, to feel a part of its vitality. But it was not the same as riding his land with the vaqueros, and Antonia knew his heart had never really been in it. He was not a meticulous man nor a careful one, and she suspected the books were not in the best of order.

When she questioned him about it, she received vague answers, and he made her feel ungrateful for asking. Antonia was afraid that he was in financial trouble he did not want to tell her about. Their conversation a month ago, when he had urged her once more to marry Ramon, had only confirmed it.

She decided to look at the books while she waited for him. Antonia found them in the bottom drawer of his desk. She felt a certain guilt as she started glancing through them. Never before in her life had she spied. But then, never before had she met someone secretly, either. Her sins were accumulating at a rapid rate.

Perhaps if she could discover the extent of their indebtedness, she would find some way to right things, and without Ramon hovering around, her father might more readily accept Tristan.

Antonia kept one ear open for the sound of the buggy as she poured over the books. It was worse than she had thought possible.

The Mexican authorities, while not taxing land, taxed just about everything on it: cattle, sheep, crops. Every sale carried a heavy tax. And the money to pay the taxes had all been borrowed from Ramon.

Like most ranches, the Ramirez holding was land rich and money poor. There were always new expenses: the vaqueros and their families, winter fodder, food and clothing. And taxes. Always taxes.

How could her father not welcome the Americans?

Tristan had offered to help and had said that he had funds. But this much? Even if there was some way to get her father to accept them.

Antonia closed the ledger. Her father was so proud of his ancestors, of the courage that brought them here and kept them here, of the land that had been in their family seven generations, of the pure Spanish blood that flowed through their veins.

He had made her proud of it, too. Until she had met Tristan, she had never expected to marry anyone but a Creole like herself. Two hundred years was much history to defy.

But she had looked at Ramon and at Tristan, and she readily saw which was the better man. Spanish blood, if corrupted, meant little.

First things first, she told herself. She must prepare the list of horses to be sold and a list of possible buyers. The American army, of course, would be the logical choice, but she suspected her father would not accept that. He would take a lower price instead. She had to convince him otherwise. If he dealt with the new American authorities, perhaps he would discover on his own that there were good, decent men among them.

When he left the hill, Tris once more followed Antonia until he felt she was safe, then turned back to where he had secured the man who had been trailing him.

The Mexican was still where he had been left, shivering with cold and terror. He didn't wish to freeze to death, but neither did he wish to face the American's hard cold eyes again. His wrists were torn with his efforts to escape and his mouth was dry.

He looked up fearfully when the tall gringo took his knife from a sheath on his belt and approached him. He flinched as the blade cut away his gag and then touched his neck. He felt a trickle of blood drip down his skin.

"Who sent you?"

Tomas Gomez had always considered himself a brave man. Until now. He did not wish to die this way. He wanted to swallow, but the knife was tight against his throat.

"Who was it?" the Yanqui devil asked again.

No one, not even Ramon Silvero had frightened Tomas the way this man did: coldness in his eyes, the unforgiving set of his lips. "Señor Silvero," he whispered.

The tight lips curved into a frightening smile.

"You are a smart man, *señor.*"

The Mexican said nothing.

"Your name, *señor?* I wish to remember it." The knife once more nicked the skin.

"Gomez." The sound was more a croak than a word.

The knife hesitated, and Gomez thoroughly expected his throat to be cut. He was stupefied, instead, when the knife moved away and cut his bonds.

"Get the hell out of here," Tris said, surveying the man with contempt. "If I ever see you again, I'll kill you."

The Mexican could barely move. His limbs were stiff and numb, and he couldn't believe the words he had heard. *"Señor?"*

"Before I change my mind," Tris added.

The man needed no more encouragement. Forcing his legs to move, he hobbled painfully to his horse, noting immediately that his rifle was gone. His pistol and knife had been taken earlier. He mounted, then looked back for a long moment at the gringo. Would this one who moved through the night and attacked like a cougar, shoot him in the back? Surely, he was a blond devil.

Tomas Gomez spurred his horse cruelly, deciding to obey. He would get the hell out of here. He cursed Don Ramon and hoped he would rot in hell.

Tris waited until the man was out of sight, then started to follow the tracks, wondering whether the Mexican would report to Silvero. When the trail started up into the mountains, he decided the bandit had taken his advice.

He smiled to himself, wondering what the rancher would think when his second man failed to appear.

There was a certain satisfaction at the thought.

Chapter Eleven

Ramon came to the humiliating knowledge he had under-estimated the gringo scout. Badly.

Gomez had disappeared as if he'd never existed. It was the third time the American had escaped him. *Por Dios,* Hampton had more lives than a damn cat.

At first, Ramon had attributed it to luck, but now he could no longer deny the fact that the gringo was good, very good.

He also knew that Hampton probably suspected him, but he had taken great pains to see that nothing could be traced back to himself or his ranch. The two Mexicans had been hired guns, both new to the area. Ramon had made sure of that.

He stalked the comfortable main room of his ranch. Hampton had been hiding something. No question about that, either. Could he be meeting Antonia again?

The very thought made Silvero's blood boil. He had wanted Antonia since she had been a bewitching child with huge dark eyes and a laughing mouth.

He wanted her laughter back. He wanted to see her eyes wide with admiration.

Dammit all. Damn Hampton.

Ramon had never loved a person other than Antonia, and he wondered what it would be like if she loved him. She might have, if it were not for the gringo. But he had seen how she looked at Hampton at the dance. He wanted her to look that way at him.

A gringo, for the love of God.

His hands clenched into tight fists as he thought of them together. He would not underestimate Hampton again. The next time, the scout would die.

"Papa?"

Don Miguel turned his attention from his dinner to Antonia.

"I've made a list of horses that can be sold," she was saying. "Perhaps then we can pay Ramon back a little of what we owe him."

Miguel shook his head. "Ramon says the Americans plan to impose even more taxes."

"Ramon says. What does Señor Bent say?"

Miguel averted his eyes. If things went as planned, Señor Bent would not be governor much longer. They would have their own governor, one who understood the old families, the old traditions.

But he didn't like the means, even if Ramon insisted it was the only way. Don Miguel did not like killing. He never had. He had hoped that Ramon might give up when part of the plot had been uncovered in Santa Fe. Instead, Ramon and the others, including the Taos priest, Father Martinez, were continuing to stir up hatred among the Indians. Don Miguel wondered if they were building a fire they would be unable to quench. He and others had been recruited to give their assurances that they would support the patriots who rose against the Americans. It was necessary, Ramon had explained, that they be as one in this.

He knew he was neglecting his ranch, leaving more and more of the decisions to Antonia, but he couldn't seem to concentrate anymore. He was tired. So tired.

His face softened as he looked at his daughter. She was so beautiful...just like her mother. There was the same glow about her now that Theresa had had when she looked at him. Perhaps Antonia's heart was softening toward Ramon. He had never understood why she didn't want to marry the young man.

"Papa?"

He shook his head, trying to remember what Antonia had asked.

"The horses?"

"Do what you think best, Antonia," he said.

"The Americans will probably give the best price."

His head spun up this time, the words breaking into his lethargy. "No," he said. "We will not sell horses to those who would conquer us."

"Are they so different from those who did rule us?" Antonia asked quietly.

"They are gringos . . . heretics . . . with manners of pigs."

"Señor Bent is quite pleasant," Antonia ventured.

"We will look for other buyers," Miguel said adamantly.

Antonia hesitated. "I don't think they're all bad. Señor Hampton, whom I danced with at Francesca's, was really quite pleasant, and Augustin admires him."

Don Miguel felt even older and more weary. He had seen the two at the dance, had seen the way they had looked at each other. He didn't think they had had a chance to be together since; the American had been in Santa Fe most of the time. But he didn't like the look in Antonia's eyes now, nor the softening of her mouth. He didn't like it at all.

His lips tightened as he remembered the other gringos, the Texans who came where they were not wanted and took from him his dearest possession. What if this American wished to take Antonia from him?

His thoughts bitter, he looked at the sparkle that had appeared in Antonia's face as she spoke of the gringo. A huge lump settled in the pit of his stomach as he realized it was not Ramon who had put the glow in his daughter's cheeks.

"You do not feel anything for this man, do you, Antonia?"

She didn't know how to answer. She had never directly lied to her father. She was, in fact, terrible at lying.

"He is, as I said, very pleasant and I like him." An understatement, she told herself. An understatement, not a lie.

"I will not have you see him," Don Miguel said with unaccustomed forcefulness.

"He is a friend of Augustin's," Antonia countered. "And of Maria Bent and Josepha Carson. I am bound to see him."

There was something in her voice that frightened Miguel.

"He is a gringo. He cannot be trusted. If Augustin is a fool, then so be it. Americans bring only trouble and tragedy."

"They're not all alike, Father." Antonia's voice was pleading. "Anymore than all of us are alike."

"They killed your mother," Don Miguel retorted, his bitterness spilling out of him like lava from a volcano. Antonia shivered. She had never heard such venom in her father's voice.

"We had done nothing to them. They came from nowhere...three men. They shot Jesus like a dog. And when the buggy overturned, they laughed when I begged them to help my wife. They laughed, Antonia."

Antonia saw tears gather in his eyes, and she ached with sympathy for him. She could understand his hatred of the Americans. Understand, but not share it.

She tried to say so. "Those men were not like Señor Bent—"

"They are all adventurers, Antonia, who care only about themselves. They know nothing of the people who settled this area, who fought for the right to live here and to keep the land."

Somewhere, in the recesses of her mind, Antonia reluctantly remembered that Tristan had left his Virginia home because of restlessness, because he wanted to see beyond the next hill.

Her face was pale, and Don Miguel wondered if he had done the right thing in reminding her about her mother. But perhaps it would convince her of the perfidy of gringos, perhaps it would save her from heartbreak.

Antonia felt painfully, hopelessly sick. There was a knot at the bottom of her stomach that she didn't think would ever go away. She wondered how she would have felt if she watched Tristan die, unable to do anything to help him. She may not have understood two months ago, but now she did.

Her father's face was drawn, his eyes full of pain. She realized how much it must have cost him to retell the story. All the bitter hurt, all the anger and all the guilt of not being able to do anything had been brought to the surface.

She had almost convinced herself that she and Tristan should declare their love, that her father would accept a deed done, but now she knew he never would. Her actions would only add to his pain. Could she take her happiness at his expense? Could she risk further danger to his health?

How would she make Tristan understand?

A terrible gnawing grief flooded her.

"I don't like leaving you here alone," Tris argued.

"Me, or Antonia?" Charles Bent asked.

"Either one of you," Tris countered with a grin. "We're not sure the plotting against you has stopped."

"Maybe these orders will help soothe things," Charles replied. "Everyone expects me to hang those conspirators. A little leniency should go a long way to show our good intentions."

"I still don't like it. You were a principal target in Santa Fe."

"In Santa Fe," Charles agreed. "Not here. This is my home, remember. I know everyone here."

"I still don't like you being without any protection at all."

Charles grinned. "I've been full grown for a long time now, Tris." He sobered. "But you be careful. There have been more attacks against you than me. Perhaps I'll be safer without you."

"True," Tris admitted dryly.

"I don't want anyone to know you're leaving."

Tris nodded. "I'll come back as soon as possible."

"Just make sure Stirling Price doesn't do anything with those prisoners. He was out for blood."

"I'll leave tonight at moonrise."

"No more stalkers?"

"Not that I've been able to detect," Tris replied. By God, he was tired of looking behind him, of doubling back to check every shadow. He had purposely stayed away from the hill, hoping against hope that Antonia would find some means to contact him. Antonia would have to make her own decision; he didn't want to make it for her.

"I'll miss you, Tris," Charles said. "You keep life sort of interesting."

Tris grinned. He would miss Charles Bent. Next to Conn, Bent had become his best friend. He liked everything about the governor: his warmth, his affection for his family, his independence. And they fought well together. There was something about depending upon each other for their lives that forged steellike bonds between men.

Tris tried to dismiss the disquiet he felt about leaving. Perhaps Charles was right. Perhaps leniency to the conspirators would finally bring around the last of the group. It might even change Miguel Ramirez's opinion of Americans, he thought hopefully.

"I'll be back in three, four days," he said.

Charles shook his head. "Don't push it. I want you to talk to Price and the other officers. Doniphan is screaming for the artillery that Price has in Santa Fe. I want to know when Price plans on sending it."

Tris agreed. Aside from his own misadventures, things seemed calm enough in Taos. Charles knew these people far better than he, and if the governor said there was nothing to worry about, then who was Tris, a newcomer, to disagree?

But despite Charles's words, Tris planned to make it a damned quick trip.

Charles changed the subject. "If Ramirez has the money problems you believe he does, I think I might have a solution. I've talked to a friend, a Creole in the Santa Fe area, who is a friend of Ramirez. He's willing to be a go-between. He doesn't like Silvero, either."

Tris's mouth crooked in a slight smile. "What can he do?"

"Ramirez usually sells some of his horses about this time of year. Our friend will offer some damned good prices, superior ones, in fact . . . on your silent behalf, of course"

Tris's smile widened. It was a step forward. Perhaps it would separate Silvero and Ramirez a bit if Ramirez could pay off his debts.

"Thank you."

"Even if it can be arranged," Charles warned, "don't be too optimistic. Don Miguel still dislikes Anglos, whether or not he's in debt to Silvero." He grinned. "I doubt even your charm will help much, although I don't think I'll bet on that." Charles winked at Tris. "If I didn't know Maria loved me, and you loved Antonia, I'd be worrying a bit."

Tris included Maria in his broad answering smile. "And you would have to," he answered mischievously as the subject of their conversation blushed. Tris's eyes went from Maria to Charles enviously. They had three children and were obviously still very much in love.

Tris hoped he and Antonia would be the same way years from now. With that contented thought, he excused himself from the table to catch some sleep. He planned to leave several hours after dark in the small hours of the night. The sky was clear; the moon and stars on the glistening white snow should provide enough light.

It was now January 17. He would be back no later than the twentieth. The ride might be just what he needed to clear his head. His impatience and restlessness were taking its toll, and he was afraid if he were in Taos much longer, he would storm the Ramirez ranch and take Antonia, willing or not. Civilization had its drawbacks. For a moment, he wished he were a Viking of old and could just carry her off.

When he started out, he felt the whisper of anticipation. As he had grown accustomed to doing in the past week, he backtracked to see whether he was being followed. He was not. He hunched down into his saddle, pulling the collar of his jacket up to his ears and his hat down over them. The night sky was bright, and the air cold and crisp. God, but he was coming to love this country, even the winters, which he had hated in Virginia. There was something about the glistening ice and snow against the vivid red rocks and blue mountains that enchanted him.

That he was completely alone was evident. The only sounds were the echo of Nugget's hoofbeats and the occasional hoot of an owl.

Tris thought of how much he had changed in the past months. He had been restless for years, and now he could think of nothing he wanted more than to stay in this place.

Dawn came, and he wished that Tonia was with him to watch the sky turn from gray to pale rose to a soft gold as the sun tipped over the mountains to shine benevolently on the frozen earth. He urged his horse into a slow trot. He wanted to make Santa Fe before nightfall.

Santa Fe was noisy. It was always noisy since the American army had descended upon it. Exhausted from the long ride, Tris decided to bunk down in the officers' quarters and meet with General Price in the morning. One way or another, he would start back the day after tomorrow.

For one of the few times in his life, he surrendered the care of Nugget to another man after innumerable instructions and dire threats. He quickly found a bed and collapsed on it, his mind too weary to think of Antonia or Charles Bent or Taos.

As Tris and Charles had anticipated, General Price was not happy with the governor's decision. There had been rebellion, and the instigators should be punished as traitors, never mind that it had been their country just weeks earlier.

But Governor Bent was the civil authority and had the right to pardon. Price would, however, keep them in the filthy jail under the Palacio until he was sure the rebellion had been smashed.

He had already sent most of his artillery down to Doniphan, who was continuing to move farther south toward Chihuahua. Except for the Christmas Day battle, Doniphan's Missourians had encountered no further opposition, but they expected a big fight when they reached Mexico. Price, however, held a large force in Santa Fe to protect northern New Mexico.

Tris collected some letters from his family in Virginia. He missed them. And he wanted a family just like his own, big and boisterous, full of the devil and as diverse as his own siblings.

Refusing an invitation to go drinking, he went to bed early. He had accomplished everything he could here and he wanted to see Tonia. He also couldn't rid himself of a certain foreboding about Charles Bent, probably because of the attacks Tris had already suffered. Apparently those had had little to do with Governor Bent, but he would still leave very early. Damn, but if he wasn't digging a trench between here and Taos.

Chapter Twelve

Ramon watched the wagons drive off without a twinge of guilt.

This was war. And there were few boundaries in war.

His one concession had been to warn the Indian leaders against killing women and children. Only the gringo men. Particularly Charles Bent and Tristan Hampton.

The wagon was full of whiskey heading for the Pueblos. The Indians were already enraged after three of their number had been jailed by the sheriff and demands for their release had been met with insults. The Pueblos were boiling over with anger and the whiskey would remove whatever inhibitions they had. It was exactly what Ramon had been waiting for.

Tonight, Taos would be a bloodbath.

And tomorrow, when they realized the governor had been killed, the New Mexicans would rise against the American usurpers and drive them from Mexican soil. Ramon had many pledges of support.

He would then be among the most important men in the territory. Perhaps he would even be made governor.

Antonia could not refuse him then.

And the American would be dead.

He hoped Miguel would remain strong, but he had seen the man wavering as the time drew closer. Miguel was well liked among the New Mexico families, but he was weak. He had always been weak. And he had a decided distaste for violence.

Didn't he know that nothing great was accomplished without it?

Perhaps, Ramon thought, he would ride over and make sure Miguel did nothing foolish. The Creoles and Mexicans were safe. He thought about the plague that swept Egypt and killed the first-born male of each family. His plan was like that plague, a disease that would strike every Anglo that had tried to usurp the rightful government of Mexico.

Antonia was exhausted. She had been riding all day with the vaqueros as they rounded up the horses. She was glad for the activity, relieved that she would have little time to think about Tristan or to even consider going to their hill. She had conscientiously stayed away from it, even as she longed to ride up there and feel his arms around her.

She had not seen or heard anything of him in the last several days. She was bitterly afraid of seeing him, of succumbing to his determined will.

It was dark when she returned to the house, and she gave her horse to Jose.

"Señor Ramon just left, *señorita,*" he said.

So she had done something right today. Antonia smiled as much as her weariness allowed and walked to the hacienda.

Luz was in the kitchen and glanced at her young mistress with a worried expression. "Don Miguel and Don Ramon waited a long time for you. They were worried."

"Where is Father now?"

"He was very tired...and very upset." It was one of the few times Antonia had heard censure in Luz's voice.

"Someone has to oversee the vaqueros." Antonia's retort was sharper than she had intended, but she was hungry and cold.

Luz dropped her gaze. "You work too hard."

"Has Father gone to bed?"

"Yes."

"I shall let him sleep, then," Antonia said, watching Luz's busy hands quickly shaping some tamales.

Antonia ate quickly, more than ready to go to bed. Her muscles were sore and her mind was tired. As she went to her room, she stopped at her father's door and heard restless noises and the clump of his crutches.

She knocked, then entered. They had never stood on ceremony.

Her father was still dressed. His face was lined and his lips were trembling. His hands shook.

When he looked at her, it was with clouded dark eyes.

"Papa, what's wrong?"

It took a moment for his eyes to focus on her. His mouth trembled even more.

"What's wrong?" she repeated.

"The rebellion," he muttered.

"The rebellion?"

"Against the gringos. It is starting."

Tonia stood in shock. "What . . . rebellion?"

"I did not know, Antonia." His voice faltered slightly. "I did not know what Ramon had planned. . . ."

"What?" Her voice was heavy with fear.

"Ramon asked for my help in uniting the Spanish families, to guarantee their support in an uprising. I didn't know he would use the Indians . . . God help me, I did not know."

"What do you mean, Father?" Her body stiffened as she knew she was about to hear something terrible.

"The Indians. They are attacking the gringos in Taos tonight."

Antonia leaned against the wall for support. "Oh, dear Mother, no." Tristan was in Taos, staying with the Bents. A half moan came from her lips. "What have you done?" she whispered.

"I was . . . trying to help drive the Yanquis from my country," he said, faltering at the accusation in her eyes.

"And you incite Indians to do it for you?" The bitter words came pouring from her lips. She had to get to Taos, had to warn Maria and Charles Bent, had to warn Tristan.

She whirled out the door, mindless of her father's pleading call.

Night Wind was tired from the long day's work. Antonia quickly saddled the next fastest horse she could find and mounted, urgently pressing her heels into its side.

It was seven miles to Taos. Dear God, let her be on time.

Charles Bent realized he probably wouldn't live through the night. The best he could do was to try to protect his wife and children. He and Maria and their houseguests, Maria's sister and Mrs. Thomas Boggs, had awakened to gunshots and yells. Dressing quickly, he had gone out to pacify the angry crowd of Indians surrounding the house. He had done the same thing many times before as a trader, but this time, there was so much noise he could not hear himself talk. And no one was listening.

He had come back inside and fetched his guns, telling Maria to start tunneling a hole through the earthen wall into the next house. He would try to delay the attackers.

But when he faced the crowd again, he knew he would never escape. Whiskey had dulled their senses. They screamed that they would not leave an American alive in New Mexico. "Since you are governor," one shouted, "we will kill you first."

Bent felt a deadly calm as he looked over the hate-torn faces of men he had considered friends. He had been wrong and Tristan had been right.

He held his guns but didn't shoot. If he did, the Indians might go after the women and children as well as himself. Over and over again, he tried to speak, but his voice couldn't be heard above the taunts.

The mob moved closer, and a lump lodged in his throat as his hands tightened on his guns. He felt a sudden overwhelming sorrow for his family. He had lived with danger all his life, and he had never feared death, but now he felt a deep sense of failure. He had worked and traded with these Indians since the twenties and had thought them friends. He had always dealt with them fairly, more fairly than many of the New Mexican ranchers had. Leading them were Romero and Montoya, two Indian leaders he had known for years.

Charles heard gunshots and screams in other parts of town, and he could only surmise what was happening. There were a number of other Americans in Taos.

"Kill the gringos," the chant went up. "Kill the gringos." There was no reason in the mob. Faces were twisted with liquor and rage and three hundred years of resentment against the white man.

The governor turned to Maria, who was hovering nearby. "For God's sake, hurry," he said. "Get the children out of here."

"Use your guns," she begged.

He shook his head. "Just hurry."

Maria joined Josepha Carson and Mrs. Boggs in digging through to the next house, using a poker and iron spoons. They heard the noise of their neighbors digging on the other side of the wall. Perhaps Charles could get out, too.

"Charles?"

But all his attention was back on the screaming, yelling mob. An arrow sped through the air, fixing itself in the adobe above Charles's head.

"We're through," he heard an exultant yell behind him, and he waited at the door, wanting his family to get through before he moved. His guns remained at his side.

He felt pain, intense fiery pain in his shoulder, then in his leg, and he saw the arrows protruding from his body like pins from his wife's pin cushion. Almost from a distance he heard the crack of a gun, and agony sliced through his chest.

He fell back through the door and a hand grabbed his hair. Another pain, worse than any of the others, swept him as he realized he was being scalped alive. Still, he tried to crawl away, to the hole, to Maria. Blood coursed down his face until he could barely see; yet he moved slowly but determinedly. A red haze blinded him and then everything started to fade, to turn gray. Some of the pain seeped away, and he was drifting. There was one more lacerating stroke, but now it seemed as if it were happening to someone else, someone else....

"Maria," he cried. But there was no answer, only blackness.

* * *

Her horse drenched with sweat and heaving with exhaustion, Antonia reached Taos and instantly knew she was too late. Even from a distance she could see the fires and hear the screaming.

Approaching cautiously, she hugged the shadows, grateful that her horse was dark and she was wearing black. Down one street, crowds of Indians were running wild, yelling exultantly and holding up their bloody souvenirs. The night was spiked with the echoing sounds of gunshots and mortal cries.

Sick with fear and revulsion, she dismounted in the shadow of a building and tied her horse to a nearby bush. The Bent home was several hundred yards away. She inched against the walls toward the house, ducking back when she saw a group of five Indians swaggering drunkenly down the street. After they passed, she continued her cautious advance. Tristan. Maria. Nothing could stop her from knowing what happened. Nothing. Terror for Tristan wrapped like steel fingers around her heart, squeezing until she could barely breathe. If anything had happened to him because of her father, she couldn't bear to live.

The door to the Bent house was open, the doorway littered with arrows and blood. Antonia wanted to fall on her knees and be sick, but she forced herself on, tracing the sticky trail of blood to the hole in the back wall.

Antonia got down on her hands and knees and crawled through it, praying each inch of the way. She came out in another room, and she stopped at the sight of the shocked white faces around the body in the corner.

She had seen death. Anyone who lived in New Mexico had seen sudden violent death: gunshot wounds, snake bites, men broken or trampled by horses. But never had she seen the kind of vicious mayhem committed on Charles Bent's body. There seemed to be hundreds of wounds, and his scalp was gone. His eyes were closed, but his mouth was still twisted in agony.

Antonia had not know him well, but she knew that Maria loved him dearly and that he was Tristan's friend.

Tristan. Oh, dear Mother, where was Tristan?

Everyone was staring at her. There were five women in the room. Maria, tears streaming down her face, was trying to clean some of the blood from her husband's body with a cloth. Her tears came faster as she spied Antonia, but she was too dazed to even wonder how or why Antonia had appeared.

"He wouldn't defend himself," Maria whispered. "He was afraid they would hurt me or the children if he did."

Antonia's heart shattered. Her father had been partly responsible for this. At the moment, she hated him, hated herself for being a part of him.

"Señor Hampton?" she finally managed to ask. Dear God, let him be alive. But he never would have left Charles Bent to die alone. Never.

Josepha Carson answered for her sister. "He is in Santa Fe, thank God. The Indians asked for him."

Thankfulness, like a storm-swollen river, flooded Antonia even though she despised herself for it. How could she feel relief when Charles Bent lay mutilated and dead before her?

Tristan's friend!

He would never forgive her for her father's part in this. He was intensely loyal to those he cared about, those he loved.

Emotions warred bitterly inside her until she wanted to scream—grief for Charles Bent, anguish for Maria, loss for herself, shame and anger toward her father. She felt herself trembling as the enormity of events overwhelmed her.

A hand reached out to give her support, but she shook it off, not able to bear the touch of these people her family had wronged. Nor could she cry. The horror was too deep, too piercing.

Maria was still trying, ineffectively, to clean the body of her husband, and Antonia heard one of the Mexicans speak, as if from a distance.

"We will bury him soon, before they come back and try to take the body. Will you come with us?"

Antonia realized the Mexicans were risking much to help Maria and Josepha. Would they hate her when they discovered her father's part? Would they resent her for participating in the sacred ritual?

Maria held out her hand. "Please?"

Antonia nodded, unable to do anything else. Taking another cloth, she helped bathe the pale, lifeless body, wondering how Maria could bear to see the many jagged wounds and the disfigured face. Yet patiently, lovingly, her friend kept at her task, fingers tender in their last ministrations.

The burial ceremony was short, the night air still cut with cries of hate and vengeance. There was no peace to soften the loss, no words of hope to comfort. Antonia stood beside Maria thinking there would never again be peace or comfort for her.

When they returned to the neighbor's home, there were other Mexicans there. Maria moved as if in a dream. The children were still awake, their young faces filled with terror and grief. Antonia tried to comfort Teresita, who was only five, but nothing could still her steady stream of tears or her cries for her father.

When dawn came, Antonia and the others heard the rest of the nightmare. All but two of the Americans in town had been killed; among the dead were the sheriff, Stephen Lee; the prefect, Cornelio Vigil; and Narcisse Beubien, son of the local judge. The prosecuting attorney, James Leal, had been brutally tortured to death, and Pablo Jaramillo, brother-in-law to Charles Bent and Kit Carson, had been riddled with bullets and arrows.

Of the two Americans who escaped death, one had been hidden by a priest, and the other, Charles Towne, had escaped on a fast mule.

The report of Towne's escape was the only good news of the morning. He would reach General Price and bring help.

Antonia stayed, unwilling to go home. She didn't think she could face her father or even share the same dwelling with him. She felt dead. She longed for Tristan, even as she dreaded to see him again.

Yet she could not betray her father, no matter what he had done.

When someone finally asked why she had come to Taos, she merely said she had heard two of their hired hands speaking of a possible uprising. She cringed each time, knowing the lies were a sin. How could she ever forgive her father? She thought of how he had held her so tenderly in his arms so many years ago, how he taught her to ride, how his eyes lit every time she came in the room.

And then Charles Bent's battered face appeared in her mind.

How could she not go mad?

It was nearing dusk. Bands of Indians and Mexicans were still prowling the streets. She had heard that some women had ventured forth to retrieve the body of Señor Leal, which had been tossed to the wild hogs in the streets. She also heard that the Indians were still looking for Hampton.

What if Tris came back, not knowing what awaited?

Still in a daze, Antonia left, doubting anyone would notice. Everyone was steeped in their own tragedy.

She found her horse, chastising herself for leaving it unattended for more than twelve hours. She had never done that before in her life. She was extremely lucky the gelding was still there.

She would take him home, see he was cared for. Then she would get Night Wind and ride out along the Santa Fe trail to meet Tristan before anyone less friendly had the same thought.

And she would say goodbye.

She would protect her father. No matter what he had done, she could not let him hang. And that meant leaving Tristan. She knew there would never be a way to bring them together now.

"How could you, Papa?" she whispered to the wind. But it had no answer.

Jose had a forbidding frown as Antonia and her tired horse approached the ranch. "*Señorita,* Don Miguel is very worried about you."

Antonia slowly dismounted and handed him the reins. "Saddle Night Wind," she said. "I'll be going back out."

"But Don Miguel?"

Antonia looked at Jose with an expression he had never seen before. "Please, Jose."

The man nodded. He would do it, but it would be a waste. When she saw her father, she would not leave. Don Miguel was very ill.

Antonia, disheveled, dirty and physically and emotionally exhausted, slowly made her way to her father's room. He was lying in bed, looking years older than he had the day before.

"Antonia." He tried to sit but slumped back. "Dear God, where have you been?"

For the first time in her life, she looked at him coldly. "Taos. I rode to warn them, but you will probably be pleased to hear I was too late. They killed Governor Bent. They scalped him while he was still alive...."

Her father's face paled and his lips trembled. "Antonia," he gasped.

"And then they tortured Señor Leal...all night they tortured him. Does that make you happy, Father?"

Rage and sorrow poured out of Antonia. Everything she had believed, everything she had loved had been devoured in flames last night.

"Antonia... Dear God, I didn't realize..."

The horror in her eyes made him realize for the first time exactly what he had done. He couldn't even use the excuse that he hadn't known what might happen. He hadn't wanted to know. He had thought that he was merely uniting the old Spanish families, that he had nothing to do with Ramon's other plans. But he should have known, should have been aware of all the possibilities. And now the blood was on his hands. He didn't know if he could live with it.

Antonia stared at his waxen face, wondering if this man who had been, in part, responsible for cold-blooded murders could be the one she had loved all these years. She ignored his outstretched hand, the tears she had been holding back now falling down her cheeks. "I don't want to be your daughter."

Antonia saw him flinch, his eyes fill with pain.

She shook her head. "I thought I knew you. I loved you. Dear Mother of God, I still love you. But I will never, never, forgive you for the horror you helped cause last night."

The words were rushing out and she didn't know how to stop them.

"I love one of the men you sought to kill. I will love him until the day I die. But now there can be nothing between us. Nothing except hate and death." She rushed out, unable to bear his presence—or the stricken look on his face.

She didn't stop to change her clothes, but added a heavy coat, then went to the kitchen and asked Luz to pack some bread and cheese and dried meat.

"Do not go," Luz begged. She had never seen Antonia like this, her usually composed face streaked with tears, her mouth trembling yet determined.

"I must," Antonia said. "I don't know when I will be back." She hesitated. "Take care of Father."

When she reached the stable, she tied two additional blankets to the saddle. Night Wind nickered as Antonia mounted and pressed her heels into the horse's side. She would go to the Rio Grande Gorge. She didn't know if Tristan would return today or tomorrow or the next day. But when he did, she would be there to warn him.

She thought about going to Santa Fe to stop him, but she might miss him, and so might Charles Towne, who had ridden for help. There were several trails, but he would have to come through those rocks. She shivered as she thought of the explanations she would **have** to make. Tristan would ask the questions. He would want to know everything. And he knew her so well. So very well.

Several times she passed groups of riders—New Mexicans and Indians—but none bothered her. They had, strangely enough, not hurt any woman.

Please, Lord, let me reach Tristan before anyone else does. Please.

When she reached a place in the rocks she thought safe, she took some bread from the saddle bags and wrapped herself in a blanket. She was tired, so very tired. It had been nearly two days since she had had any sleep. She started nibbling on the bread, more to keep awake than from hunger. She wondered if she would ever be hungry again. She kept seeing the governor's body, kept hearing the cries.

The day turned gray as frothy clouds whirled above in angry races with each other. The wind grew colder, and she pressed the blanket closer to her body, willing herself to keep her eyes fixed on the trail below.

The cottonwoods and aspens swayed with the wind, singing a haunting melody of their own. The sky grew a dark, ominous, purple. It suited Antonia's chilled and lonely spirit as she thought that nothing would ever be right again.

She didn't realize she had dozed until she heard the clattering of hoofbeats. Instantly alert, she listened as the sound grew louder.

Tristan. She knew it. Somehow she sensed it. Her body grew rigid and she fingered the rifle she had brought with her.

The *clip clop* of hoofs was louder now; the rider was making no effort at caution.

She started to scramble down, to meet him at the bottom when she heard the gunshot. It echoed through the rocks, and she realized someone else had staked out the gorge. Perhaps they were waiting for Tristan, perhaps for anyone. Thank God, they had not seen her.

Antonia thought of Charles Bent once more. She would not let it happen to Tristan. She crawled upward among the rocks, moving silently across rough terrain now darkened by a cloudy sky.

She heard another shot, then a third from a different location. Wanting to hurry but afraid she would betray her presence if she did, Antonia slowly inched herself to a high position, then looked down.

A figure lay beside a golden horse and another man was stumbling down to reach him, a gun in his hand. Antonia didn't wait to see more. She sighted her rifle, her finger curling around the trigger.

Images moved in her mind. Images from last night. Blood and violence and terror.

She squeezed the trigger.

The man fell, and another stood, looking down in surprise before scanning the rocks. Antonia quickly drew back and reloaded the rifle. When she looked again, the second man was gone.

Antonia waited, every second a lifetime as she wondered how badly the figure below was hurt. She heard a noise above and to the left, and she swung the rifle in that direction. The man had not seen her. He was searching, but her black riding costume blended with the darkening landscape. He, on the other hand, was wearing a white shirt and it stood out like a beacon.

Once more, Antonia aimed. The man went down to his knees and then fell over.

She waited for several minutes, but no one else appeared. The evening silence was absolute. Even the night birds were still. The only sound was the whistling of a defiant wind.

Antonia hurried down, falling, stumbling, rolling. Rocks grazed and cut her arms, but the pain was nothing compared to her worry for the man below.

When she reached him, he lay still. Blood clotted at a wound on the side of his head, but his breathing was regular and when she knelt down and put her ear to his heart, the beat was strong.

We must get away from here. It was obvious someone had set guards over the passage, and she had no idea when they were scheduled to be relieved.

But how? He was so large.

"Tristan?" She called to him over and over again, but he was unconscious and nothing seemed to stir him.

And where could she take him? Certainly not home. She couldn't be sure where the vaqueros' loyalty lay... to her father or to her.

It would be cold tonight. Despite her many clothes, she was chilled to the bone, and Tristan needed warmth. She would have to find a cave. There were many in these rocks. She needed only to find an empty one; she didn't fancy happening on to a bear.

She eyed him speculatively. He was wearing the same sheepskin jacket he had on the last time she saw him. His hat had come off when he fell, and his gold hair was bright even in the evening gloom, except where the blood seeped from his wound. For a moment, she was reminded once more of Bent, and she shivered. She would never forget that sight.

Tristan's stillness frightened her. She was so accustomed to his energy, to his restless, impatient movements.

Night Wind was still some distance away, but she dared not leave Tristan even for a few moments. She went to his horse and, ignoring the nervous movements of the golden stallion, found some rope. She tied the end to Tristan's hands, then she went to the other side of the horse, using the animal's back as leverage as she pulled with all her strength. Tristan's body slowly started to unfold, and she prayed the stallion would remain still and not move. Finally she had Tristan draped halfway across the saddle, and she went back to the other side, and boosted him further up, tying him securely.

She took the reins and led the horse to where Night Wind was tethered. Taking those reins, she whispered softly to both horses, grateful that they had been together previously and now showed no animosity. As silently as possible, she led the horses into the mountains.

Chapter Thirteen

Antonia didn't know how long it took her to find the right shelter. She only knew she was getting colder and colder, and that Tristan wasn't waking up. Yet she was desperately afraid to stop in the open.

She finally found what she was looking for. It was a shallow area with an opening wide enough for the horses, and it was far from the main trail. She led the horses in and untied Tris from the saddle, cushioning him with her own body as he dropped.

In the last faltering light, she studied his wound and discovered there were more than one. A bullet had grazed one side of his head, and contact with the ground when he fell had apparently bruised the other. The blood was drying on his scalp, and neither injury looked death threatening. She started to untie his hands, then thought better of it. What if he insisted on going into Taos? Knowing him as she did, it was not unlikely.

Charles Bent had been his friend. Tristan would be terribly angry, terribly hurt, and could easily do something reckless.

Oh, dear Mother of God, what if he ever found out about her father's role in all this?

Painfully, Antonia came to a decision. Tristan's wrists were raw from having been pulled by the rope. She untied them, wrapped them in cloth torn from her undergarments, then retied them. She then used the additional rope to tie his ankles.

Antonia quickly started a fire. When she finished, she took her canteen from the saddle and washed Tristan's face, calling to him softly at first, then sharply. There was a slight movement, then a second, stronger one. He groaned, and she could see him trying to move his hands. His eyes fluttered open, vivid in the flames of the fire. Confused, he again tried to move his hands and discovered them tied. His eyes, the look in them mirroring his confusion, moved rapidly and found Antonia.

"Tonia?"

She touched his face soothingly. "It's all right. Stay still."

But he continued to search the cave, looking for whoever had tied him. He found no one.

"What . . . in the hell?"

"You were ambushed," Tonia said.

Tris tried to remember. God, this was becoming a habit. And not a very pleasant one. Every time he had come to Taos, he had been set upon. He struggled to sit up, and pain ripped through his head. He probably should have taken more precautions, but he didn't think anyone knew he was traveling. Damn. He closed his eyes, trying to puzzle through what had happened. Why was Tonia here? Why was he tied? Just what in the hell was going on? The pain in his head made it difficult to concentrate.

He held up his hands. "Cut me loose."

Her eyes were luminous in the firelight. Instead of doing as he commanded, she looked away.

His voice softened. "Tonia?"

Despite the quiet tone, there was an irresistible demand in it. She turned to look at him.

"I have to tell you something." Her voice broke.

Tris was suddenly filled with dread as he recalled those doubts he had of leaving Taos. His voice was dangerously soft when he answered. "What, Tonia? What do you have to tell me?"

Tears hovered in back of her eyes, but she knew she couldn't shed them, not now. By sheer strength of will, she held them back. Her voice was low but steady. "There's been—there was . . . trouble in Taos." She watched as Tristan went completely still, every sense alert. He waited for her to go on.

"The Indians...they... Tristan, they killed Governor Bent."

Tristan might have been a statue he was so motionless. His eyes turned to blue ice. "What happened?" His voice had the staccato of pistol shots. "Exactly what happened?"

"Sheriff Lee arrested three of the Pueblo Indians and wouldn't let them go when their people demanded their release. The Indians killed him and all the Americans in Taos. Señor Leal, the judge's son, all of them."

"And Charles?"

"He wouldn't defend himself. He was afraid his wife and children would be killed." Antonia couldn't bear to tell him how Charles had died.

Tris's jaw set and a muscle moved compulsively in his cheek. "I should have been there."

"Then you, too, would be dead."

"Has anyone sent for troops?"

"Charles Towne escaped and went for General Price. I thought you might have met him on the way."

He shook his head. "How did you ...?"

"They are looking for you, for any American, but particularly for you," she said. "Maria said they asked for you. I had to come warn you, and then I heard shots."

"You ...?"

"You were on the ground. I killed them."

He closed his eyes, trying to remember. But all he recalled was riding along. He didn't even remember a shot. "Them?" he said, narrowing his eyes.

"There were two of them. They didn't know I was there until one went down to check you."

Tris considered the information. He looked at her, wondering how the slender woman beside him could kill two men and sound so matter-of-fact about it. And then he saw the blankness in her eyes, and knew she hadn't really comprehended the fact yet.

She had killed for him. He understood her well enough to realize the pain that would cause later ... when some of the shock was gone. Tris swallowed, hurting for her, while fierce pride ran through him that she would risk so much for him. Then other emotions crowded his heart and mind. Deep pain for Charles and Maria. Rage for those who had killed him. A sense of failure.

He lifted his bound hands. "Why...?"

"I was afraid you would try to go into Taos. You can't. Many New Mexicans have joined them, and they are roaming in bands. They will kill any American they see."

He was slowly absorbing the information, putting together the bits and pieces. She was right. He thought about Charles Bent and the other Americans, and his fury grew, needing some outlet. He fought the ropes without success before turning back to Tonia. "Untie me," he demanded in a low voice.

"Not until you promise to stay here until your troops come." Her voice quavered under his demanding look, but the determined set of her chin told him she would not change her mind.

"I can't stay here."

"One way or the other, you must," she replied.

"How long have I been here?"

"Not long...the bullet grazed your head. I think the fall made you unconscious."

He watched her carefully in the flickering light. There was something in her voice that disturbed him, something she was not telling him. And suddenly there were dozens of questions in his mind. How long had she been waiting for him? How did she know where he was?

Tonia shuddered at the thought of lying to Tris. He looked hard and ruthless, all the gentleness gone. If he learned of the plot, she had little doubt that he would go after the leaders. She felt like a rabbit being struck senseless by the eyes and motion of a snake. His eyes, which had once shone with such tenderness, had become flinty and dangerous, his mouth tight, the strong chin set.

It was his stillness, however, that was the most frightening. Antonia knew he was weighing every aspect of his current situation and liked it not at all.

Her fingers tingled with the need to untie him, and she knew that was exactly what he intended. He was willing her to obey.

"What will your father think of your being gone so late at night?"

That question was so sudden that she almost blurted out an angry, hurt reply. At this moment, she didn't care what her father thought. She wondered if she would ever care again.

But she did care what happened to him. She could not allow anything to happen to him. No matter what he had done.

Unable to face Tristan, terrified that he would see something in her face, she sprung to her feet, hiding in the shadows. "He doesn't know," she lied.

"But when you're gone in the morning? Or do you plan to leave me alone, tied?"

"No."

"Tonia, look at me." It was a command she was unable to refuse. She turned slowly back to him.

"There is something you're not telling me."

She was silent.

"You said you talked to Maria. When?"

"This morning."

"Why were you there?"

"I—I heard some vaqueros talking...I wanted to warn Maria. But I was too late."

"I thought the Indians here were peaceful."

"They usually are."

"Have they attacked any of the ranchers? The New Mexicans?"

She shook her head, afraid to speak.

"You said they were also looking for me." His voice was unmerciful as it bored in. "Did Silvero have anything to do with this?"

"All Americans...they were looking for all Americans," she replied in a low voice, avoiding a direct answer. If Tris went after Ramon, he might also find her father. The last remnants of hope faded from her. He *would* find out. It was just a question of when. "I must get some more wood," she said, trying to change the subject. She could bear no more questions.

"I'm thirsty," Tris said.

Antonia stopped in midstride. "The canteen is next to you."

He held up his hands. "I can't hold it with my wrists tied."

Antonia bit her lip in frustration. She didn't want to get close to him right now. But, of course, he would be thirsty and she could not deny him that small request. She went over to where he had struggled to sit up, his back against the cave wall. She knelt, picked up the canteen, removed the cap and held the container to his lips.

He drank greedily, his hands steadying her own as she held the canteen. And then, they tightened around hers. Despite the rope, his fingers were able to trap her wrists, and he pulled her down.

When Antonia recovered her balance, her face was level with Tristan's, and when she tried to twist away, she found that her wrists were caught tighter than ever.

"Let me go," she pleaded.

"When you let *me* go," he retorted.

"Will you promise not to go to Taos?"

"No." The word was flat and conclusive.

"Then I won't untie you."

"Then I won't let you go."

It was, Tris knew, a stalemate. But he also knew his own will, and as much as he loved Antonia, he didn't care for her evasions or tying him like this. He didn't like the feeling of impotence, of being out of control.

He felt her body tense as his grip continued as firmly as before, and then she seemed to slump. Her eyes, at first defiant, were filled with pain, and Tristan couldn't help notice the depth of it. It deflated his own rage.

Tris moved his hands. "Cut the ropes and we'll talk. I promise I won't do anything reckless." It was as close to a pledge as he could make.

It was more than she had expected. And she couldn't leave him bound forever. He was right about that.

"There's a knife in my belt," he added, not giving her a chance to think.

"No, there isn't," she said with a slight smile, the first of the night.

Tris's eyes narrowed as he glanced at the empty sheath on his belt. She was thorough, he had to give her that.

Antonia still hesitated. He had always appeared dangerous to her, but never so much as now. Even uncomfortably tied, he radiated a fierce untamed energy.

Tris noted her hesitancy and dropped his voice a note lower. "I do promise, Tonia."

Their eyes met, and she knew she had no choice. She might as well have been his prisoner for the power he exerted over her. She had to believe him.

She slowly, reluctantly, went to a corner of the cave. He watched as she dug the knife up from a corner. She hadn't taken any chances.

His wrists ached as the rope fell away. Part of his mind registered the cloth wrapped around them for protection and how carefully she had tried to keep from hurting him. Nonetheless, he was stiff from his fall, and the ropes had only compounded his discomfort. Slowly, he tested his arms, then his legs. As he stood, he felt the weakness. But the strength came back, and images returned to his mind.

Images of Charles Bent.

Antonia, who had watched his every move, knew exactly what he was thinking. And she shivered.

Tris saw the movement and reached out, pulling her into his arms, needing her warmth and closeness to ease some of the desolation he felt. She moved as near to him as possible, wanting, needing his touch, but desperately afraid of it and where it would lead.

Their needs ignited together. Their lips touched in tender violence, as each of them sought to soothe the pain of the past hours.

Tris's mouth moved hungrily, his tongue seeking to join her with him, to bring back some of the innocence he felt they had lost, to banish the belief she was hiding things from him.

He wanted to seize the life that now seemed more fragile than ever.

His hands were possessive, his mouth avaricious, his loins aching with a desire such as he had never known before.

His tongue probed, spreading a honeyed teasing warmth throughout her body. The warmth became heat and then fever as she molded her body to his and felt the hardness of his frame, heard the rapid beat of his heart and breathed the fine leather scent of him.

Antonia's hands searched under his jacket, following the lines of his chest, his strong muscled shoulders, the back of his neck. It was as if they had a life of their own, as they explored in a way that both shocked and amazed her. As her hands moved, so did her tongue, meeting his equally until they were both caught in frantic whirlpools of desire that could no longer be stopped.

Tris unbuttoned her coat, searching and finding her most vulnerable spots, moving with experience and impatience to the rounded mounds of her breasts, silently cursing the layers of cloth that protected them.

He drew back, catching her hand in his and bringing it to his mouth before shrugging off his coat, grateful for the heat of the fire, although the heat in his own body, he decided, would probably provide enough warmth for both of them. Slowly, he took off her coat, his hands stroking, touching as he did so. He could see her eyes in the firelight, and as he continued to undress her, slowly unbuttoning her short jacket, he paused occasionally to seek an objection in them, but there was none. When he was through, he gently placed a blanket around her while he discarded his deerskin trousers, all the time watching for fear or hesitancy or denial, but seeing nothing but love shining in her eyes.

Tris knew he should stop, and perhaps he could have if she had shown a trace of reluctance, but there was none and he sensed that her need for contact, for joining, for loving in the most beautiful, intimate way, was as compelling as his own. His hands loved her, his eyes said things his voice never could, and his body bent to hers.

Nothing could be this wondrous, Antonia thought. Tris's fingers moved exquisitely along the side of her breasts, finally cupping them as his mouth went down and played with nipples grown hard with passion. She gasped at the feelings he aroused, tumultuous, swelling, raging feelings that pushed her body to his in response.

She felt his manhood touch and play and tease her as her body screamed for relief from the need to become a part of him.

Nothing mattered now but their joining. Something wild and primal surged through her, and her hands clasped his back, bringing him fiercely to her, cherishing his closeness, writhing under the marvelous magic of his hands.

"My love," she heard him whisper. "It will hurt...."

But nothing could hurt as much as this aching inside, this hungry seeking of body and heart. She answered him with a low cry—part plea, part pain, all desire—as her arms tightened around him. She felt his tongue, now gentle, dart featherlight along her face, her neck, her earlobes. Her body arched instinctively toward him, and she felt his body shuddering in an effort to keep control, to go slowly.

Then she felt his warm coursing strength enter her. At first there was fierce, stabbing pain, but she drew her arms tighter around him, and drew him deeper inside. All the sensations she had felt before paled in the glorious splendor that suddenly possessed her body as he moved, slowly at first and then with more urgency, and became as one with her.

The pain receded and its memory was gone, swallowed in the sunburst of ecstasy that fell in great golden drops around her. She gasped with the intensity of it, the sheer awesome beauty as he plunged deeper into her, reaching the very core of her soul in great shuddering movements, each one creating sensations greater than the last, until she thought she could bear no more.

But still her body reached for him, meeting his as it came down in one crashing roll of thunder that whirled her upward into a swirling vortex of dazzling colors and exploding sensations, until she collapsed in hundreds of tingling vibrations.

She felt him quiet inside her, and an incredible sweetness filled her as they lay joined. She never wanted him to leave. Never. His body shuddered with the aftermath, and she knew a bittersweet joy that she could affect him so. Her heart twisted as she realized she had to savor these sensations, to lock them in her memory, because this might well be the last time she would know them.

It was as if Tris sensed her agony. His eyes, which had closed in peace, now opened, seeing the mist of tears that hovered in hers. He started to withdraw, but she held him there, loath to let him go and lose his warmth. He smiled at the gesture, a smile full of love and deviltry. It was a devastating combination, and if Antonia were not already lost beyond reason, she would be now.

His mouth touched hers with tenderness and love, and then once more he moved, this time separating from her. Antonia felt a great sense of loss until he smiled, a tender beautiful smile that was like a rainbow after a storm.

"We might just freeze to death," he said, "and I have no intentions of losing you now." He gathered the blanket around her, then dressed quickly as she, too, started to feel the chill. She huddled in the blanket as he fed the fire until it was once more blazing brightly.

Tris sat next to her, his head still aching from the blow, and marveled at how the pain had disappeared moments earlier. He pulled her next to him, feeling a wonderful peace as her body snuggled naturally into the crook of his arm.

There were still nagging questions, and his guilt resurfaced. Not because of Antonia. They would marry now. What had happened between them had been too beautiful, too right to be a sin. His guilt was for the death of Charles Bent. He couldn't help but feel that if he had been here, he could have done something. He had sensed danger and he should not have disregarded it.

His arm tightened around Antonia. Charles Bent had made it possible for him to be with Antonia, to stay in Taos. He owed the governor. The fact that Antonia said the New Mexicans had joined the Indians meant that the massacre was part and parcel of a careful plot. If it took him the rest of his life, he would find the leaders and see them hung. He would revenge Charles. He could do nothing less.

Wondering only briefly at how love and hate could abide side by side within him, he pulled Antonia to him and lay down next to her, his arms around her. He closed his eyes and went to sleep.

Antonia, however, didn't sleep. She didn't want to lose a moment of knowing the touch of his body against hers, the possessiveness of his arms, the warmth of his easy breathing against her face. She would have this night, every moment of it.

Chapter Fourteen

Tris woke with the first glimmer of dawn's light in the cave. It took a moment to orient himself. He felt a softness in his arms that took some of the chill from the ground. Hair tickled his cheek, and warm curves fitted into his own craggy angles.

He didn't want to move, even when his mind started working and he remembered every word Tonia had said the night before, along with those he sensed she hadn't.

He didn't want to move. Damn his soul.

He had taken Tonia last night, something he had vowed not to do until they were married. And he had done it in the aftermath of Charles's death. A death he should have somehow prevented.

And now he lay here, doing nothing.

Tris gently disengaged himself from Tonia, trying not to disturb her quiet sleeping, trying to ignore the persistent longings of his body, trying to separate Tonia from all the other thoughts crowding his mind.

Why? That was the most important question. Why had Charles Bent been killed?

He stood up, his head throbbing, and went to the opening of the cave. It was cold, freezing cold. The fire was almost dead and he piled it with brush and wood he found outside the cave and watched as the flames reached playfully upward. Then he walked back to the mouth of the cave.

The sun was just coming over the horizon, and a quiet lonely pain flowed through him. He had always had friends, but few like Charles. Perhaps it had been their joint fascination for this land, their sense of adventure, perhaps even Charles's understanding of his love for Tonia. Perhaps the fact they had saved each other's lives. Perhaps their sense of shared responsibility.

Whatever it was, Tris knew that part of him felt terribly empty, and he hated the impotence that accompanied the feeling. Tonia was right. He could do little by himself at the moment. And he wanted to. God Almighty, he wanted to.

If bands were roaming the countryside unchecked, he would have to wait until he joined General Price. Then he could be of use as a scout.

His stomach twisted. He didn't want to wait. He couldn't wait, dammit. God alone knew how long it would take a troop of men to make its way through the frozen country.

He wished he could shake the feeling that Tonia knew more than she was saying. Could she be protecting someone? Silvero? But she had certainly demonstrated no liking for the man. Her father?

The thought was like a knife running through him. But it would explain several things, particularly how she knew so much. Yet her father was ill, he comforted himself. It was obvious he couldn't get around well, and Antonia had said his heart was bad.

Tris turned to her. She looked so lovely, so peaceful. Her dark hair was loose and spread over the ground like a piece of rich black velvet, her lips still swollen from their kisses.

He thought about his promise to her last night that he would not do anything reckless. But he couldn't stay safe, not when murder was being done and rebellion brewed. It should be easy, with Antonia here, but even these minutes were an agony of guilt to a mind that demanded action.

He walked over to Antonia and knelt beside her, the back of his hand touching the softness of her skin. Her eyes opened ever so slowly and he saw the lazy awareness in them as she smiled in remembrance of the night. It was all there, all the fierce tenderness they had shared, the completeness of their union, the incredible loving they had explored. She stretched like a contented cat, her long lashes dipping over the dark eyes.

Tris sat down, pulling her into his arms, wondering how anything could feel so good, so right, as she snuggled inside the embrace. Yet a streak of impatience made his body tense, separating one part of him from another. One part wanted to stay here, like this, forever; the other wanted to follow a more violent pursuit.

Antonia, only partially aware of the battle being fought within him, tipped her head upward, and her lips invited his to join once more.

But his touch this morning was distracted, and she knew it instantly. The kiss was light, and she knew why. Her joy fled and left her bereft. Something in her wanted to die as she felt his hurt and anger over Governor Bent's death. She couldn't help but feel she was betraying him by not telling him what she knew.

Tris appeared a stranger, unreachable, despite the warmth of his arms. She wanted to know that stranger, but she had no right. Her father was his friend's murderer, had tried to murder Tristan, and she could say nothing.

Closing her eyes, she prayed to the Holy Mother that the outside world would go away and she could stay here forever…like this. She did not expect her prayer to be granted, and wretchedly she reopened her eyes as she sensed the growing tension in his body.

"Tell me exactly what happened in Taos," Tris said, as she had known he would. This time he would not be satisfied with the sketchy information she had given him yesterday.

"I—I told you last night."

The grimness around his mouth became more pronounced. "I want to know who you overheard, what exactly happened to Charles, to the others, how many are involved."

"What will—will happen to them?"

"It's treason, Antonia. Like it or not, the United States is now the legal government."

"But they consider themselves Mexican citizens…."

"Who?"

"The Pueblos," Antonia blurted out helplessly.

"I thought they didn't like the Mexican government."

"They...I...heard they are afraid you will make them move...like the Creeks and the Cherokees and—"

"And how do they know about the Creeks and the Cherokees?"

"I...don't...know...perhaps from the school, the priests."

"You said you overheard the vaqueros talking. How would they know that the Indians were planning to attack?"

"I don't know," Antonia said desperately. "Perhaps they heard some Pueblos talking about it."

"Silvero," Tris said softly and unexpectedly—so unexpectedly that Tonia stared at him with eyes she was afraid said more than she wanted to.

"Was Silvero involved?" Tris persisted.

"It was the Indians," she replied wretchedly. "Maria said it was the Indians."

Tris stared at her, and all the softness was gone. She was a terrible liar. Her lips trembled with the lie. His anger competed with his sympathy as he felt her shiver in his arms. After last night, he couldn't doubt that she loved him. Why couldn't she confide in him? Who was she protecting? He tried another tack. "What exactly happened to Charles?" If he had sought to soothe her, he couldn't have chosen a worse question. Tears crept into her eyes. "Tonia?" His voice was quiet but demanding.

Her voice shook and the words came very, very slowly. He had to lean down to hear them, they were so soft. "They killed the sheriff, then they came for Governor Bent. He tried to talk to them, but they would not listen. He would not use his guns...there were too many of them and he was afraid they would come after Maria and the children. He let them...kill him to save the others."

Tris leaned back his head, as if her words were too heavy to bear. He didn't want to hear anymore, but he had to. He had to hear it all.

"How did he die?" The pain in his voice doubled Antonia's agony.

"There were...arrows and—and...he was scalped."

"Oh, God," Tris moaned. When Antonia finally had the courage to look at him, she saw tears in his eyes. She had never seen tears in a man's eyes before, and she didn't know if she could bear it. Her hands found his and clung to them, trying to give him comfort when she had so little for herself.

Moments went by and they seemed like hours. He could not know how responsible she felt.

"The others?"

Antonia barely heard his words. She didn't want to answer.

"Tonia. The others?"

"They were...they were... Dear God, they were tortured."

He cursed under his breath. When he spoke aloud, there was steely resolve in his voice. "I will find them. So help me God, I will find them. Those who did it and those behind it." Through a haze, she heard his words and she shivered at his quiet rage. Her Tristan, her laughing, loving Tristan, sounded like an avenging angel, or a devil, and she had no doubt he was capable of anything at the moment.

"Your vaqueros," he said. "I want their names."

Antonia went as still as a statue. "It was...just rumors."

"Their names, Antonia."

It was one of the first times he had called her Antonia, and his tone sent chills down her spine. It was as if he were a different person, someone she didn't know at all.

All she could do was shake her head.

She felt his hand tighten around her balled fist. "I will find out," he said finally. And she knew he would. And what was left of her world would collapse.

Tris took his hand away from hers and caught her chin, forcing her to look at him.

"What aren't you telling me, Antonia?"

She knew it was time to tell him of her father's part, to ask him to spare him, to tell him it had been Ramon's doing more than her father's. But the warmth had left his eyes, and she wondered if there was any compassion in him.

"I have told you all I know," she murmured, and Tris saw the misery and determination in her eyes and knew he would get no more.

He disengaged himself and stood. "I'll take you home."

"No," Antonia cried.

His eyes were weighing her, and she knew he found her wanting.

He took her hand and guided her to her feet and looked down at her. "Trust me, Antonia. I won't hurt you. I would never hurt you."

But how could she trust him? He had his duty to find those he considered traitors and those who had killed his friend. How could she put him in a position where he had to choose... between her and his personal honor. For she had no doubt that honor meant much to him. She would destroy him.

She would destroy herself first.

Antonia lied. "I do trust you. And I told you everything."

A muscle twitched in his cheek, and his eyes grew even colder. If she could die, she would gladly have done so at the moment.

Without any more words, he gathered what few belongings they had.

Antonia watched, her face pale. "You promised."

"I promised not to do anything reckless. And I won't. I'll be very careful. I'm a scout, remember. And I'm a cautious one."

"I won't go with you."

"You will, Antonia. I'm going to see you home safely, and I'm going to talk to your vaqueros."

"Why don't you wait?" It was an anguished cry.

"Because then I might never find out who and why."

"The why is obvious," Antonia said. "There are a lot of New Mexicans—Spanish, Mexican and Indians—who are afraid of the United States, of its appetite."

"Its appetite? Who have you been listening to?" Tris's face was creased into hard lines. His hands went up to her arms and held them tight. "Who, Antonia?"

Antonia felt his fingers bite into her. Her fear turned into anger at the piercing look in his eyes.

"Let go of me."

The words were so cold that Tris dropped his hands, and the two stood there, transfixed.

Antonia's chin was tipped and her eyes misted with tears.

God, but she was beautiful.

Tris's eyes were as cold as the deepest mountain lake, and his jaw was thrust forward.

Holy Mary, but she loved him.

"Tonia..."

"Tristan..."

Tris finally opened his arms, and Antonia needed no further invitation. As she stepped into them, they closed around her, comforting and soothing.

Trust. He needed it like a drowning man needed to breathe. *Talk to me.* The words were in his mind, but he could not utter them. He had given her the chance, and now only she could break the silent barrier between them.

Everything he was thinking was evident in his touch, and Antonia felt its heavy weight. If only she were the culprit, she would confess readily enough. But she could not give him her father.

"I love you," she whispered, but she knew it wasn't enough, that it would never be enough.

"Is it your father?" The words were so abrupt that her head jerked up and she knew he must see the truth in her eyes.

"My father?"

"Was he involved?"

The truth was in her face, and Tris stood there stunned. It had crossed his mind several times but he had always dismissed it. He now knew why. He hadn't wanted to consider the implications.

"Good Christ," he whispered.

Antonia didn't want to look at him, but her pride forced her to.

"He is involved, isn't he?" Tris said through his teeth.

Antonia silently pleaded with him not to force an answer, but his face was sculpted in stone.

Her silence was enough. Tris spun around and leaned against a wall, one hand clenching the rough stone until his fingers were white.

He wanted to curse the rock, the cave, the earth, the heavens. To avenge his friend, he would earn the hatred of the woman he loved. To do his duty, he would have to mortally wound the one person he had vowed not to hurt.

"Silvero?" he finally said, turning to watch her. He had asked before, and he now remembered he had not received an answer.

Antonia could not betray Ramon any more than she could her father. No matter what they had done. She could despise their actions as murderous and cowardly, but she would not give them over to their enemies to be hung. Whatever she thought of Ramon, however much she detested him for involving her father in this, she could not condemn him. She had known him all her life, had played with him, had been given his love . . . as much as he could love.

Tris's face was as white and stiff as the chalked edge of a granite cliff. His eyes were full of quiet fury as his question went unanswered.

"Did you know ahead of time?" He could barely say the words, yet the question had to be asked.

Pain, such as she had never known before, hammered at Antonia's chest until she thought it would explode. How could he ask such a thing? She had told him that his name was among those to be killed. Did he truly think she could be accomplice to his murder?

There was nothing left. Nothing . . . if he could think such a thing.

"Answer me, Antonia."

"No," she screamed. "No, no, no." She crumpled to the floor of the cave, tears streaming down her face even as she tried to hold them back. Huge sobs rocked her body as she thought how thin their love had been, how fragile.

Tris's eyes glittered with mist of their own. It had been a stupid question. But he didn't understand anything. He didn't understand why his best friend was dead, or why he hadn't anticipated it, or how a plot of this magnitude could be undertaken without someone discovering it.

Again he thought of Charles Bent. Scalped. Killed within the sight and hearing of his wife and children. He hated Bent's murderers and, God help him, that meant Antonia's father.

And Antonia was right. There *was* nothing he could do now except wait for General Price. He knew the identity of two of the ringleaders. The others could be easily found.

At what cost?

He whirled around and strode out of the cave, welcoming the cold blast of an icy wind.

"I'm sorry, Charles," he said to the wind, "I'm so damned sorry."

He didn't know how long he stood there before Tonia joined him, standing quietly, miserably at his side.

Nothing in his well-ordered life had prepared him for this. How he had longed to make his own way, to get away from the shadow of his father, regardless of how much he loved him. Now, more than ever before, he longed for his father to be at his side.

"Tristan, what are you going to do?"

Antonia's soft voice was like a volley of shots, each one catapulting itself ruthlessly into his mind and heart.

Tris turned and looked at her. Her noble pride he loved so much was gone; there was pleading in every feature of her face.

She had saved his life yesterday. She had ridden out in the cold and waited, and she had killed for him, knowing as she did that he would hunt those responsible for the rebellion.

And then last night. Realization hit him with the impact of a sledgehammer. All the time they were making love, she had known. Doubt crept into his heart. Had she made love to save her father? He closed his eyes, trying to erase the thought, but it would not go away. Oh, dear Christ. Could he ever look at her again without seeing Charles's face or remembering his death?

Despair filled him. He had never felt so empty in his life…so hopeless. "I will not hurt your father," he said finally with a lifelessness that pierced Antonia far more than anger. "I won't say the same for Silvero."

"You won't tell them?"

Them. His people. His superiors. His loyalty. Once again his insides twisted. He tried to justify his decision. *How could one crippled old man matter?* But it did. He knew it did. Justice. Justice for Charles. Justice for his government. Retribution.

He would have to kill Silvero. If he told Price about Ramon Silvero, he would inevitably have to tell the general about Ramirez.

Tris, already hardened by the past months, felt himself grow icy with resolve. He had never before set out to kill a man, coldly, deliberately, even gladly. It was the last emotion that frightened him the most.

Antonia saw the change come over him with his decision.

Maria Santisima, his expression was just like Ramon's. He was a stranger she could no longer trust.

The ride seemed endless. Tristan could not be dissuaded from accompanying Antonia home, regardless of the danger, and she was terrified of what might happen.

She could only try to believe him when he said he would do nothing to harm her father, but he was so hard, so cold.

Tristan was cautious. He would not allow the simmering anger within him to blind him to the danger. He had no doubt that he was a marked target, and he did not intend to let anything happen to him until he dealt with Silvero.

At one point, they saw a cloud of dust in the distance, and they turned and circled, going several miles out of their way.

As they neared the Ramirez ranch, Tris turned to Antonia for the first time during the miserable ride. "Your vaqueros?"

"They obey me as much as they do my father," she replied. "They will not attack you."

He nodded, accepting her words.

He remembered the hacienda from the first visit. It was sprawling and low with a certain comfortable elegance. There were several heavily lathered horses near the barn, evidence of hard riding. The few vaqueros in sight stared, then started for her, but at Antonia's shake of the head, they returned to their business. One went off at a trot to the house.

When they reached the front door, Antonia turned to Tris. "What are you going to do?"

"I want to talk to him." His words were raw and angry.

"Tristan . . ."

"I gave you my word," Tris said roughly, his soul torn between Antonia and the man who was at least partially responsible for his friend's murder.

"Please . . . he is old, sick, he did not know what he was doing. . . . I will see that he does not do any more harm."

But Tris was already off his horse. He offered his hands to her, catching her lightly as she slipped down. When she looked up at him, she knew she would not change his mind.

His eyes softened slightly, and one of his hands reached for her face, caressing it with fingers that trembled with emotion.

"Antonia." The voice from the direction of the house was weak, and Tris turned toward the withered form of Miguel Ramirez struggling toward them on his crutches.

"Jose," the older Ramirez called, and a Mexican vaquero came running, a hand on the pistol at his side.

"Take him," the older man called as other vaqueros started gathering around.

Tris went for his pistol, but Antonia put her hand on his wrist. "No," she said in a strong clear voice.

Don Miguel's face paled. "Antonia, get out of the way."

"No, Father. You will have to kill me first."

"Antonia, you don't know—"

"I will tell the Americans everything," Antonia interrupted.

Tris heard the strength of her voice, but her hand was trembling. Admiration for her registered in his mind.

The older man seemed barely able to stand as he turned to Tristan.

"What do you want?"

Tris looked around at the curious faces surrounding them. "I think it would be better said inside, Señor Ramirez."

His eyes sparking with anger, the older man turned and went inside, leaving Antonia and Tristan to follow.

Antonia's eyes were large and apprehensive. She stood silently while her father sat down in the chair with wheels and sighed heavily.

"I have been worried half to death about you," Don Miguel said slowly. "The vaqueros are out looking for you, and you bring this . . . Yanqui here." He had been half out of his mind with fear during the long night, fear for her safety, fear that he had lost her. Now the fear turned to anger as he saw the tall American and remembered the other Yanquis so many years ago. His words erupted before he could stop them. "What disgrace have you brought on our name?"

Antonia looked at him with disbelief. All the pain and anguish and fear of the past few days exploded once more, now aimed against her father.

"Disgrace," she said bitterly. "Any disgrace of mine would be mild compared to what you have brought."

Don Miguel's eyes went quickly to the tall American. "Antonia!"

"He knows, Father. He knows everything. How you helped plan the insurrection—"

"You told him this?" There was stunned disbelief in his voice as he watched the American's eyes pin him against the chair.

"She didn't have to," Tris interrupted. He turned to her. "Leave us alone, Antonia."

She hesitated.

"It will be all right."

Antonia looked at her father. There was impotent anger on his face. Anger and a hopelessness that drained her own anger. He looked a hundred years old.

"I will stay," she insisted stubbornly.

"Antonia," her father said. "Please . . ."

She had seldom heard her father beg. She wondered how much more he could take. How much any of them could take.

"You promised!" she whispered to Tristan, but his expression was as closed as her father's. "I will wait outside," she finally said, knowing the silence would continue for as long as she was there.

Tristan had promised. But was he the same man he had been yesterday?

Unwilling to eavesdrop but afraid to leave the area, she hovered nearby in the kitchen.

"What are you doing with my daughter?" Some of the rage had drained from the old man and there was sorrow as well as anger in his voice.

Tris regarded him levelly. They had seen each other twice, once at the hacienda when Tris had been told he was unwelcome, and once at the dance when the Creole had glared at him.

He's Tonia's father. Think of that. Don't think how much you would like to put your hands around his throat and shake the breath from him.

"Tonia came to warn me," he said finally. He watched as the older man started to rise, then fell back.

"I don't believe you," Don Miguel challenged.

Tris raised his eyebrow, the lazy insolent gesture belied the fact that he was barely maintaining his control.

"She was there, you know," he said softly. "In Taos, where she saw the results of your plotting."

Don Miguel winced, remembering the words of his daughter when she had returned from Taos, the images she had presented. He had regretted his participation in the rebellion with Ramon almost from the beginning, not because of the objective, which he still firmly desired, but because of the means. It *had* been cowardly, but he was not about to admit his regret to this Yanqui.

The corners of his mouth twitched with resentment and dislike. "You are invaders," he grated out in a whisper. "You do not belong here."

Tris's searching look was measured. Tonia's father. How different were father and daughter. One so gentle, the other so full of hate. How could he ever reconcile them? Was it even possible?

"You are guilty of treason," he said coldly.

Don Miguel drew himself up proudly and for the first time, Tris felt a touch of admiration for him.

"I am a patriot. You can do as you will," the Creole said.

"The others?"

The older man remained stiffly silent.

"You could hang," Tris said grimly. "You *should* hang."

"I am an old man," Don Miguel said. "And I do not particularly wish to live among Yanquis."

"And what about your daughter?"

The Creole's look became fierce, but pain still showed deep within it. "It appears she has made her choice." His words were so bitter that Tris wanted to step back as if from a blow.

"You forced her decision," Tris said calmly.

Don Miguel's gaze dropped. He was suddenly very tired. Hate could only sustain one so long. Had he sacrificed Antonia's love for it? He was very, very afraid he had.

"I cannot stop you, *señor,*" Don Miguel said with resignation, but not defeat. "But you realize you will never have all of Antonia. She will never forget her heritage, her blood, her religion." His unspoken threat hovered between them. Antonia would never forgive Tris if he let anything happen to her father.

Tris's jaw locked. He had never really felt hate before until yesterday, but he hated the man in front of him. Miguel Ramirez was using his daughter, a daughter he had professed to love. Tris had been told of Ramirez's hate for Americans, but he hadn't fully understood its strength.

"Why?" he said. "Why do you hate us so much?"

"Because you care for nothing . . . you spoil everything you touch . . . you destroy. There is no honor in you."

"And there's honor in you?" Tris returned bitterly. "Honor in inciting others to do your dirty work? If that is honor, then I'd rather not have any."

Don Miguel's voice was weary when he finally spoke. "I did what I had to for my country, for my family, for my home." He raised his eyes and stared at Tris. "Now do what you must."

The challenge had been made. Tris had not expected this bold defiance. Tonia had told him her father had been ill, and he did look pale and weak, but his hate made him strong, and Tris didn't know how to fight it.

He only knew he couldn't hurt Tonia and that this man, no matter how wrong, was dear to her. "Do you have any idea," he asked in a low, tense voice, "what you have done?" His hand trembled with emotion. He wanted to hear one word of remorse, or regret.

But there was none. Don Miguel would not allow this enemy to see his own uncertainty, his doubts. His pride would not allow it.

Tris lowered his eyes. "I will say nothing about your part," he said. "But God alone can help you if I hear of any further...activities."

"I don't want your silence...or your help...Yanqui."

Tris clenched his teeth and a muscle jerked in his hard jaw. "I love your daughter, Señor Ramirez. Because of that, and only that, I will protect you. I hope that you roast in hell for what you've done, but I won't make Antonia suffer for it."

"You will never have her, Yanqui. I will make her see...no Yanqui can be trusted. Now get out of my home."

"I will go," Tris said slowly, "but only because I have other business. I'll be back. You can be sure of that."

He didn't trust himself to say anything more. Curbing the waves of fury flooding him, Tris opened the door and saw Tonia standing there, her usually determined face pale with apprehension.

Tris went to her, and raising a finger, he ran it gently down the length of her face, soothing the anxious furrows. His doubts about her motives last night vanished at the desperate love that shone in her eyes. He had just seen what she had lived with all these years, the anger that had been part of her life. He wondered how she could have ever loved him at all, when all her life every mention of Americans had been laced with hate and distrust.

He leaned down and kissed her, quietly, possessively, letting her own lips respond before he stepped back.

"I'll be back for you," he promised, and then he was gone, leaving only a cold, barren emptiness behind.

Chapter Fifteen

Hate. Tris had known the word all his life but had never truly understood its meaning until now.

He had seen its destructiveness in Miguel Ramirez, and now he felt its sickness twisting inside himself. He despised his own weakness, but the hate would not let him go.

It was midmorning, and a cold drizzle kept his senses awake and alive. From a bright sunrise, the day had deteriorated into cloud-filled gloom, a setting that entirely fit his mood.

His hand went to the pistol strapped at his waist. He meant to kill this morning. Perhaps that act would drain the poison eating at him. Another voice told him it would not.

But, dammit, he had to do something or go crazy.

He knew the weather would slow any troops from Santa Fe. The mountain passes were icy and treacherous and although one man on a fast horse could make Taos in a day, it would take an army three or four. By then, Tris reasoned, Silvero might have fled.

And Silvero was his!

But the demons that drove him did not dim his caution. Tris realized he could not ride up to Silvero's ranch.

He had scouted out the property weeks ago. A mesa overlooked the ranch, and the trail was bordered in some places by clumps of trees. Silvero was so damned good at ambushes, it was time he was on the receiving end of one.

Tris found the place he thought would serve his needs, and dismounted. He tied Nugget to a tree and climbed a small bluff until he reached an excellent vantage point. He doubted whether Silvero would be watchful; the Creole apparently believed all the Americans in the area were dead, and it was obvious American troops could not have arrived yet.

Yet the man had to know the Americans wouldn't allow such an atrocity to go unpunished. Could Silvero really believe they would accept the rebellion as the work of the Indians alone?

Tris had seen the resolve on Miguel Ramirez's face, and he could only suppose that Silvero was driven by the same strength of purpose.

How could they be such damned fools? Santa Ana had been defeated years ago by the Texans. This time, the entire force of the United States was directed against him.

Tris lay on the ground, cursing its icy wetness. From his vantage point he could see approaching riders as well as departing ones. He wondered how long he would have to wait for Silvero. And whether Don Miguel Ramirez would try to warn him. Perhaps he had been a fool to leave Ramirez alone to do more mischief, but there had been no alternative other than kill the man or to bring him along. He had to trust Antonia's influence to keep her father and their vaqueros in line.

Tris tried to relax but his body was wound like a tight spring, and the cold seeping through his clothes did little to help. Think of something else. Think of the rich, green valley of home.

Home. A house full of laughter and warmth and love. The contrast with his current situation struck him with a certain poignancy and pain. Then he remembered Tonia's eyes and the way he felt when he was with her—the soaring joy and exquisite tenderness—and he knew anything was worth being with her again. Someday, some way, they would share their own home full of laughter and warmth and love.

He turned his attention back to the trail.

Tris didn't know how long he had lain there. The clouds in the sky so completely blurred the sun that time was no longer evident. It must have been hours before he saw movement around the ranch house. He moved slightly, feeling stiff and sore from the cold and immobility. Let it be Silvero, he prayed.

His heart plummeted, however, as figures approached down the trail on horseback. There had to be thirty at least, and as they came closer, he could see they were all heavily armed and carrying large packs. Tris sank into the mesa, grateful his clothing matched the winter gold of the ground. He fingered his rifle, wanting badly to sight it on the rider in black who rode at the front of the troop. But that would be suicide, and he didn't want Silvero that badly. He had too much to live for. And he wanted to know where Silvero was going.

Tris pulled back from the edge, keeping well out of sight until the riders had passed. He started to snake his way back down when he heard additional hoofbeats. This time it was two riders, one an Indian, both coming from the Silvero ranch and traveling leisurely. If he hurried, he could intercept them. Ignoring the ache in his legs, he quickly reached his horse and mounted, pushing the animal into a gallop.

He was able to circle and wait for the two in a small stand of pine trees. His cold command stopped them immediately; his eyes left them no doubt that he meant what he said.

One was a Mexican vaquero, the other a Pueblo Indian. He ordered them both from their horses and commanded the Mexican to tie the Indian's hands and feet. He then tied the Mexican's hands behind him and pulled his knife, placing it at the man's throat. It had worked before, he figured. It would probably work again.

"Where is Silvero going?" he grated out.

The man looked at him in terror.

"Where?"

"The Yanqui army is coming. Señor Silvero is going to meet it."

"And you?"

There was silence, and Tris pressed the knife deeper.

"To get the others."

"Who?"

The man shook his head.

"Damn you, who?"

Tris again increased the pressure and the man reluctantly named four New Mexican families in the Taos and Valdez valleys.

"Where are they going?"

"La Canada," the New Mexican screamed, naming a small town not far north of Santa Fe. "They plan to meet the army there."

Tris sheathed his knife. His personal needs no longer mattered; Silvero would have to wait. He had to get to General Price and tell him about the New Mexican force. He gathered the weapons he had taken from the two men and started for their horses.

"Señor?"

He turned back.

"You will not leave us here, *sí?*"

He wanted to. God, how he wanted to. Let them suffer just a little of what the Taos Americans had suffered. But damn if he could. Instead, he cut a two-foot length of rope, tying each end to the ropes that bound his prisoners' hands so that they were now linked together. Then he took a knife he had found on the Indian and threw it, embedding it in a tree thirty feet away.

With bound hands and feet, it should take the men hours to reach the knife and cut themselves loose, but they would, eventually, if they worked together. And Tris would have their horses.

"Señor?" the Mexican pleaded again as he already felt the cold entering his body.

"I would get started if I were you." Tris's voice was harsh, and the two men knew they were lucky to be alive. "I know your faces," Tris added. "If I see either of you again, I'll see that you hang."

With that final warning, he mounted, taking the two extra horses with him. He couldn't take them far; they would slow him down and make him more conspicuous. In several miles, he would set them free.

He thought about the ride ahead, nearly eighty miles through enemy territory. He was hungry, tired and cold. But he had no time to consider any of those problems. Nor, at the moment, Antonia. He had to reach General Price.

After Tris had gone, Antonia had entered her father's office. All the anger and defiance had taken its toll. Don Miguel's eyes were dull and listless. His shoulders were slumped, and his face was creased with lines.

Every word the Yanqui had said had been a blow. Somewhere in the past weeks, he had lost his honor. And now he had probably lost his daughter. The last day and a half had been the worst hours he had ever spent in his life, even worse than those when he had lain helpless with his dead wife.

"Antonia." His eyes pleaded with her to talk to him, to understand.

She looked at him, remembering the good times, the gentle times. The times she had leaned against him in the saddle as they rode the ranch, the affection they had shared around a camp fire at night, the unqualified love he had given her over the years. She remembered the terrible accident when he was crippled, and she knew she could never turn her back on him, no matter what he had done.

She knelt at his knee and put her head on his lap as she had when she was little. "Oh, Papa," she said. "Papa."

Don Miguel closed his eyes and felt the wetness in them. He did not know the last time he had cried. Not when Theresa died; then he had been too filled with rage, too stunned, too lost. But the tears came now. The hate in him was gone, and he felt empty. So damned old and empty. And tired. For the love of God, he was tired.

Antonia didn't know how long they stayed there. No one interrupted them, not even Luz. But a cry from outside finally separated them. "Riders!"

Don Miguel straightened, pushing his shoulders back. He didn't know who was coming, perhaps soldiers to arrest him.

But it was Ramon who came through the front door, striding his way through the house, his black eyes glittering with excitement.

Antonia stood, taking a place next to her father, eyeing her neighbor with distrust.

Ramon ignored her and spoke to her father. "I need your vaqueros," he said without preamble or greeting. "There has been word from Santa Fe...the Americans are marching here. This is our chance to drive them from our land."

"No."

Neither Ramon nor Antonia believed what they were hearing. The denial was laced with a strength that Antonia had thought was gone.

"Miguel...I must have them." Ramon's voice was full of confidence. Don Miguel had been just as anxious as he to rid this area of the hated Americans.

"It is over," Don Miguel said. "I will not ask my vaqueros to die for a lost cause."

Ramon's face filled with confusion. "What...?"

"We have been fools, Ramon," Don Miguel said slowly. "We have been fools to think we could win. We have sown a terrible crop."

Ramon's eyes moved from Miguel's implacable face to Antonia's surprised one. He did not miss the sudden gladness that shone in her eyes.

"The Yanqui," he said bitterly. "It is the American scout, isn't it?"

A flicker of agony crossed Miguel's face. He would not risk losing his daughter completely. He had already lost her respect. He would risk no more. Even if it meant accepting the Yanqui, even if it meant giving up his lifelong vendetta. Sometime during the last hours he had finally come to understand that love was more important than hate.

"Traitor," Ramon spit out.

Miguel's gaze didn't waver. He *was* a traitor. Dear God, whichever way he turned, he was a traitor. But at the moment, his daughter was the most important thing. He had forgotten that for a while. He reached out his hand and clutched hers.

"If any of my vaqueros wish to go with you, they may do so," Miguel said finally. "I will not order it."

Ramon's eyes went from father to daughter, then back. A sudden suspicion grabbed him. The men he had posted in the canyon had been reported killed by the vaqueros sent to relieve them. "Has the American scout been here?"

The silence answered his question.

"Does he know your part in all this?" Ramon asked with a sneer. "Does your daughter?"

"I know everything," Antonia finally spoke.

"Then you know your father is as guilty as any of us . . . that he will hang if we don't defeat the Yanqui army."

"He said—" Antonia stopped and cursed her own words. She had wanted to defend Tristan but immediately realized what she was admitting. That Tristan was in Taos . . . that he knew about Ramon. Had she just signed Tristan's death warrant?

"And you trust him?" Ramon asked angrily. "You are a bigger fool than I thought, both you and your father." He turned. "I have no more time to waste. Wait here for your arrest, for your hanging. You will see. But I will fight."

The door to the office slammed behind him, and Miguel and Antonia were once more left alone. As they heard the drum of many hoofbeats echo through the ranch house, Antonia's hand tightened on her father's. "Thank you," she said.

His eyes found hers. "Are you sure that your Americano can be trusted?" The idea went against years of belief, years of hate, but God help him, he did not want to hang. There could be no more ignoble death, and Ramon's last words ate at him.

There was no doubt in Antonia's mind. "Yes, I am sure," she said.

It took Tris two days to reach General Price. He had had several pieces of hardtack in his saddle bags, remnants left from his journey from Santa Fe, and some water, nothing more. He hadn't needed any more. He hadn't been able to eat.

He had spent the time on the trail devising suitable lies for General Price as to how he had come by the information he had. If there was one thing in the world he despised, it was lies, no matter how worthy the cause, and he didn't feel Miguel Ramirez was worthy at all. It galled him to have to protect Ramirez, and, in doing so, protect Ramon Silvero. Thank God, he hadn't had much time to think about it.

The hills and canyons had been filled with resurgents. It had seemed as though all of New Mexico had been hurrying to join the rebellion. He had wondered if Ramirez's men were among them, and swore bitterly to himself.

There had been a haze over the mountains that had been both a blessing and a curse. It had made him fairly invisible, but it had also been difficult to see anyone else. He had been afraid he would stumble into the enemy.

He had taken all the back trails and sometimes ridden where there was no trail at all, the brush and trees cutting into his legs and face. He had stopped frequently, listening for the sound of other horses, for the movement of trees, for voices. When night came, there had been no moon or stars to light the treacherous way and he had dared not start a fire to thaw his frozen limbs. Instead, he had huddled under blankets in the protection of a clump of trees, too tense to sleep.

On the second day, he was up with the first gray of dawn, stiff and sore and hungry. For several hours, he had pressed Nugget hard, believing that few others would be about so early. As morning faded into a similarly gray day, he had started taking precautions again, once darting into almost impassible brush when he heard the sound of horses. His hand quieting Nugget, he had heard the riders pass and judged the number at sixteen. He knew he would have to circle even more, delaying his report. He had sworn, knowing his time was running out.

Tris had reached Price's first sentries at dusk and had demanded to be taken to the general. He had not engendered confidence in the private charged with taking him to the general, and the soldier kept his musket steady on Tris's back, but Tris had been too damned tired to care.

General Price was in an ugly temper. The day had been a nightmare. He had been horrified by the reports from Taos and, for a while, had been disbelieving. When he had finally realized that the stories were true, he had hastily ordered into

Santa Fe various units that were scattered throughout the territory as grazing parties and town garrisons.

Fretting over every lost moment, he had gathered three hundred and fifty men and four mountain howitzers and started his march over frozen rugged terrain, hindered every moment by the heavy equipment.

And he was moving blind. He didn't know how many New Mexicans were involved in the rebellion or what his troops faced, but was only consumed by a burning rage for the atrocities committed on the governor he served and other Americans.

War was one thing. This wanton killing another. And he ached to punish.

It took him a moment to recognize Tris Hampton. The scout's face was gray with cold and covered with stiff bristles. His eyes were harder than anytime Price remembered, his mouth set in a bitter grim line.

"Hampton, I'm glad to see you. I was afraid they might have killed you, too."

"They came damned close a couple of times."

"It's true then, all of it?"

"It's true," Tris said slowly. "Governor Bent, the sheriff, the judge's son. Every American they could find."

"Mrs. Bent?"

"They didn't hurt any of the women or children."

"Thank God for that, at least." Price looked at Tris's fatigued face. "What news do you have for me?"

"There's a large force waiting for you, just ahead at La Canada."

"How many?"

"I don't know, but the mountains are crowded with them. I would say hundreds, perhaps thousands. How many men do you have?"

"Three hundred and fifty, but we have howitzers."

Tris nodded. The odds weren't bad. The Americans were far better armed, and the Missourians were a hell of a bunch of fighters.

"Anything else you can tell me?" General Price probed. "Who started this?"

Tris just shook his head wearily.

The general looked at him sympathetically. He knew how close Bent and the scout had become. "Get some sleep, Tris. I'll send some of my scouts farther ahead. We'll stay here until they report."

Tris nodded, grateful for the reprieve from any further questions and the chance for some sleep.

"And, Hampton . . ."

Tris turned back to the general.

"Thank you."

Tris tried to smile, but his lips wouldn't cooperate. Again, he nodded, and after seeing Nugget rubbed down and fed, he found a dry wagon, crawled inside and went to sleep.

They met the New Mexicans, who had gathered two thousand strong, the next afternoon.

Tris had slept most of the night, then rose early and rode out to scout. He was with two others when they saw the New Mexican force tucked in the broken hills.

The battle was quick and ferocious. General Price's howitzers and cavalry quickly flushed the rebels from the hills, breaking their lines and sending them back into the mountains.

It was Tris's first organized battle, and he felt the camaraderie as the Americans marched steadily forward, one group kneeling and firing as the other reloaded. Their inexorable discipline and forward movement unnerved the untrained enemy, and he saw them turn and run, leaving their fallen behind.

Tris looked for Silvero, first among those shooting, then the wounded, the dead and finally, the prisoners. The Creole wasn't there.

He returned to General Price's headquarters after the battle. "We'll have to fight them all the way through these canyons," the officer was saying. He looked up. "Hampton, where's the best place for them to make a stand?"

Tris bent over the map, studying it carefully. He finally pointed to a spot on the east side of the Rio Grande, behind a mountain. "If I were to select a spot..."

"Can you scout it for us?"

Tris nodded. He wanted to keep busy. He wanted to find Silvero, preferably alone, although that prospect was growing increasingly unlikely.

Progress, the next several days, was painfully slow. The Taos road was primitive, and snow and ice often obscured it. The scouts, and even some of the main army, could see the rebels scurrying over rocks, moving easily ahead. General Price was becoming increasingly irritated.

He was calmed slightly with the arrival of a company of the First Dragoons and another company of Missouri volunteers. He now had nearly five hundred men.

But the road through the high mountains was sometimes two feet deep in snow and difficult for his infantry and guns and wagons to traverse. The army proceeded at a snail's pace until they reached Embuda Pass, the place pointed out by Tristan.

The New Mexicans were waiting once more.

This time, Tris rode with the Dragoons, sweeping down on the positions after the howitzers had done their work. Once more, the New Mexicans broke and ran. And still there was no sighting of Ramon Silvero.

Tris questioned prisoners to no avail. Some said the rancher had been with them; others had not seen him. It was as if he were a ghost. A ghost that haunted Tris day and night.

It was clear that General Price intended little mercy toward the rebels. The ringleaders were to hang, their property confiscated. He intended to end the conspiracies and plotting with one bold stroke. And he intended to punish.

"I'm going to finish this once and for all," he told Tris, his usually good-natured countenance lined and determined. "We were much too lenient the first time. And Governor Bent paid for it."

"It was his decision, too," Tris said mildly.

''And it was a mistake. Good Christ, what they did to him. I'll find out each of their names and, God help me, they will die for it.''

A coldness that did not come from the weather enveloped Tris. How long could he protect Miguel Ramirez? Who, other than Ramon, knew of the man's involvement? Probably all of the principal conspirators. It was bound to come out sooner or later.

Antonia. He knew she would never forgive him if her father was killed, no matter how she felt about what had happened. He could only hope Silvero or anyone else who knew of Ramirez's role was not taken alive. It was a damned small hope.

General Price encountered no more organized opposition, although there was a spattering of gunfire from an occasional sniper. The force entered Taos four days later without another major confrontation, but they quickly learned the rebels were preparing to make a stand in the Pueblo of Taos, the principal home of the Taos Indians, just north of the town.

They also learned that nearly all of the rebels holed up in the Pueblo were Indian; most of the Creoles and Mexicans had disappeared.

Tris asked to be relieved; his scouting talents were no longer needed. But for once, General Price was unaccommodating. He was going to stamp out the rebellion ruthlessly, and he wanted every able bodied man available to see that none of the rebels escaped.

Small details were sent out to gather up those insurgents who were not at the pueblo, and Tris was attached to the Dragoons. He was soon caught up in the planning, acting as courier from one unit to another.

He comforted himself that Miguel Ramirez should be safe enough while Price's attention was fixed on the pueblo. When it was over, he would try to convince Antonia's father to head south toward Mexico until some of the American anger was spent. Not that the man would listen to him, but perhaps he would listen to Antonia.

The Indian rebels had taken shelter in the centuries-old twin pueblos that faced each other across a wide plaza broken by the

Taos Creek, and in an adobe mission church that was part of a walled enclosure joining the pueblos. All scouting reports put their number at an estimated seven hundred.

Tris and General Price eyed the buildings cautiously. The pueblos and the church were natural fortresses, with holes on the parapet and in the walls through which the rebels could shoot.

General Price ordered the buildings surrounded so that no one could escape, and then called out the howitzers. Tris watched restlessly as the guns pounded the church. There were flashes of red and black and brown against the white snow as the sounds of cannon fire and the screams of the wounded split the crisp cold air.

Tris didn't know how long it continued... it seemed forever. The roof of the church caught fire, and he joined a storming party. The interior was full of smoke and dust, of dead and dying Indians. It was a scene from hell, and Tris knew he didn't ever want to return. The fury in him for the murderers of Bent died at the sight of such pain and agony. There were shouts from outside, then heavy gunfire and more screams, and he and others made their way out of the church, finding bodies everywhere. A group of fifty Indians, who had tried to go over the wall, lay at the bottom, shot by Price's troops.

Dead and dying were everywhere. But again there was no Silvero, though Tris no longer expected to see him. The man was too wily to get caught in this trap.

Several minutes later, white flags were flying over the pueblo, and Tris made his way to Price's location.

It was near nightfall when Price gave orders to stop firing. He would meet with elders of the Pueblos in the morning. As Tris approached him, the general sank down on a stool.

"Hampton," Price said. "Good job."

Tris grinned wearily. He had been here nearly eighteen hours now and was totally exhausted, but he had to see Antonia, to warn her.

"We arrested that Ramirez you warned us about," Price added. "Lieutenant Baker's on his way to Santa Fe with him now."

"Ramirez?" Tris's face tightened in sudden apprehension.

Price stared at him. "A message . . . it came through a Mexican who said he was loyal to us. He said you instructed him to tell me a Señor Ramirez was one of the ringleaders."

"No," Tris said. "I sent no such message."

Price's face was wreathed with confusion, then shrugged. "Perhaps he got the name wrong. It doesn't matter. The man confessed."

"Why Santa Fe?"

"I want names from him, the extent of the conspiracy. The dungeons at the Palacio should be an effective persuader. From what Lieutenant Baker said, he didn't seem to be swayed by the prospect of hanging."

He wouldn't be, Tris knew. Ramirez was too proud to give away his fellow conspirators. He doubted whether imprisonment would be a stronger incentive.

And then the import of all Price had said struck him. Dear God, Antonia must believe he was the one who had informed on her father.

Silvero. It had to be Silvero. But why? Why would he betray his friend?

And then Tris understood.

Antonia!

Chapter Sixteen

It had been a terrible morning. Antonia had paced the hacienda, then the area outside the corral, waiting for Tristan to appear. She wanted to ride out, but she was afraid she might miss him.

Nearly a week had passed since he had left, and then this morning a vaquero had brought word the American army had arrived.

They were all tense...Antonia, her father, the vaqueros. Occasionally a rider arrived from another ranch, and they were updated on the news. The Americans had surrounded the pueblo, where most of the rebels had fled.

Why hadn't Tris appeared? Antonia kept asking herself. Had he been hurt? Wounded? Had he changed his mind about not turning her father over to the authorities? Her father obviously thought so, but then he didn't know Tristan.

Her heart jumped when she heard the sound of approaching horses in the afternoon. Stepping to the window, she saw four men in blue uniforms; Tristan was not with them.

Fear clutched at her as she watched one of them pull out a gun as they approached the door. It was not a polite knock, but a commanding pounding on the door, and she went slowly to open it, nodding Luz aside.

The faces of the soldiers were hostile, their stances wary and tense.

"Señor Miguel Ramirez?" the leader asked.

Antonia drew herself up. She didn't care for his manner at all. "Why do you wish to see him?"

"I'm Lieutenant Baker, miss. We have information Señor Ramirez was involved with the killing of Governor Bent."

Antonia stepped back, her face whitening. "What information?"

"From one of our scouts, miss."

"Who?" she whispered.

"A man named Hampton, miss," the officer said impatiently. "Now where is Señor Ramirez?"

Antonia couldn't speak as she slowly absorbed the impact of his words. It was as if her life was draining from her. The hurt was so strong that a certain numbness took over. It was the only way she could survive.

Are you sure your American can be trusted?

Yes, I am sure.

You are a bigger fool than I thought. Both you and your father.

Her father's words. Her words. Ramon's words. All of them skipped through her mind. Ramon was right. What a fool she had been.

The American was getting impatient. "Search the house," he told his men, his eyes glancing over Antonia's agonized face without sympathy. He, too, had heard all the bloody details of the massacre.

"In here," called one of the men at the door to her father's office, and Antonia came alive again.

"What are you going to do?"

"He's under arrest," the lieutenant said curtly, trying not to notice how pretty the girl was.

"He's an old man," she said. "He cannot travel."

"But he can plan revolution and murder?" the lieutenant replied.

"Whoever accused him lied," Antonia said desperately, but she was pushed aside and could only follow the soldiers into the study.

Her father was sitting, his back straight, his eyes fierce and proud and she was reminded of how he had been years ago . . . before the accident. Like a proud eagle.

"Don Miguel Ramirez?"

Her father nodded.

"You are under arrest."

"May I ask the charge."

"Treason and murder."

"You can commit treason only against your own country. I was defending mine."

"Then you admit being involved in the rebellion."

Don Miguel shrugged. It was no use to deny anything.

"And the others?"

"I can speak only for myself."

"General Price means to see you all hang. If, however, you reveal the names of others, you might survive."

"In prison?"

"You might be freed," the lieutenant said, glancing once more at the young woman standing so rigidly beside the old man.

"At the expense of others? No, Lieutenant," Don Miguel said gently.

Antonia had never been quite as proud of him. No matter what he had done before, he was acting the man now.

While Tristan was too cowardly to come with the men he had sent to arrest her father. A sob caught in her throat.

The lieutenant looked at her. "You may get him a coat."

"I will come with you," she said, her chin setting determinedly.

"No, miss, you will not," the lieutenant said firmly.

"He's right, Querida," her father said gently. "Someone needs to take care of the ranch."

"No," she said.

"Please," he said. "Stay here. I will be all right, and I will feel better if someone is here. You can, perhaps, reach some friends and tell them what has happened."

Ramon. He was talking about Ramon. Perhaps Ramon could offer men, help, advice. If he, too, weren't captured. She would find Ramon and beg for his help.

Antonia nodded reluctantly. "I will get some warm clothes for him."

The lieutenant nodded. "Make it fast."

She found her father's fur-lined boots and coat, and helped him put them on.

One of the soldiers approached her father with rope in his hand, but the lieutenant waved him away. The Creole looked too feeble to cause much trouble.

"Thank you," Antonia said softly, grateful her father would be spared the bonds.

The lieutenant's eyes softened for the first time. The girl looked so damned sad. Then he hardened again. Before coming here, he had seen Maria Bent and the sorrow and tragedy in *her* eyes.

Don Miguel stood awkwardly, unwilling to admit weakness. Only Antonia knew how much effort it took for him to stand alone, balancing himself against the desk. The lieutenant started to take her father's arm when Antonia cried out.

"He needs his crutches."

The lieutenant stopped, a certain chagrin on his face as he realized how weak his captive was. He waited as Antonia helped her father tuck them under his arms. The officer nodded his understanding and waited impatiently as his captive struggled the few feet toward the door.

"Can you ride?"

Don Miguel sent him a withering look. It would be painful, painful beyond the man's comprehension, but he would do it. He had little left beyond pride.

Antonia embraced him, not caring what the Americans thought. "I will call upon our friends for help, Father," she whispered. "And then I will come to Santa Fe."

Her father nodded, his eyes dark and hooded. She wondered if he was thinking about the American scout, and she was grateful he did not tell her how terribly wrong she had been to trust the man.

Instead, he hobbled to the door and to the horses saddled in front of the hacienda.

A number of vaqueros were outside, waiting. Several started to draw their pistols as Don Miguel was led out, but he shook his head even as the four soldiers started for their own weapons.

He could not fight the entire American army, and he did not wish to run away. He looked at the hacienda once more, the place where he had lived his entire life, the place of so much sadness, so much joy. He straightened his shoulders and shrugged aside an American who neared to help him mount. Instead, he nodded to one of his vaqueros to help him.

"Take care of Señorita Antonia," he charged the man after he had mounted painfully. At the man's nod, Don Miguel placed his hands on the saddle horn as the reins were taken by an American private and his horse was led from the house.

From Antonia—and the betrayal of Tristan Hampton.

Two miles away, Ramon watched as the five riders turned toward Taos.

Recognizing Don Miguel, he was struck with unfamiliar pangs of guilt. But he felt confident the Americans would not hang a sick elderly man.

Ramon knew he had lost everything. He had cursed those who had run from the American guns, and those who had not joined him in rising against the Americans despite their pledges of support. Even Miguel. The thought eased his guilt.

It would not be long now before the Americans discovered the part Ramon had played in the rebellion, his full role as one of the leaders. His lands, and probably his life, would be forfeit.

He had no more choices. He would have to disappear into Mexico and start a new life. It would not be easy. His family had lived here for hundreds of years. He had expected to see his son born here, his and Antonia's.

But he would have Antonia. The very image of her made everything else bearable. He could not live without her, no matter what he had to do to make it possible.

She would never be happy with the Gringo, he told himself. They were too different, while he and Antonia shared so much.

Ramon had seen his rival during the battle at La Canada, and it was then, that he had devised the scheme to turn Antonia from the hated American.

He had to restrain himself from riding down to the Ramirez ranch immediately. He would give Antonia time to worry about her father, to consider the gringo's betrayal. The arrest was already the gringo's deed in Ramon's mind. If it hadn't been for his presence in Taos, none of this would have been necessary.

It had been so easy. He had paid the Mexican well to deliver the message to the gringo officer and then disappear. The messenger had said that a Señor Hampton had discovered Miguel Ramirez had planned the American killings. The general had been so busy with the Pueblo Indians that he had ordered Ramirez's detention without question.

Ramon saw riders come from the direction of the Ramirez ranch toward his own property and knew Antonia was probably seeking him. He spurred his horse to intercept one of them.

"Don Ramon," the vaquero called out with relief. "I was sent to find you. The *señorita* . . . she needs you."

She needs you. He had wanted to hear that for years. He kept the triumph from his eyes and nodded solemnly, turning his horse toward the Ramirez ranch.

Ramon had never thought Antonia fragile before, but now he did. Perhaps it was the barely controlled emotion that glittered in eyes that were usually so calm.

He gently put one arm around her shoulders. "I was coming to warn your father that we must leave New Mexico when I met your vaqueros."

Her great brown eyes were clear of tears, but he couldn't mistake the pain in them. She wanted to tell him he had been right about Tristan, but she couldn't force the words. Her agony at the betrayal ran too deep. There was no longer anything to believe in. First her father and his part in the massacre, then Tristan. Even now she couldn't quite believe it, wouldn't have believed it, except for the lieutenant's own words. How could he have made them up?

"What can we do about Father?" she asked haltingly.

Ramon heard the broken words and knew she was grieving as much for the loss of the Yanqui as for her father. He wished to the bottom of his soul that she could feel such pain for him.

"There will be a price on my head, too," he said. "I've been evading the Americans all day. There are too many to help your father here."

"Then what?" It was a cry of desperation. It was all her fault. If she had not fallen in love with Tristan, if she had not let that love blind her to everyone's warnings . . .

"There is one chance, Chula."

Antonia looked at him with sudden hope. All her reservations about Ramon were gone. She had been wrong about Tristan. Perhaps she had also been wrong about Ramon. Her eyes begged him for help.

"Santa Ana," Ramon said. "He is my friend. And he has American prisoners. Perhaps he will exchange them for one as loyal as your father."

"But that will take so long. . . ."

"Not if we travel fast."

The words slowly penetrated Antonia's mind. "Mexico. Go to Mexico?"

"It is your father's only chance," Ramon said.

"With you?" Her words held so much doubt they were like blows to Ramon.

"Santa Ana has a weakness for beautiful women," he insisted softly. He hesitated, adding painfully, "You need not worry about unwelcome advances from me, Antonia. I have sorely regretted that episode on the hill, and, again, I pledge it will never happen again. I swear to God. I want only to help your father."

Antonia's eyes set solemnly on him, wanting to believe, but no longer sure of her own instincts. "Jose will go with us," she said.

A stone dropped in Ramon's stomach. But he didn't know how to deny the request. "But we must go now."

Antonia turned to go pack what few things she could carry. She hesitated at the stairs. "Thank you, Ramon," she said softly, and then turned before he could see the tears in her eyes.

Oh, Tristan, how could you? How could you?

Two hours later, they were making their way over a little-known trail through the mountains, to the left of the Taos Road to Santa Fe. They would skirt through Comanche country, traveling over some of the roughest terrain in the southwest, Ramon had said.

Antonia didn't object. It was what she needed now. Challenge, hardship, discomfort. She needed them to keep from lying down and dying, for that's what she wanted to do. As the hours went on, her grief turned to bitterness and then to the hatred she had always eschewed. Hatred for Tristan Hampton.

Yanqui. Betrayer. Enemy.

It was dark before Tris reached the Ramirez ranch. He had been riding like hell, and his horse was lathered and breathing hard. There were no lights anywhere . . . not at the barn, not in the house.

He pounded at the door and finally, after minutes that seemed hours, it was opened by a large, grim-faced woman.

"Señorita Ramirez," he said.

Luz recognized the tall American and had heard enough to want to slam the door in his face. She tried to do it. But he caught it midway and jerked it open.

"Your *señorita,* where is she?"

"Gone," Luz said impassively, though her eyes glittered with dislike.

"Where?"

Luz just stared at him dumbly.

"Where, damn you?"

"She did not tell me, *señor.*"

"Did she go with anyone?"

An indefinable emotion flickered across the woman's face. Luz did not like Ramon Silvero. But then, she did not trust this Yanqui, either.

"For God's sake, tell me," Tris said.

"I know nothing."

Tense with frustration, Tris pierced Luz with his eyes. "I know what she must think. It's not true. I did not betray her father, dammit. Silvero did."

The words jerked the impassive stare from Luz's face. For some reason she believed the Yanqui. She had seen such happiness on Antonia's face recently. Until today.

Luz looked straight into the Yanqui's eyes. His gaze was steady, without a flicker of deceit. She noted the muscle that strained in his cheek as he tried to curb his angry impatience, and the firm set of his mouth.

Luz made her decision. "She went with Don Ramon. I don't know where. Jose went with them."

"Jose?"

"One of Señor Ramirez's horsemen and my husband. He will take care of her."

"Where did they go?"

"I don't know, *señor*. She did not say. But I think it had something to do with her father."

Tris cursed long and fluently.

"Try to remember," he insisted. "Did they say anything?"

"I just know they took food, *señor*. Enough for a long trip... much dried meat and hardtack."

"Clothes?"

The woman nodded. "*Sí, señor,* she took several riding outfits and a dress... I asked why so much."

"And what did she say?"

"That she was going a long way—" The woman's eyes cleared.

"Something else?"

"She told us not to worry if she was gone for a long time, that Manuel should take charge. She told us that everything will be all right." The woman's eyes filled with tears. "But how can it be, *señor?* The soldiers have taken Don Miguel. And..."

"And what?"

"I don't trust Don Ramon.... I'm afraid for the *señorita*."

Tris's lips twisted into a hard line. "I will find her. You can be assured of that."

"And Don Miguel?"

"I will do what I can," he promised.

Tris rode to Taos, quickly finding out that Don Miguel, along with several other suspected conspirators, had been taken to Santa Fe for extensive questioning. The prisoners' positions as respected ranchers were saving them, for the time being, from the fate of the Indian leaders who had actually murdered the Americans.

The ringleaders were surrendering, and their hanging was all but a surety. They would be tried, according to law, but the judge was the father of Narcisse Beaubien, one of those tortured and killed. There was little chance of mercy.

Meeting with General Price, Tris found out the extent of the battle just fought. The general had lost ten men and had fifty-two wounded. The Indians and Mexicans had lost a hundred and fifty and more than that number had been wounded.

"One of the leaders apparently escaped," Tris said.

Price raised an eyebrow.

"A man named Silvero. I believe he was one of the ringleaders and is now heading south. I would like permission to go after him."

"I don't want to lose you, Hampton. I'll send a detail."

"Begging your pardon, sir, but I think I have the best chance to find him."

Price eyed him carefully. "Could this be personal, Hampton?"

"Charles Bent was my friend, sir," Tristan said simply. He was not going to elaborate on the other reason.

"I've lost enough good men today. I don't want to lose another," Price said.

Tris smiled faintly. "I'll try to see that doesn't happen, sir."

The general considered his scout. His determined chin was set, his eyes were glacial. "You'll go whether or not I give permission," he commented.

"Yes, sir," Tris answered, knowing he was inviting arrest. He had a contract with the army.

Price's lips turned up in a smile. "I appreciate honesty," he conceded wryly. "Get the hell out of here, then, and get back as soon as possible."

"Thank you, sir."

"And I want this Silvero alive, Hampton."

"If it's possible."

"Alive, Tris."

Tris nodded. "Another thing, General . . ."

Price fixed his scout with his most intimidating scowl.

"Lieutenant Baker is taking a New Mexican, a Señor Ramirez, to Santa Fe."

"And . . ."

"He's old, sir, and ill. I think Silvero just used him."

"And you're asking for leniency?"

It galled Tris to agree. The death of Charles was still in his mind. He had seen what the killing had done to Maria Bent, and Antonia's father had been at least partly responsible.

"Yes, sir, I am," he said slowly.

"Something else that's personal?"

"Yes, sir," Tris said.

"You don't want to say what it is?"

"No, sir."

Price shook his head, wondering why he liked the scout so damned much.

"It will take a while for him to come to trial, Hampton. You should be back in time to have your say."

Tris knew that was the best he would get. He nodded and left the tent.

There was little sense in going after Ramon and Antonia now. It was close to midnight and heavy clouds blocked the light from the moon. At least Antonia had Jose with her. Tris decided to get some sleep and leave at dawn. He could only hope he could pick up the trail. Thank God for Conn and his lessons. He would need every one of them.

Chapter Seventeen

Doniphan's army was deep into Mexico when they heard of the Taos Massacre. Conn absorbed the news in grim silence. There was no word of Tris Hampton, but he could only assume the worst. He knew that Tris had been assigned to the governor.

The feelings of loss and guilt were shattering. He knew his sister would never forgive him, nor would he forgive himself for bringing Tris here.

And he knew he had to discover what had happened to the man who had become so important to him.

Colonel Doniphan had to come to a decision. The Missourian was originally to meet an American force under General John Wool in Chihuahua. Now he received word that General Wool had been diverted eastward to assist General Zachary Taylor. If he were to continue southward and take the city of Chihuahua, he would have to do it with his one thousand men, most of whom were infantry.

The colonel put it up to his men, warning them that they would be going two hundred fifty miles into enemy territory, over land with little or no water.

When the Missourians voted to continue farther into Mexico, Conn had the devil's own decision to make. His duty lay with Doniphan, but he had to find out what had happened to Tris.

It ended up being easier than he thought. Doniphan knew him and knew about Tris, and thought he could accomplish several objectives by sending Conn north. The colonel needed to get word to Price in Santa Fe about his plans to continue on into Mexico, and to convey his need for more artillery. The country between El Paso and Santa Fe was alive with Apache, and no one knew the land better than Conn O'Neill. He asked Conn to take the dispatches and request for reenforcements to General Price.

Torn between wanting to go south where a battle was brewing and heading north to find out about his nephew, Conn reluctantly agreed. He would return as soon as possible.

"I'm depending on it," Doniphan said.

"You have my word. Six weeks, no more."

"That nephew of yours will be all right," Doniphan said. "He's as damned capable as you."

Conn's mouth turned up slightly in self-effacing humor. "That good, huh?" he grumbled.

"Near on," Doniphan said. "Damn, but I'll miss you."

"I'll be back before the fight," Conn said again.

"I don't doubt it," the Missouri colonel said, knowing how much Conn had looked forward to facing the Mexicans. He had never seen anyone with a grudge quite as large as his scout's. O'Neill had taken the Alamo very personally.

"How soon will those letters be ready?" Conn said.

"In an hour. I'll ask the cook to put together some food for you."

"Thanks," Conn said.

"I wish you good luck and Godspeed."

"I'll need both," Conn replied somberly, his smile gone.

An hour later, he rode out, intending to make at least fifty miles a day. It would be a killing pace, but he hoped to get to Santa Fe within eight days.

He was unused to prayer, but he said one, nonetheless, feeling the strangeness of it in his throat.

Antonia was numbed by fatigue. Every time Ramon or Jose asked her if she wished to stop, she shook her head. Perhaps if she were tired enough, she wouldn't think, wouldn't remember, wouldn't keep seeing the golden image of Tristan Hampton.

They avoided the regular trails, and swung far east of Santa Fe, entering Apache country.

When she allowed herself to think at all, Antonia was consumed by doubts. Perhaps she should have gone to Santa Fe. Could her father's health withstand imprisonment? Perhaps she would have been a more effective advocate for him in person.

But then she would probably come face-to-face with Tristan Hampton, and she didn't think she could bear that.

Ramon had been going out of his way to be kind. She often found his dark eyes studying her, and he was always there to help her on and off the horse. Never did his hand linger longer than was proper, and she wondered whether she had misjudged him all these years.

Only once did he bring up the subject of the American scout, and he dropped it immediately when he saw her tortured eyes.

"It was his duty," Ramon said softly.

But he said he would say nothing, she wanted to scream back. *And I trusted him. My father trusted him because of me.*

She didn't want Ramon to be reasonable.

Ramon had turned away from the tears in her eyes and didn't mention the American again.

On the fourth day, she was so tired, she could barely hold on to her saddle. The few hours they rested, she slept listlessly. She barely ate, her eyes had dulled. Both Ramon and Jose tried to tempt her with pieces of roasted rabbit, but she only looked at them with indifference.

She leaned against a cottonwood along a stream, and worried about her father.

"You can do nothing for your father if you give up, Chiquita," Ramon advised. "You must eat."

Antonia nodded, knowing he was correct. She forced the food down, chewing slowly. She had to be strong for her father, but the emptiness was so deep that she wondered how she could survive.

She had never indulged in self-pity; she had, in fact, often silently criticized her father for doing just that. The little strands of steel in her hardened as something in her started fighting back.

She slept that night, not as she had before the murders in Taos, but assuredly better than she had in the past few days. And as light crept back into her soul, she began to wonder.

Antonia remembered Tris's gentleness in the cave. He couldn't have feigned that. Nor the obvious turmoil he felt at being caught in the middle . . . between his government and her father. Somehow she knew he would have told her if he had changed his mind.

But why would the American officer lie?

If she had received the information from Ramon, then she would have been quick to disbelieve, but it had come from Tristan's own people.

When she rose the next morning to a pristine sky, doubts clouded her mind. She had accepted evidence presented to her without giving Tristan the benefit of the doubt. But was she doubting herself now only because she wanted to believe so badly? To believe in Tristan?

As they pushed their horses continually southward, she darted glances at Ramon's somber face. There was nothing in it to indicate deceit or guilt, only a concern for both her welfare and her father's.

What had he said earlier? About Tristan's duty? She tried to remember whether she had said anything to him about Tristan's part in her father's arrest. If not, how would he know?

Think, Antonia. Think.

Her head hurt with the possibilities. How could Ramon have been involved in her father's arrest? They had been lifelong friends with the same commitment to Mexico. It was too terrible to consider.

Worse than thinking that Tris had betrayed her?

Her legs tightened against Night Wind. She would find out the truth. She had to.

Tris's heart wrenched as he left the isolated farm of a Mexican couple. He was a good three days behind Antonia and Ramon. They were traveling much faster than he had thought possible.

If only she had believed in me, he thought. He had never felt so alone, and he wanted to scream to relieve the pressure boiling inside him. How could she have believed he would betray her? How could she run away from him? With Ramon? He felt sick and defeated.

He knew the evidence against him had been damning. But her lack of trust still hurt.

He had to find her.

Ramon was clever, far cleverer than Tris had given him credit for. He had hidden his tracks well, and only through dogged perseverance had Tris finally picked up the trail. It was headed straight through Apache country to Mexico.

He had first gone to Santa Fe to see whether Antonia had arrived to be with her father. Before leaving, he had visited Ramirez in his cold, dank cell in the Palacio. Strangely enough, Tris had not received the hostility he had expected.

Ramirez had listened to him, to his denials, to his promise that he would do everything possible to help him. The older man's face had creased in worry at the news of Antonia's disappearance, but to his own fate, he seemed indifferent. He had never liked Ramon's plans, and Antonia's condemnation had only multiplied his own guilt. Conspiracy had never sat comfortably with him, and now he was glad it was over.

In response to Tris's charge that Ramon had betrayed Don Miguel and taken Antonia, he looked at Tris with steady dark eyes. "He will not hurt her," the older man said. "Ramon has loved her all his life. It is why I wanted their marriage. I believed that Antonia could gentle the hardness in his heart." In that moment, Tris knew the older man thought Ramon capable of the betrayal.

"Or harden her own," Tris said bitterly.

"Do you really think that is possible?" Ramirez said with a sad smile. "She wanted to hate me, and she could not. She loves so well, so fully."

"And you, Señor Ramirez, how do you feel about me?"

"I would be less than honest to say that you are what I want for my daughter," Don Miguel said slowly. "I love my Church, my country, and you share neither. But Antonia has showed me the bitter fruit of hate. I came very close to losing her forever, and she is the light of my life." He paused a moment, then continued. "I have much to answer for . . . to her, to my God. If you are the man Antonia has chosen, I will not interfere."

"If I can find her," Tris replied harshly.

A wry smile played on Ramirez's lips. "Something tells me you will, Señor Hampton."

"Do you have any idea where they may have gone?"

"Mexico," Don Miguel said. "They would go to Mexico. Ramon is a distant relative of Santa Ana. He will go to him."

Tris stared, surprised at the information readily given him. His blue eyes met dark ones and a flash of understanding passed between them, so fleetingly that Tris wondered whether he had imagined it.

Don Miguel leaned against the filthy wall of his cell. "I'm an old man, Señor Hampton. It does not matter what happens to me. But I want happiness for Antonia." He continued painfully. "Do not think she is the daughter of a cold-blooded murderer. I wanted the Americans gone from my country, but not this way. I say this not for myself, but for her."

Tris nodded slowly. He could not doubt the intense sincerity of the words. He turned and left, watching as a guard closed and locked the cell door behind him. He took out some coins. "See that he gets some blankets, some decent food," he said.

Mexico. But which trail? And how fast could two men and a woman travel? Thank God for Nugget. Tris had packed his few belongings rapidly and headed south.

He had found the first signs of them three days later, three days of crisscrossing, of questions, of following dead-end trails. Of being haunted at night by visions of Ramon and Antonia together, of the man forcing himself on her. Only Ramirez's assurance that Ramon would do nothing to hurt Antonia kept Tris from going mad.

Once he had found their tracks, he had hunted relentlessly and knew he was gradually overtaking them. He had been three days behind, then two and now, he knew from the age of the horse droppings, only one. In another few days he should reach them…just before they entered Mexico. As he had every night, he rode until his horse desperately needed rest; his own needs didn't matter. He kept a dry camp and went without fire, for he didn't want to attract Indians or outlaws. There were deserters from both the Mexican and American armies, and they were as ruthless as the Apache that haunted the canyons and rocks of southern New Mexico.

On the seventh morning, he had gone ten miles or so when he saw the remnants of their fire. Dismounting, he felt the ashes. They were cool, but the horse droppings nearby were less than several hours old. He remounted and once more turned south. He had gone barely a mile before he saw additional tracks of approximately twenty unshod horses and they were fresh.

Apache.

Tristan's hands dropped to the neck of his horse, and sent Nugget into a gallop. Dear God, let him be in time.

Ramon carefully watched Antonia. They had stopped at a watering hole and she was leaning over, filling the canteens. He knew it was one of the few sources of water in the next hundred miles. They would fill their canteens and be on their way again.

He had felt her measuring gaze for a long time. In the beginning, he had thought she would turn to him, accept the comfort he offered. But that had not happened. During the first four days, she had seemed lifeless, and since she had regained some of her spirit, she had distanced herself from him.

How he wanted to take her! But he remembered the day he had tried and the revulsion in her eyes, and he didn't think he could stand to see it again.

He had to be patient. She was hurt now, feeling betrayed. It would take time for her to trust. When he proved he could help her father, she would be grateful. She would forget about the gringo.

Ramon had made his plans. He had money in Mexico City banks, some made from his dealings with the Indians, some stolen here and there from taxes. He had enough to start a new ranch, a profitable one that would never again be endangered by the Americanos. And he would have Antonia by his side. He would build an empire for Antonia and his sons.

Ramon wished he knew what Antonia was thinking. But aside from periodic querying looks, she had said little, insisting that they press on.

Antonia took out a small piece of cloth and washed her face with the dirty stream water. She was beautiful, so proud and regal.

She saw his eyes on her. "How much farther, Ramon?"

"A day, perhaps less, into Mexico. Several more days to find Santa Ana."

"Do you think he will help us?"

He wanted to put his arms around her, to pat her face comfortingly. Instead, he merely inched a bit closer. *"Sí,"* he said simply.

"How do you think the Americans learned about my father?"

The question was unexpected and speared him with its import.

"I suppose there were many who suspected. He never kept his dislike of the Yanquis secret."

Antonia waited for him to implicate Tris, but he didn't.

It was that one comment he made three days ago that gnawed at her. *"It was his duty."*

She decided she could go no longer without knowing. "You knew Señor Hampton told the authorities?"

"The American scout?" Ramon said with feigned surprise. "But how would he know?"

The question rang false, and both he and Antonia knew it.

The emptiness that Antonia felt previously was nothing to that which now settled inside her. Shame washed over her in great waves as she thought how little trust she had given Tristan. Where was he now? What had he thought when he heard she had left with Ramon? How had he felt knowing she trusted Ramon more than the man who endured the enmity of her father and had sacrificed his own honor for her?

She bent her head in grief and self-recrimination.

"Antonia?"

Antonia forced herself to compose her face before she looked up. She had rushed to judgment with Tristan. She would not do the same with Ramon, although she was becoming increasingly convinced that somehow he had arranged her father's arrest.

But how? And why? She did not for one moment believe that her father's and Ramon's friendship had not been real. Perhaps Ramon really thought he could save her father through Santa Ana, using that as a tool to wedge himself into her heart.

Perhaps she would have been grateful enough, and sufficiently hurt by Tristan, to have finally accepted him.

Dear Mother of God, she was weary of conspiracies. Her mind sped ahead. She would stay with Ramon . . . she had no choice at this point. No matter who had informed on her father, his sole chance now lay with Santa Ana and the president's willingness to exchange Americans for those loyal to him in Taos and Santa Fe. She would stay with Ramon until that mission had been accomplished.

And then what?

The future stretched out bleak and lonely. The ranch would be confiscated no matter what happened to her father. It had been her home, her life for so long. Until Tris came, and now he was gone, too. If she was right, if somehow Ramon had planned her father's betrayal, then Tris could never forgive her, would never trust her again. She would lose something so rare, so precious. After tasting splendor, how could she live without it?

"Antonia?" She heard Ramon's voice again, persistent and questioning.

"I was just thinking about my father," she said, needing a reason for the tears hovering in her eyes. "I don't know if he can withstand prison. He is so ill." She would not even let herself think of hanging. They wouldn't. Not even the Americans would hang a sick man.

Ramon put a comforting hand on her shoulder, and Antonia steeled herself against flinching. She needed him now. But if she ever found out that what she suspected was true, she would kill him.

"He will be all right," Ramon said. "I promise you, Chula. I will never let anything happen to you or your father."

"What will you do after he's released, Ramon? You can't go back."

"I have some money in Mexico," he said. "I will build a big new ranch, and you and your father will live with me. It will be your home, too."

Ramon was careful not to propose. She was still too shattered by the American's betrayal. He must give her time. He had not missed the flare of suspicion in her eyes, but it was gone quickly enough. And he had protected himself. She would never know, and he would make her happy. Once they were all in Mexico, she would forget the American bastard, and her gratitude and dependence would change to love.

But, the devil take it, it was harder and harder not to pull her to him, to take what he wanted as he had all his life. She would be worth the wait. When she melted in his arms, his restraint would be only a memory.

He looked for Jose, who was taking care of the horses. It was hot, after the ice and cold of Taos. The sand was burning under their feet, and it was difficult going for their mounts. They would stay here until late afternoon when the air cooled. The moon was full, and it would be easy traveling at night. He wondered only briefly if the gringos had dared to track them into enemy territory. He doubted it. The scout would be under orders, and the military would fear more rebellion in the north. And he had taken precautions, using little-known trails, and traveling through Indian country. It was risky, but he had dealt with Indians all his life, and thought he could do so now.

"Señor!" Jose's voice was sharp with warning.

Ramon looked to the vaquero. The man was pointing to a hill in the distance.

Putting his hand to his eyes, Ramon squinted against the bright afternoon sun. He could barely make out riders, sitting motionless on their mounts overlooking the water hole.

Ramon had not lived all his life in New Mexico without recognizing the careless poise of Apache. His throat constricted. He had had profitable relations with the Apache of the north, but he knew each band was fiercely proud of its own independence. The friends of one were not necessarily the friends of others.

And then there was Antonia. How could he parley with them in front of her without her learning of his past transactions?

He looked at her and saw that her eyes, too, were on the riders. They flickered over to him in question.

"We'll try to outrun them," Ramon said. "Our horses are all strong."

Antonia nodded, struggling to keep the fear from her face. She had heard so many stories, so much talk of what Apache did to white women. And her father? He would wait and wait, until...

"What should I do?" she asked in a quiet voice.

"They probably know we've seen them, but don't hurry, just move as we usually do when we break camp."

It was the hardest thing Antonia had ever done, but she packed unhurriedly and watched as Jose saddled her horse. She accepted Ramon's hand when she mounted, all the time trying to keep her eyes from the riders to the west.

They slowly rode out of the clearing, keeping their horses at a walk.

Antonia brought her horse apace with Ramon's. "Why don't they come?"

"They are playing with us, Chula," he said. "Trying to frighten us into wearing out our horses. There are probably other Apache among these canyons."

Antonia's hands tightened on the reins, and Night Wind sidestepped in protest.

"Easy, Antonia." Ramon gave her a small confident smile. "We have guns. I doubt they do." He hoped to hell they didn't have the rifles he had sold to the Apache outside Taos. That would be a tragic irony, he thought with a tight, grim smile.

There was still negotiation. But he had damned little to negotiate with. There was really only Antonia. He looked at the proud figure beside him.

He would die first. And he would kill her before he let them have her.

Chapter Eighteen

Conn reached Santa Fe in a record five days. He had worn out his horse, and he felt none too spritely himself, but every time he had stopped, a voice within taunted him and spurred him ahead. He was needed. How . . . why, he did not know. He just knew it to be so.

It was sixteen days after the massacre when he reached Santa Fe, five after Tris had left. Part of Price's command had returned; another part, including General Price, was still in Taos.

Conn quickly found out what he needed to know. Tris had escaped the massacre but was now chasing one of the ringleaders south. By careful questioning, he also discovered that Miguel Ramirez was in prison and his daughter was missing.

It did not take Conn long to surmise that Antonia had been taken by, or gone with, Silvero, although no one else mentioned such a possibility. Other than Charles Bent, he was the only man who knew of Tris's obsession with the Ramirez girl. Conn didn't want to think it might be anything more. If the girl had gone willingly with the New Mexican rebel, then he could see little future with her for his nephew.

The relief he felt at Tris's narrow escape at Taos was quickly swallowed by new apprehension. Tris had managed to get word to Price's headquarters that he had found Silvero's trail and was heading south. The trail was east of the Rio Grande, and the country hostile and exceedingly rough. Worse still, it was Apache country, and the Apache were particularly active now that war between the Mexicans and Americans made any concentrated effort against the Apache impossible.

He exchanged his horse for a fresh mount and bought a second one to take with him. He would make better time that way without ruining either animal. As far as headquarters was concerned, he was merely heading back south to meet Doniphan. He didn't bother to explain he would be taking a different trail.

Conn took only hardtack and jerky with him. He did not intend to stop long enough to build a fire. After a couple of hours of sleep, he retrieved his horses and headed south at a canter.

Ramon, Jose and Antonia traveled without apparent hurry but at a consistent pace, aware every moment of the Apache following at the same pace behind them.

"Why don't they do something?" Antonia finally asked.

Ramon looked at her. Her hair was in a braid that had twisted around and lay against her breast. She had taken off her jacket and only a soft silk blouse separated his eyes from the flesh he envisioned in his mind. Despite the dust and perspiration that covered them both, she was incredibly desirable.

She was also, at the moment, completely dependent on him, and she quickly obeyed his every command.

"When they are ready, Chiquita," he said, looking toward a canyon south of them. It was dusk and the horses needed rest. Perhaps they could find some protective rocks for the night.

He was grateful they had filled their canteens earlier. They would have enough water for themselves and the horses for the time being. Tomorrow, however, would be another matter.

Ramon decided not to say anything to Antonia, not unless they found a safe place to stop. His eyes moved swiftly from rock to rock as, an hour later, they started through the mouth of the canyon. He finally found what he was looking for, a large outcropping of rocks big enough to protect the three of them and their mounts.

There was one disadvantage. They could be cut off at both ends of the canyon. But just as he was thinking that, he saw riders approach from the far end. They were already trapped.

He heard Antonia's gasp, but didn't bother to acknowledge it. He grabbed her reins and headed upward, his horse stumbling and turning its head in protest. He heard rock falling behind him and Jose's Spanish curse as the man's horse slipped.

They finally reached the rocks, and all three dismounted rapidly just as several arrows passed harmlessly by. Antonia grabbed for her rifle as the two men went for their pistols. Antonia took the horses behind a boulder and tied them to a bush, then dropped next to Jose.

Apache milled around below them, and Ramon took aim and shot, hitting one. The rest hurriedly moved out of range, several pointing toward them and gesturing.

Antonia counted ten of them below. There were more at either end of the canyon, probably about twenty in number. None, she thought gratefully, seemed to have a rifle. But an occasional arrow bounced around them, and Antonia knew a deep heart-wrenching fear.

To die before seeing Tristan again. That was the greatest agony of all. He would never know how much she loved him, how much she regretted her own actions. She tried to think of his eyes, warm and tender and full of passion, but she could only envision their coldness, the icy glare that had frozen her with its intensity. She had experienced it when he had talked of Ramon, and now she had chosen Ramon over him. Or at least it would seem so to him.

And she could never explain. An arrow sped overhead and she tried to sink farther into the ground.

"Your rifle," Ramon commanded, reaching for it. He and Jose had left their rifles in their saddles, and Jose was slowly moving from their protective location toward the horses.

Antonia moved her rifle, knowing that Ramon meant for her to hand it to him, but she did not. Instead, she aimed at one of the Indians, who seemed to be the leader. She tightened her finger on the trigger and hesitated. Until she had killed the men ambushing Tris, she had never aimed at a human being before. But she had had plenty of practice with animal predators.

"Antonia!"

Her fingers closed on the trigger and she felt the shock of the rifle's report against her shoulder. She looked down again and saw the Indian falling, slowly, as if suspended in some way. She heard a cry from behind her and knew it was Jose. She felt Ramon's body cover her as the air seemed alive with arrows. His weight was heavy and suffocating, and she couldn't breathe, but she knew he was protecting her, offering his life for hers. Conflicting emotions ran through her mind as the whistle and thud of arrows created a deadly symphony around them.

All of a sudden, all was silent. The heavy weight on her moved, and she felt free as her face turned up to the moonlit sky.

"Ramon?"

"I'm all right, Chiquita."

"Jose?"

Jose's voice came through the night air like the whisper of a wounded bird. "My leg..."

Antonia evaded Ramon's arm and crawled up to where Jose was doubled over. The wound was pouring out blood, and she quickly took his bandanna and tied it just above the wound, twisting it to cut the supply of blood. Together, they crawled back to where Ramon was watching below.

"The rifles?"

"I couldn't reach them," Jose said, panting.

Without thinking, Antonia darted toward the horses fifteen yards away, believing an arrow would strike her any second, but there were none. She reached the horses and pulled out the rifles and saddlebags with additional ammunition. She fell to the ground and inched her way back to the two men.

Ramon's black hair shone in the moonlight and his dark eyes glittered with anger and admiration. "That was foolish, little one."

Antonia ignored him. She looked below and realized why there had been no arrows. The Apache were leaning over their fallen leader. She watched as several leaned down and picked the body up gently, placing him carefully on his pony. There was no movement from the Indian.

"Perhaps they will leave?"

Ramon looked at her. "They will mourn him tonight and take their revenge tomorrow. The Apache can wait. We have no place to go," he added bitterly. "They have cut off the exits to the canyon."

"You don't think they will attack tonight?"

"No. Get some rest, Antonia."

"I'll take care of Jose first."

Ramon shrugged. He knew it would do no good to protest that Jose could take care of himself. He nodded and watched as Antonia carefully wrapped the vaquero's leg. The arrow had gone completely through and Jose had broken off the head and pulled the shaft out. Two gaping wounds bled profusely every time the tourniquet was released. The arrow had apparently ruptured an artery. Jose's face was pale, his teeth clenched in suffering.

"I am sorry, *señorita*," he murmured before losing consciousness.

Antonia kept working, but the bleeding continued, and when her eyes met Ramon's dark ones, he shook his head. Antonia wet a cloth and washed Jose's face, watching it grow paler and paler, his skin clammy.

"You must sleep, Antonia," Ramon insisted. "I will watch him."

But Antonia couldn't. It had been her stubbornness and stupidity that had brought Jose out here. She wondered how she would tell Luz, and then realized she would probably never have the opportunity to do it. Dear Jose.

She took out her rosary and said a prayer for him, holding his hands until they went slack and the life drained from his eyes. She closed them and made the sign of the cross.

Antonia didn't know how long she sat there, but she finally felt a hand on her.

"You must get some rest, Antonia," Ramon said in a gentle voice she had never heard before.

"I cannot," she whispered.

"We will need all the strength we have tomorrow," he said. "I'll take the first watch and wake you in three hours." And still she hesitated. "For God's sake, do as I ask."

It was the pleading in his voice that convinced her. Just as she had never heard gentleness in his voice, she had never heard him plead before, either.

Antonia nodded slowly. He passed a canteen to her and she took a swallow. It was whiskey, not water, and she sputtered even as she felt its warmth seep into the cold, frightened part of her.

Although she didn't think she could fall asleep, it wasn't minutes before she had. Ramon watched her eyes close reluctantly, and he leaned back against the rocks, part of his attention on the stillness below, part on Antonia.

By bringing her here, on this trail, he had most likely signed the death warrants of both of them. He did not recognize the Indians below; they were none of those he had done business with. And with Antonia's killing of the man who was apparently their chief, there was no chance of negotiation or mercy...if there had ever been one. He doubted strongly there had been.

With their guns, they could hold off the Apache for a day, perhaps more, but their lack of water would do what the Apache could not. They could expect no assistance.

Once more his gaze went to the sleeping woman beside him. She was so beautiful in her sleep, the long dark lashes like strands of fine silk against her face. So brave. So spirited. If only she had loved him, he could have been anything, accomplished anything. A deep regretful sorrow filled him. He had never meant for her father to die. He had been so sure he could win Santa Ana's assistance. But now they would never reach the Mexican leader.

His hand reached out and touched Antonia's ebony curls. He wanted to feel her cheek, her skin, but he was afraid he would wake her. She needed this brief time of sleep. His hand went to his pistol and he thought about killing her now. He would have to do it sooner or later; he would never let the Apache have her. And he had to do it while he still could, before he was killed.

He thought of the deep brown of her eyes and how transparent they were. He remembered how they used to regard him so admiringly as a child. When had that look turned to contempt?

Ramon thought of the power he had had, of the money he had accumulated. He would give it all up for one real smile from Antonia. He thought of the men he had ruined, of the conspiracies he had fermented, of the lies he had lived. He thought of tomorrow, of death, and he knew real fear... not of death, but of judgment.

His fingers tightened around a wayward curl. "Forgive me, Antonia," he whispered.

Tris heard the echo of a shot. It was impossible to tell the distance in the still, clear night.

But he felt a chill run through him.

He had pushed his horse unmercifully, but now he asked even more of Nugget. The plain was broken by canyons, and the shot had echoed, disguising its exact location. He had easily followed the tracks, both shod and unshod, as they crossed and recrossed until dusk fell. Now it was more difficult, and he just bloody well didn't have time.

Tris was only too aware of how badly outnumbered Tonia's party was. There were only three shod horses and at least a dozen unshod ones. Pretty poor odds, even if Ramon and the Ramirez vaquero did have guns.

Tris spoke to Nugget, urging the horse on cautiously. The gunshots probably meant that Silvero and Antonia had stopped. And Tris didn't want to bungle into a party of Apache.

Another gunshot rang out, this time fairly close, and he saw the silhouette of a canyon ahead. He knew it probably offered one of the few defensive positions available and thought it likely Silvero had chosen it. For the first time since he met the Creole, he hoped like hell that Silvero was competent.

There was a third gunshot, and he knew he had guessed right. He studied his options. They were damnably few. Riding in would accomplish little. If the Indians didn't shoot him, Silvero probably would. He needed to cut the odds.

There may be another way into the canyon. It might be guarded, but possibly not as well as this one. He would have to ride until he found it. But, Dear God, that would take time. He wondered if he had any.

Still, it was the only chance he had.

Soothing his tired horse, he dropped back to a walk. He didn't want the sound of hoofbeats echoing as the gunshots had. Forcing himself to be patient, he moved south, keeping in the shadows of the canyon. He could only hope the Apache felt little need for sentries.

Each moment seemed like an hour, especially when the air stilled and there were no more gunshots. Was Antonia dead? It was a thought so painful he quickly dismissed it. *Stay alive, Antonia. Stay alive, and believe in me. Believe in me.*

The moon was bright, the stars even brighter. Every shadow was ominous and deadly.

He finally reached the other side of the canyon and dismounted, tying Nugget to a small bush. As Conn had taught him, Tris moved as silently as a wisp of cloud across the sky.

He saw the fire first, the flames shooting up into the sky, and then the figures around it. He counted five and then another two, who were on guard.

He lowered himself to the ground and, after covering his face with dirt, crawled forward, his eyes seeking any movement, the slightest brush of a shrub, the merest breath on the wind.

He finally found what he sought. Next to some horses was a solitary figure. Tris took the knife from his belt and crawled across the grass. A movement stopped him and he froze, trying to disappear in the sparse shrub that was the only life in this godforsaken place. He heard voices, then one of the men seemed to be moving away.

Wait, he told himself. Be sure. He counted seconds, then moved slowly toward the dark blur that blocked the moon. He stood quickly, his hand going to his victim's mouth as the knife went into his throat. There was a slight gurgling sound as the figure went slack and Tris lowered him to the ground.

One.

He moved slowly in the direction in which the other man had gone. Another figure. Tris wiped his knife in the sand and once more went for the Indian's throat.

Two.

There were five Apache remaining at this end of the canyon, and he had no hope in hell of continuing his present silent success. The others were grouped together.

He crawled back to the Indians' ponies and carefully untied their ropes. With a slap on one and a holler, he sent the ponies rushing in the direction of the fire as five Apache scattered to get out of the way. They were all silhouetted by the flames.

He shot four times, three shots hitting targets. The two remaining Indians dived into the shadows.

He waited. They waited. One of the ponies came wandering back, and an Apache dived for his back. Tris shot as he did and saw the rider fall and the pony bolt forward.

One. There was one left at this end of the canyon. He wouldn't even think about the other end. Not now.

It was a waiting game now. One against one.

Nothing moved.

There was a moan in the shrubs to his left. Then a call, the sound of a coyote, from some distance away. But no one answered.

Tris remained still until he heard the slightest whisper of movement to his right. He twisted around, rolling away from it as a knife went into the ground just inches away from him. The figure twisted toward him once more, and the Indian frantically tried to reach the knife in the ground. Tris gave him no opportunity. His leg went out, tumbling his assailant. As Tris was about to use his own knife, the Indian was on him, an iron hand grabbing his wrist and pinning it to the ground. The man's strength was formidable, and Tris could feel the muscles straining as he pressed against him.

Tris went slack for a moment, and the man's grasp faltered in surprise. Tris twisted his leg around the Apache's, forcing him over on his side, and rolled on top of him.

The knife was clenched by both of them and the battle became a test of sheer strength and determination, each knowing that the prize was life.

Tris gained the advantage. As one hand battled for the knife, his other went around his opponent's throat and he pressed tightly, ignoring the beating on his chest, the frantic kicks that tried to unseat him. Slowly, the Apache's strength faded as he fought for breath, and his hand relaxed.

Tris took the advantage. He shook the Apache's fist loose from the knife and he plunged it into the man's chest, hearing the agonized grunt as the Apache made one last attempt to get free. And then the movements weakened until they were no more.

Tris pulled slowly off the man's body and lay on the ground, trying to slow the rapid movement of his heartbeat. It had been so close.

The call from the other end of the canyon came again, and Tris answered it with a like sound, hoping it would suffice. If not, he could be knee deep in more Apache, and his strength was almost gone.

He felt a wetness on his shirt and, feeling pain for the first time, he put his hand there.

Removing his shirt he checked the wound. There was a long jagged slice down his side. It was bleeding steadily. He tore a strip from his shirt and tied it tightly around his waist before leaning back once more, trying to regain some of his strength.

He would take an Indian pony into the canyon. Hopefully the Apache would think he was one of their own. Once there, he would try to locate Antonia's position and pray to God she was still alive. The chances were good that she was; otherwise, the Apache would not be guarding the canyon.

And Silvero? God help him if he got in the way.

Tris painfully rose, once more hearing the moan of one of the wounded. It was fainter now, and he ignored it. Tonia was the only person of importance at the moment, and he had to get to her before he lost much more blood.

He hoisted himself onto one of the Indian ponies, taking two more with him in case Tonia and the others had lost their horses. He knew he might need three, but he didn't think he could control that many. Two were difficult enough with his sapped strength.

Tris started down the canyon, leaning over the pony's neck. He was larger than most Apache in height and build, and he tried to disguise it as much as possible. He wished he had taken a moment to rub more dirt in his sun-lightened hair, but it was too late to think of such things now. God, but he hurt.

He could hear the lonely *clip-clop* of hoofs beneath him, and each seemed as loud as a cannon charge. Once more he heard the coyote call, and he answered. He was a third of the way in, and then nearly half. The red walls were almost black in the moonlight. He searched them relentlessly, looking for a perch or position that could hide three people.

There was a fire at the end of the canyon, and he saw figures rising to their feet, standing curiously. Another minute, and they would be reaching for their weapons.

And then he saw it. The flash of moonlight on a gun above. And it was pointing at him.

His eyes immediately found the steep path up. "Antonia," he yelled. "It's Tristan."

He turned his pony toward the outcropping, praying it and the ponies behind him could make the climb in the dark. He heard the guttural shouts below and sensed quick movements.

Something stirred above, and he leaned even closer to the neck of his horse just as a bullet hit a rock nearby. He was a perfect target for Silvero.

Antonia woke to the sound of her name. For an instant, she thought she was still sleeping, that she had summoned Tristan in her dreams. She heard a curse in Spanish, and she sat up abruptly. Ramon was at the edge of the rocks, aiming at something below. She heard the shot and then its echoes. She crawled over to him and looked down.

She could never mistake that golden hair. Tristan. He had come. She looked at Ramon, who was once more aiming his gun at the horseman now just feet away.

"No," she screamed, and her hand pushed the pistol away as Ramon fired, the bullet going harmlessly into the air. Whatever gentleness was in Ramon last night was no longer there. It was as if an evil demon had taken over his body. His face was twisted with hate. He started to take aim again, but her hand reached for the gun and she fought him like a wildcat.

"No, Ramon," she said again, this time her voice low with intent. "I love him."

The words were like a bullet in Ramon's gut. His hand lost its strength and the pistol dropped to the ground as Tristan reached them and a shower of arrows started coming toward them.

Antonia got to her knees, mindless of the flying arrows, mindless of Ramon. Tristan. He had come for her.

"Get down," Ramon yelled. She felt something push against her back, felt the weight of a body as she fell. Stunned by the fall and the weight on her, she lay motionless, barely sensing the jerk of the body on top of her as the world went black.

Chapter Nineteen

Four arrows jutted from Silvero's still body. Tris gently turned him, checking his neck for a pulse and finding none. The man's eyes were closed, the expression blank. All the hatred he held for Silvero drained from him. The Creole had taken death meant for Tonia, and he had done it without hesitation.

Tris turned to Tonia. Her pulse was strong and her breathing easy. His hands ran over her body; he could find no injuries.

He looked up. A wisp of a cloud was crossing the moon, extinguishing some of the light. There was another cloud nearby, and Tris prayed for more. Taking advantage of the shadows, he hunted among the rocks for a canteen, finally finding one tucked away near the place he had first seen Silvero.

He dampened his bandanna and washed Tonia's face with the warm water. He touched his side; the pain was now a steady throb, and the bandage was covered with blood. He had to get them out of here and get some attention himself.

"Come on, Tonia," he whispered. "Wake up, love."

His desperation seemed to communicate itself to her, and she stirred slightly, her eyes slowly opening. They settled on his face.

"Ramon . . . he's trying to kill you."

"I know, love," he whispered. "He's dead." Tristan hesitated. "He saved your life."

"Ramon?"

"Ramon," he confirmed. "He covered your body with his own."

"Dead...?"

He heard the confusion in her voice. "Arrows," he said, not wanting her to think he had killed him, although he had been quite ready to do just that.

"He said he loved me," she said slowly.

"He proved he did," Tris replied tenderly. "When it was important, he proved he did."

She looked at Tris with dark eyes full of churning emotion. She wanted to ask him a million questions, but she knew this was not the time. She wanted, most of all, to be in his arms, to feel his protection, his warmth.

But he drew away, once more looking toward the sky and the scant cloud cover that might mean their escape. "Jose?" he asked, although he had already guessed when he saw no sign of the man.

"Dead," she said in a low voice. "He's behind the rocks, with the horses."

"They're all right? Your Night Wind?"

"As far as I know."

"We have to ride for it," he said. "Can you do it?"

She hesitated. "Ramon and Jose?"

"We'll have to leave them."

"I can't."

"Then there will be four bodies here instead of two," he said, forcing a hardness into his voice.

Antonia stared at him, her eyes welling with unshed tears, all of them, he knew, for someone else. Tris's throat constricted. He would have resented it bitterly moments ago, but perhaps Silvero deserved tears now.

Finally, she nodded. She crawled over to Ramon and put her cheek against his. "Thank you," she whispered.

She then gave her hand to Tristan, and he saw her mouth firm with determination. She nodded.

"We'll take your horses," he said. "They'll last longer than the unshod ponies. As we go down, I'll scatter the Indian horses. They should confuse our trail."

"Your horse?" she said.

"Nugget? He's waiting outside the south end of the canyon. We'll pick him up on the way." He paused. "When you mount," he continued, "ride like hell. Don't stop, no matter what. If something slows me, you keep going. I'll catch up. Do you understand?"

"Yes." It was said in a small voice, and not a very believable one.

"You could kill us both if you don't," he said.

She would do nothing to put him in more danger. "Yes," she said with more conviction.

He had one last thing he needed to say. He may not have another chance. "Tonia, I love you. I didn't tell the army about your father." It was difficult to say, but the pain in his side was worse, and he didn't know whether he would make it out of here alive.

"I know," she said, wondering at the faltering voice. "I knew almost as soon as I left."

He bent his head to hers and kissed her. It was desperate and sad and tender, all at once, and Antonia wanted to grab him and hold on. But all too quickly, he let her go and stood back, his eyes once more scanning the surroundings. The rocks were dark now, the clouds completely covering the moon.

Tris and Antonia snaked their way up the few yards to where the horses were hidden, and Tris helped her mount with the last strength he had.

"Don't forget your promise," he whispered. "Don't stop for anything."

He mounted Ramon's horse, the best of the two remaining mounts, and untied the third, slapping his rear to send him down the path. Antonia went second, and Tris followed, stopping only to release the Indian ponies, and then all of them were slipping, sliding down the steep decline.

Tris watched as Tonia reached the bottom and Night Wind stretched out into a gallop. But as his mount reached the canyon floor, several Indians grabbed for him, for the reins of his horse, for the saddle. He had reloaded the pistol before going to the horses, and now he fired, scattering the figures. When one tried to swing up behind him, he hit him with the butt of the gun and then he, too, was galloping down the length of the canyon as screeching war cries rose behind them.

At the mouth of the canyon they were met by silence. Tris stopped, watching Tonia streak ahead, and he rode to where he had left Nugget. He slid to the ground and jerked Nugget's reins from the bush. Mounting quickly, he felt new blood pushing against his makeshift bandage.

He returned to the canyon mouth and saw several Indians emerge from the opening. Only three bullets were left in the gun, but they wouldn't expect him here, not coming from this direction. If he could hit several of them, it would stop the others for a few minutes and give Tonia more time.

Tris took aim at the first rider and pulled the trigger. The Indian's horse faltered and fell. Tris cursed. His hand was no longer steady. He fired once more, missing again, but it was enough to make the Apache retreat into the canyon.

Tris tightened his knees against Nugget and chased after Antonia, Silvero's horse racing at his side.

His vision blurred, and he had to trust the horse to follow Antonia as his hands lost the reins and his fingers clung desperately to Nugget's mane.

Antonia heard the shots behind her and slowed Night Wind. *Don't stop...don't stop...don't stop.* Tristan's words echoed in her mind just as the shots had resounded in the canyon.

But what did life mean, what did anything mean, without him? She still couldn't quite believe this wasn't all some hideous nightmare where everything exploded in blood. Except for Tristan. Except for his love and protection. Even after what she had done, he had come for her.

And Ramon, who had given his life for her. Poor Ramon, whom she could never have loved. She swallowed, trying to keep back the tears she was afraid would blind her.

The darkness turned to a deep blue-gray as the clouds left the moon behind and there was some light again. She looked behind and saw a rider on a golden horse following her, and her heart freshened and filled with hope.

She slowed and looked back again, this time noticing the strange way he was crouched over the horse. Something was wrong, very wrong. She reined Night Wind to a walk and concentrated on the rider. He was no longer tall and proud in the saddle, but bent over and swaying, as if he would fall at any moment.

Dear Mother of God, he had been hurt.

His warning, her promise, no longer mattered.

She drew her horse up and waited. He was barely conscious and holding on only by sheer determination. Why hadn't she noticed before—or had he been injured during the wild ride through the canyon?

With a sickening dread, Antonia remembered Jose and how he had bled to death.

She leaned down and grabbed the trailing reins of the horse Tris was riding. They couldn't stop here, not out in the open. But it was equally obvious he couldn't go much farther.

There were no other riders visible. She quickly calculated the odds. She and Ramon had killed several of the Apache, and Tris must have killed several more since he had three of their ponies. Would they lick their wounds and retreat or come after them?

She couldn't take the chance.

They were in the rugged foothills of the Guadalupe Mountains, an area full of hidden canyons and broken ground. There should be any number of places to hide. A cloud drifted over the moon again, darkening the landscape, adding shadows to the stunted junipers and cat claws.

Tris was mumbling jumbles of words that meant little. She had to get him safety. She had to get him water. She found a break in the hills littered by stones that she hoped would hide their tracks. She followed the natural path until they reached a wide overhang of rock with a barrier of shrubs surrounding it. She led the horses under the overhang and dismounted. As she had done weeks earlier, she helped Tris from his horse.

There was writing on the overhang, Indian symbols, but they seemed ancient and there was no evidence of recent habitation. She peered into the opening and saw only a yawning hole in the ground, reaching almost to both sides of the cave. They would have to stay under the overhang. The interior, she feared, held dangers of its own.

Antonia took the blanket from Nugget's back and placed it under Tris's head. The horse was nuzzling his still master as if puzzled at his lack of response. Antonia, sick with anxiety of her own, gave the horse a brief reassuring pat before kneeling beside Tristan.

She quickly found the dark stain on his shirt and pulled the garment's now ragged edges up to reveal the makeshift bandage. Her hand felt the stiffening cloth, and she realized how long he had been hiding his injury. He had had no time since their flight to dress the wound.

In the moonlight, she saw the purpled ribs and other assorted bruises and winced. How had he managed to accomplish everything he had? The pain and the effort must have been gargantuan.

His face was pale, but at least his wound was not bleeding as profusely as Jose's had.

As morning light creeped under the overhang, Antonia looked at Tristan with anguish.

He had used all his strength in extricating her last night. There must be so little left.

He lay very still, just as he had during the last long hours of night. She had sat next to him, washing his face with the limited water they had, wishing desperately there was something else she could do.

The knife wound was open and sore looking, the skin around it fiery. It needed stitching, but she had nothing to use, and she could only try to pull it tight together with a bandage. She could see by the cloth it was still seeping a terrible watery orange liquid.

She had never felt so helpless in her life. She knew the rudiments of medicine, knew some of the benefits of roots and plants, but there were none of them around, and she had no medical supplies. Even Ramon's whiskey was gone, the canteen left back at the canyon. She could try to sear the wound, but she was afraid he was too weak to stand the pain and shock.

Antonia had removed the shirt from him, and now as light revealed the tan chest with the golden curly hair, she saw a recent scar on his arm. It must have been the wound Maria Bent had mentioned. Somewhere else, she knew, was a scar from an arrow.

How much could one body withstand?

All of it because of her, because of Ramon. And in return, she had given so little, not even her trust. He should despise her. Yet he had said he loved her. Had it been only to give her strength?

Her hand touched his cheek. It was so clammy. It broke her heart to look at him. "You can't leave me now," she whispered. "You can't."

The legend. She thought of the horrible legend she had once believed so romantic. When the original Tristan had thought his beloved had failed him, he had turned to the wall, and died.

"I love you, Tristan," she said desperately. "I love you. I'm so sorry I didn't believe in you...so sorry." She moved her hand down to where his touched the ground, and she grasped it, trying to transfer some of her life to him. She wanted to cry, but her grief was too deep for tears, her fear too great. Instead, still clasping his hand, she put her head on his chest over his heart and listened to every beat, for they said he was still alive. In her fear, she thought she heard the rhythm slow, and she prayed. She prayed as she had never prayed before.

Conn had lost track of the days. He had traveled day and night, and both horses were exhausted. But something he couldn't identify kept pushing him.

He had developed a pattern of riding one horse ten miles, then the other. He never stopped for more than two hours, and then he would take a quick nap while the horses ate. It was as if he had an internal clock that kept him from sleeping beyond the allotted time.

He had lived his life this way, often with only an hour's rest, and even then a part of him was alert. That was why he was still alive after three wars and a life spent on the frontier.

It was a strange life for a boy raised on a South Carolina plantation with all the luxuries and niceties of wealth. But from the time he had gone to fight with Andy Jackson in the War of 1812, the wilderness was in his blood, its call undeniable. He had tried to settle down in South Carolina, but within weeks he was restless and unhappy. He always wanted to see beyond the next mountain, to test his skills against the wilderness and against other men. Conn no longer thought anything of killing an enemy; compassion was a weakness, mercy often a fatal error. He had given up both years ago.

Those qualities were where he and Tris differed. Although Tris had amply demonstrated he could be diamond hard, he would always have a streak of decency and generosity in him.

Conn knew they were weaknesses that could damn well kill his nephew . . . if they hadn't already.

Conn had seen much of himself in Tris: the faraway look in his eyes, the need to find his own destiny, the zest for danger. He had ignored those qualities that he had long eschewed in himself but which were so compelling in his nephew.

Conn couldn't help feeling that Tris was in deadly danger, and that it was his fault. He knew he would never forgive himself if Tris died.

It was noontime when he saw the tracks he was following merge into others. Many others, some unshod. Muscaleros Apache, goddammit.

The tracks led to a canyon, and he approached cautiously. There were ashes from small fires and tracks converging and crisscrossing each other. His eyes caught the movement of buzzards and his nose filled with an unpleasant odor. He didn't need to be told what it was. He had experienced it too many times before.

Filled with dread, he made his way to where he had first sighted the ugly black birds. There was an outcropping of rocks, and a number of tracks leading to it. He dismounted; the horses needed a rest, and he could make it as easily on foot.

The smell grew stronger, and Conn tried to prepare himself. He had seen many dead men before, including friends and comrades, but now . . .

There were two bodies, both naked and mutilated, their scalps gone. But neither had Tris's build or tawny chest hair. Conn hadn't realized he had held his breath, but now he released it in one long sigh. Apparently Tris had escaped, probably with the woman, although the Apache could have taken her. Conn knew they would not have taken his nephew; the Apache didn't take male prisoners.

He wished he had a shovel. He didn't like leaving the two men to the buzzards. No one deserved that. He compromised with himself by covering the bodies with rocks, knowing that coyotes would probably uncover them. But there was nothing else he could do.

Conn slid down the hill. He saw blood, a lot of blood, and suspected the Indians probably met more opposition than they had bargained for. He supposed they had taken their dead back to whatever camp they had. Or gone after Tristan?

Where in the hell was his nephew?

He studied the mishmash of tracks and saw none that matched Nugget's. He knew them well, for they had been a major part of his lessons when he was teaching Tristan to track. There was a broken edge on one of the shoes. It hadn't been enough to replace the shoe, but it was distinctive. Unless Tris had had the shoes replaced.

The tracks also showed that horses, both shod and unshod, had moved fast toward the end of the canyon. He followed those. Some veered in an erratic pattern, and he guessed they were riderless. Another seemed to go around the point of the canyon. He followed those, then picked up Nugget's tracks. He also saw blood.

Leaning over his horse to follow the broken horseshoe tracks, he moved as quickly as possible, hoping like hell the Muscaleros had a large number of warriors to mourn and would take the time to do it properly.

* * *

The day was fading quickly. The sun had started its charge toward the west and the hot air had cooled. A slight breeze ruffled the junipers.

There was little change in Tristan, except his breathing seemed more shallow. He moved occasionally, twisting his body as if in agony, and Antonia could only try to keep him still, afraid that the least movement might start the bleeding again. They were running out of water, and she was terrified that if she left, Tristan might stumble into the huge hole just inside the cave or that the Apache might come.

What if they did come? What could she do alone?

Her fingers shook as she inspected the bandage again. It was soaked with a bloody discharge, and beads of sweat were forming on his body. She wondered about changing the bandage, but feared she would reopen the wound. If only she had some help. If only Tristan could tell her what to do.

All her independence, her hard-earned skills were nothing now. He was going to die. And she needed him. She needed him so badly.

"Tristan," she whispered. "Please help me, Tristan."

His eyes fluttered open and hope flared briefly in her, but then they closed as if the effort was too great, and she was totally alone again.

Antonia sensed, more than heard, the rider coming. She reached for the pistol she had carefully reloaded and hid herself in the shadows where she could see Tristan and anyone coming toward the overhang.

Fear clawed at her. It could be no one but the Apache. She looked at Tristan and knew a bittersweet sadness for what had been and could never be again. But she would protect him with her life.

She didn't hear any footsteps, but she finally saw the cautious movements of a man in buckskins. There was a pistol in his hand. He was wearing moccasins, the reason he was so quiet, she supposed. An old bent hat reached down over his forehead, but she could see stubbled blond cheeks.

An army deserter? A trader with the Indians? Who else would be traveling alone in Indian country.

Was he alone?

She waited for several seconds, watching as the man neared Tristan, the gun still firmly in his hand.

"Stop right there," she said, her voice as steady as she could possibly make it.

The man looked at her, and she saw his eyes were as blue as the deepest New Mexico sky. His mouth was grim, his face dirty and marked with a week's growth of beard. Yet there was a certain familiarity about him, and she looked from Tris back to the intruder. The hair color was different. Tris's was more tawny than blond; this man's more like wheat. But the facial bones were much the same.

"What's wrong with him?" The deep male voice was curt, without fear.

"A knife wound," she answered, automatically responding to his question as if it were a command. The piercing gaze of the stranger's eyes would let her do nothing else.

"You're the Ramirez girl?"

Antonia could only nod.

"Put that fool gun down."

"Who...?"

But she already knew. It had to be Conn, the uncle Tris had told her about. The family resemblance was strong, although there was no gentleness in the hard mouth...or anywhere in his face.

The gun fell from her fingers. "Thank God," she whispered.

"God didn't have a damn thing to do with it," he said abruptly. "Thought I taught Tris better than to chase after a fool female, especially one who runs away with another man. Had to come see for myself." The look he gave her was one of pure contempt, and she shivered under its hostility.

But it didn't matter. Nothing mattered but Tris. "Please help him," she whispered.

Without giving her the dignity of an answer, he stooped, his hands feeling Tris's face, then his chest and finally the blood-covered bandage.

"Get some water," he said.

"It's all gone."

"There're a couple of canteens on my horse...about a hundred yards to the east. Get both of them along with my saddlebags." He didn't look at her; his eyes were intent on Tris's flushed face.

Antonia hurried, almost tripping over several rocks before locating the horses, which had been tied behind some bushes. Both carried saddlebags and canteens. She grabbed them all, grateful beyond belief for the angry glowering presence of the man Tristan admired above any other. He would be able to save Tristan. No one, not even death, would dare defy him.

She hurried back to the cave. The older man didn't seem to notice her return. His hands were busy undoing the bandage. They went still when he uncovered the ugly open wound.

"When did this happen?" Only then did she realize he had probably been aware of her every movement.

"I don't know," she said. "Sometime last night."

"You don't know?" The harsh tone was condemning, but then everything about the man was intimidating, even to Antonia, who wasn't easily cowed.

"Ramon Silvero and I were trapped in a canyon not far from here...Tristan was already wounded when he came in to get us."

"Silvero was one of the men back there?"

"Yes." Her voice was so low, it was like a whisper of wind.

"I hope he was worth this," the man said in a tense voice.

Antonia was silent for a moment. "Will he...Tristan...will he be all right?"

Conn looked up, his face harsh, his eyes like a frozen lake. "Do you care?"

There was a wealth of censure in his features, but it was no more than she had already bestowed on herself.

"I love him, *señor*."

"You New Mexicans have a strange way of showing love," he observed dryly. There was no sympathy in him, but then she didn't feel she deserved any.

"What can I do?"

"There's a needle in the older set of saddlebags, a needle and thread in a small pack. Find it. Then build a fire." He looked up again. "You *can* build a fire?"

"Yes, *señor,* that I can do." She didn't wait for another comment, but quickly found the little sewing kit and went back out to look for wood and brush to start a fire. She returned within minutes. In several more, a fire was blazing.

"Stick the needle into a stick and heat it in the fire," the buckskin clad man ordered, "and hand me the canteen with initials carved on it."

Again Antonia hurried to obey. She would obey the devil himself if he could help Tristan. She was beginning to think this man must be a close copy of the former.

"You got a weak stomach?" the man asked.

"No," Antonia replied.

"Good. Grab his arms and hold him. I'm going to wash that wound with alcohol and if anything wakes him, that will. Hold him as still as you can.

Antonia braced herself on her knees, each hand taking one of Tristan's.

Conn looked up. At least she wasn't excitable. Her mouth was set in a determined line, her eyes half closed in concentration.

He poured the alcohol. It had to be agony in the raw open wound, and he felt Tris jerk as a groan like that of an anguished animal rose from his throat.

"Easy, Tris," Conn ordered. "Easy." There was another frantic movement as the liquid seeped down, cleansing the wound.

Tris felt part of himself come alive as the flames consumed him. The agony was everywhere, waves and waves of pain and fire. He tried to escape, but hands held him, and he was too weak to break loose.

"Tris." He heard the familiar deep voice, but it had no meaning for him.

"Tristan." The second voice was like cool water, gentle and sweet. He reached for it, but it disappeared in another explosion of pain. He fought to find the source of the sound, to see the speaker, but he was falling, falling back into a gray netherworld.

"Oh, dear Mother," Antonia said, unable to stand his pain. Her hands started to tremble.

"Didn't think you would have the grit," Conn observed nastily as he calmly threaded the needle.

Antonia's hands tightened again around Tris's wrists. She could do anything for him.

She watched grimly as the needle went in and out, binding the edges of the wound together. Every once in a while, Tris's body would jerk, as if in reaction to the punishment it was taking. Antonia hung on fiercely, whispering desperate words of comfort.

At last it was over. Tris's face was soaked in sweat, and when Antonia looked at the man above him, she noted his face was just as wet.

Her eyes pleaded with him to say Tristan would be all right, even while she knew no one could say that with certainty. Tris's survival now depended upon how much blood he had lost and whether infection had taken hold. The rough American, at least, had improved the odds in that battle.

"We'll need more water," Conn said, jerking Antonia from her thoughts. "I'll take the canteens and see if I can find some."

He would also take a good look around, but he didn't see any need to tell her that. Or anything else, for that matter.

Antonia looked up briefly. Filled with gratitude for his help, she merely nodded, satisfied to sit at Tris's side. She saw the American's eyes on her as she took Tris's hand, her fingers caressing it.

Conn thought about telling her to stay put, but saw her watching Tris and knew it would be unnecessary. It would take a tribe of Apache to pull her away. He had been mildly surprised at her steadiness moments earlier, but then she was frontier bred.

She was pretty enough, Conn noticed, even travel stained and dirty, and her eyes were remarkable. She had not done badly with Tris before he came, considering how little she had. Some of his hostility faded, but enough remained to keep his back stiff as he stalked away.

Antonia was unaware of his action. Her only concern was soothing the lines of pain from Tris's face and washing him with the remaining water in the one canteen his uncle had left. Without thinking, she started to croon to him, an old Spanish lullaby promising wonderful dreams.

Chapter Twenty

Tris drifted between unconsciousness and semi-consciousness for the next few days, and Antonia didn't move from his side except to see to her personal needs. She bathed as much of him as she decently could, hesitant to do more with Conn O'Neill there. She spooned him soup she'd prepared from a rabbit Conn had brought back, patiently letting the broth drip slowly into his throat while he barely responded.

She would look at the handsome face and wonder if she would ever see it light up again with love.

Despair had settled in her heart, a constant ache that wouldn't go away. She felt so unworthy of him. She had discarded him so easily, ready to believe the worst, despite the magical night they had shared.

Tris's uncle had disappeared repeatedly during the past three days, never saying where he was going, but suddenly reappearing with a plant that he made into a salve and rubbed into Tris's wound, or with a rabbit when she never heard a shot, or with water she didn't know was available.

He said little to her, except for an occasional order. He watched her steadily, but there was no emotion in his eyes. It was as if she were a temporary annoyance to be tolerated. His eyes warmed only when he saw Tris stir for the first time, and his hand went affectionately to his nephew's shoulder. There were no words of comfort or reassurance, but Antonia could almost feel the regard that flowed between the two.

She had never felt so much the outsider, so awkward. She would have resented Conn his silent condemnation if she had not agreed with it or if he had not saved Tris's life...which she was sure he had. She could never have managed alone.

She bore the tall American's scrutiny with her own impassivity, knowing she had probably lost Tristan forever, but comforted by the fact that he would live.

She could not even think about her father. It was just too painful. She knew she had little hope of saving him now, and Tris's needs were so much more urgent at the moment. Her divided heart could stand only so much.

And then, of course, there was Ramon. He had lied to her, he had betrayed her father and in the end, he had sacrificed himself for her. She had known him all her life, and now she mourned him.

The threat of Apache was still with them, although she suspected that was why Conn was gone so much, to scout the area. In one of the few conversations they had had, he had asked in detail about the number of Apache who had attacked her party and how many she thought they had killed or wounded. She had reckoned about four.

"And Tris?"

She shook her head miserably. "I don't know."

She had then risked his grim countenance and looked directly at him. "Do you think they will keep looking for us?"

"You can bet on it, missy," he said curtly. "They probably think there're just two of you left. And from what you said, you might have killed one of their chiefs. They won't like that."

"Can they find our trail?" she asked.

"I wiped it out completely," he said. "Found some of the horses Tris scattered and sent them in another direction, but they'll be back looking."

He left again, as if he didn't want to talk to her, and she curled in a ball of misery at Tris's side. It would be days before Tris could ride.

Tris woke fully conscious. As his eyes focused, he recognized Antonia. He tried to smile, but it was more a grimace.

"Conn," he whispered. "I thought . . . I heard him. . . ."

"He's gone for water," Antonia said, not sure whether he had or not, but wanting to calm Tris's anxiety.

"How did he . . . ?"

"He trailed you," Antonia said. "He saved your life."

His eyes closed, then opened. "Are you all right?"

She nodded miserably, wishing she could change places with him.

It was apparently all he needed to hear. His eyes closed again and his breathing came easier.

When Conn returned, he had two rabbits in hand and he gave them to Antonia without a word, leaning down to check on Tris.

"He woke up," she said, almost shyly. "He remembered hearing you."

Conn nodded and leaned back against the wall of rock.

Antonia wanted him to say more, to share her joy that Tris was improving, but there was an iron reserve in his manner that made her silent.

When Tris woke again, he smiled weakly at Conn, who grinned back in the first open expression Antonia had seen. It disappeared as quickly as it had come.

"What happened at the canyon, Tris?" he asked.

"There were Apache at both ends. I circled around to the south and was able to get most of the group at that entrance, but one jumped me. I finally killed him, but not before he used his knife."

"How many did you down?" Conn said.

"Seven," Tris replied apologetically. "I missed two shots later."

"Only seven?" Conn said, raising an eyebrow. "I didn't teach you so well."

Tris's mouth creased into a painful smile. "I'll do better next time."

"See that you do," his uncle replied, his voice just slightly chiding.

Conn sat back on his hands, thinking. He had seen tracks of approximately twenty horses. The girl thought her party had killed four. Tris another seven. Probably half the original war party.

It was a damned good thing the Apache couldn't get along with each other and raided in small individual groups. Still, they would be aching for revenge at this point. Thunderation, but Tris had done well. Conn couldn't stop the rush of pride that flooded him. His nephew had done more than well.

During the afternoon, Conn noticed the intent searching looks Tris gave the Ramirez girl. He wasn't entirely sure he wanted to leave his nephew to the wiles of the Creole, but the air was explosive with unsaid words.

His natural restlessness, along with Tris's pleading look, soon dispelled his reluctance. Conn shook his head, his mouth quirking up cynically at one end, and left. They could always use more food, and he had several traps set.

Once Conn was gone, Tris turned to look at Antonia. Although there were deep shadows under her eyes, she was lovely as always. She looked infinitely tired and sad. There was still pride in the way she held her chin, but she had lost some of her fire.

"Your father is fine," he said gently. "I saw him in Santa Fe."

"They will put him on trial?"

"Not for a while," he said, "and even then, they may decide not to. The Indians directly responsible for the killings will hang...and quickly...for murder. But there's considerable doubt that treason charges will stand against the others. They have never accepted citizenship. There's already an argument in Santa Fe that you can't commit treason against a government you haven't recognized and which hasn't officially recognized them. It seems General Kearny's declaration doesn't have the effect of law."

"But the murders...?"

"There's nothing to link your father directly to the murders," Tris said quietly.

Antonia closed her eyes. Nothing, except her father's conscience and her own. And Tristan. He would always know the truth. And then the full import of his words struck her. It had all been for nothing: her hasty trip with Ramon; Jose's and Ramon's deaths, Tris's injuries. All for nothing.

She rose blindly, unable to return his steady gaze, unable to answer the questions that still remained in his eyes.

Grief heavy in her voice and her heart leadened with guilt, she finally found the courage to ask the question. "Why did you come after me?"

"I was afraid for you." It was simply said, and whatever was left in her to break shattered now.

She swallowed painfully. There was a lump in her throat so large she was sure she could never breathe again.

"Come here, Tonia." His voice was gentle, so gentle it was irresistible. Without a will of her own, she returned to his side.

His hand reached out for hers. It was cold despite the warm day.

"Tonia. I know what happened. Lieutenant Baker told me of the message he received. I realize how it appeared to you."

"I should have known."

He tried to move, and a new surge of pain ran through him. He couldn't prevent a small groan, and Antonia's hand tightened around his fingers. "Damn," he said, his teeth clenching tightly.

"You should get some more rest," Antonia said softly.

"How long has it been?"

"Three days."

"When did Conn arrive?"

"Two days ago."

"You brought me here?"

She nodded.

"This is getting to be a habit . . . you dragging my unconscious body around." His mouth lifted slightly at the corners.

Antonia let a tiny smile of her own creep into her eyes. "You do not take very good care of yourself. . . Tristan." She needed to say his name, to hear the sound of it on her lips. She frowned again as she thought of the questions he hadn't asked.

But they needed to be answered.

"Ramon said he could help my father . . . that Santa Ana would exchange him for another prisoner."

Tris wanted to tell her that Ramon was the one who informed on her father, but he didn't know for sure. He had no evidence.

He didn't need it. It was Antonia who said the words. "I know now it was Ramon who had my father arrested...." Her voice quivered. "I am sorry, Tristan... I should not have believed it."

No, he wanted to shout. *You shouldn't have.* Not after the night we had together. He had not thoroughly realized how much her lack of faith had pierced him. No matter how he had rationalized it on his trip south, there was a bitter hurt inside that hadn't gone away. He wondered if it ever would.

Looking into his eyes, Antonia wondered the same thing. Part of the openness she had so loved about him was gone. For the first time, he had hidden part of himself away from her.

She wanted to cry. She took her hand from his and, for something to do, offered him a drink of water.

For something to do, he took it.

Conn felt the visible strain between the two when he came back. Tris appeared to be sleeping, but Conn knew his nephew had been feigning when his eyes opened slowly.

"Anything out there?" Tris asked.

"Like Apache?"

"Like Apache."

"Not where I can see them."

"But they will be back."

"Probably," Conn said cheerfully.

Tris tried to rise. "We need to get out of here."

"Don't be a fool, Tris. You couldn't go more than a couple of miles. We have shelter here."

"But if they come looking?"

"I didn't see any sign of Indians around here. Could be the cave is bad medicine. Anyway, we're as safe here as anyplace until you get better."

"And then?"

"And then we'll make a run south...try to link up with Doniphan. They have a supply route up to Santa Fe... someone's always going up and down."

"Why not directly back to Santa Fe?"

"Two reasons. The area north of here is crawling with Apache. You're damn lucky you didn't run into more of them."

Tris grimaced. "And the second?"

"I'm supposed to meet Doniphan."

"Mexico is south."

"So it is," Conn replied with satisfaction.

"There are angry Mexicans in Mexico."

"So there are," Conn replied with even more satisfaction.

"And you think it's healthier to tramp through Mexico than go north?"

"Yeah."

"And what about Tonia's father?"

Conn shrugged with indifference. "I have to meet Doniphan, and I sure as hell won't let you two travel through Apache country again on your own."

It was the end of the discussion, and Tris knew it. So did Antonia.

She might have argued with Conn O'Neill if he had shown any anger toward her, but he hadn't. It was as if he didn't care whether she was angry or not, whether she felt anything or not. And she knew from his set jaw he wouldn't change his mind. She also knew she and Tristan, in his condition, had no chance alone.

For Tris's sake more than her own, Antonia tried to please Conn. But no matter what she did, she couldn't coax the smallest smile from him. She had built the fires, dressed and cooked the rabbits he brought, sewed Tris's shirt as best she could and kept everything as clean as possible. All without even the slightest nod of approval.

And she wanted it badly. It hurt unbearably to know the older scout thought so little of her, thought that Tris had been a fool to chase after her, thought she was unworthy of his nephew.

There was also a new reserve about Tris, despite his soothing words. It was like a stone wall, and she didn't know how to restore that magic bond they had once had. The attraction was still there. She could feel its pull and see the wanting in his eyes, but something else was missing, something precious was gone.

Ramon still hung between them. She knew Tristan wondered about her decision to go with him and the manner in which he died, but she couldn't really talk about it. Not yet.

So the wall remained. He said no words of blame, and her hands were gentle when she touched him. But the silver chain that had bound them heart and soul had weakened, and neither knew how to mend it.

The next three days moved slowly for Antonia, although she rejoiced with the ease of Tris's recovery. He had tremendous recuperative powers. It was that will of his, she thought. He never gave up on anything. Except, perhaps, her.

Conn was a stifling presence when he was there, but more often than not, he was gone. Antonia believed he was ranging farther and farther out, trying to track the Apache. He usually said little when the three of them were together. Once, when she returned from attending to her private needs, she heard him telling Tris about the battle at Valverde on Christmas Day. His voice reflected more feeling than she had heard before, and she felt a trembling inside at a man who came to life only when talking of battles and death.

But she couldn't avoid noticing the closeness between the two men, and she wondered whether Tris had more of Conn O'Neill in him than she had suspected.

Madre de Dios, but she had had enough of death.

Only when Conn was gone could she relax a little, and then not altogether.

One day when she was changing Tris's bandages, she wondered where the old independent Antonia had gone, the Antonia who had managed a large ranch, who had been afraid of nothing.

Now she was terribly afraid. Afraid of losing her father, afraid of losing Tristan, afraid of being alone after knowing the glory of being one with the man she loved.

And hadn't trusted!

It was as if Tristan had read her mind. She felt his eyes intense on her, and she looked up from the makeshift bandage she had just finished tying.

"Would you come with me on a short walk?" His eyes had recaptured their glitter, like the sun on a restless sea, and she nodded, her eyes full of questions.

He grinned, and even with a week's growth of beard, Antonia thought he was still the most handsome man she had ever seen.

She watched him rise awkwardly. He was still in pain but he needed to work off the stiffness and test his strength. He wavered just a little, and she took his arm, placing it around her shoulders to steady him.

The sun was bright and she felt him hesitate, soaking up its warm rays. She looked up at him, catching his eyes watching her intently.

It had taken Tris days to sort out his own emotions. Part of him, the logical part, knew Antonia had had every reason to believe Ramon. The emotional part had been wounded severely. He had not known how much until he had seen Ramon and Antonia together.

But each time she had touched him, Tris had watched her eyes fill with love and unhappiness. And each time, some of the anger and hurt drained from him. She was so stoic against Conn's distrust. She did everything asked of her and more, without complaint or question.

He remembered the time she had saved his life in the Rio Grande Gorge and he wondered who he was to judge. She had saved his life not once but twice. She had given him the same loyalty she gave others in her life. It was only when those loyalties clashed, when she had had to make an instantaneous choice, that she chose the person she thought the weakest. And now he longed to touch her again, to soothe away the grief lines around her eyes and see her smile again.

They walked together up a small rise, Tris's arm still around her shoulders. He sat and pulled her against him, wincing slightly at the pain that was still with him when he moved. Antonia trembled in his arms, and he knew her uncertainty because he felt the same. He had been so damned judgmental...in his thoughts, if not his words, and he knew she had recognized it. There was a quiet dignity about her, a refusal to make excuses or explanations. That pride touched him deeply.

Suddenly nothing mattered except her. He had never fully understood or accepted her complete loyalty to her father, a man he thought flawed. But he had seen in her father that same pride, and had even felt a certain admiration for the man in his prison cell.

If positions had been reversed, if it had been his family involved, wouldn't he have grasped at any straw to save them?

He thought about the wall he had erected and felt a rush of shame. His arms tightened on her, and he realized how much thinner she was than she had been weeks ago. She had gone through hell and he had not been there to help, except at the end.

"I'm sorry, Tonia," he whispered.

Antonia shuddered and the tears she had been holding back for days spilled over.

Her thin body moved with great sobs Tris could feel but could not hear, for she held them within. "Oh, Tonia," he said softly, his own soul in anguish at her quiet agony. His lips touched her hair, the tear-soaked cheeks, traveling in feather-light movements across her neck in comforting caresses. "Don't, Tonia. Oh, God, don't. I love you."

But the tears continued and she could not stop them. They had been held for too long, through the killing of Governor Bent, the arrest of her father, the terrible revealing trip south with Ramon, the death of first Jose and then Ramon and the unbearable hours when she was afraid that Tristan, too, would die.

She felt his hands. Gentle on her, as they once had been, as they were that night when they made love, as she had dreamed they would be again, and it was more than she could bear. The tears came faster.

His lips moved toward her own, and she lifted her mouth to him. Her lips trembled, then met his in an explosion of joint need. Each movement created more and more hunger as his tongue probed, tender at first, and then fiercely possessive. His fingers wandered over her wet cheek, creating little streaks of burning sensation where they touched.

But the surface sensations were nothing to the warmth that flowed between them. Antonia could feel its strength growing and her own hands could no longer stay away from him. They whispered her love as they moved slowly along his neck and back. They touched and teased and worshiped, and Tris thought what a fool he had been to think anything had changed between them.

He knew now that love would never change. They were vital to each other's survival.

Tris tore his mouth away from hers and kissed away the tears moving down her face. With an index finger he touched her kiss-swollen mouth, pausing to study every beloved detail before leaning down and covering it once more with his own.

The kiss said so much, promised so much.

And then his lips were gone, but his arms were around her with the same half gentle, half fierce possessiveness. Antonia carefully leaned against him, loving the feel of his hands as they stroked her arms, claiming her so completely.

"Oh, Christ, I love you," he said at last. "I couldn't bear the thought of you with Ramon, of not seeing you again."

"I missed you every second of every minute. I couldn't stop thinking of you. I wanted to, but I couldn't," Antonia replied.

"Promise me you will never leave again." There was such aching need in his voice that she was afraid her tears would start once more.

"Never," she swore. "Nor you," she added quickly.

"Nor me," he agreed.

They sat needing no more words, only the joy of being close to each other.

* * *

When Conn returned again, he knew instantly something had changed. The tension between his nephew and the girl was gone and Tris's eyes were glittering with satisfaction.

It was, however, no time to remark on such a change. He had ranged northward and with his sea-glass had spotted a group of Apache slowly sweeping their way south. It was obvious they were looking for Tris and Antonia.

"Can you ride?" he said abruptly.

Tris caught the concern in Conn's voice and nodded.

"Fast?"

"Fast enough."

Conn nodded. He didn't have to ask the girl. The fact that she had made it this far told him all he needed to know. He had a rather reluctant admiration for her spunk.

But he still didn't trust her, not altogether. She was New Mexican, which was too close to Mexican to suit him. He didn't trust any woman very far, and a man in love even less. That she had infected Tris with heart sickness did not sit well with him.

But at least she wasn't a complainer, he thought as she watched him quietly.

"When?" she asked.

"As soon as it gets dark."

Conn dropped a bundle of canteens on the ground. "I dismantled the traps and covered the trail." He looked over at Antonia. "What food do we have left?"

It was one of the few occasions he had addressed her directly, and for the first time she felt less awkward around him. "About a day's supply of hardtack, a few pieces of cooked rabbit."

"It will have to last at least two days," he said curtly. "By then, we should be far enough away to hunt."

She nodded and started to pack their meager possessions.

They left at dusk, Conn riding behind with a piece of sagebrush tied to his horse to brush away their tracks. Although they moved steadily, the pace seemed painfully slow to Antonia. She rode beside Tris, watching as his mouth turned grim with pain. She agonized with every rolling movement of his horse and wondered how he could bear it.

They continued on through morning, when Conn caught up with them. At the sight of Tris's unnaturally stiff posture, Conn called a halt when they reached a small stream.

"Can he rest a few hours?" Antonia asked, knowing that Tris would never make the request himself, regardless of how much he might need it.

Conn nodded. "We should be in Mexico now. I doubt if the Apache will search this far south, but now we have to watch for Mexican troops. They don't treat prisoners kindly." He threw a quick challenging glance at Antonia, but she merely nodded.

They rationed the remaining hardtack, each taking only enough to quiet the rumbling in their hungry stomachs. But they drank their fill. Antonia, who had not been able to wash for a week, looked joyfully at the thin stream of water. There was not enough for a bath, but at least she could clean her face and hands. She had never felt quite so dirty.

Both Conn and Antonia insisted that Tris rest while Conn scouted the area. Antonia took the bandage from Tris's side and nodded with approval. The wound was still seeping a bit, but the skin around it was no longer an ugly red. Whatever Conn had used was working.

She watched as Tris, unable to stay awake, slept restlessly. His mouth had relaxed and he looked incredibly young and vulnerable. Dear God, how she loved him. It was still difficult to believe he loved her after everything that had happened. It was, in fact, a miracle. She crawled next to him, placing her hand in his, and slept.

That was the way Conn found them. Tris had moved, unconsciously wrapping his arm around her, and her hand still clutched his. For a moment, Conn felt a streak of envy pierce him before he shrugged it off. He had made his choices long ago.

He let them sleep, his eyes occasionally glancing at their peaceful expressions.

He wondered how long that sense of peace would last.

Chapter Twenty-One

Days started running together. The three rode all night and slept during the day.

As at the cave, Conn would often disappear without explanation and silently rejoin them. Antonia had never met such a taciturn man, and she wondered if part of his reserve was due to her presence or if he was always that way.

Since they never knew when Conn would reappear, Tris and Tonia had little privacy, even when he was gone. Their hands met, their eyes promised, their bodies ached, but any more had to wait.

It was easier now for Antonia. The promise of what lay beyond the journey filled her heart. Tristan was so much better, and it would not be long before they could be together... forever. She would let nothing interfere again. Not even her father. She would even take Conn O'Neill with some degree of equanimity.

Because she knew he was important to Tris, she desperately wanted Conn's approval, but it seemed hopeless. He avoided her even more now than he had at the cave, and his eyes were always cold when he looked at her. But she tried. She assumed care of both her horse and Tris's, carefully rubbing them down each morning, regardless of how tired she was. If Conn allowed a fire, she gathered the wood and started it. She tended Tris's wound and attempted to anticipate their every need. She offered to share sentry duty, but was curtly refused.

She knew they were traveling southeast toward Chihuahua, and she wondered if the fact they were in Mexico had increased Conn's natural suspicion of her.

After two days, Tris rode easier and took up sentry duty during half of the day. Food remained a problem since Conn had limited the use of firearms. The sound carried too far in this country.

On the third day, they found a stream and Conn, who seemed to have any number of practical items in his saddlebags, produced a hook and caught some fish. He then built a small fire and heated stones in it. Digging a small pit in the ground, he lined the bottom with heated stones and placed the fish on top, covering them with a water-soaked piece of material. They would steam without the smell of smoke or of cooking fish.

They all ate hungrily and had enough left for the next day. Conn hoped they would soon meet with American troops.

After supper, Conn appeared more relaxed than usual. He had scouted during the morning, mostly to the north and west. He figured the American troops were not far to the west.

Twilight came fast and they prepared to leave. Conn saddled the horses, and Tris checked their guns as he always did before starting on the trail. It didn't seem to matter that he had checked them the night before and that they had not been used since. Being prepared had become a habit.

Antonia was tired and dreading the night's ride. She had not slept well during the day, and neither, she knew, had Tristan. Although he appeared much better, his face was still drawn. But the smile was back.

Antonia accepted Conn's help in mounting. She was afraid that if she didn't Tristan would try to help, and she knew he wasn't ready for that.

It was turning cool again, as it had every night. She pulled her jacket around her and urged Night Wind forward, stopping abruptly when Conn and Tristan did. In the plain before them, where there had been nothing hours earlier, the last vivid colors of a setting sun framed what seemed to be the entire Mexican army.

Tris and Conn reacted instantly, turning their horses, but there was a group of mounted men, led by a man in a blue-and-red uniform, trotting toward them with pistols drawn.

Conn cursed long and bitterly. He looked at Tris and knew his nephew couldn't stand another wild gallop across the rugged landscape. And he couldn't leave him.

Antonia looked at him for a long minute. "Trust me," she said simply.

Conn didn't have any choice. He nodded, wondering every second if she would betray them. Both he and Tris watched as she moved her horse ahead and rode out to meet the band of riders.

The officer's hat came off in a flourish, and the two talked with gestures for several moments. Neither Conn nor Tris could make out the words, but the officer kept looking their way and nodding. Antonia graced him with a smile, and the man bowed in the saddle and leaned over, taking her hand to his lips.

Conn heard Tris growl behind him and he felt idiotic beyond measure for trusting the woman. But then the Mexican soldiers and the Ramirez woman were all riding toward them, pistols holstered and smiles on their faces.

The officer reached them first and bowed. *"Señors,"* he said with a measure of welcome.

When Antonia spoke, her voice was controlled and her expression blank. "I have explained to the soldiers that the Americans have arrested my father and that you have graciously offered to provide me with protection on my journey to seek assistance from Santa Ana. Lieutenant Alvarez has heard of the San Patricio Battalion you both wish to join and how bravely they fight for Mexico. He welcomes us to travel with them and to join the officers at dinner tonight."

Before either of her companions could react, she turned back to the Mexican officer. *"Señor,"* this is Conn O'Neill and his nephew. And this is Lieutenant Pedro Alvarez."

Conn was stunned. He had heard of the traitorous San Patricio Battalion as he knew Tris must have. Composed mostly of Irish deserters from the American army, its members had joined the Mexicans, some for land, some because of supposed grievances in the American army. Whatever their reasons, they had proved to be some of the deadliest and most competent fighters in the Mexican army.

He did not, however, like being identified with them. Everything in him rebelled against the association: his dislike of the Mexicans, his strong sense of loyalty, his hatred of deserters. Yet he immediately understood the brilliance of Antonia's plan. He returned the lieutenant's bow with a graciousness that stunned both Tris and Antonia.

"We are honored," he replied. He knew the courtesies; he just damn well didn't like using them.

Antonia smiled at him for the first time, and he suddenly understood why Tris was so taken by her. There was a quiet, serene beauty that could make a man ache.

Just as that fact was registering in his mind, he watched her turn back to the lieutenant, her eyes filled with admiration.

"We are very grateful, Lieutenant," she said softly.

"I would be so honored if you would consent to ride with me, *señorita*," he said.

She smiled in agreement, then turned to Conn. "Lieutenant Alvarez's troops have been sent from Chihuahua to Buena Vista to meet Santa Ana. It is thought there will be a large battle there."

Despite himself, Conn had to smile. She had found out in minutes what a dozen scouts probably had not. So Santa Ana was stripping Chihuahua. That should make Doniphan's job much easier. He reined his horse next to Tris, but avoided his nephew's glance. He didn't think he was quite ready for the satisfied smirk he suspected was there.

The three of them feasted well at the table of senior officers. There were a number of camp followers with the troops, but no ladies, and the officers were hungry for the company of one. Tris and Conn, much to their surprise, appeared just as welcome.

Asked their reasons for leaving the American army, they both gave the one they knew would be understood: discrimination because they were Irish and Catholic. The Americans looked down on the Irish, Conn said bitterly, just as they did the

Mexicans. They shared much with their Mexican brothers, Conn added, warming to his role. And, of course, Santa Ana had promised them land, land of their own.

The Mexican officers, in return, told of some of the exploits of the San Patricio Battalion, particularly their expertise with cannons against American troops. Tris, knowing Conn as he did, said a few silent prayers, but his uncle seemed relaxed. Conn asked about Chihuahua and why Santa Ana was draining Mexican troops from the area when he had heard an American army was approaching that way.

"Ah," one of the senior officers said, "the governor thinks those gringos will be no trouble. General Conde is marching from Mexico City, and together with the governor's militia, they will have three thousand men. Enough to swat a few gringo fleas, no? I hear he has filled a whole wagon with lariats to tie the Missourian prisoners to their saddles. But let us not talk of grim matters with such a beautiful woman at our table."

It was Tris's time to tense and Conn's to worry.

With a tight rein on their emotions, they all managed to survive the dinner, and Antonia finally pleaded exhaustion. A chorus of voices offered their tents, but she merely smiled graciously and said she had grown used to the ground and to her protectors. They would leave early in the morning, she said, because she was worried about her father. The troops were moving too slowly with their artillery. Again there were protests, but tears crept in her eyes and she said surely they must understand a daughter's love for a patriot father.

The plea was sentimental enough to touch each heart. They insisted on giving the three plenty of food and promised to see her at Santa Ana's headquarters.

"I'll be damned," was all Conn could say as they rode unmolested out of the camp next day.

Tris merely raised an eyebrow and grinned.

For Antonia, the day was much the same as the others: riding, riding, riding until she thought she would be happy never to sit a horse again, even Night Wind. If Conn O'Neill had maintained a hard pace earlier, it was a deadly one now as he sought to get his information to Colonel Doniphan.

Every muscle in her body hurt, and she could barely hold her head upright.

And after leaving the Mexican army, she discovered her heart was still divided. What if Tristan was wrong about her father's safety? What if the Americans did decide to bring him to trial? And how long would he remain in prison? How long could he survive there? Perhaps Ramon had been right, perhaps Santa Ana would have helped her father. Perhaps she had condemned her own father. She tried to dismiss the thoughts, but they wouldn't go away.

She took some satisfaction, however, in the fact that Conn's hostility had lessened. Not disappeared, but at least weakened. And then, of course, there was Tris. He, too, had eased, and each time she looked at him, his eyes were warm and laughing despite the pain.

They sighted Doniphan's army late the next day.

When they reached the first tents, Antonia was astounded at the seeming lack of discipline or even cleanliness. There were few real uniforms. Many of the soldiers wore buckskins; other were clad in bits and pieces of clothes. Their hair and beards were untrimmed and they were largely unwashed.

As the three of them rode through the camp, there were any number of rude and loud comments, and Antonia wondered how such slovenly men could defeat the disciplined troops such as they had met a day earlier, especially if the Americans were outnumbered three to one. She prayed that Tris would not stay for the battle that appeared to loom ahead.

It was dusk when they reached Doniphan's tent. A guard alerted the tall Missouri colonel, who came to the entrance. His face wreathed in smiles as he saw Conn and Tris.

"My God, I'm damned pleased to have you back, O'Neill. And you too, Hampton. Glad to see you're still alive. We had heard—"

"I know," Tris said. "Conn told me." He dismounted and took the colonel's hand.

Doniphan looked beyond the two men to Antonia. "And the young lady...?"

"Señorita Antonia Ramirez," Conn replied lazily as Tris helped her down.

"We usually don't have such lovely ladies in camp," Doniphan said with courtesy.

"Especially ones who dined with Mexican officers two nights earlier," Conn said with another of those rare smiles Antonia was beginning to like.

Doniphan raised one heavy eyebrow. "And what were *you* doing at the time?"

"Dining with them," Conn replied with a grin.

"Conn O'Neill... dining with the Mexican army? I have to hear more about this."

"You will," Conn promised with an unusual gleam in his eyes. "Is there an officer you can trust with this lady while we talk, perhaps help her with some water and food?"

Antonia didn't want to leave them and started to protest, but Tris shook his head. He had a plan, but he didn't want to get Antonia's hopes up. He took her hand. "I'll be with you shortly."

"But—"

His hand went up to her cheek despite the crowd gathering around them. "Shortly," he repeated.

She stood frustrated, knowing she could easily be prevented from entering the tent. She had hoped to plead her father's case with Colonel Doniphan. She had heard he had much influence.

"Ma'am?" A young officer, one of the few in proper uniform, appeared. "You can use my tent. I'll have some water brought to you."

Antonia looked angrily at Conn and Tris, finally shrugging her shoulders, but not in defeat. She would talk to the colonel later.

Doniphan laughed as they entered the tent. "I don't think I want to be either of you when you see her again."

Conn looked at Tris and another grin started. "I'll let him worry about that." The smile disappeared and Conn quickly related the news they had learned in the Mexican camp.

Far from being concerned about the increase of enemy strength, Doniphan leaned back and laughed at the images presented to him. "My God, I wish I had been there. O'Neill in the San Patricio Battalion! It's a wonder you didn't have apoplexy in front of them all."

"I do admit to feeling a little...odd," Conn admitted wryly. "But they eat well. It was the first decent meal I've had since we started south from Santa Fe."

The two men smiled at each other in understanding. Doniphan's men were not known for their cooking abilities.

And then Doniphan's chuckle turned into a full belly laugh. "Damn, I can't wait to tell that story...the scourge of the Mexican army dining at the table of senior officers. Some of their heads will roll for that one." When his laughter died, he sat straight again as a thought occurred to him. "How in God's good earth did they believe you?"

"The girl," Conn said, hesitating only slightly as he saw Tris stiffen. "She's the daughter of one of the Creoles accused in the Taos conspiracy. They believed her."

Doniphan's eyes narrowed and the laughter was gone. Charles Bent had also been his friend. "Perhaps you should tell me the whole story."

Conn did, as Tris listened carefully, but his uncle told it dispassionately and fairly, probably better than he could have. The dry recital of events...how Antonia had originally set out to find Santa Ana and then sacrificed her own plans to help the Americans...was certainly more potent than his own impassioned pleading would have been.

And he didn't miss the wry admiration in Conn's tale, which surprised him. Conn had certainly shown none to either him or Antonia on the trip.

"I can see we owe Señorita Ramirez a certain debt," Doniphan observed after he listened in silence. "What do you suggest?" he said, turning to Tristan.

"Your help in obtaining a pardon for her father," Tristan said quickly. He knew the Missourian had friends in Washington.

Doniphan eyed him carefully. "Charles was your friend, too."

Tris nodded slowly. "God knows I can never forget how he died. But Señor Ramirez has been sick, and influenced by Silvero. He was tempted and led into the conspiracy out of patriotism. I can't see any good rising out of making him a martyr."

"And his daughter did do this country a service," Doniphan said. "One deed wipes out the other, is that it, Hampton?"

"Yes, sir. I think so."

"I'll do what I can, Hampton."

Which was a great deal, Tris knew. He excused himself, half smiling at Conn's sly wink.

Antonia was pacing restlessly in the tent. She had washed, but ignored the food sitting on a camp table nearby. She kept wishing she had insisted on staying, although it probably would have done precious little good. Damn men, anyway.

She sensed Tris's presence, although she had not heard him enter. She wondered whether she would always feel the electricity and excitement of just being near him, even when she was angry. She turned slowly, reluctant to give up her resentment at being so summarily dismissed, but wanting badly to feel the warmth of his arms. She had missed it in the past several days.

His eyes were serious, but his mouth was creased in a tender smile. He opened his arms and she fell into them, some of her anger draining as he clasped her tightly, burying his face in her hair. "I've missed this," he groaned.

Then he forced himself away, taking her chin in the palm of his hand. "Colonel Doniphan's going to work for your father's pardon," he said abruptly.

"What does . . . what does that mean?"

"Colonel Doniphan is a very popular man, both in New Mexico and in Washington. He usually gets what he wants."

Her eyes beamed brightly. "Oh, Tris, thank you."

"Don't thank **me**," he said, "although I wouldn't mind claiming the reward for it."

Her mouth curved up with the question.

"Conn," he said with a broad smile. "Conn pleaded your case, and very nicely, too."

She stepped back, amazement on her face. "But I thought . . . he didn't like me."

"You never know what Conn thinks," Tris admitted dryly. "I thought he believed I was the most inept, clumsy oaf he'd ever had the misfortune to meet until I overheard him tell General Kearny that I was 'fair competent as a scout.' "

" 'Fair competent,' indeed," she said indignantly. "I would like to see him kill seven Indians by himself."

"Oh, he's done that and more, I'm afraid," Tris said. "I still have a long way to go to best him."

He had said it in jest, but Antonia's face went white. Her hands clenched and she stepped back.

"Tonia?"

"Madre de Dios," she said furiously. "Haven't you been hurt enough? What is it that makes men want to kill, kill, kill?" Her eyes blazed, and she looked beautiful.

So beautiful he couldn't resist seizing her in his arms again, despite her attempt to stop him. He quieted her struggling as his mouth touched hers.

The fire started deep inside her, and a storm raged in her heart, but instead of quenching the blazes, it seemed to breathe even more life into them.

She closed her eyes in mute surrender and her body snuggled next to his, feeling the yearning of his manhood, the taste of his hungry lips.

"Your wound," she whispered.

"To hell with my wound." He almost added that it wasn't nearly as painful as some of his other parts at the moment. Instead, his tongue gently probed her mouth, awakening sensations she had felt might be gone forever. Now she was greedy for them, and her tongue did its own invasion as she held herself tightly against him, as if to make them one again.

With a moan, Tris moved his lips. His mouth traced her cheek to her neck, leaving searing kisses in its wake. He started nibbling on her ear, feeling her tremble with the waves of sensation. "Dear God, Tonia," he whispered.

He wanted her. He had never wanted anything so much in his life but over the roaring in his ears and the loud beat of his heart, he could hear the camp noises outside and knew they might be interrupted at anytime. He could not do that to her.

Instead, his arms went tighter around her and he held her as if he would never let her go.

Antonia felt the love and need flowing between them and knew she would never be alone again.

Tristan knew his restless search was ended. It hadn't been adventure he sought but a place for his heart.

They were still holding each other minutes later when they heard Conn's cautious voice from outside the tent, telling them they had been invited to dinner with Doniphan.

Tris groaned with reluctance, but he knew they needed the colonel just now. With a bittersweet smile, he took her hand and they went out to meet Conn.

The battle of Chihuahua took place five days later. Antonia, jointly anxious to see her father and worried sick for Tris's safety, had pleaded with him to take her back to Santa Fe. It had been like talking to a stone wall. He felt well enough to participate, and the odds were such that every man was needed.

The young American officer insisted that Antonia keep his tent as long as she stayed, and she saw little of Tris. He was often out scouting with Conn, and was strained and tired when he returned. There was no time for them to be alone, and Tris was reluctant to do any more to damage her reputation. It was bad enough that she had ridden alone with two men for weeks. Only Doniphan's obvious respect for her quieted the comments.

So she waited fearfully. She had few hopes that Tris wouldn't be in the middle of the battle.

On the eve of the fighting, he just held her, feeling her apprehension and fear. "I have more lives than a cat," he tried to reassure her.

"And you have used most of them up," she retorted.

"This will be the end," he promised. "My contract with the army will be up soon, and the colonel is sending me back to Santa Fe."

It was the closest they had come to talking about a future since she had gone with Ramon. Her eyes lifted hesitantly to meet his.

"Where . . . ?"

"Your ranch . . . if you and your father will agree," he said slowly. He had been thinking about it for a long time. It would be difficult to make peace with her father, but he knew Antonia would not leave him. He also knew she loved the ranch.

"But it will be confiscated," she said, fearing to hope.

"Then I'll buy it," he said.

The thought was too wonderful for her to comprehend. She had dreaded leaving the only home she knew, the land she had loved. But so much had happened to him here. How could he want to stay?

It was as if he read her mind. "This land gave me the most precious gift in the world," he whispered softly. "It gave me you."

Mist formed in her eyes, and she thought how many tears she had shed in the past six months. But these were happy ones. Such very happy ones.

Until she thought about tomorrow.

Her fear was so profound, she didn't want to let him go, and they sat outside the tent until the first rays of dawn came. Tris held her gently, telling her of all the fine things that were ahead of them, the children they would have, the moments they would share.

At sunrise, Conn came for him, and she watched as Tristan checked his weapons.

When he was through, he kissed her lightly, afraid that anything more would increase her fear.

The noise came from everywhere: the jingling of spurs, the sound of hoofs, the ominous clicks of muskets and rifles being checked. In the distance, she could hear the sound of bugles from the enemy camp. She had already heard that the Mexicans were flying the black flag, which meant "no quarter." She shuddered as she remembered what had happened at the Alamo.

The camp emptied slowly with only a few hostlers remaining. The hours crept by slowly and she could hear the sound of artillery and rifles. Each shot might have been one aimed at Tristan. She wondered how she could get through the day.

"Dear God, protect him," she prayed over and over again. "Protect them all."

It was late afternoon before a galloping rider came in. "Victory," he screamed to the all-but-empty camp. "We've taken them."

Antonia rushed up to him, her face twisted with anxiety. "Injured?" She couldn't say the word *dead*.

"Just a few, ma'am. Our scouts discovered their left side was undefended . . . they didn't think we could go that way. But we did, by golly damn, and our artillery just rained on them."

Our scouts. That meant Tris was probably in the middle of the battle. "Tristan Hampton," she said. "Have you heard anything of him?"

"No, ma'am," the rider said. "I'm sorry." And then he was gone to tell the others of the great victory.

Antonia knew she could wait no longer. She went to Night Wind and saddled her. Before anyone could stop Antonia, she pressed her knees against the mare's side, galloping toward the sounds she had heard all afternoon, reining in only when she saw a golden horse ridden by a man with golden hair racing toward her.

Joyously she urged her horse to a gallop and the two met in a pale stream of light from the setting sun.

Epilogue

The two men sat their horses in easy companionship as they looked out over the Shenandoah Valley at the wide river below.

Just as Tris remembered, the scene was utterly peaceful. The mist softened the boundaries between the sky, the blue-gray of the river and the rich green of the land.

His hand tightened around the small boy seated on the saddle in front of him, and the lad leaned back against him, snuggling his body against his father's.

Tris knew complete contentment as his hand moved to young Chase's dark hair and ruffled it lovingly. He leaned over.

"This is where your papa grew up," he said in a soft, loving voice.

"Green," the boy said.

"Very green," Tris said with a laugh. The boy had been fascinated on their long journey as the land had turned from red and gold to gray and finally this lush green.

"You have another adventurer here," Reese Hampton said.

"Dear God, I hope not," Tris said with another laugh.

Reese openly studied his son. There was something harder about Tris, harder and stronger, yet his smile was much the same, especially when Tris looked at his wife or child. Reese knew he had made the right decision years ago. He had often wondered over the past five years. But after one searching look at his son, he saw the same happiness he himself knew in his marriage and family.

And no one could ask for more.

He leaned over and put his hand on Tris's shoulder with affection. "Your Antonia is beautiful. And this little imp...is, well, quite magnificent."

"I hoped you would approve of your first grandchild."

Reese gave a satisfied grunt. "And Francis and Annabelle each have one on the way," he said, naming Tris's brother and sister, both of them married last year. "At long last. Your mother has not been pleased at the slowness of her family in producing grandchildren. Perhaps now I'll have some peace."

"Surely she doesn't blame you," Tris chuckled.

"Ah, but she does. She chalks it up to English reserve."

"And you?"

"To American stubbornness," Reese grinned. The matter of national foibles had long been a Hampton family debate.

Tris's chuckle turned into full laughter, and he felt Chase starting to giggle also.

"It was good to have you home," Reese said as he regarded his son and grandson with welling love. "We will miss you."

Tris's laughter died. They had arrived two weeks ago, and tomorrow they would leave for their home in New Mexico. There was sadness in leaving...yet he was eager to return to the ranch where he had placed his roots. "You will have to visit us in Taos. It's a beautiful land, Father."

Reese sighed. He had hoped to convince Tris to stay in Virginia but he had known it was hopeless after only a day. New Mexico was in Tris's blood.

"Perhaps we will," he conceded. "Rafe is more than capable of running the farm. Perhaps next year."

"A promise?"

"A promise," Reese confirmed. "I wouldn't mind seeing some of these Indians of yours."

"Still a sense of adventure, huh?"

"It runs in the blood, son."

"I think I've had enough to last a lifetime," Tris said slowly, and there was a trace of sadness in his voice that Reese understood.

Reese was silent for a moment. "When you see Conn again, tell him he has my everlasting gratitude."

Tris raised a golden eyebrow quizzically. "You better do it yourself. I don't think he'll believe me."

Reese gave him a half smile. "It will be damned difficult, I'll tell you that. Ruin a damned good feud." The smile disappeared. "Did you ever make peace with your father-in-law?" It was a question he had not wanted to ask in front of Antonia.

Tris hesitated. It had not been an easy relationship...his and Miguel's. Tris had never been able to forget Miguel's part in Charles Bent's death, although he had come to believe that Miguel never knew about, nor intended, the bloody massacre that Ramon Silvero had unleashed. "Of sorts. I don't think he ever quite forgave me for being American, and I could never quite forgive him his involvement with the rebellion, but we adjusted for Antonia's sake. At least he saw his grandson before he died. I think that made him happy."

"Even though he's half American?"

"Even half American. He would sit there for hours holding Chase, and Chase always quieted with him...as if he knew Miguel wasn't well. There was a special bond between them. I think it made Miguel's last days contented."

"And you never thought about returning to Virginia?"

Tris shook his head. "The ranch was Antonia's home, and now it's mine. There's something compelling about New Mexico...its color, its energy, its challenges."

"Samara asked me to try," Reese explained with chagrin, and the two men smiled in complete understanding.

"I'll never forget this valley," Tris said, his eyes fogging a little. "And I'll make sure my children will know it. Perhaps one of them will return."

"Perhaps they will," Reese said, his own eyes a bit misty.

"I'll race you back," Tris said.

"You're on," Reese replied, and the two men, one tightly holding on to his son, pressed their horses toward the farmhouse, leaving a trail of harmonious laughter in their wake.

* * * * *

HARLEQUIN
American Romance®

RELIVE THE MEMORIES...

From New York's immigrant experience to the Great Quake of 1906. From the Western Front of World War I to the Roaring Twenties. From the indomitable spirit of the thirties to the home front of the Fabulous Forties. From the baby boom fifties to the Woodstock Nation sixties... **A CENTURY OF AMERICAN ROMANCE** takes you on a nostalgic journey through the twentieth century.

Revel in the romance of a time gone by... and sneak a peek at romance in a exciting future.

Watch for all the **A CENTURY OF AMERICAN ROMANCE** titles coming to you one per month over the next three months in Harlequin American Romance.

Don't miss February's **A CENTURY OF AMERICAN ROMANCE** title, #377—TILL THE END OF TIME by Elise Title.

A CENTURY OF
AMERICAN ROMANCE
1970s

The women... the men... the passions... the memories...

Take 4 bestselling love stories FREE

Plus get a FREE surprise gift!

Special Limited-time Offer

Harlequin Reader Service®

Mail to

In the U.S.
3010 Walden Avenue
P.O. Box 1867
Buffalo, N.Y. 14269-1867

In Canada
P.O. Box 609
Fort Erie, Ontario
L2A 5X3

YES! Please send me 4 free Harlequin Historical™ novels and my free surprise gift. Then send me 4 brand-new novels every month. Bill me at the low price of $2.89* each—a savings of 36¢ apiece off cover prices. There are no shipping, handling or other hidden costs. I understand that accepting the books and gift places me under no obligation ever to buy any books. I can always return a shipment and cancel at anytime. Even if I never buy another book from Harlequin, the 4 free books and the surprise gift are mine to keep forever.

*Offer slightly different in Canada—$2.89 per book plus 49¢ per shipment for delivery.
Sales tax applicable in N.Y.
Canadian residents add applicable federal and provincial sales tax.

247 BPA YA33 (US)   347 BPA YBCP (CAN)

Name _____ (PLEASE PRINT)

Address _____ Apt. No. _____

City _____ State/Prov. _____ Zip/Postal Code _____

This offer is limited to one order per household and not valid to present Harlequin Historicals™ subscribers. Terms and prices are subject to change.

HIS-BPADR   © 1990 Harlequin Enterprises Limited

Coming in March from

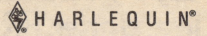

HARLEQUIN®

LaVyrle Spencer's unforgettable story of a
love that wouldn't die.

SWEET MEMORIES

She was as innocent as she was unsure . . . until a very special
man dared to unleash the butterfly wrapped in her cocoon and
open Teresa's eyes and heart to love.

SWEET MEMORIES is a love story to savor that will make you
laugh—and cry—as it brings warmth and magic into your
heart.

"Spencer's characters take on the richness of friends, relatives
and acquaintances."   —*Rocky Mountain News*